A RIPPLE FROM THE STORM

By the same author

DORIS LESSING

A RIPPLE
FROM
THE STORM

BOOK THREE
of the 'Children of Violence' series

HarperCollins*Publishers*

HarperCollins*Publishers*
77–85 Fulham Palace Road,
Hammersmith, London W6 8JB

Published by HarperCollins*Publishers* 1993
1 3 5 7 9 8 6 4 2

First published in Great Britain by
Michael Joseph 1958

A catalogue record for this book is
available from the British Library

ISBN 0 246 10905 X

Set in Melior

Printed and Bound in Great Britain by
Hartnolls Limited, Bodmin, Cornwall.

A Ripple from the Storm

Part One

There is no passion for the absolute without the accompanying frenzy of the absolute. It is always accompanied by a certain exaltation, by which it may first be recognized and which is always working on the growing point, the focal point of destruction, at the risk of making it appear to such as have not been warned, that the passion for the absolute is the same as a passion for unhappiness.

LOUIS ARAGON

Chapter One

From the dusty windows of a small room over Black Ally's Café it could be seen that McGrath's ballroom was filling fast. Groups of people clogged all the pillared gold-painted entrances of the hotel.

Jasmine said composedly: 'Jackie's very late,' and, having neatly fastened the windows and turned herself around, she smiled at Martha. Martha smiled back with affectionate devotion. The devotion was no less because its quality had changed. Three months before, she had regarded this competent girl with awe: Jasmine was not afraid to stand on a platform before hundreds of people; she understood that mysterious process *organization*; and people always suggested her first if a secretary were needed. Martha had been used to watching her descend demurely from a platform with her files and papers or selling pamphlets at the door, feeling that she must be of an entirely superior order of person, not because she was competent, but because competence was the result of years of service in public causes of one kind or another.

Now Martha could do these things herself. She had learned without knowing she was learning by being with Jasmine so much of her time. She understood she had become for others what Jasmine had been for her when the pretty English schoolteacher, Marjorie Pratt, her fine blue eyes alive with admiration, had said: 'I do admire you, Matty, for not being afraid of doing these things in public.' At which Martha had felt an affectionate pity – not for Marjorie, who would herself soon acquire these so easily acquired qualities, but for herself of three months ago.

9

Martha said: 'William's late too. They've probably got some sort of meeting in the camp.'

Again the two girls exchanged a warm smile. In it was the affection every member of the group felt for the others: a communal tenderness. But there was more: Jasmine and Martha, both with lovers from the airforce, had a special tie. They did not speak of what they felt: their men would most likely be posted soon, and they would be left alone: their happiness was lit by the foreknowledge of loss. Or rather, this was what each felt on behalf of the other, a gentle protectiveness for the other's situation, as if for someone weaker; and all these emotions were part of that greater elation on which they had all been floating now for months, ever since the formation of 'the group'.

The small grimy room had in it a small deal table, a couple of hard benches and some unpainted chairs, This was the group's headquarters and home. It was also the scene of Jasmine's love, for there was a campbed folded against the wall beside the filing cabinet. To Martha, with her painful need to admire someone for qualities she could never possess herself, it seemed natural that Jasmine's love should be at home here, camped among the files and papers of the world Revolution. On those rare nights when Jackie was free from the camp and Jasmine from her family, here it was that they lay in each other's arms. To Martha, her own love seemed domestic and ordinary in comparison.

Jasmine was independent of her family because – or so it seemed, she was so bound to it. The Cohens had heard of their daughter's affair with this disreputable character from the camp, and confronted her with their knowledge. She had said calmly, Yes, she intended to live with Jackie Cooper when the war was over. Yes, she did know he was married and had children. 'You can't expect them to understand,' she had remarked, telling Martha of the unpleasant scene. 'I did explain it was a question of the revolution, but I saw it was no use.'

It seemed that the parents, both in tears, had officially disowned Jasmine, an entirely ritual act, for she still lived at home. But they would not speak to her. 'I can't leave home,' she explained, 'because it would be such a disgrace for them in the community.' (She meant the Jewish community of this small town.) 'That kind of thing is very important to them; they simply can't help it.' To protect her parents from the results of their own attitudes, she was prepared to live at home like an outcast, treated as if she did not exist. Martha admired her for this chivalry she was convinced was far beyond herself.

Her own mother had also cast her off, in a letter of the same ritual quality. Martha, Mrs Quest had announced by registered letter, was no longer her daughter. Unable to discover the right answer to this, Martha had done nothing at all. Besides, she was so busy she had no time to think about it. As a result, Mrs Quest had come bustling one morning into the furnished room Martha now lived in, saying: 'Dear me, how untidy you are!' That final casting-off letter might never have been written and posted. And Mr Quest, meeting Martha, outside the chemist's shop near the house, had announced vaguely: 'Ah, there you are, old chap! How's everything with you, all right?' In this way he had been enabled not to make judgments or to take a stand. But this meant that Martha could no longer go to her father for his advice and support. She scarcely admitted to herself that she needed it. But on occasions like this, when Jasmine and she were alone, engaged on some 'group work' – they were at the moment stacking pamphlets and books on the Soviet Union into a suitcase for the meeting – they were likely to discuss their parents. They were talking about the difficulties of 're-educating the older generation to socialist ethics', and what sort of work would be best suited to the capacities of Mr and Mrs Cohen, Mr and Mrs Quest – work which would release them into being much better and nobler people than they were now; while they simultaneously worried about the unpunctuality of their lovers.

At last they heard voices from the pavement below and they went to the window and peered out. Beside a taxi stood William and Jackie; the taxi driver was standing with them; and Jackie had his arm on the black man's shoulder and was

talking directly into his face, his own forceful face expressing an intimacy of persuasion. The black man was nodding,
but seemed uneasy; and Martha and Jasmine also instinctively cast wary glances up and down the street in case
anyone was watching the scene. Jasmine leaned over and
said in a cautious voice: 'Hey there, Jackie, be careful.' Jackie
glanced up and nodded, but continued his emotional pressure on the driver. Martha therefore called down to William:
'We're going to be late.' She could see that the young man
had been trying to hurry Jackie; for now he smiled quickly
up at them both, as if glad of their moral support, and said
something to Jackie, who was irritated at the interruption,
but he gave a final squeeze to the black man's elbow, smiled
warmly into his face, and then turned and vanished into the
doorway of Black Ally's. He must have forgotten to pay the
taxi-man, for William now did so. The taxi drove off and
William again looked up at the two young women, who
could hear Jackie's steps on the wooden stairs, with a small
smiling upwards grimace, which was a warning. Then he
too disappeared into the doorway. Martha and Jasmine
turned back into the room, looking severe. All kinds of
loyalties prevented them from speaking; but Martha's look
said to Jasmine that it was her task to deal with the situation.

Jackie Bolton came in with his soft wolf-tread, unbuttoning the jacket of his uniform with one hand, while he laid
the other on Jasmine's cheek and smiled into her eyes. The
publicity of this love gesture embarrassed Martha; she knew
that it was partly designed to make her feel jealous of
Jasmine. She looked away, for William was coming in.
Immediately William said: 'Don't settle yourself down,
Jackie. We're all late.'

Jackie Bolton, smiling, finished removing his jacket, and
settled himself on a bench by the wall. Martha saw he had
been drinking. Now both she and William glanced at Jasmine, waiting for her to speak. Jasmine was flushed, her
small round face distressed. Martha could feel her struggle
in herself.

For months no one had said what they felt about Jackie
Bolton. Without him, there would never have been 'the

group'. That quality in him which enabled him to inspire others seemed to put him in a category outside criticism; for to criticize Jackie – so he made them all feel – was to criticize the revolution itself. But two days before, Jasmine (flushed and unhappy then as now) had stood up at a meeting and said in her quiet way that she felt Comrade Jackie had a great defect, which was that he had anarchistic tendencies. If the other comrades agreed with her, then Jackie should accept the criticism and try to change himself. The other comrades did agree with her, with a spontaneity that embarrassed them all. Jackie Bolton had, as usual, heaved with silent laughter; but he had at last admitted, although with reluctance, that he had to accept a unanimous vote.

Since then, his manner had held an angry and deliberate sarcasm; he had missed three meetings, saying he was busy in the camp; and Jasmine, William and Martha all knew that he was late tonight and apparently determined to be later still because he had been criticized.

Now he was watching Jasmine with the look of one ready to be betrayed.

'Jackie,' said Jasmine firmly, although her voice was unsteady, 'you know you shouldn't go talking to Africans like that in public. We're all trying to be so careful.'

Jackie looked for support to both William and Martha, failed to find it, and turned his eyes up, grinning, at the ceiling.

'If you want to talk to African contacts, you should get them up here, where no one can see.'

'That man is worth all the group put together,' said Jackie. 'He's driven me into town several times now. He's got an instinctive understanding of the fundamentals of politics.'

'But Jackie, of course he would have. That's not the point.' Jasmine was nearly crying.

William came in to support her. 'Now look, Jackie, it's just plain bloody silly.'

'That's enough from you, Sarge,' said Pilot Officer Bolton, laughing.

The familiar joke made them all laugh with relief.

Martha said: 'You promised you'd be here last night to discuss the tactics for the meeting this evening. And now there's not much time to explain, is there, Jackie?'

'William's given me the gist,' said Jackie airily, and proceeded to put back his jacket and button it.

There was a pause, while Jackie surveyed them, grinning, challenging them to do their duty and criticize him further.

Jasmine said, in a disappointed voice: 'It's eight. We should be getting to the meeting.'

The suitcase with the literature lay open on the table. Jackie Bolton examined it, hands in his pockets. 'Where's the Marxist stuff?' he demanded.

'We took a decision about that,' said Jasmine, very firmly. 'No Marxist literature for the Help for our Allies Meetings. It's the wrong tactics.'

'Bloody social democrats,' said Jackie. 'You're as bad as the Left Book Club crowd.' He heaved out another laugh, challenged them with his eyes, but let it go: Jasmine was waiting by the door with her hand on the light switch. William fastened the suitcase, and they all went out, carefully locking the door.

In the street they became two couples. Jasmine put her hand in Jackie's elbow, but he appeared not to feel it, and she let it fall again. Jasmine and Jackie walked with a yard of pavement between them, in front of Martha and William, who were arm in arm.

When they reached McGrath's, Jackie said abruptly over his shoulder that he had something to discuss with Jasmine. William and Martha watched the other couple settle themselves in at a table under the noisy orchestra. They felt sorrowful disapproval because of the way Jasmine had succumbed to Jackie.

The ballroom was jammed with lines of chairs, all full. It was the Annual General Meeting of the Society. The gathering was essentially respectable. Or, as Martha put it, after a single confirming glance: The Help for Our Allies Audience. She had ceased to feel a secret disquiet because of the way people fell automatically into groups: a law expressed, in this instance, by the way audiences for Help for Our Allies,

Sympathizers of Russia, or the Progressive Club could be recognized at a glance, all drawn together by some invisible bond, although they thought that an individual act of will had made them choose this or that allegiance. Martha was convinced she now understood this law.

On the platform this evening were Messrs Forester, Perr and Pyecroft, together with some prominent businessmen, a couple of members of Parliament, and two clergymen. Martha listened to three sentences from Mr Perr's opening speech, knew what would follow and ceased to listen.

The hotel management had forgotten to provide tables for the sale of literature. She went in search of them with William. By the time the tables were set out at either side of the entrance, and arranged with pamphlets and collecting tins, and saucers full of change, and she and William had taken their places behind them as salesmen, Mr Perr had finished speaking and Mr Forester was giving the Secretary's Report, which was an account of garden parties, fêtes and the like. The object of this society was to raise money for Russia (the word had been chosen because it had none of the disagreeable associations of the phrase *The Soviet Union*) and a very large sum of money had in fact been raised which would in due course reach Russia in the shape of medical supplies. The treasurer, Mr Pyecroft, now proceeded to analyse the figures.

These three men, the three officers of the society, sat prominently around a deal table at the front of the platform. Behind them sat the bank of respectable patrons.

The boring part of the meeting was now over. The next item on the agenda was 'policy'; and everyone expected a fight. It was not, after all, enough simply to call the Soviet Union *Russia*.

Boris Krueger stood up from somewhere in the middle of the packed hall and proposed that the society should produce a book consisting of articles about Russia, financed by gift-advertisements, for mass sale. The committee had discussed this proposal one evening the week before from eight until three in the morning, with heat and ill-feeling. The faction represented by Messrs Perr, Forester and Pyecroft said that to sell a book of articles would be interpreted as making propaganda about Russia. The faction represented by Krueger, Anton Hesse and Andrew McGrew said it would be purely factual and nothing to do with propaganda. The real battle was over who was to control this society. That there was a battle was not understood by the respectable patrons, who did not attend the committee meetings. Since the committee could not agree, the battle was to be fought out now by the membership. Boris Krueger's proposal was the flinging down of a gage in public.

Again Martha did not listen to what was being said: the shortest acquaintance with politics should be enough to teach anyone that listening to the words people use is the longest way around to an understanding of what is going on.

Mr Perr's long lean body, now upright behind the table, was writhing with affronted rectitude of purpose; the light flashed continually from his agitated spectacles. Then Mr Forester's equally angular shape jerked itself into various postures expressive of outrage. Mr Pyecroft rose beside them. For a few moments the three men were jerking up and down from their seats like three puppets manipulated by the strings of annoyance. Their faces, however, continued to appeal to the audience with intimate, deferential, but warning smiles.

Martha could see that the people packed on the chairs below the platform had responded to Boris Krueger who had spoken well and calmly, his pale, fattish, intellectual face making no concessions of appeal to them. Now they were feeling disquieted because of the excessive reaction of three officers.

Boris rose to his feet again, not to put forward any new arguments, for he repeated in different words what he had said before, but in order to reimpress his calm and objective image on the audience. The three men on the platform remained seated, in postures of warning anger, while half a dozen people got up one after another around the hall, to say that to produce such a booklet would cost nothing, since the printing would be a gift; and the distribution would of course be done by members of the society. An ironical voice shouted that the articles would cost nothing either, since obviously there were plenty of people prepared to write them for nothing! But everyone in the ballroom laughed at this: it was the laugh that occurs at a public meeting when something has been said which might have been dangerous: a laugh a little too ready, a little too loud, and accompanied by dozens of pairs of eyes seeking each other for confirmation. It was noticeable that at the laugh the three figures on the platform assumed more easy postures: in short, they would accommodate themselves to the mood of the meeting. They had been too ready to see danger.

Mr Perr stood up to say, in the easy amiable tone of his chairman's address, that he would of course accept the majority opinion. Before he sat down, people were jumping up all over the hall to make suggestions about the practical side of the proposition: the thing had been accepted, in fact, without a vote.

At this moment Martha saw Jasmine and Jackie enter a side door. Jackie's jacket buttons were undone again and his dark and satirical face was already expressing every sort of contempt. The man's capacity to impress himself was such that although he had made no sound coming in, all the people on his side of the hall had turned to watch him, and the men on the platform were exchanging warning glances.

Jackie Bolton made his way to an empty chair, excusing himself smilingly, and every time he did so, he caught the eyes of the person he was disturbing and held them until he chose to nod and look into the next face. He seated himself in such a way that everyone expected him to rise to his feet for a speech.

Meanwhile, Jasmine had taken a chair beside Martha at the literature table. Her face expressed exactly what Jackie's did: a conspiratorial contempt. It cut the current of sympathy between the two girls; and Martha whispered: 'I hope he's not going to speak. It's not necessary now.' Last night the group had decided that Comrade Jackie would get up to speak only as a last resort; and only to put forward facts, not to make revolutionary speeches! It was to be hoped that

Jasmine had explained all this to Jackie while they were drinking in the other room?

'Oh,' said Jasmine composedly, rolling her eyes, 'it won't do them any harm to hear some home truths about themselves.'

Jackie's voice could already be heard. He was standing, or rather lounging, at the back of the hall, and he was making that speech they had all decided it would be disastrous for him to make. Jackie had two voices. One was the most correct and colourless version of upper-class speech that could be imagined. He could use it blandly: in order to neutralize himself and his over-colourful personality. And he could use it with undertones of satirical comment, as if to say: This is what you sound like. (He also used it, as Martha had noted with resentment, when he was alone with a woman.) His other voice was the cockney of the streets he had come from and when he chose it he was a different person. The exaggerated contempt he carried with him in his other role became a shoulder-shrugging barrow-boy's good-natured anarchy; his whole being became alive with darting critical comment. He sometimes dropped into his cockney voice from the pilot officer's voice, becoming the working-man with admirable effect.

But tonight he was drunk and the two voices, the two personalities, slurred together. He was delivering an attack on the officers and committee of Aid for Our Allies. They were all cowardly, lily-livered social democrats; he, Jackie Bolton, in the name of the oppressed masses of the world, demanded a radical change of policy, the end of weak-minded shilly-shallying ... He might have gone on for several minutes, but the chairman rapped on the table. Jackie Bolton heaved out his silent sarcastic laugh. Now Boris Krueger stood up, no longer calm and dignified, speaking directly to Jackie, saying that he would be the first to sympathize with anyone who wished to deliver the oppressed masses of the world from their chains, but this was neither the time nor the place ... The chairman rapped again. Neither Boris nor Jackie sat down: they were facing each other over the heads of the silent and unhappy crowd.

'If you don't sit down I'll . . .' began the chairman; and stopped himself. He had lost his temper, and Jackie Bolton laughed out openly at the sight.

'Sit down,' shouted the chairman.

'I understand,' said Jackie pleasantly, 'that you have agreed to publish the booklet. In that case I propose that a sub-committee to produce it be formed. I put forward the following names to be voted on.' The names he proposed were: Jasmine Cohen, Anton Hesse, Andrew McGrew, Martha Knowell, Marjorie Pratt and – here his shoulders shook with sarcastic good-nature – 'Myself.'

Mr Perr stood up and said that a vote had not yet been taken on whether this magazine should or should not be produced. The whole body of people stirred and shifted uneasily, as if they wanted to leave. At this William got up from behind his literature table to say that surely it had been understood before Pilot Officer Bolton's remarks that there was no need for a vote? He could not understand why a vote had suddenly become necessary. He sat down again, offering Martha a conniving, cheeky smile. She understood that he had been coming to the rescue of a fellow-serviceman, and that he disapproved of Jackie as much as she did. But she did not like the schoolboy's smile; she was ashamed of any association with Jackie Bolton – and ashamed of being ashamed, since, as a member of the group she was responsible for him.

The three men on the platform had their heads bent together. Mr Perr got up and said that he found it quite impossible to serve on a committee which was being made use of by communists for their own ends. Either they must be got rid of or he would offer his resignation. He remained standing while Mr Forester and Mr Pyecroft also offered their resignations. There was a long embarrassed silence, while they gazed authoritatively at Jackie, apparently expecting him to resign.

Meanwhile, Jasmine was making agitated signs at Jackie to the effect that he ought to resign, for the sake of keeping the society together. But he returned an openly defiant stare.

The silence continued. Then the three men expressed

their apologies, and went out of the hall, leaving the officers' table empty. It seemed no one knew what to do next.

Anton Hesse got to his feet; but Boris Krueger was before him. Boris said it was very unfortunate that this had occurred; and everyone must hope that Mr Forester, Mr Perr and Mr Pyecroft would reconsider their decision. In the meantime they must elect a temporary chairman so that the meeting could elect new officers. At this, a clergyman from the bank of respectable patrons got up to say that he was quite unable to understand the storm which had blown up out of a blue sky but it seemed to him essential that the society should continue, since it was performing a useful service for the war-effort, and he would like to second the last speaker's suggestion that a temporary chairman be elected. He would like to suggest Mr Krueger.

He was speaking in an affable, apologetic public voice. The expressions on the faces of the respectable patrons were affable and apologetic. People were nodding and smiling in an attempt to make humour save the day. But it was no use: everything was false and unpleasant.

Boris Krueger, since there were no dissensions, climbed on to the platform and said that while he hoped everyone agreed with him that every effort should be made to get the officers to reconsider their decision, he called for nominations from the floor for alternative officers. He waited, standing.

No one spoke. There were perhaps six hundred people crammed together under the chocolate and gold ceiling in McGrath's ballroom, and they were all silent.

Then Anton Hesse got up and said in his correct manner that perhaps some of the patrons would consent to act as officers? From this Martha understood that Anton was afraid they would lose all their respectable patrons. Boris turned to consult the body of twelve or fourteen people, sitting behind him. They shook their heads, one after another; but it was not possible to tell whether this was because they were too busy to do the actual work, or whether they were considering offering their resignations. On most of their faces strong distaste was mixed with the humour they still continued to offer to the members. Again Anton rose to urge the Reverend Mr Gates (the man who had just spoken) to be chairman. Mr Gates, after a pause, agreed to act as chairman temporarily, and Anton sat down, with a look of satisfaction which explained to Martha that she had under-estimated the danger of the entire body of respectable patrons resigning *en bloc*. She had learned to have the deepest respect for Anton's political flair in spite of, perhaps because of, the cold formality of this tall, stiff German who frightened her a little even now, after seeing him every day for months.

Boris Krueger stood down and Mr Gates again called for nominations. A man nobody knew suggested that the last speaker should be secretary. Anton got up and said very smoothly that he was a German, technically an enemy alien, and it was clearly undesirable that this society should have such a person as a secretary. He sat down. The cold bitterness behind his words was such that everyone in the ballroom felt positively guilty. A young girl stood up and said impulsively that she could not see why one of Hitler's victims should not be the secretary of a society whose aim was, after all, wasn't it? – to defeat Hitler. But the silence which followed was uncomfortable. Rumours pursued all the foreigners in the town to the effect that they were enemy agents, and Anton Hesse was no exception. Boris Krueger, knowing this, knowing that he too was popularly supposed to be in the pay of Germany, stood up to give public support to Anton, in spite of the fact that political bitterness had prevented the two men from speaking to each other for some months. Boris said that Anton was right: he was a foreigner himself, and therefore able to make such remarks without being suspected of prejudice; and he would like to take this opportunity of saying how fortunate it was Mr Gates had agreed to be chairman, because it would be highly undesirable for a foreigner to be chairman, even temporarily, of a society such as this. He had intended to sound magnanimous, but he smiled uncomfortably around the audience, his spectacles gleaming. Mr Gates thanked Mr Krueger for his remarks 'with which he did not necessarily agree' – and again called for nominations. And again there was silence.

At this William proposed Jasmine as secretary. She had resigned from the position three months before because she was also secretary of Sympathizers of Russia, but when a dozen hands shot up from the hall to second the proposal she nodded a demure agreement.

There remained the position of treasurer. It was agreed that the committee should be empowered to co-opt one.

Mr Gates then announced the next item on the agenda which was an address by Mr Horace Packer, MP, on the course of the war on the Russian Front. There was a storm of relieved applause; the people who apparently had been on the point of slipping away from the hall now settled themselves again in their seats.

Jackie Bolton, who had been sitting and smiling as if the unpleasantness had had no connection with him at all, now rose with a conspicuously negligent ease and began squeezing his way out along the row of chairs. He came to where Martha and Jasmine were, laid his hand on Jasmine's shoulder and said: 'I have to be back in camp by twelve. We must have an urgent group meeting. Get them all together, will you?'

Jasmine, visibly torn by the conflict of her love for him and her complete disapproval, said uncomfortably: 'But, Jackie, how can we possibly go now?'

'Oh, find someone else to do the literature.'

'We can go to the office when this is over.'

'No. We'd better meet in the park.'

'But why?'

'It's safer,' said Jackie, with weary importance.

Jasmine's eyes and Martha's met involuntarily out of embarrassed disapproval of these histrionics, but Jasmine said: 'Very well, but we had better all leave separately.'

Jackie Bolton went out, with the eyes of all the people in the hall on him. Jasmine proceeded to write a series of little notes: to Andrew McGrew, Anton Hesse and Marjorie Pratt; folded them up, and handed them to people at the ends of the rows of chairs the addressees sat in, as if she were releasing into the air three carrier pigeons. Then she approached a young aircraftsman who had been anxious to help in the past, asked him to guard the literature sales, and, having made all arrangements, nodded at Martha and William. Martha, William and Jasmine quietly left the hall after Jackie. Already Anton and Andrew and Marjorie were reading their notes and looking towards the door. 'The group' – conspicuous with discretion, were leaving the meeting in a body.

Jasmine found Jackie smoking moodily on the pavement outside McGrath's. This time it was he who approached her elbow with his hand – not in apology, for one would never expect that from Jackie Bolton, but in a laughing declaration of intimacy. Jasmine said at once: 'Jackie, you've behaved very badly.' He laughed at her, and the two set off together towards the park. Martha and William followed. Inside the ballroom Mr Horace Packer's statements were earning great applause. There were continuous storms of clapping. From outside it sounded like heavy rain on a tin roof: the small overall rattling of individual drops striking metal together in a swelling and subsiding din of sky-flung rain. Martha instinctively glanced up at the sky, which was clear and moonlit.

'Why the park?' she demanded, irritably humorous.

'He's got news. He really has.'

'*What* news?'

'Oh, perhaps it'll come to nothing.'

All Martha's dissatisfaction with Jackie, and with William for associating himself with Jackie, culminated in: 'He's got no sense of discipline at all. He's just an anarchist really.'

But at this William said in the tone of a man humouring a woman: 'Why are you so cross, Matty?' And he did a couple of dance-steps along the pavement.

Feeling herself to be humoured, she remembered how often recently William had reminded her of Douglas. She therefore humoured him by telling him a chatty and gay story about something that had happened that morning in the office, because – although she had not yet admitted this to herself, it was not worth disliking William when he was bound to be leaving her so soon.

Exchanging amiable bits of news, they reached the big

open gates of the park. Ahead, dark spires of conifers reached up into the moonlight. Under the trees, Jasmine's pale dress spotted with shadow and with moonlight drifted beside the black lean shape of Jackie. A springy mat of pine-needles gave under Martha's feet, and she watched her black shadow shift and break along the dark trunks of the trees.

The two couples met where a white path blazed in the bright light, bordered thick with clumps of canna lilies sculptured out of shadow.

'The others won't know where we are,' said Martha.

'Then they'll just have to look for us,' said Jackie, laughing.

There was a bench set in the grass beside the path. Jackie stepped high over the clumps of lilies to sit on the bench. On the back was written: For Europeans only. Instinctively he straightened himself, and turned away from it. His face in the moonlight showed a sharp and angry repugnance. When he noticed the others had watched him, had noticed what he felt about the segregated bench, he said histrionically: Bloody white fascists. Then, for the first time that evening he looked uncomfortable, and walked away ahead of them to where a small Chinese-looking pavilion stood at the end of the path, surrounded by flower-beds. The night-air was thick with mingled scents. From this pavilion a band from the African regiment played on Sunday afternoons while the people of the town lay about on the grass, or sat in deck-chairs, eating ice-cream, smoking, gossiping.

Jackie sat on the chill dry grass beside the pavilion and the others joined him. Almost at once William leaped up and said he must go and see if he could find the others. He went off. There was an officiousness in his bearing which Martha disliked, and chose not to notice; but Jackie looked after him, smiling, and said: Sergeant Brown, Administration. His dark face was hallowed into dramatic lines and folds by the sharp moon. He smiled at the two girls, one after another, as if he owed allegiance to neither. Suddenly he was simple, natural and direct. He was a man who would always be at his best alone with women.

'When I leave here,' he said quietly, 'what I'll remember will be this park.'

He spent whatever free time he had in the park, lying on the grass with an anthology of poetry.

Jasmine's breathing changed; he heard it, remembered that after all she was interested in the possibility of his having to leave, and laid his hands on hers.

He looked straight up into the starlit solemnity of the sky and began to quote:

> How to keep – is there any any, is there none such,
>   nowhere known some, bow or brooch or braid or
>   brace, lace, latch, or catch or key to keep
> Back beauty, keep it, beauty, beauty, beauty, from
>   vanishing away?

His voice was drowned by the whine of aircraft engines: an aeroplane, landing lights flicking, went past overhead.

Jackie said in cockney: 'Half of a wing of one of those mucking machines would rebuild a whole street in that mucking slum my mother's in.' He was coldly, deadly serious. He waited until the aircraft had dipped, a silver shape in the silver light, past the trees and continued with the poem in his other voice. The rest of the group, shepherded by William, were approaching through the shadows, but Jackie went steadily on, and not until Anton Hesse, Marjorie, Andrew and William stood over them did he acknowledge their presence by raising his voice at them:

> Come then, your ways and airs and looks, locks,
>   maiden gear gallantry gaiety and grace . . .

He stopped and added laughing: 'But that is counter-revolutionary of course.'

Andrew, gruffly annoyed, said: 'What's this, a poetry-reading?'

Anton Hesse, his rough pale hair as white as sand in the moonlight, his eyes glinting with white disapproval, said: 'Why have you convened a meeting here? What is the reason for fetching us all up here and leaving the other meeting?'

25

Jackie said: 'Because I thought it would be more pleasant to sit in the park than in that dirty little office.'

Jasmine said with determination: 'We should elect a chairman.' Her tone said plainly that she did not intend to be moved, by the poetry or by anything else, away from her determination to criticize Jackie.

'Andrew,' said Marjorie. They all agreed. They were now sitting in a circle on the grass.

'Now, Comrade Jackie,' Andrew said in blunt annoyance, 'you convened this meeting. I should like to say first that if you really fetched us here because you wanted to admire the moonlight then I, for one, wish to pass a vote of censure.' The formal chairman's voice sounded so absurd here, in the spaces of the big park, that he added, smiling: 'But only as a matter of form.'

They all laughed and became, instantly, 'the group'.

'Anyway,' said Jackie, 'all those social democrats and Trotskyists are spying on us. I caught Boris sniffing around in Black Ally's Café yesterday.'

The group tightened still further out of its units.

'I brought you here,' Jackie said, lowering his voice, 'to say that I've found out that all of us service types are likely to be posted at any moment.'

'What makes you think that?' demanded Corporal McGrew. He was shaken; alone of the airforce men he liked his stay in the Colony and did not want to leave.

'I got young Peters in the canteen and screwed it out of him,' said Jackie. There was a chorus of contemptuous exclamations. A great many men from the camp attended the Progressive Club meetings. They were mostly aircrafts-men and of a type: this last was not clearly understood, however, until a certain Sergeant Peters began attending their meetings: he was so unlike the others that comparisons were forced on them. He was a clipped, almost mincing young man with a habit of leaning forward over a question, head on one side, a disagreeable smile on his small pink lips, saying: 'Do I take it that you mean to imply . . . ?' Jackie Bolton, whose particular genius it was to establish a swift persuasive intimacy with people, had gone home one night on the camp bus with this youth who was being querulous because Andrew McGrew had said across the floor at the meeting that he was a typical member of the corrupt petty bourgeoisie. Sergeant Peters was slightly drunk. He had told Jackie that he had been appointed by the camp commander to attend all the 'Red' meetings in town so as to take down the names of all the airmen present. He turned in a list of these names, with a short précis of what each had said, after every meeting. He was unaffected by Jackie's jovial contempt for him; and a remarkable situation developed where, while informing on his fellows to the commander, this instinctive spy would then immediately go to Jackie Bolton and tell him everything he had said, for as he explained: 'If the Labour Government gets in and you Reds take over, things might be quite different at Home and I don't want to be on the wrong side.'

'He told me that I and William are for the high jump. The CO's got it into his head that we are extremely subversive.'

'Judging from the way you went on tonight I'm not surprised,' said Andrew.

'Yes,' said Jasmine firmly, bracing herself to criticize her man, although she was fighting down tears because he was leaving. 'We've got to discuss your behaviour, Jackie.'

'What it amounts to is this,' said Martha. 'That because you are leaving you don't care what sort of difficulties you make for us.'

'Oh, I can't be bothered with all this small-town nonsense,' said Jackie airily. And he got up from the grass and strolled off towards the pavilion, hands low in his pockets, whistling.

The six people who remained were silent: they were agreeing without words that since Comrade Bolton was leaving them, they would let it all drop.

Comrade Bolton was now strolling beside the clumps of moon-blotched lilies as if enjoying a pleasant evening walk.

Anton Hesse, who had not said a word until now, demanded: 'Comrades, I must have permission to speak.' He was coldly, contemptuously angry: his anger tautened their sense of responsibility.

27

'Comrade Anton,' said Andrew, with the small tinge of irony his manner always held when Anton was in question.

'We have been behaving like a bunch of amateurs . . .'

'I agree,' interrupted Jasmine eagerly. Her eyes were following Jackie's dark shape at the far end of a path; her face was contracted with pain, yet she was listening closely to the argument: 'We've made every mistake we could make. We had decided, quite correctly, that the Aid for Our Allies should be kept respectable and unpolitical, that its task was to raise money for medical supplies for the Soviet Union and nothing else, and that it should be run by that bunch of social democrats – under our guidance, of course. Now, because of Comrade Bolton it will most likely lose all its sponsors; Trotskyist Krueger will have control of it because he's in with Gates, unless Jasmine makes it a full-time job controlling it: Jasmine has allowed herself to be secretary again when she already has far too much to do.'

Here Jasmine said demurely: 'Oh, I don't mind. I can manage.'

'No,' said Anton sharply. 'That is nonsense. The essence of good organization is never to do anything oneself that someone else can do as well.' Here they all laughed, but Anton said, 'Yes, yes, yes. You laugh. But you wouldn't laugh if you had learned anything at all. The basic trouble is, we have neglected our theory. The sort of thing that happened tonight is a direct result of not seriously analysing the situation . . .'

Here they smiled: the phrase, analysing the situation, was peculiarly Anton's.

'Yes, comrades. Analysing the situation. And now. It will soon be eleven o'clock. The airforce comrades must get to their buses. But I propose that we convene a meeting to fundamentally reorganize the work of this group. Because things cannot continue like this.'

Here Jackie Bolton returned to the group, and seated himself beside William instead of beside Jasmine. The two men already had a look of being distant from the rest. They all realized that Jackie had been making his farewells to the park and, in a way, to them all: he was already thinking of the next place the fortunes of war would drop him into.

'Very well,' said Andrew. 'I agree with Comrade Anton.' Andrew and Anton always agreed with each other although they could not address two words to each other without the hostility sounding in their voices. 'We must have a special meeting. I take it everyone agrees. Tomorrow night there is the committee meeting of the Progressive Club. The night after there is a five o'clock meeting of the Sympathizers of Russia. At eight o'clock at our office there will be a special business meeting of the group. Attendance obligatory. No excuses will be accepted.' He stood up, saying to the other two men from the camp: 'We'll miss our bus.'

The three airforce men became a group separate from the civilians, led by Jackie, who said in cockney: 'Cerm on, mates, cerm on, get moving naow.' They went off into the shadows under the trees. Anton and the three women remained. Anton nodded at them, formally, as was his way, and he departed in another direction, without offering to see any of them home. Now the girls separated: Jasmine to her home where she would be met by silence; Marjorie to the boarding-house; and Martha to the room she was renting in the house of the widow Carson which was very close, being opposite one of the gates of the park.

Martha said to herself: I must walk slowly and enjoy the moonlight. She was conscious that the moment she left the group she felt as let down as if a physical support had been removed. 'I'm not alone enough – I should enjoy it when I am.' But she was almost running across the park. As usual a demon of impatience was snapping at her heels, pushing her into the future. Her dissatisfaction at the evening, at Jackie Bolton, at the months of her life in the group had crystallized in the form of words Anton Hesse had used. They had been behaving like a bunch of amateurs. Well, the day after tomorrow some serious analysis would set them on the right path; as these words slid through her brain it was as if they rolled up the past months and pushed them away. Two days ago, walking through the park with Jasmine, the girls had agreed, as if talking about some period a long way behind them, that they had been very romantic and irresponsible when they had joined the group. That conversation with Jasmine now seemed a long time ago. So much experience and active learning had been crammed into each day of the four months since she had walked out of her husband's house that she thought of herself as an entirely different person.

The white gates of widow Carson's house gleamed just ahead. Now Martha did walk slowly. She knew that as soon as she got inside she would fall over on to her bed and sleep, and she had to think: she was thinking that she had been informed William was leaving, and she ought to be unhappy about it. But she was not. She was relieved. Two days ago William had come to her room to say that 'he had reason to believe' that Douglas, her husband, had put pressure on to the camp authorities to get him posted. More, that 'he had evidence' that Douglas was thinking of citing him as co-respondent in a divorce case. Martha had listened to this, conscious of dislike for William. Her own contempt for any forms of pressure society might put on her was so profound and instinctive that she as instinctively despised anyone who paid tribute to them.

When Douglas had threatened her with the machinery of the law, she had shrugged and laughed. When William spoke of 'getting legal advice' and she understood that he was enjoying the idea of a fight with Douglas over the possession of her – then, for a few moments, she had seen the two men as one, and identical with the pompous, hypocritical and essentially male fabric of society. That was why she now felt relief at the idea of William's going. Yet, in the eyes of this small town, 'Matty Knowell had left her husband and a child for an airforce sergeant.' She succeeded in suppressing her amazed dismay at this view of herself by the device of never thinking of the people who, so short a time ago, had made up her life. She lived in 'the group' and did not care about the judgments of anyone else. She felt as if she were invisible to anyone but the group.

Outside the Carson gates she stopped. This was because what she referred to as 'coping with Mrs Carson' was becoming more of a strain daily. So much of a strain in fact that now she abruptly swerved off so as to walk around the block and collect her energies for what might follow.

When Martha rented this room she had informed the widow that she intended to live with William Brown: she had spoken defiantly: for the moment Mrs Carson represented the society she despised. But Mrs Carson had merely seemed puzzled. The irregularities of behaviour under the outward forms of conformity in this small Colonial town might be more easily tolerated than in, let us say, a small town in Britain, but they did not take the shape Martha insisted on for herself. The widow Carson did once inquire if Martha was going to marry Sergeant Brown when the war was over, but Martha said, obviously irritated, that she didn't know. Mrs Carson sighed and remarked that her own daughter, now happily married to a Johannesburg businessman, had been unhappy in her first two marriages. Martha did not seem to see any parallel. It had crossed Mrs Carson's mind that perhaps Martha believed in free love? But the phrase had associations which did not fit in with Martha's manner, which was alarmingly unfrivolous. She therefore ceased to think about it; she returned to her private preoccupations and was interested in Martha only in so far as the young woman would enter them with her.

The first night Martha was in Mrs Carson's house, she had woken at two in the morning at a noise in the passage outside her door. She found the widow, a gaunt figure in a cretonne dressing-gown, her grey hair in draggle-tails around her bony grey face, with her ear bent to the keyhole of the door that led to the veranda. Mrs Carson had taken her arm between two trembling hands and demanded: 'Did you hear a noise?' Martha had recognized a form of neurosis only too familiar to her. The widow Carson's life was a long drama played against fantasies about her servants. She never kept one longer than a month: they left for the most part in a state of bewilderment.

Mrs Carson had been left well-off by her husband and only let a room because she was afraid to be alone at night. She always sat up until Martha came home, alone or with

William, then dragged heavy iron bars across the doors and fitted specially-made steel screens across the windows. She went to sleep in a fortress. Yet more than once Martha had seen Mrs Carson, late at night, standing motionless under the big jacaranda tree at the gate, watching the house. She was engaged in some dream of a black marauder breaking into the house in spite of all its bars and barricades and finding it empty. As for Martha, she slept as usual with her windows and doors open, but promised Mrs Carson to keep the door between her own room and the rest of the house locked.

Collecting herself to face Mrs Carson was not an effort, for charity's sake, to sink herself in the sick woman's private world, but rather an effort to test her own vision of the world against the other. Mrs Carson, she told herself, was the product of a certain kind of society, and the Mrs Carsons would cease to exist when that society came to an end. Her patience with the terrible obsessed woman was because she saw her as a variety of psychological dinosaur. But more than once, after sitting with Mrs Carson behind barred windows and doors, assuring her that no black man with evil intentions lurked outside, she had returned to her own room invaded by despair. The wings of elation had folded under her. She even caught herself thinking: Supposing she's stronger than we are?

Therefore, before entering the big empty house at night, when she was by herself and not supported by William, she always hardened herself and strengthened the buttresses and arches of her own dream: over there, she thought, meaning in the Soviet Union – over there it's all finished, race prejudice and anti-Semitism.

She made the trip around the block fast, shivering a little, for the moonlight lay cold everywhere, and she had no coat. She intended to go as silently as possible to her own room, but the front door stood slightly ajar, and she knew Mrs Carson waited just inside it. She cautiously pushed the door in on the darkened passage, and the widow said: 'Oh, is that you, dear?' Martha felt her arm encircled in a bony trembling grasp and said cheerfully: 'Yes, it's me.' She switched on the light with her free hand, so that the passage showed its polished bare boards, its fading pink-flowered wallpaper, and a great glaring brass bowl on a wooden stand, filled with marigolds and zinnias. Mrs Carson wore her cretonne dressing-gown, and her head was covered over with curlers. 'You didn't see anything as you came in?' she demanded, her face white and gaunt, her eyes gleaming dark in deep sockets.

'Nothing. There really isn't anything. You should go to bed now.'

'Today Saul looked at me in a very strange way.'

'I expect you imagined it.'

'I'll give him the sack in the morning. He's got ideas in his head. I can see he has thoughts in his head.'

'I'll bar the door for you and then you go to bed,' said Martha.

Mrs Carson said: 'Thank you, dear.' She sounded, as always, disappointed: Martha had not said what she wanted to hear. Suddenly she remarked, in an ordinary voice: 'You've got a visitor.'

'Who?'

'Yes, you've got a visitor.' Then, her voice returning to the dragging insistent note of her obsession: 'You won't forget to lock your door tonight?'

'No, I promise.'

Mrs Carson knew that Martha slept with the door open, but as long as she heard in words that it was locked, she was satisfied, apparently.

'I'll sack Saul in the morning. There was quite a nice-looking boy who came around this afternoon looking for work. I'll give him a try.'

Martha's visitor was her husband.

Douglas was sitting with his back to the window in such a way that he could watch both doors. From his attitude, which was tense and suspicious, Martha saw that he must have been there some time, and that while he was waiting he had, as she put it, 'been working himself up into a state'. His face had the swollen reddened look which meant she could not take anything he said seriously.

He said: 'I'm sorry if this is an inconvenient time to call.'

She said nothing, so he insisted: 'It might have been inconvenient.'

'Not at all,' she said, falling automatically into meaningless politeness.

He brought out, self-consciously bitter: 'William might have been here.'

'Well, obviously,' said Martha coldly. She sat down across the room from him. Her knees were trembling and this annoyed her. It had taken her a long time to admit that she was physically frightened of Douglas, but admitting it made things worse, not better.

She had seen him three times since leaving his house.

The first, about a fortnight after leaving him, he had come one Sunday morning to ask her to go for a drive with him. His manner had been simple and pleasant and she found herself liking him. She would have accepted if it were not that she had a group meeting that morning. After he had left her, she was thinking of returning to him. For some days she was very unhappy: the simple friendliness of his manner had made it possible for her to think of the child. Most of the time she was very careful not to allow herself to think of Caroline. Once, missing Caroline, she had borrowed Jasmine's car and driven several times up and down past the house, to watch the little girl playing in the garden with the nurse-girl. The sight had confused her, for she had not felt as unhappy as she had expected. She had continued to drive up and down past the house until she saw a female figure through a window and believed she recognized Elaine Talbot. Afterwards, the thought of Caroline caused her acute pain. A cold shell she had been careful to build around her heart was gone. She longed for her daughter, and was on the point a dozen times of telephoning Douglas to say she would come back. During this time she was more in love with William than she had ever been. She was rocked by violent and conflicting emotions, vulnerable to a tone in William's voice, or the sight of a small child playing on the grass verges of a street.

This period of misery had come to a sudden end when about three weeks later Douglas had rung up from the office to demand an interview. As soon as she heard his voice she felt herself harden. She went to his office where he had gone through a scene which she had recognized from the first word as something he was acting out for his own benefit. He questioned her with a fervid cunning about what he referred to as 'her activities', watching her all the time with widened glaring eyes, and finally informed her that he was only 'checking up' since he had a full report on her behaviour from a private detective. This was so much more dramatic than she had expected, that she was sorry for him, and said, almost humorously, that surely a detective was unnecessary since she would be only too pleased to tell him everything she was doing. 'After all,' she pointed out, 'I have told you everything, haven't I?' He ground his teeth at her, but it was as a matter of form: the whole scene had the rehearsed quality she had expected as soon as she had heard the 'official' tone on the telephone.

The third time he descended abruptly at eight in the morning and she knew that this was the result of a sleepless night thinking about her. He informed her that in the year before she had left him, she had bought goods to the value of £20 at the shops, and as he was incurring a great deal of extra expense due to her having left him, he felt 'it was the least she could do' to pay it back. He produced an account like a shopkeeper's on a sheet of stiff paper: Item one pair of shoes; Item one sweater, 25s; and so on, handing it to her with a sentimental and appealing smile. His lips trembled; he was nearly in tears.

She took the account and said she would let him have the money as soon as she could. She was earning at that time £15 a month. He continued to gaze at her appealingly, and she said, suddenly very angry: 'I'll pay it off at a pound a month,' and looked to see if he would be ashamed. But he again gave her the sad trembling smile and said: 'Yes, Matty, that-that-that would-would be a-a help.' The stammer told her that all this was part of a pre-imagined scene.

When she had told Jasmine about it, the girl's look of amused discomfort made her feel angry with herself: she knew she should have told Douglas to go to hell; and by acting in the way she had she had made herself part of his hysteria.

'But Matty, you couldn't have agreed to pay it? He earns so much money.'

'Well, yes, I did.'

'Then you're mad too.' Jasmine gave her the twenty pounds, told her to pay Douglas and be done with it. Martha sent Douglas the money, got a stiff but sentimental letter of thanks back, and because of Jasmine's reaction to the incident, and her own shame, promised herself 'when she had time' to examine the emotion she called pride.

This, then, was the first meeting since she had sent him the twenty pounds.

'What did you want to see me for?'

'There's this question of divorce.'

'Yes?'

'I intend to cite William as co-respondent.'

For a moment she was frightened: then she understood she was not frightened, her heart was beating out of anger. She had become skilled in listening to her instinctive responses to Douglas: If I'm not frightened, she told herself, then it means he is lying. I don't believe him. Why don't I? After a time she was able to see it: Of course he wouldn't cite William – he would never admit publicly that his wife had left him for a sergeant in the airforce – that's the way his mind works. So he's trying to find out something else. What is it?

'Of course you must cite William,' she said. 'It would be much quicker that way.'

He went red, and blurted out: 'Of course if he were posted suddenly it would make divorce proceedings difficult.'

'Yes, I suppose it would.'

'Desertion is quick and civilized. But if you contested it, then it would be difficult.'

'I deserted you,' she remarked; reminded herself that there was something she ought to be understanding; considered, and finally said to herself: That's it. He's afraid I'd divorce him for that girl in Y— But how could I? I didn't condone it

– or did I? I couldn't have condoned it, legally, or he wouldn't be afraid.

Again she was dismayed by the depth of her contempt for him. She got up and said: 'If you divorce me for desertion, I won't contest it. Why should I? I don't care about it one way or the other.'

He remained seated, staring, his fat lips trembling. She saw that he had imagined this scene differently. He had gained what he wanted, but not as he had wanted it.

'I'd like to go to sleep,' she said.

He remained seated. 'I'll see the lawyers tomorrow and if it's easier to cite William, I'll let you know,' he said.

He's trying to make me plead with him not to involve William, she thought. He was watching her with a self-consciously wistful smile. She said nothing. His face swelled into hatred and he said: 'It would serve him right.'

'What for?'

'Breaking up our marriage.'

But not even he could believe this. He hastily looked away, and said: 'The lawyers will write to you. We must have no communication of any kind until the divorce is over.'

'Of course.'

He lingered by the door, again wistful. She thought: I've lived with this grown-up schoolboy for four years, and we've had a child together. I ought to feel something that I don't: I ought to feel degraded or ashamed or regretful – something like that. Well, I don't. It simply didn't concern me. While this thought went through her mind she felt her knees shaking again, and she understood she was terrified. His sideways glances at her were full of an avid hate: it was ludicrous, the effect of the ugly eyes in the formally senti-mental and appealing face. She thought: If I don't say the right thing, he'll embrace me or hit me – it will be horrible. There'll be a horrible scene. She said, 'I'll ring you up in a day or two and ask what the lawyers said.' Her voice was casual and friendly. His face changed and became stiff. He nodded, and went out, carefully closing the door after him as if locking her in. And when she tested it she found that he had turned the key in her lock.

Now she wanted to cry. But she would not allow herself tears. Just as tenderness, moments of real emotion with William left her exposed to her need for Caroline, so did tears, even brief tears, open her to a feeling of deep, impersonal pain that seemed to be lying in wait for her moments of weakness like an enemy whose name she did not know, but whose shape and attributes she was learning because of its shadow, deepening steadily outside the bright shell she lived within.

She went to sleep at once, without thinking of Douglas.

These days she always woke early, and with delight, no matter how late she had been in getting to bed. For the first time in her life waking was not a painful process of adjustment. The shrilling and twittering of the birds who filled Mrs Carson's garden every morning, or the roar of aircraft overhead, sank into her sleep like a premonition of the day's excitements, and before she had opened her eyes she was already poised forward in spirit, thinking of the moment when she would rejoin the group and her friends.

Before she could join them, of course, she had to put in an obligatory eight hours in the office. She had returned as junior typist to Robinson, Daniel and Cohen, now reduced because of the war to Mr Robinson. Mr Max Cohen was two years dead of a heart attack. Mr Jasper Cohen was helping to run the army in North Africa. Mr Daniel was fighting in it. Mr Robinson's young, lean, tightly-sprung body must conceal some weakness, for it was known he had tried to reach the war and failed. When Martha had applied for a job in her old firm she had done so thinking of the gentle kindliness of Mr Max Cohen. There was such a shortage of women workers for the offices that Mr Robinson was pleased enough to see her. That Martha disliked him as much now as she had always done seemed irrelevant, when her working life was irrelevant to her real interests. There were two women in the office now, herself and Mrs Buss. That two women were enough was because of the efficiency of Mrs Buss, who never let Mr Robinson or Martha forget this truth, which led to her salary being increased almost monthly. Neither Mr Robinson nor Martha begrudged her this: in fact Martha imagined that when he signed the pay cheques and handed hers to Mrs Buss he must feel embarrassed because he was paying for her entire life: her devoted, jealous watchful interest was concentrated on Mr Robinson, not as a man, but as the unworthy representative of the absent senior partners. Sometimes he remarked, almost resentfully, that there was no need for her to work at nights, or arrive at the office so early in the mornings. Whereupon she faced herself at him like a quarrelling little bird, and said: 'Mr Robinson, I know my job. I had my training in Britain, not like these Colonial girls.' 'Oh well,' he would say, escaping hastily, 'I suppose it's all right, if you don't mind.'

Mrs Buss tolerated Martha; it was because the Colonial spirit she despised was too strong for her. Martha had been married to one of the up and coming young men of the town, and would probably marry another. Society, it seemed, owed her this job as an interim support, and efficiency was scarcely demanded of her. Mrs Buss felt that Martha was one of the drones – 'one of the marrying kind,' as she put it, with kindly but critical titter, although not married at the moment. She, Mrs Buss, was not, although she had a husband. On this basis the two women enjoyed an amiable working relationship.

On that day Martha worked through the lunch-hour, not for Mr Robinson, but addressing envelopes for the Sympathizers of Russia. After lunch she was telephoned by Jasmine who said that Jackie Bolton had telephoned her; he and William were posted and leaving that night for some necessarily unnamed destination. They must all meet on the station for the farewell at six. The two girls consoled each other and agreed to meet at the group office after work. There they sat, smoking, for once idle, out of a feeling that their impending loss must be paid due to in some way. They were talking of how the four of them would meet after the war, and continue this friendship which was subordinate to the Revolution. They did not specify the country where they would meet: the world was open to them. As Jackie often remarked: When you're a communist you can go to any country in the world and be with friends at once. When members of the group talked of the future, it was as if they were interchangeable with each other, one country the same as another: they were part of the great band of international brothers, and as they talked their eyes met, exchanging looks of infinite devotion and trust.

Now Jasmine and Martha leaned at the window looking down into the street, and both their minds were so occupied with visions of the future that the fact their lovers were leaving them in an hour seemed unimportant, even proof of their belief that the time was coming soon when pain would cease to exist.

A small ragged, barefooted black child, pot-bellied with malnutrition, hesitated on the opposite corner outside McGrath's holding a note in his hand. He had been sent by his white mistress on some errand and could not find the right address. Martha and Jasmine smiled at each other, saying in the smile that because of them, because of their vision, he was protected and saved: the future they dreamed of seemed just around the corner; they could almost touch it. Each saw an ideal town, clean, noble and beautiful, soaring up over the actual town they saw, which consisted in this area of sordid little shops and third-rate cafés. The ragged child was already a citizen of this ideal town, co-citizens with themselves; they watched him out of sight around the corner smiling: it was as if they had touched him with their hands in friendship.

Soon, the entrances of McGrath's were again clogged with people, this time because it was sundown hour, and they knew that if they were to be in time to see William and Jackie off they should leave for the station. At the station the train for the South already stood waiting. Down the long platform stood groups of men in uniform, waiting.

When the two men arrived, it was in separate groups, one of officers and one of airmen. They stowed their belongings away in the train, and slipped away to join Martha and Jasmine in a compartment where it could not be seen that the natural divisions of wartime organization were being flouted. The four of them sat laughing together, while the two men, half-sardonic, debated where they wished to be sent, like tourists choosing a holiday place. William settled for India; Jackie for the Mediterranean. In the next compartment a group of aircraftsmen were chanting in a variety of British voices: *Join the army and see the world.*

The train whistle shrieked, but Martha and Jasmine, with a long experience of seeing trains off from platforms, did not move. They were both of them instinctively avoiding an emotional farewell. At last they leaped off the train when it was moving, and turned to see the faces of Jackie and William already absorbed into the mass of faces that crammed all the windows. The train trailed off, as they had seen it so often before, across the soiled and factory-littered veld, leaving a long smudge of wind-torn black smoke across the clear calm sunset sky.

Chapter Two

Anton said: 'Has anyone prepared an agenda?' and Andrew remarked in reply: 'It was you who convened the meeting, Comrade Anton.'

'Yes, that is so, that is so.' He had been leaning back against the wall on the bench, arms folded, watching the others come in: Andrew, Martha, Jasmine, Marjorie. Now he unfolded himself upwards off the bench and into the chair behind the small white deal table, with the movement of a hinged knife opening and shutting. He watched them all in silence, waiting. The large electric bulb over his head cast a strong white light and made him even more fair and pale than usual, taking the colour from his ice-blue eyes. Recently the women had been remarking to each other: 'I hope Anton looks after himself.' Or, 'He doesn't look strong, does he?' Yet he was a strong man: he had the strength of extreme control, and the contradictions in the face added to the impression. The structure of bone was firm, narrowing too sharply towards the small pointed chin, yet it was an obstinate chin. The skin which covered the thin flesh was fragile, very white, and scored with dozens of minute dry lines which quivered into tense meshes around the eyes and mouth, particularly the mouth, which, though not small, added to the impression that the upper half of the face was too spacious for the lower. Yet it was a mouth continuously focused with the pressures of his self-discipline.

His contained intensity never failed to make people feel uncomfortable. Sometimes, after he had finished speaking, they might exchange a small grimace – not critical, they did not feel that – but as if they were confessing: 'Heavens, we'll never be able to live up to *that*!' But if there was irony in it, it was a criticism of themselves and not of him who took upon himself a burden of self-discipline and thereby released them into the freedom to be comparatively irresponsible.

There was something of this quality of ironical admiration in the air now, as they waited for him to begin speaking. But it seemed he was in no hurry to do so, and Jasmine at last said demurely: 'Comrade Anton will now analyse the situation.'

He lifted the icy shaft of his gaze at her, and said: 'No, comrades, I will not. It seems to me that no one here' – and now he looked with accusation at Andrew – 'has ever considered what an analysis of the situation – a real, Marxist analysis of the situation means. At least, our situation in this country has never been analysed. Not once. We have been too busy to think. Yet a real communist never takes an action which does not flow from a comprehensive understanding of the economic situation in a given situation and the relation of the class forces. We have merely rushed into activity spurred on by revolutionary or so-called revolutionary phrases.'

The contempt in this, aimed at the absent Jackie Bolton, affected Jasmine, who looked wistfully towards the place where he had always sat, crouched in a gap between a cupboard and the wall, radiating calm sarcasm.

Martha was thinking uncomfortably: It's all very well, but all this time Anton has been sitting here, listening and watching but he waited until Jackie actually left before exploding like this.

Andrew said comfortably: 'You are quite right, comrade. But things have happened very quickly, and they've got out of hand. Now we must pull ourselves together. And I wish you would make a statement of some kind that we could use as a basis for discussion.'

'Got out of hand,' said Anton impatiently. He had a way of isolating an idiom, listening to it, and giving it back to them for consideration. 'Got out of hand is correct. If things have ever been in our hands. We are running the progressive bodies in the town. But how? Why? Above all, how?'

'Well, well,' said Andrew gruffly. 'Well, well, well.'

'Perhaps, Comrade Anton, you could make an analysis and we could discuss it,' said Marjorie hurriedly. Anton patently softened as he glanced at her. Marjorie's small, fair fragility, her intense sincerity, seemed to put her, for Anton, outside ordinary criticism. They all felt it; so, obviously, did he, for now Comrade Anton collected himself from his moment of weakness, gave his cold circling glance around the room and said: 'We are supposed to be communists. Yes, that I believe is what we call ourselves. I'm not going to analyse the situation, comrades. That is something which is serious and will take time and thought. But I am now going to explain what the word communist means, and we can then, if we consider it desirable, begin to analyse the situation.' Again he collected them all into his concept of nobility by the circling sweep of his eyes. 'A communist, comrades, is a person who is utterly, totally, dedicated to the cause of freeing humanity. A communist must consider himself a dead man on leave. A communist is hated, despised, feared and hunted by the capitalists of the world. A communist must be prepared to give up everything: his family, his wife, his children, at a word from the Party. A communist must be prepared to work eighteen hours a day, or twenty-four hours, if need be. A communist is continually educating himself. A communist knows that in himself he is nothing, but in so far as he represents the suppressed working people he is everything; but he is not worthy to represent the working people, unless every moment of his life is dedicated to becoming worthy of them. The working people of the world are the inheritors of all culture, all knowledge, all art, and it is our task to explain this to them, and they will not listen to us unless we ourselves are people they can respect.'

Here the three women looked towards Andrew who was after all just as much of a communist as Anton. He was leaning comfortably back on his bench, pipe in his mouth, contemplating Anton and nodding from time to time.

'A communist,' Anton said, 'must remember that if he has personal weaknesses, it will be laid at the door of the Party.

A communist must always order his private life in such a way that the Party cannot be blamed for it. A communist must so respect himself that when he goes to the workers he is not afraid to look them in the eyes.'

The word communist, repeating itself through Anton's sentences, was a reiteration of responsibility and goodness; and Martha could feel the exaltation that seemed to be the natural air of this small dirty room heighten. At the same time there was something lacking. It was, after all, a very empty room with Jackie Bolton and William gone. They were not, tonight, 'the group'. They were five people.

Marjorie said hurriedly: 'Comrade Anton, I think we ought to recruit more comrades because it seems to me – I mean, the things you are saying . . . there ought to be more of us.'

Comrade Hesse smiled gently at her confusion, but at once collected himself. 'It does not matter how many we are. When Lenin began, there were probably no more than we are here.'

Instantly they were transported into the very heart of their vision: during the last few decades when people in the West have suddenly become communists, they have always been contemporaries of Lenin. They felt themselves to be in a vast barbaric country (though not their own) sunk in the sloth of centuries, members of a small band of men and women with rifles in their hands, prepared to die for the future. They pictured themselves, moving fugitive from one hiding-place to another; saw the mob of ragged workers storming the Winter Palace; heard Lenin say: 'Comrades, we will now proceed to build socialism.'

Andrew said gruffly: 'I don't mean any disrespect to anyone if I say that no one here is Lenin.'

They laughed and the mood was broken.

Anton did not laugh. His face tightened, and he said: 'If two communists find themselves together on a desert island, or in a city where no other communists exist, then their duty is to work together, to analyse the situation, to decide on the basis of their analysis what is to be done.'

'We are all in agreement with you,' said Marjorie excitedly, looking for confirmation at the others, who nodded.

'But I do think we should recruit more people,' said Jasmine. 'We all know people who are ripe.'

'You can't recruit just any Tom, Dick or Harry,' said Anton.

They felt awkward. They were sitting here now because they had been touched by that great world conflagration which was *the Revolution*; they might just as well, they felt, have been unlucky and not met people who could have inspired them into understanding. There must be dozens, hundreds of other people waiting for the touch of the holy fire. But if Anton did not share the feeling, did it mean he thought they, too, were unworthy to be sitting here at all? What else could it mean?

Andrew said with the gruff disapproval that told the others he was in total disagreement with Anton: 'We have obviously got to recruit more people. We can't run a communist group with five people.' He took in half a dozen breaths of smoke from his pipe, let it out through clenched teeth, and said: 'I know a couple of lads from the camp who'll muck in.' He then occupied himself with tapping, examining, handling his pipe, giving all his attention to it. They had come to understand this was his way of controlling his temper; and now knew that he was more than usually irritated with Anton.

Martha said hastily: 'We all know people, don't we?' – glancing with apprehension at Anton, as they all did, who remarked: 'Before bringing anyone here, they must first be discussed and approved of by the whole group.'

'The whole group,' said Andrew, 'five people. Of whom one, myself, is in the RAF and an outsider; one an enemy alien; one' – he smiled affectionately at Marjorie – 'a newcomer from Britain, and we all know that our Colonials regard everyone from Britain as wrong-headed. One' – here he gave a comradely nod at Martha – 'has recently behaved in what people regard as a scandalous manner. In fact the only person here who is absolutely sound, respectable and without blemish is Jasmine. I think we should bring some more people in, see how things go, and then make a decision.'

'See how things go,' said Anton, handing the phrase back to them. 'That is what we have been doing, and look at the results. We must do either one thing or the other – have a properly organized communist group, with rules and discipline, or we should stop this play-acting.' He spoke with impatient contempt.

'We can't have a properly organized group without people to organize,' said Jasmine. Anton was silent, and they understood that he would rather the group were disbanded.

'But we've got all these organizations on our hands,' said Martha. 'We're irresponsible to suggest dropping them.'

'No one's suggested dropping them,' said Anton. 'If you're referring to Aid for Our Allies, Sympathizers of Russia and the Progressive Club, then all we need is to have a co-ordinating discussion once a week. We don't need an apparatus of organization for that.'

'But you're talking as if we have to decide whether or not there is a communist party? But the vote was taken last year. This is a communist party.'

'We've just been running around like a lot of chickens – without discipline, without analysis, like chickens.'

'We've been meeting, we've been discussing, we've taken decisions,' said Marjorie, sounding positively tearful.

'Decisions? We've taken decisions and no one has obeyed them. We've been a bunch of anarchists.'

'The way to end anarchy,' said Jasmine, 'is not to abandon organization, but to strengthen it.'

'I must say that that is my opinion,' said Andrew. 'I cannot see how Comrade Anton can suggest a new vote or decision now. We voted once before. Formally this is a communist group. Now let us make it one.'

Anton was silent. At last he said: 'Very well.' He was silent again, and said: 'We have a committee. I suggest the committee meet. Jackie's gone ...' His expression said plainly how pleased he was that this was the case. 'But there's Andrew, myself and Jasmine.'

'But there are three committee members for five people,' said Martha. Anton shot her an angry glance.

'The committee's silly,' said Marjorie. She blushed at her

own agitation, while Anton smiled towards her. 'I consider it is not correct to have a committee while there are so few of us,' she said in a responsible way. The others smiled at each other, with fondness.

'Very well,' said Anton, 'but first, before recruiting cadres – that is, if we do recruit them, we've got to reorganize our existing responsibilities. We have to do something about the Aid for Our Allies.'

'We've got control of it in our hands,' said Jasmine. It was the last time she was to speak in Jackie Bolton's voice. The ghost of Jackie Bolton was exorcized, and for ever, by the way Anton said: 'Yes, yes, yes, we have control of it.'

The triple 'yes', was the nearest he ever got to humour: it was in fact an ironic, critical deadly assent that always made people shrink inwardly. 'That's nothing to congratulate ourselves about. There's nothing easier than to get control of organizations. Any fool can do it. It's a question of understanding the psychology of a crowd, or a public meeting. If a drunken fool wants to make himself important and play the revolutionary, it's not a matter to congratulate ourselves on.'

Jasmine's face was burning. At moments when Marjorie showed distress, Anton seemed almost to protect her until she had recovered, but it appeared he felt no such chivalry for Jasmine. He continued to stare at her, while he said: 'I think it is likely that *Comrade* Bolton has wrecked that organization. It remains to be seen whether he has completely wrecked it. It will certainly never be the same again. We have to see what we can do. The first thing is that there must be a respectable secretary.'

When anyone but Anton used the word 'respectable', it was with a small smile like a jeer; Anton used it like a measure of status. 'The former committee was ideal. Perr, Forester, and Pyecroft were the right officials. *Comrade* Bolton saw fit to force their resignation against the unanimous decision of this group.'

'But now that Trotskyist Boris Krueger is in control – and he will be, since he's a friend of that old fuddy-duddy Gates, we'll have to get it out of his hands,' said Marjorie.

Anton said: 'Yes, yes, yes.'

Jasmine asked at last: 'Have you reassessed Boris's character, Comrade Anton?'

'I see no reason why Kreuger should not be in control.'

Again Jasmine said, querulous and puzzled: 'But Comrade Anton, he's a Trotskyist.'

There was a long uneasy silence. For the months of what they all privately thought of as 'Jackie Bolton's régime' neither Anton nor Andrew had demurred when Jackie had jeered at Boris and his wife. The jeer had been collective, and automatic.

Anton said at last: 'Boris is an opportunist and so is his wife. But he's quite capable of running Aid for Our Allies.'

Guilt stirred in them. After all, Boris had been a personal friend. They had liked him – in a former incarnation. But Anton's attitude was more than an insult to them; it was frivolous. For months they had abused Boris Krueger and his ally Solly Cohen. They had even (if it is possible to cut people with whom one constantly sits on committees) cut them both. So whether or not Anton had seen fit to reassess his estimate of Boris it was too late. Andrew spoke. When he did so it was in a change of role: after all, he too had concurred with Jackie, called Boris a Trotskyist. Now he spoke ironically: 'Comrade Anton, you might have expressed yourself on this point before. And the fact is that any proposal we make on any committee, Boris always is in opposition. That goes for Solly Cohen and for Betty Krueger. Will you please consider that fact for a moment?'

'Boris has been trying to keep Help for Our Allies moderate, and to restrict its activities to its purpose, which is to raise money for the Soviet Union. Also to run this magazine, which we all agree is a good thing, combining factual propaganda and fund-raising. In my opinion Boris's line has been right and ours wrong.'

He now steadily regarded them. They were too confused to say anything.

'But aren't they Trotskyists then?' asked Marjorie earnestly, blushing.

It was a remarkable fact that none of the girls knew what

a Trotskyist was; they had accepted it as a term of abuse. For that matter, they knew nothing about Trotsky, except that he had tried to wreck the Russian Revolution. They associated the word with something destructive, negative, oppositionist for opposition's sake – with the cautious temporizing of the Perrs, Foresters and Pyecrofts, with the tendency of Boris and Betty to insist continuously on not alienating the citizens of the town by being too extreme; and with the way Solly Cohen would come to all their meetings and rise to make speeches about the Soviet Union full of facts and figures which contradicted their own. It was a fact more remarkable than any other that 'the group' spent most of their time plotting ways to circumvent the 'Trotskyists' – though the people they called 'Trotskyists' had little in common, and were in fact hostile to each other. Between the 'Perrs, Foresters and Pyecrofts' and people like Solly Cohen and Boris there was mutual contempt; and in fact there was a gap much wider between the first group and the second, than between Solly and Boris and themselves. Above all, between the attitudes of mind of the mass of the people living in the Colony, either white or black, and the small number of people that made up the 'Trotskyists' and 'the group' was a gulf so deep that from the other side of it the various sects making up the Left were practically indistinguishable, and described impartially as 'Reds' and 'Bolshies'.

Now, for over an hour, the five people in this room discussed what their 'correct attitude' should be to the 'Trotskyists' and emerged with the following conclusions: that they should be watched; that they should not be allowed to gain control of anything; that they should not be allowed to know that the group existed; that they should be 'exposed' at public meetings when they made statements detrimental to the honour of the Soviet Union. They were all deviationists, social democrats, left-wing sectarians, right-wing temporizers – these terms were flung about at random and without further definition. Simultaneously, however, they should be 'worked with' and 'made use of'. As for Boris Krueger, he was misguided but fundamentally sincere (Solly

Cohen was not sincere) and should be given to understand that they, the group, considered him appropriately placed on whatever position he might be able to get for himself on the Aid for Our Allies Committee.

It was now ten o'clock, and Andrew had to catch his bus to the camp. He rose, putting his warm pipe away as if it were a friend with whom he intended to have further, private conversation.

Anton said: 'Yes, but we have not come to any fundamental decisions.'

'What decisions?' asked Jasmine, who imagined, as they all did, that their firmness of mind about the Trotskyists amounted to a decision about policy itself.

'Comrades,' said Anton, 'there are at the moment five of us. It appears that we consider it necessary to recruit further cadres. We should know what we want to recruit them for. I suggest we each now give a brief account of our responsibilities and party work.'

Andrew, still standing, took the pipe out of his pocket and lit it.

'Comrade Andrew – since you seem to be in such a hurry.'

'Comrade Anton, I don't organize the bus service. However, I'll shoot: in camp I run the library. I think I may say it is the best library of any camp in the Colony. Except the camp outside G—, which is run by another communist. I have all the progressive and left-wing literature available, and my collection of the British and French classics is, considering how hard it is to get them now, not bad at all. I run twice-weekly lectures on British literature and poetry, and they are attended by anything up to a hundred of the lads. I run a weekly study class on the development of socialism in Europe, attended by about twelve men. I run a weekly Marxist study circle attended by six. I'm on the committee of Aid for Our Allies. I do a great deal of self-education. I think that's all.'

'Good,' said Anton. 'You may leave.'

'Thank you,' said Andrew, and departed with visibly controlled exasperation.

'Marjorie,' said Anton.

'I'm a librarian for the Sympathizers of Russia and Help for Our Allies.'

'Good, but you are developed enough to take on more. Martha.'

'I'm on the committees of Help for Our Allies and Sympathizers of Russia and the Progressive Club, and I'm organizing the sales of *The Watchdog*.'

'Good. That seems well balanced. You are not to take on any more. And you should attend to your self-education. Jasmine?'

'I'm secretary for Sympathizers of Russia, Help for Our Allies, the Progressive Club. I'm organizing the exhibition of Russian posters and photographs. I'm librarian for the group and group secretary.'

Martha and Marjorie laughed. Anton did not laugh. He said: 'Since I am an enemy alien and am forbidden political activity, my list is scarcely as impressive as Jasmine's.' He was examining Jasmine critically. 'Comrade,' he said, 'this must stop. This is nothing but slackness. No one can be secretary of more than one organization and do it efficiently. You will hand over the secretaryship of the Sympathizers of Russia to Matty, and the secretaryship of Aid for Our Allies to Marjorie.'

'It is, after all, a question of elections,' said Martha.

And now Anton stared at her. 'Comrade,' he said, 'a communist can always get himself elected. We are always the best people for the job. We are always reliable, punctual, and prepared to work harder than anyone else. If we are not better than anyone else, we are not communists at all. We do not deserve the name.'

He began collecting his papers together. 'I declare the meeting closed,' he said.

'But, comrade, we have made no decision about these people we are going to draw into the group.'

'Yes, yes, yes,' said Anton, moving towards the door.

'But we have taken a decision to bring them in.'

'Not more than one person each,' said Anton. 'I shall give a lecture on the broad outlines of dialectical materialism. That means there will be no more than ten of us, at the outside. We must keep control of what we are doing. We must stop all this girl-guide running about. We are revolutionaries. So called.'

Marjorie said, affectionately mischievous: 'Anton, you should have more tolerance for us. We must seem pretty poor stuff to you after your experience, but you don't bother to hide it.' She was blushing again, because of the effort it took her to tease him.

He allowed himself to smile. Then his face stiffened, and, looking before him at the dirty wall, he said in a soft exalted voice: 'Yes. It is hard to become a real communist, a communist in every fibre. It is hard, comrades. I remember when I first became a communist, I was given some words to learn by heart, and told to repeat them whenever I became filled with doubts or despondency.' He raised his voice and quoted: 'Man's dearest possession is life; and since it is given to him to live but once, he must so live as to feel no torturing regrets for years without purpose; so live as not to be seared with the shame of a cowardly and trivial past; so live that, dying, he can say: All my life and all my strength was given to the finest cause in the world – the liberation of mankind.' His face was strained with exaltation. He turned and went out, without speaking.

'But I know that,' said Marjorie, aggrieved. 'I've got it written out and pinned over my bed.'

'So do I,' said Jasmine.

'We all know it by heart,' said Martha. They all felt misunderstood by Anton, and held to be smaller and less heroic than they were. 'It was the first thing of Lenin's I ever read,' she added.

'Well, we'll have to live up to it,' said Jasmine, speaking, as usual, in her demure, almost casual way.

The three young women went together through the park, talking about the Soviet Union, about the Revolution, about 'after the war' – when, so it was assumed among them all, a fresh phase of the Revolution would begin, in which they would all be front-line fighters, fighters like Lenin, afraid of nothing, and armed with an all-comprehensive compassion for the whole of humanity.

Chapter Three

Martha spent a good deal of time anxiously during the next few days because it seemed that she alone among 'the group' knew no one who was 'ripe'. She had no relationships with anyone but the group, Mrs Buss and Mrs Carson. True that in her capacity as member of so many committees she had been presented suddenly with several dozen new acquaintances, all in love, in their various ways, with the Soviet Union because of the new, exultant public spirit; all willing to attend an indefinite number of meetings and lectures on the most diverse subjects. But she did not think they were 'ripe'. She felt guilty that she had not been 'working' on them, so that at least some may have made the journey from a willing compliance with the yeasty new mood to the utter self-abnegation which was the essence of being 'ripe'.

The people who were going to be brought to the decisive meeting all had close personal ties with members of the group. Martha pondered over this, and decided she was at fault because she had spent too much time with William; that the ardour she had devoted to William would, had she been a real communist, as Anton used the word, have been spent on several people. But it was only with half her mind she was able to believe she had been at fault. If she had longed for nothing else steadily all these years it was for a close complete intimacy with a man. She realized it was not Jasmine who had made her a member of the group, but William. If, then, she wished to influence other people to join the group, she would have to give them what she had given William? But it was impossible.

There is a type of woman who can never be, as they are likely to put it, 'themselves', with anyone but the man to

54

whom they have permanently or not given their hearts. If the man goes away there is left an empty space filled with shadows. She mourns for the temporarily extinct person she can only be with a man she loves; she mourns him who brought her 'self' to life. She lives with the empty space at her side, peopled with the images of her own potentialities until the next man walks into the space, absorbs the shadows into himself, creating her, allowing her to be her 'self' – but a new self, since it is his conception which forms her. Such a woman is recognizable often enough not by her solitude but the variety and number of her acquaintances and friends with whom she may be intimate but who, as far as she is concerned, do not 'really' know her.

Martha knew, with William gone, she was not so much lonely as self-divided. Her loneliness, the moments when she said to herself, 'I am lonely,' had a pleasurable pain; her old enemy, the dishonesty of nostalgia, was very close, and the ease with which she succumbed to it made her irritated with herself. For she was being nostalgic for something she had already outgrown. Her 'self' with William was something she had never been before, it was true: they had been like two children, playing inside the shelter of the group, they had been almost brother and sister. They had spoken of meeting after the war, but that was in their roles of being in love, being lovers, and it was not the truth. Already Martha was impatient to be rid of that image of herself, so much less than she was capable of being. But who, next, would walk into the empty space? She knew of no one; not one of the men about her now fed her imagination, or at least, not more than for a few moments of fantasy.

Meanwhile, she told herself, she must become a good communist. And she must recognize that while she had certain capacities as a communist others would always be beyond her. For instance, she could never 'work' on people. She would find Anton at some suitable moment and ask if a real communist, a good comrade, could simply admit to herself that she had limitations.

The thought of this interview with Anton gave her sensuous pleasure. The individual members of the group had all exchanged personal confessions, in a compulsive desire to share everything of themselves. Anton did not. One could not imagine him doing so. At the end of a meeting, or during an interval between meetings, when the others sat around in couples, talking of their pasts in a way which made them offerings to the future, he would dryly excuse himself and go off back to the hotel room where he lived.

But they all knew that in the same hotel stayed the Austrian woman Toni Mandel; and while his private life was certainly his own affair (even though they all insisted their private lives must be subordinated to the group) they could not help feeling she was not worthy of them. At meetings she would clutch his arm with both hands, looking up into his face with a great deal of arch vivacity. Walking along the pavements towards or away from meetings she tripped beside Anton, letting out small cries of laughter. She was an elderly girl, rather lean and dry, wearing strict broad-shouldered suits in the style of Marlene Dietrich; her fair frizzy hair bounced and swung below her collarbones on either side of a long face irregularly patched with colour, which peered and poked and bridled and coquetted with life from behind stray locks of hair. It appeared that never for a moment did she feel free from the necessity of being gay. But once or twice, at meetings, when conversation and intimate whispers really were not possible, Martha had observed that this woman tended to stare in front of her, her mouth fallen open a little, her eyes fixed. As for Anton, he would regard the Austrian with a small smile which was tender, indulgent, fatherly; but Martha felt that this protective smile was for the arch little girl, and not for the haunted woman who was a refugee from Europe like himself. It was precisely this intuition that enabled her to think of discussing her deficiencies with him.

They had arranged to meet at six before the decisive meeting. On that afternoon Martha was busy delivering bundles of *The Watchdog*, the communist paper from down South, to various cafés and restaurants and stores which had agreed to sell it. Jasmine, who had been selling twelve copies of it for years, had handed over the organization to

Martha, clearly feeling that she would do better to keep it in her own hands. Martha now sold fifty dozen. The glories of Stalingrad had created inexhaustible stores of goodwill and tolerance towards the inflammatory doctrines of *The Watchdog* in the bosoms of a couple of dozen penny-splitting shopkeepers. Martha had only to enter one of the Greek or Jewish cafés, or Indian stores with a bundle of *Watchdogs* whose headline was likely to be: *Red Army Recaptures Rostov* or *The Heroic Defence of Kharkov*, to find the proprietor smilingly agreeable at the idea of selling them for her. On this afternoon she set off on her bicycle as usual for the lower part of the town, going from one store to another. They were crowded with Africans. Their doorways were hung with bicycle frames and garlands of tyres, ropes of beads, garlic and lengths of bright cheap cotton. Each had a portable gramophone set on the pavement outside it, and the thin tinny jazz vibrated among the sunwaves which oiled and shimmered over the pavements and mingled with hot heady sweaty sun-fermented smells of the lower town. Sometimes a black man danced beside the gramophone, patting and feeling the pavement with his great cat's feet, rolling his shoulders and his eyes and hips in a huge good-nature of enjoyment, while his eyes swivelled among the groups of passers-by, men and women, inviting them to join in, or at least to share his pleasure. Or he would look sombrely before him, nostalgic, Martha was convinced, for the veld. For she could never enter the lower town without being attacked by longing for the veld, and for her childhood. In each store she lingered a while at the counter among the bales of cottons and the jars of poisonous-bright sweets, sniffing in the smells of strong cheap dyes and sweat and soap, talking to the soft-faced smiling young Indian assistants, some of whom came regularly now to the Progressive Club meetings. Finally, her handbag heavy with small change, she directed her bicycle back towards the respectable part of the town, and with reluctance. On this afternoon it was nearly six when she had finished, and she was cycling past the station when she saw Mr Maynard at the wheel of a car parked outside the Magistrates' Court. Beside him sat

Mrs Talbot. Mrs Talbot was now cutting Martha; or rather, when her beautiful grey eyes happened to encounter hers – one felt always by accident – they assumed an expression of stunned grief, and lowered themselves, while her face put on a look of sullen withdrawal. She was wearing a grey silk suit, and there was a bunch of dark violets at her throat, and her pale face glimmered through a mist of dark pink gauze which emanated from some point towards the top of her head, where there were more violets. Clearly she had been one of the assistants at a wedding where Mr Maynard had been officiating. The wedding guests, stiff in dark suits from which sunburned hands and faces incongruously protruded, or in floral silk dresses and unaccustomed gloves and hats, were still dispersing along shabby confetti-dappled pavements. Mrs Talbot must have climbed into the car, Martha felt, as fast as she could, to save the scene embarrassment because of her incongruity in being part of it. Now she had one agitated hand on Mr Maynard's dark-clothed arm, and he was leaning forward, his heavy, dark-jowled face above hers. 'She's asking advice about investments again,' Martha decided; for she had observed that Mrs Talbot was never so helplessly feminine as when doing this. She passed the car in such a way that Mrs Talbot would not have the irritation of having pointedly to ignore her existence; but Mr Maynard's melancholy bloodhound's eyes rolled towards her and he said through the open window: 'Wait for me, I want a word with you, young woman.' Martha nodded, annoyed because of the 'young woman', but aware it was for the benefit of Mrs Talbot who – she perfectly understood the justice of this – would always exact from other people temporary fallings-off from their usual standards of behaviour. Martha wheeled the bicycle along the edge of the pavement and waited until Mr Maynard came level with her and said, with nothing of the 'young woman' in his tone: 'Can you rest that machine a minute? I want to talk to you.' Martha put the bicycle against the wall, and climbed into the car beside him, her arms full of *Watchdogs*.

Mr Maynard sat frowning. He was annoyed, but not with

her. 'What's this I hear,' he said at last, 'about you refusing to give young Knowell a divorce?'

'I can't imagine.'

'It did not strike me as likely, I admit.'

'I've got to be somewhere at six,' said Martha.

'I took it for granted you would have to be somewhere – you always have. But it's already past six, and you might as well make your apologies for a worthwhile lapse in punctuality.'

Martha thought of Anton waiting for her, fidgeted, and sat still.

'It has been put to me,' said Mr Maynard, abrupt because of his dislike at having to say any of this, 'that you have allowed it to be understood that if young Knowell starts divorce proceedings against you you will start counter-proceedings against him on the grounds of adultery.'

Martha was half-numbed with anger and distaste. She said: 'In other words, Mrs Talbot is frightened that her precious Elaine might be cited as co-respondent and has asked you to plead with me.'

'You could put it like that.' She turned her face away from him, fiddling with the door-handle as if about to jump out of the car. At the look of angry repulsion on her face he said quickly, laughing: 'Any intelligent person knows that when two people get divorced, even if they are normally the most delightful and veracious couple in the world, not a word either of them says is to be believed.'

'In that case, I don't know why you bother to ask me questions.' She opened the door and was about to leave him.

'No, do wait a moment. Do wait.' He, in his turn, had coloured: the handsome, heavy face was suffused with blood. He passed his hand over his eyes, which were closed. 'I'm sorry,' he said. 'I've been put in a false position. I don't know why I agreed to talk to you at all – but I suppose I must. Take me as an emissary. Just tell me, there's a good girl, and let's get it over with.'

'All this business makes me sick,' said Martha. 'I don't know why it has to be so – disgusting. I saw Douglas a few days ago, and he said he would divorce me for desertion and I agreed. Why shouldn't I agree? I'm not going to get mixed up in all this.'

'Mixed up? But aren't you?'

'No, I'm not.' At his ironical expression she went on: 'If they want to make something ugly of it it's their affair.'

'Not yours?'

'No. If Douglas tells Mrs Talbot I'm making a fuss it's not because he wants an excuse not to marry Elaine, I'm sure he does . . .'

'Why? I'm not sure at all.'

'Obviously. The sooner he marries someone else the sooner his pride will be soothed, won't it? Obviously he'll marry someone or other before the year's out – and there's Elaine all conveniently on hand. He'll marry the day after the decree's absolute, just to show everyone.'

'You mean, to show *you*?'

'*Me?*' said Martha, genuinely surprised. 'Why me? He doesn't care about me. He cares what people will say, that's all.'

'Ah,' commented Mr Maynard.

'And if Mrs Talbot knew anything about Douglas she'd know he's only saying I won't divorce him so that she and Elaine can feel terribly sorry for him, that's all.'

'I suppose it hasn't occurred to you that Douglas will never forgive you for not asking him to be chivalrous and allowing himself to be divorced?'

'You mean, he won't forgive me for not giving him the opportunity of looking noble in front of Mrs Talbot and Elaine – he'd get months of self-pity out of it.'

'*That* degree of contempt is really not forgivable, you know,' he commented at last, his voice ironically aggrieved as if it were he whom she accused.

'Oh *Lord*, all I want is to be rid of the thing. I keep telling you . . .' She stopped. After all, she had had no opportunity of telling him anything, and the *you* was collective, her old life which was in no way connected with what she was now.

'Ah,' said Mr Maynard, this time finally. He examined his fine handsome hand, back and front, for a few moments.

'Well, your attitude seems to be clear, and I'll take a suitable opportunity to convey your message to Mrs Talbot.'

'I haven't sent any message to Mrs Talbot.'

'You can't expect her to approve of you.'

'I don't see why not. Now she can have what she's always wanted – that Elaine can marry Douglas. God knows why she wants it, but I always thought she did.'

'Yes, I think you're right. About this you're very probably right.' Martha turned her eyes on him, startled: the way he had said it applied a degree of knowledge – at the moment ironic – of Mrs Talbot that she had never suspected. He raised his eyes from a contemplation of his fingers, saw her look and said hastily: 'Mrs Talbot and I are old friends.'

She shrugged, impatient at the idea that he might imagine she was interested one way or the other.

'Well,' he said, annoyed at her shrug, 'I shall never succeed in fathoming the complicated depths of your morality, but if you're shocked, as you appear to be, then I can only say you are quite devoid of a sense of humour.'

Again Martha shrugged. He examined her, noted she was pale, much thinner than he had ever seen her, and her mouth was set over unhappiness.

'You miss your daughter?' he inquired.

'No,' said Martha decisively, wincing.

'Ah,' he said, on a softer note. 'Well, well. And you are going to marry that young man of yours?'

'What young man? Oh, you mean William?'

'I didn't know there was another I might mean.'

'He's been posted. For taking part in politics,' she added.

'Quite right too.'

'If people can die for politics I don't see why they shouldn't be allowed to take an active part in them.'

'How naïve. Is that the line of that rag there?' He reached over for a limp copy of *The Watchdog* and regarded its exclamatory front page with raised black brows.

'So crude,' said Martha.

'Quite. I prefer my left-wing propaganda put into decent English and appearing in unobtrusive paragraphs in the serious weeklies where only reactionaries like myself can see them. I like them to begin: "According to our correspondent it is believed that there might be a possibility . . ."' He smiled at her, inviting her to smile back. She did not smile.

'Why do you call it propaganda? And, anyway, it's not meant for you.' She took back the paper and folded it into the pile of others.

'It's not, I should have thought, for you either.'

'What's the time?' she asked.

'Come and have a drink at the Club?'

'At the Club!' she said derisively.

'Then come and have a cup of tea at Greasy Dick's.'

'I'm late, I told you.'

'Are you making many recruits among the working masses?'

She grinned at him, for the first time, saying nothing.

'Well, are you?'

'I must go.'

'No, wait a moment.'

'Why, is there anything else?'

'Actually there is. It's about Binkie. You do, perhaps, remember my son?'

'Well, of course.'

'He has informed us that he intends to marry someone called Maisie. Do you know her?'

'Don't you? She was going around with Binkie for months.'

'We were not aware of it. But it appears she is already twice a widow?'

'Oh, so that RAF type got killed after all?'

'As you remark. The RAF type got killed. And so did her first husband.'

'Well, that's not her fault, is it?'

'Binkie is on leave and he insists on marrying Maisie at once. I saw her and when I asked her if *she* insisted she replied that she didn't mind. Is she always so enthusiastic about her fiancés?'

'Well, yes. She's – good-natured,' said Martha.

'Good Lord.'

'What do you want to find out about her?'

'My wife has been in tears for three days now, but she is clearly on the point of finding Maisie a sweet girl. What I want to know is, shall I find her so?'

'She's not of your class,' said Martha, 'if that's what you mean?' She was conscious, in using the word to him, of paying tribute to old habits of their friendship: she had learned to use it politically and not socially. Again she felt dragged back into something she had outgrown, and resented him for it.

'No, I do not. She may not be my class, but she is certainly Binkie's. I want to know if she'll be a good influence – you know, settling, soothing, that sort of thing. Or will they get divorced again on his next leave?'

'They've known each other for years. But why don't you talk to Binkie about it?'

His face went dark and he said: 'I find it impossible to *talk* to anyone whose language consists entirely of primitive cries of pleasure or pain. Not that I am able to distinguish between them, of course.' He leaned forward and laid a large hand on her knee. 'My dear, would you go and talk to her for me?'

'You want *me* to go and ask her not to marry Binkie?' said Martha, shocked.

'Why not? If she doesn't care whom she marries? And I gather that's what you meant? As far as I can see they're getting married because they got tight together last week and the idea occurred to them.'

'But Mr Maynard, judging from what you've said to me in the past, you think marriage is so idiotic anyway ... and what difference does it make? If Binkie doesn't marry Maisie he'll marry one of them.'

'One of *who*?'

'The gang – the crowd. The group.'

'You mean there's nothing to choose between them?'

Martha made an impatient movement with her whole body, and said: 'Mr Maynard, I never see any of that lot these days. I don't know why you ask *me*? I haven't seen Maisie in months – except in the street. And I think it's absolutely revolting that you should ask me to go and put pressure on her. It's a disgusting thing to do, you know.'

'I can't see why,' he said tiredly, 'I really can't. But if you feel it is, then there is nothing more I can say.'

She opened the door and slipped out on to the pavement.

He started the car, and turned to say: 'I want to give you some advice, young woman. You'd better leave the Kaffirs alone. And you don't suppose they understand one word of what you say to them, do you?'

Martha said politely: 'The only language they understand is the sjambok!'

'Good God,' he exclaimed, really angry, speaking from his depths. 'What do you suppose you are going to change? We happen to be in power, so we use power. What is history? A record of misery, brutality and stupidity. That's all. That's all it ever will be. What does it matter who runs a country? It's always a bunch of knaves administering a pack of fools. Look, young woman. If, for reasons that escape me, the process of government interests you, if you really want to have a finger in the pie, then all you've got to do is to play your cards right, and put yourself in a position where you have power. For a woman it's easy. You should marry a politician and run him – easier to marry, in this town, where everyone knows everyone else's business, than to remain someone's mistress. If you really want to do the dirty work yourself, then you drop all this socialist nonsense and become a town councillor and eventually get yourself elected . . .' He stopped at the look of revulsion on Martha's face. He was filled with a sense of injustice; he had spoken seriously, to an equal.

As for her, she regarded him steadily like a specimen of horror from a dead epoch; she was positively pale with disgust.

'All right,' he said. 'All right. But you might remember this: while you are running around shouting about socialism and all the rest, this isn't Britain which makes allowances for social adolescents. This country's a powder-keg and you know it. The whole thing can go up at any moment – and if you imagine that a horde of savages wouldn't cut your throat as well as mine, then you're a fool.'

Martha thought that he looked like a bloodhound as he leaned across the front seat of his car towards her, the deep-set heavy-lidded eyes fixed on her in an irritated gloomy insistence that she must agree with him. She understood he was speaking as one white person to another; and that he knew so little of what she stood for that he could not imagine the appeal would seem contemptible, even irrelevant. She felt as she did when she was with Mrs Carson: she was listening to a voice already dead; as it were the record of a voice which had once made sense.

He even seemed to her rather pathetic. 'I'm so awfully late,' she said. He kept the pressure of his gaze on her for a while, his lips compressed; then he arranged the weight of his well-dressed limbs behind the driving-wheel, nodded a formal good-bye and drove off.

Her bicycle leaned against the brick wall of an Indian shop with several others. An Indian youth was leaning in the doorway of the shop framed by dangling beads and spices, watching a couple of black children who squatted on the pavement spinning the pedals of the bicycles; the pedals of half a dozen machines were being kept in flashing motion, dull reddish circles in the light from the sunset. The children hopped from one to another like frogs, spinning the pedals. The moment the Indian youth saw her there he came officiously forward, dragged the black children to their feet, and knocked their heads together. 'Kaffirs,' he said, 'run away from here to the compound. Run away home, black Kaffir-dogs.' He watched her obsequiously for a favouring smile from the white woman. Martha collected her bicycle, frowning, trying to show that she did not appreciate this gesture, and cycled away fast. Behind her she could hear the shrill voices of the children: 'Jewboy Indian. Jewboy Indian.' And the Indian shouted back: 'Dirty little Kaffir-dogs.'

Martha was suddenly depressed. She thought of Mr Maynard, and of the incident with the bicycle, and felt the depression deepening. It was probably, she decided, because she was tired and had not eaten that day. And she was nearly three-quarters of an hour late for Anton.

Black Ally's was full of grey-blue uniforms and she could not see Anton. At last she caught sight of him in a corner, eating with a book beside him. He set aside the book as she arrived at his table. He said: 'I've nearly finished.'

'I was kept by Mr Maynard.'

His eyes focused into suspicion and he said: 'I hope you were careful.'

She said, laughing: 'He was saying we mustn't upset the Kaffirs.'

'Who's *we*?'

'But Anton, they aren't idiots. They must know there's a group or something like it.'

'We have taken a decision that the group should be secret.'

'But Anton, what's the use of taking decisions if . . .' But she was unable to go on, because of the intensity of his eyes fixed on her: 'Decisions are decisions and must be carried out.'

She was now conscious of falling below his level and her own when she used humour to soften his intensity: 'He said that in Britain it would be all right to be socialists, but to be socialists here meant upsetting white supremacy.'

'Yes, yes, yes.' He continued to eat, unsmiling, watching her. 'And now what was it you wanted to ask me?'

She had not imagined that the 'personal talk' with Anton would arise like an item on an agenda; she now felt frivolous because she had been looking forward to something different. She said hurriedly: 'Well, it doesn't matter. Personal problems are not important anyway.'

'Yes, yes, we all have our personal problems,' he remarked between one measured mouthful and another. Then, at the sight of her face, he laid down his knife and fork, and summoned words to his aid. 'The personal life of a comrade should be arranged so that it interferes as little as possible with work,' he said. A group of aircraftsmen got up from the next table, and reached out over the heads of Anton and Martha for their caps and jackets which were hanging on a stand in a corner. They grinned at Martha out of the camaraderie all the men from the camp offered 'the Reds' in the town. She grinned back and noted that Anton was disapproving. He continued however: 'For a woman things are more difficult than for a man; and that is why a woman comrade is entitled to help from her male comrades. The problems of women, in my opinion, have not been given sufficient thought in the movement.' The pronouncement gave Martha a feeling of being liberated into understanding and support, and she waited, hoping Anton would continue. But he was looking around for a waitress. 'What do you want to eat?' he inquired.

'Oh – but you've finished, it doesn't matter.'

'You've eaten a lot of bread. And I suppose you'll say it's enough and go upstairs to the meeting. Did you eat at midday? No, probably not. In my opinion, you should make sure of three good meals a day and enough sleep. Yes, yes, you can run around like this for five years, not sleeping and not eating, and then you end in a sickness and are a burden to your comrades. To preserve health is one of the first duties of a comrade.' This was said in the same way as he had spoken about women: but now she was irritated, thinking that her mother might have said the same sort of thing. She thought: At my age (she was now twenty-three) I should have got over this automatic resentment and desire to escape every time someone puts pressure on me. It's a reflex from fighting my mother. She said: 'I'll try to do better and be more sensible.'

The waitress came over. She had been at school with Martha and they smiled at each other. She held the menu card for Anton in a way that Martha could see meant she was ironically impressed by this queer foreign bird. 'The young lady will have a large portion of stew and vegetables,' said Anton. 'And some stewed fruit.'

The waitress transmitted the order to a black waiter who was passing, like a manageress; and went to flirt maternally with a table full of aircraftsmen. Her tone to the black waiter was automatically sharp and disdainful. Martha noted this familiar phenomenon for the thousandth time, and told Anton about the incident with the Indian store-hand and the black children. Discouragement returned as she talked about it; and Anton listened in silence, finally saying, because she obviously demanded some comment from him: 'Capitalism creates divisions between human beings which will vanish on the advent of socialism.'

The black waiter deposited a plate in front of her. The waitress interrupted her sparring with the airmen to inquire: 'Everything all right, Matty?' and then, to the waiter, 'Jim, I keep telling you not to . . .' With a sharp gesture of impatience she followed the waiter, who had gone hastily to the screen that hid the kitchen door. From behind the screen their voices came: 'Jim, I keep telling you, if I've told you once I've told you a hundred times about the knives and forks.'

'Yes, missus, but the boss said.'

'I don't care what the boss said. *I'm* telling you.'

'Yes, missus.'

Martha said obstinately: 'I sometimes think a good deal more than socialism is needed to cure this place.'

'Socialism,' said Anton, 'will cure everything.'

'You haven't lived here, you don't know.'

'I have the advantage of having been one-fourth a Jew in Nazi Germany.'

This impressed her again with the richness of his experience as compared with hers, and she abdicated, saying nothing further, concentrating on her food.

'You will ruin your digestion,' said Anton. The tense mouth creaked into a small fatherly smile.

She thought: I wonder if he tells that silly Austrian woman about her health and her digestion? Her look at him must have been too openly speculative, for his face changed. 'And who are you bringing to the meeting tonight?' he asked. It sounded almost accusing; but not, as Martha's instinct told her, on political grounds: she said flirtatiously: 'No one. It seems I was too occupied with William to do my work properly.'

He held his eyes on her, so that she felt the heat creep up her neck, and said: 'As I said before, women have special problems.' But this time she did not like it: the heat in her face was for distaste of him. She said: 'I don't think I want any stewed fruit,' and got up. He collected his papers, paid for his meal and hers, and followed her to the pavement where she stood, back to the café door, looking at the street. She was thinking: After all, he's been with that Austrian woman for a long time ... If he's interested in me (and her instinct told her he was) then perhaps I have something in common with *her*. The thought made her despise herself; for while she pitied Toni Mandel she did not respect her. She reflected: It would be so much more convenient for Anton if he had me instead of her: his life wouldn't be in two parts. The cynicism of this surprised her, and she said aggressively: 'Why don't you bring Mrs Mandel to the group?'

He said: 'There are people unfitted for politics. She is not a political person.'

'I thought you said that everyone must be political, that everyone is. You once said that if you were put alone with any person in the world on to a desert island for a week you could convince them of the rightness and logic of communism.'

'Yes, yes, yes. But meanwhile we must make allowances for circumstances.' Now they were climbing the dark stairs. 'So you are not bringing anyone? Do you know who the others are bringing?'

'I saw Marjorie today. She's bringing Colin Black.'

Even in the dark of the stairway she could feel that he had stiffened. 'And who is Colin Black?'

'You've seen him at club meetings. He's her boy-friend.'

She remembered the special quality of Anton's regard for Marjorie, and she thought: Perhaps he's been thinking of taking her on? But he must have noticed that she and Colin were always together? Now the light from the open door of the office shone on to Anton's face and it was set hard. The office was full of people, Marjorie among them, who was sitting next to Colin. Usually Anton greeted her first, Martha remembered: this time he did not greet anyone but went stiffly to the table, seated himself, and arranged his papers without looking around at the others who, because of his unmistakable command of them, fell silent as they waited where they had arranged themselves on the benches around the walls. On each face was a look of joyful expectancy; and Martha's spirits rose out of the conflict of doubt and despondency she had felt below, in Black Ally's and on the pavement. She sat down, examining the new faces.

She knew them all, save for the airmen who were with Andrew, five men in the thick grey uniform, and sitting together with the look of a group within a group. Colin, Marjorie's young man, was a fat, dark, solid, spectacled civil servant who surveyed them all in turn, solemnly, between affectionate glances at Marjorie. On her other side was an extremely pretty slim dark girl who was a secretary in one of the commercial offices. Her name was Carrie Jones. Jasmine had brought an African whom none of them had seen before, a large man who sat benevolently watching them. Jasmine was also responsible for a married couple, Marie and Piet du Preez. He was a great beefy good-natured fellow, one of the prominent officials in the white trade union movement. His wife was a serious, pleasant-faced woman who looked as if she were dressed for an afternoon tea, wearing a tight floral dress and white high-heeled shoes. On the other side of Piet sat a small lad, an urchin of seventeen or so, a protégé of his, presumably, from the trade union. He had a red and uncomfortable face, peeling from sunburn; aspiring earnest grey eyes; and his hair, rough-gold-surfaced from sunlight, was plastered down with cream, but plastered in vain, for it was already rising in thick lively tufts from his crown.

These fifteen people regarded each other with respectful interest, in such deep silence that the chatter and clatter from Black Ally's below filled the room together with the smell of food which competed with the chalky office smell.

Andrew McGrew, who had taken off his jacket and made himself comfortable by rolling it into a ball and stuffing it into the small of his back, took the pipe out of his mouth long enough to nod at Anton and say: 'Let's shoot.'

Anton had been showing by the set of his shoulders and his lowered hostile head that it had been agreed there should be no more than ten people here tonight. He said without looking up: 'First it should be made clear on what basis we are assembled.'

Andrew said impatiently: 'Everyone is here because they believe in communism.'

There was movement around the room, and small exclamations of agreement and interest. Anton's pale eyes now raised themselves and moved from one face to another: 'Yes, yes, but we must make our basis for being here clear.'

Andrew seemed about to speak, frowned irritably, and decided against it. Jasmine hastily said, obviously trying to ward off any friction between the two men: 'It was decided to bring people to this meeting who wanted to be recruited as members. And it was decided that you should give a short lecture on Marxism.'

Anton said stubbornly. 'It is essential to know whether the people in this room consider themselves recruits as members or not.'

'I think Mr Hesse is quite right,' said Piet du Preez. 'Speaking for myself, I'm not sure where I stand. I don't mean about communism. I got mixed up in the Party down South last year, and it seems OK to me. But we ought to know about this group. There's a lot of talk in the town. But is it a formally organized communist group or a discussion group?'

Anton said nothing. Jasmine therefore looked towards Andrew who said: 'This is a communist group. A secret communist group. But the lads here from the camp came along simply to listen and see if they wanted to join. Comrade Anton seems to think that he shouldn't speak at all until he knows whether people want to join.'

'In that case,' said Anton, 'it should be defined as follows: the people here have come to listen to a discussion on Marxism, after which they will decide whether or not they will join the group.'

'But that's what we said all the time,' said Marjorie, amused and impatient. Martha had observed that the girl had been trying to catch Anton's eye to gain from him his usual fatherly approval of her, and was now hurt because his eyes met hers without any sort of acknowledgment. He said coldly: 'Precisely so. But we have to know exactly how we stand. And now I shall speak for three-quarters of an hour on Marxism, with particular reference to the dialectical materialist conception of history, after which there will be discussion. Then the people present will decide whether or not, on the basis of what they have heard, they wish to join.'

'Actually,' said the pretty dark girl, leaning forward, 'most of us know about the Party, don't we? I was recruited in London last year. Well of course I was on holiday so perhaps it doesn't count, but I do know a little, and I thought most people here did.'

Anton, controlling irritation, slowly turned over papers.

Andrew asked: 'Is there anyone here who has not had some connection with the organized communist party?'

The lad near Piet went dull red. Piet good-naturedly jerked his elbow into him, and put up his hand like a schoolboy and said: 'I haven't done anything yet.'

At which the African, Elias Phiri, nodded in reply to Andrew's glances and said: 'I'm ignorant of these matters. But I am very interested.'

They regarded him with a warm sympathy: after all, it was on behalf of his people they were all here. He accepted their glances with a broad smile.

'Now we all know where we are,' said Andrew. 'The lads here have had experience in Britain. But it does no harm to have the principles stated.'

'None at all,' agreed Anton quietly, holding them with his eyes, one after the other. He began: 'Comrades, this is the dawn of human history. We have the supreme good fortune and the responsibility to be living at a time when mankind takes the first great step forward from the barbarity and chaos of unplanned production to the sunlight of socialism – from the babyhood of our species to its manhood. Upon us, upon people like us all over the world, the organized members of the communist party, depends the future of mankind, the future of our species.'

He spoke slowly, drawing the sentences out one after another from his brain where they were stored waiting, and handed them to the listeners, his voice measured, unhurrying, not cold so much as anonymous.

Martha found herself leaning forward, tense, on her patch of hard bench. When she looked around, the others were in the same condition of joy and release. It seemed to her this unhurrying voice was cutting the past from her, that ugly past which Maynard had described that afternoon as a record of misery, brutality and stupidity, 'a bunch of knaves administering a pack of fools'. It was all finished. She was feeling a comprehensive compassion: for the pitiful past, and for the innumerable unhappy people of the world whom she was pledging herself to deliver.

Also, the calm voice was linking her with those parts of her childhood she still owned, the moments of experience which seemed to her enduring and true; the moments of illumination and belief.

It said: 'Comrades, the infinite complexity of events, each acting and interacting, so that there is no phenomenon in the world which is not linked with and affects every other – in nature nothing happens alone . . .' and she was returned to a knowledge of the thrust and push of knitting natural forces which had grappled with the substance of her own flesh, to become part of it, in the moments of illumination in her past.

It said: 'Comrades, men make their history . . .' and she felt her shoulders straighten, with an influx of strength, as if she had been given a gage of trust. So had she felt years ago when the Cohen boys at the station put books into her hands, as if they were giving her a key and trusting her to use it well.

It said: 'Comrades, the bourgeois illusion of eternity, the illusion that the present system of government is permanent . . .' and the terrible fear that haunted her, the nightmare of recurring and fated evil was pushed by the words into a place where it was no longer dangerous.

It said: 'The motives of men making history in the past were often good; but the ideology of reformers often had no connection with what they actually accomplished; this is the first time in history that men can accomplish what they mean to accomplish; for Marxism is a key to the understanding of phenomena; we, in our epoch, see an end to that terrible process, shown for instance in the French Revolution, when men went to their deaths in thousands for noble ends – in their case, liberty, fraternity and equality, when what they were actually doing was to destroy one class and give another the power to rob and destroy. For the first time consciousness and accomplishment are linked, go hand in hand, supplement each other . . .' And Martha felt as if a light had been turned on for her: she might still admire the great men she had been used to admire; they had been misguided, that was all. And she herself need not dwindle out (like her father, for instance) savage with the knowledge of belief betrayed. There could be no more misguided passion for the good, or soured idealism.

She was swung, because of the calm and responsible certainty of Anton Hesse's voice, on to a state of quiet elation and purpose. She knew that everyone in the room felt as she did. She was linked with them all, and from the deepest needs of her being. The people in the room, listening, exchanged small trusting smiles with each other; eyes, meeting, pledged faith with each other and with all humanity.

Anton Hesse spoke for more than three-quarters of an hour. It would not be said of him that he was carried away – he was not; but his words had the power and passion of the great men from whom he had taken them; and the confiding silence of the fifteen people listening released in him a faith in them which had most certainly been missing when he had begun to speak. His very pale-blue eyes, shining from the white light over his head, moved from one face to another – not in any sort of appeal; but in certainty, because the words he used were a proof of goodness and trust.

He finished with a quiet: 'And now, comrades, I have laid before you the barest bones of that structure of thought, Marxism. You must not imagine that I have done more than sketch in an outline. If we are to be serious, we must study. We must study hard.'

He let his shoulders loosen and his head drop to his papers, which he shuffled together, as if anxious to be off.

'I should like to congratulate Comrade Anton on the best brief outline of Marxism I have heard,' said Andrew. 'I suggest we appoint him forthwith as Education Officer.'

'Agreed,' said Jasmine promptly.

Anton said patiently and ironically: 'Comrades, may I point out that in the Party one does not appoint an Education Officer, or any other kind of officer on a wave of enthusiasm.'

'Quite right,' said Andrew. 'I apologize.'

'Is there anyone here who does not want to join the group?' asked Jasmine.

No one spoke. After a moment it was seen that they were all looking at the African Elias. He smiled and nodded. Andrew said: 'I think I can speak for the lads from the camp.' The four airmen with him all nodded.

'So there's no one who wants to stay out. Well, of course not,' said Marjorie excitedly.

One of the airmen, a young Scotsman with flaming hair, turned red and said with a consciously rueful despair: 'But man, I'm no scholar. If it is going back to school, then I'm willing enough. I left my schooling at fourteen, but I'm an ordinary working lad, that's all.'

At which the urchin Tommy Brown said: 'I think the same. I'm not up to all this. I mean, I liked what you said, but I left my schooling at fifteen.'

Anton sat up, fixing his eyes first on the young Scotsman, then on the young Colonial. He said: 'Comrades, do I understand you to say that the *workers* are not capable of studying? Of education?'

'Ah, heck now,' said the Scotsman. 'No one says a word against the workers while I'm by. But all this is too high-falutin' for me, it's the truth.'

'No, it is not the truth,' said Anton Hesse. He leaned forward, holding Murdoch Mathews from the slums of Glasgow with his eyes, while the young man writhed under the cold stare. 'Comrade, when you speak like that, it means that the propaganda of the capitalist class that the workers are not fit for the best, has affected you. You are a victim of their propaganda. As a worker, you are fit only for the best.'

Murdoch, having tried to exchange humorously desperate glances with Tommy the urchin, who was too serious to be humorous, said: 'For all that, I don't understand half of what you say, comrade.' His tone was still weakly rueful. Under the peremptory urging of Anton's eyes he sat up, however, and said differently, in a manly responsible tone: 'But I'm willing. I'm willing to learn if you are willing to teach.'

Comrade Anton turned to Tommy. 'Comrade Tommy, did you really not understand what I said?'

'I understood the general thing,' said Tommy apologetically. 'But a lot of the words you used were too long.'

'Then I'm sorry. You must correct me in future. It was always my worst fault. But in a foreign language it is not always the easiest, to find the right words.'

'You speak English better than me,' said Tommy, with a mixture of admiration and hostility.

'Foreigners always speak English better than the English,' said Marjorie, with such a warmth of admiration for Anton that he glanced up, giving her the small paternal indulgent smile she was used to receive. But Colin Black was admiring her with his eyes; Anton's face darkened, and he said, looking around the room: 'And so now, are we all going to work at our theory?'

At this, one of the airmen, who had not spoken at all, a very tall untidy youth with a pale bony face under a lank mass of black hair, said: 'I would remind you, comrades, that theory should be linked with practice.'

Anton said: 'You've been in the Party?' He did not say *of course*, but it was in his manner: the young man's tone had been as authoritative as his own.

'Three years,' said the airman.

'You are quite right. We do not forget the unity of theory and practice. But before we put our ideas into practice, we need to know what our ideas are. In short, we need to analyse the situation . . .' He acknowledged the indulgent glances of the old gang – Jasmine, Martha, Marjorie and Andrew – with an impatient movement of his shoulders. 'We need, I say, to analyse the situation. Before we can analyse it, we need to discuss it. Before we can discuss it, we need to organize ourselves in such a way that the group has the benefit of the experience and knowledge of every comrade in it. Therefore, we need now to discuss organization.'

'For the want of a nail the battle was lost,' said Marie du Preez, smiling humorously. But the humour faded from her face as Anton turned to her and said: 'Precisely so. We are Marxists – or so called. We therefore apply our minds to an existing situation and act accordingly.'

Marie gave the smallest swallow of resigned amusement, while her husband grinned broadly sideways at her lowered cheek.

'Yes, yes, yes,' said Anton, and waited.

'I formally propose,' said Andrew, 'that Comrade Hesse should put forward his plan for the organization of the group.'

'Agreed,' said Jasmine. No one disagreed.

Anton proposed that there should be a formal group meeting every week, attendance obligatory, for group business, reports on work done, criticism and self-criticism. Also, that there should be a meeting every week, attendance obligatory, for Marxist education. Also, that there should be a meeting every week, attendance obligatory, for education in political organization.

'That's three evenings,' said the stern dark young man. 'Some of us don't get that off in a week.'

'And what about my girl-friend?' said Murdoch, waggishly; but Anton said: 'Never mind your girl-friend,' and he subsided, with a loud sigh.

Three evenings being out of the question, and it being pointed out that this small group of people were committed to running half a dozen of the town's most lively and demanding organizations, it was agreed that there should be one obligatory group meeting, which would combine education with organization. That the airforce men should get lectures on Marxism from Andrew in the camp. That the group should be secret. That there should be no membership cards. That they would be bound only by their agreement to obey discipline and the will of the majority.

'Why should it be secret?' inquired young Tommy Brown at this point. 'I mean to say, this is a democracy, isn't it?' There was a shout of laughter at these words, and they glanced at the African Elias, who said good-naturedly, 'Yes, this is a democracy all right.'

'I see what you mean,' said Tommy uncomfortably. Then he leaned forward across the others, and said earnestly to Elias: 'I'm sorry, Comrade Elias. I've got a lot to learn yet.'

Elias waved his large hand at him benevolently.

'Having agreed that this is a democracy, and that a Party would not be allowed to exist, we shall keep it secret,' said Anton.

Bill Bluett, the stern airman, said: 'There's nothing much secret about it – I heard there was a group months ago in the camp.'

'Since we seemed unable to decide ourselves whether there was a group or not, we are not surprised you are confused,' said Anton. 'But in future we must behave like revolutionaries and not like a lot of chickens.'

The group rose from the hard benches, stretching and rubbing themselves. Elias said he must go at once. They all felt bad; he was going first, they knew, because it would be so awkward for them when they descended the stairs in a body and probably decided to go together to a café where he would not be allowed to enter. They all warmly said good night to him, shaking his hand. It occurred to them as they did so that they would not shake each other's hands: the effort to avoid some forms of racial discrimination leads often enough to others.

Elias went; the airforce men departed to their bus. The civilians remained, and, finding it painful to part, went downstairs to Black Ally's for coffee, where they talked, as always, with a painful yearning nostalgia about the Soviet Union.

The du Preez left first – the married couple. Then Marjorie departed with Colin. The small grimaces and raised eyebrows that followed their departure said that the group acknowledged these two as a good couple; the excitable charm of Marjorie seemed a satisfactory match with the phlegmatic common sense of Colin.

Anton, Jasmine, Martha, Tommy and Carrie remained.

Tommy, red with earnestness, his hair in tufts all over his head, was talking to Jasmine about the deficiencies of his education. She promised to meet him tomorrow at four, after work, to discuss a reading list. Carrie was keeping the pressure of her very pretty dark eyes on Anton. Martha thought she must be attracted to him, and was surprised to feel a small pang of jealousy. This made her abrupt and awkward in her manner to Anton. But neither of the two young women had the benefit of their emotions, for Anton rose, saying calmly: 'I must get my sleep,' and left them with a formal nod.

And now it was midnight, and there was no excuse to stay longer. Assuring each other of their reunion at the earliest possible opportunity next day, they parted.

Martha found Mrs Carson standing in her darkened kitchen in nothing but a thin nightdress, her ear pressed to the crack of the door which led into the garden, shivering with cold and with enjoyable fear. This evening it was easy for Martha to soothe the poor woman, and to persuade her into her bed.

Chapter Four

Cecil John Rhodes Vista spreadeagled at its upper end into a moneyed suburb known by the citizens as Robber's Roost. In the lower town it expired in a sprawl of hot railway lines and a remnant of oily evil-smelling grass-laden soil, beyond which, side by side, lay the white cemetery and the Native Location.

Before it came to the railway lines, the Vista ran for several hundred yards bordered by hovels, shops and laundries, and it was one of the four parallel streets known collectively as the Coloured Quarter. Along these four streets Martha sold *The Watchdog* from house to house. In theory this activity was to take two hours once a week. But in practice it took three or four afternoons, and three of the RAF men had been allotted to help her. Since the Coloured Quarter was out of bounds to the RAF for the purposes of discouraging immorality and miscegenation, the three joined a large number of RAF men who kept civilian clothes hidden in various nooks and corners of the town and changed into them so that they could visit their Coloured friends or women.

The rendezvous for *The Watchdog* sellers was an Indian shop near the end of the Vista. At six o'clock one afternoon, Martha had deposited the four dozen copies of the paper the shop sold for her, and was idling outside it, looking for her colleagues, when a small girl came running across the street, her thin hips pistoning through a large rent in her dress. 'Missus, missus,' she said: 'Mam wants you.' A hundred yards away Murdoch Mathews came into sight surrounded by a swarm of small boys who were shouting joyously: '*The Watchdog!*' 'Uncle Joe,' 'Stalingrad.' His lean jerky body was swathed in clothes three sizes too large, borrowed from Anton, and with his flaming hair and sun-hot face he was so spectacular a figure that groups of people had stopped to stare all down the street. These streets were wide, three times as wide as those in the upper town, for they had been built in the days when ox-wagons were expected to turn in them: ox-wagons often still did. A strip of tarmac, car-wheels width, held the dust down in the centre, but on either side the rutted gritty earth was thick with a haze of dust, reddened by the glare of the setting sun, which must have been shining into Murdoch's eyes, for she had to gesticulate several times before he saw her. She indicated that he should wait for her; he replied in a hushed shout that he would wait around the corner where he could not be seen, and went around the corner, followed by the stares of several dozen interested people.

Martha followed the child across the ruts and furrows of the road into the entrance of Mansion Court. The court was built on a common pattern of the old days fifty years before: single rooms opening off a three-sided veranda. The square in the middle was a filthy dust, and covered all over with washing-lines. Sitting in the middle of the court on a candlebox was a fat dark woman, whose ancient hat was skewered to her head with broken knitting-needles. She stared suspiciously at Martha from small, squashed-up, yellowing eyes, and said: 'Why can't I have a paper, why can't I have it?' and held out her hand for a *Watchdog* as if her being given it were a test. Her eyes became even more suspicious when Martha held out her hand for the penny.

'Didn't a man come around with *The Watchdog* this afternoon?' asked Martha – for this street was supposed to have been covered by Murdoch.

'A man never came. Men are not wanted here. The police don't want men here.' And then, insistent and suspicious: 'When will I get my room in the new flats?'

'I haven't anything to do with the housing.'

'You said I could have a flat when I signed the papers,' she said, fanning some flies away from her face with the *The Watchdog*.

'If the man didn't sell the papers in this court, then I'd better do it now.'

'Yes, we all want new rooms in this court,' said the woman.

There were twelve rooms to the court, and over a hundred people living in them. The first door, standing open, showed a man in his shirt-sleeves lying, arm over his face, on the bed; a woman knitting as she sat on the floor, four children, a baby in a candlebox, and a half-grown girl in a pink celanese petticoat who turned her head with a wide swing of her thick black plait as she hooked up a dish-cloth on a peg already loaded with clothes. The woman on the floor said to the dozing man: '*The Watchdog.*' He brushed the sleep off his face with his forearm, plunged his fist into his trouser pocket, brought out a sixpence, took the paper, gave Martha a comradely nod, and fell backwards on to the bed again, arm over his face. The next room was locked, but felt as if it were full of people, listening, waiting for her to go away: they were afraid of the rent collector or a summons, and Martha quickly passed on to the next room. Six men squatted around the floor in the space between two beds, dicing, with a pile of pennies beside each. There were two babies asleep on one of the beds, and a woman asleep, rolled in a blanket, on the other. A young man rose, leaned across the heads of the dice-throwers, handed over two pennies, took two *Watchdogs*, said: 'How's the Reds this week?' and settled down to his dice. Martha went on, accompanied by the small girl who had summoned her from the Indian store, and who was hopping on one leg after and around her, watching her with steady curiosity from very bright black eyes.

The next door was closed, but did not have about it the feeling of people waiting behind it in anxiety. Martha knocked, and it was opened by a young white man who said in a Yorkshire voice: 'Come in, we was waiting for you and all.' Martha saw he had taken her for a white-skinned Coloured girl; but when he saw *The Watchdog*, the moment's flash of suspicion on his face went, and he said: 'Oh, *The Watchdog*. T'revolution for me, right enough.' He took the paper and gave her a shilling, shaking his head when she offered change. Behind him through the half-open door Martha saw two half-naked girls, and another young man on the bed. One of the girls came, rested her naked breasts on the shoulder of the man at the door, and shouted over his head to the woman sitting on the candlebox: 'Mam, did you buy the bread?' The woman, without turning her body around, but with prim hoity-toity movements of her shoulders said: 'Dirty bitch, I'll put the police on to you.' And she continued to fan herself with *The Watchdog*. 'Did you see the police?' said the RAF man to Martha, one ally to another.

'No,' said Martha. 'There's two in the next street.'

'Then we'd better get moving on.' He hastily pulled the door inwards, saying: 'I'll be along to one of the meetings one of these days, you'll be seeing me.'

Here the small sparrow-like girl, still hopping on one leg, said to Martha again: 'Mam wants you.' Martha had imagined the woman on the candlebox was her mother, but now the girl darted off across the court shouting excitedly, 'Mam, mam, mam.'

A half-open door across the court shifted and a youngish tired-looking woman put her face around it. She said to Martha: 'Are you the Welfare?'

'No.'

'I thought you was the Welfare,' she said disappointedly.

'Can I do anything?'

The woman promptly opened the door. It was a small room, identical with the others, rough-plastered, with a red cement floor which was cracked. Small black ants swarmed along the cracks. There were clothes hanging from hooks and in a low bed a long knobbly body under a patched sheet. A shock of black hair protruded from the top of the sheet. The body was heaving with sharp, hard and irregular breath.

'The Welfare said they would come this day,' said the woman, looking at the bed. At which the sheet fell back and showed a very thin young man, in a grey shirt, which was open down the front, showing a cage of knobbed ribs. His face was extremely thin, his black eyes fevered and enormous. His skin had a dry greyish look.

'What do you want?' he asked Martha angrily.

'She's not the Welfare lady,' said the woman. 'It's my son,' she said to Martha. 'He's very sick.'

He said: 'I told you, I'm not going to hospital.'

'It's your sickness makes you talk,' said his mother. She stood at a short distance from the bed, hands folded before her. Her feet, in canvas shoes, moved irritably on the cement. Martha was reminded of a gesture of her mother's: the way she would sit smoothing the stuff of her dress on her knee with the flat of her hand, over and over again, in a tired irritable gesture. So did the feet of this woman move on the floor, in a compulsive, pawing way, like a horse which has been standing too long. She said to Martha: 'It's his sickness makes him bad. It makes him hard to please.'

A spasm of anger crossed the bony sick face. The boy flung himself down again, his back turned, and again became a heavily-shrouded body breathing hoarsely.

'Shall I fetch someone for you?' asked Martha.

'The Welfare said they would come this day.'

During this conversation the small girl twirled and twiddled her thin black legs as she hung from the door-knob, her eyes fixed relentlessly on Martha's face. 'Oh, leave off,' said her mother, and smacked her lightly across the face, to relieve her own exasperation. The child moved her face sideways, automatically, from the sting of the blow, and continued to dangle from the knob, splaying out her legs over the floor.

Murdoch's flaming mop of hair appeared on the veranda.

'What's up?' he said.

Martha went to the veranda and the woman followed them. Her eyes moved from Martha's face to Murdoch's in a patient undemanding query.

'A good day to ye,' said Murdoch to her. 'How's the patient?' His tone struck Martha as facetious, but the woman said, moving nearer to Murdoch, 'It's his chest, it's not doing better.'

'TB,' said Murdoch to Martha, and the woman nodded, adding practically: 'He will die soon, I think.'

Martha was shocked by the directness of this, but Murdoch nodded and said simply: 'Aye, and he'd be better in hospital, with the right things for him.'

At this moment a large car stopped outside the entrance of the court, and a well-dressed young woman got out of it. Martha recognized Ruth Manners, now a young matron with children: two small girls sat in the back of the car with a native nanny. She came picking her way across the court on large well-polished shoes, and did not raise her eyes to see the group of people until nearly on them. She recognized Martha, and gave her a polite smile, while her pale cautious eyes were animated for the space of a startled second at the sight of Murdoch, before she decided that he, like Martha, was outside her radius of interest. On Murdoch's face was a wild irreverent grin: 'The Welfare,' he said, audibly and derisively.

Ruth Manners ignored him, and said to the woman: 'How is he?'

'Very bad, miss.'

'Has he changed his mind about coming into hospital?'

'No, miss, sorry to tell you, he hasn't, the sickness has him unreasonable, miss.'

Ruth Manners looked full of patient distaste for the whole situation. She asked in cold clear tones: 'Shall I try and make him see reason?'

'If you like, miss, but he's not himself.'

Martha and Murdoch stood to one side while the young woman went to the doorway and stood looking down at the long knobbly form under the white sheet.

'Ronald,' she said, or rather stated.

The form did not stir.

'It's the Welfare,' said the mother helplessly, but on a note of warning.

There was a growl and a mutter of obscenities from under the sheet. Ruth came back and stood in front of the mother, her expression of distaste even more marked. 'You must see,' she said in a high patient voice, 'that there's nothing at all we can do. Is he taking his medicines?'

'Yes, miss, I make him.'

Ruth Manners continued to stand, frowning, looking around the court as from a long distance. Suddenly all her distaste focused: her pale eyes under the black crooked brows moved in a snap towards Murdoch and Martha; her face contracted with hatred, and she said: 'I suppose you communists have been putting ideas into his head.'

The colour flamed into her thin angry cheeks and she walked stiffly back to her car.

Murdoch grinned and said: 'It's the Red Hand again. Man, but we get into everything, we're under every bed.'

The woman, tugged backwards and forwards out of her stoic and patient stance by the pull of the lively swinging little girl on her hand, said: 'There was a baas here yesterday talking to Ronald. Ron liked him. Perhaps he could make him go to hospital.'

'Who was it?' asked Martha, slowly translating the 'baas', in her mind, into who it must be – one of the men from the camp.

The woman, with her eyes on Murdoch's extraordinary assortment of clothes, said with delicacy: 'I think he was from the camp too.'

'What did he look like?'

'He was selling your newspaper.'

'We'll see if we can find out who it was,' said Martha,

She and Murdoch left the court together, while the patient tired woman and the lively child looked after them, and the woman on the candlebox shouted: 'You promised me faithfully my room. You promised it.'

'I don't see who it can be,' said Martha, 'unless Bill's been doing our street. And by the way, you should have done this court – you forgot it.'

'I was getting around to it, I was getting around to it,' said Murdoch instantly, in an aggrieved voice. He had a way of suggesting he was unfairly accused at the slightest suggestion of criticism, but he was, above all, humorous. Now he grinned clowningly at Martha and said: 'Give me a chance, comrade. I was having a talk to a nice girl in the street behind this one.'

Martha asked: 'What girl,' realized that she was thinking

'white' – because her first thought had been, there are no girls in this area, meaning white girls, was shocked at herself, and out of her guilty anger said: 'You know quite well the group has taken a decision you're not to have affairs with Coloured girls, it's against the group decision.'

'Have a heart,' he said, 'I was only talking to her.'

He looked as guilty as a schoolboy, and Martha, disliking herself, said: 'But in any case, why shouldn't you? It's a bad decision, it's undemocratic.'

'Och, we should listen to Anton now, he knows his stuff, he's the real mackay,' said Murdoch with sentimental earnestness, and Martha, irritated by the sentimentality, said: 'But Anton doesn't have to be right all the time, does he?'

A tall lanky figure approached along the dusty broken pavements, wearing clothes several sizes too small. It was Bill Bluett.

'Wotcher,' he said, lingering at a short distance. His face was stiffly serious, but he winked at Martha with a panto-mimic sideways twist to his mouth. 'Finished?'

Martha said: 'There's a man in there who's ill and he won't go to hospital.' Bill Bluett responded to her agitated voice instantly, by saying with a soft jeer: 'Dear me, naughty naughty. These people don't trust hospitals. They should be taught for their own good.'

'She's right,' said Murdoch, one airman to another. 'He should be in hospital.'

'Of course he should.' The voice was still a soft jeer. Bill Bluett had cast Martha in the role of 'middle-class comrade' and never let her forget it.

She said to Bill: 'Was it you who made friends with him? His mother said there was someone.'

'Perhaps I have.'

'But why be mysterious about it?'

Bill Bluett, patiently explaining to an imbecile, said: 'These people don't like going to the native hospital, being treated like that.'

'Obviously not – on the other hand I don't see it's sensible to die before you need for a political principle on this level. He's not going to hospital because the Coloured people don't want to be treated as "Kaffirs". They want their own hospital.'

Bill Bluett and Martha, natural antagonists since they first set eyes on each other, faced each other now, frowning.

'OK, OK,' he said. 'Nothing like an intellectual for reducing everything to its principles. But he won't go. And that's all. He's one of the few around here with any political understanding at all. He influences quite a few of their lads. I've dropped in on their sessions once or twice. What would he do in hospital?'

'Perhaps he wouldn't die so quickly?'

All at once Bill decided he had sufficiently made his position clear, for he gave her a warm grin, and said:

'OK, Matty, I'll go and smooth his brow for you. But first there's another little problem. There's a bloke in the next street who's going to have his furniture taken away if he can't raise two pounds by six o'clock this evening. That's half an hour from now. We're quite a bunch of charity workers, aren't we? Fork out.' He pulled his trouser pockets out and picked out a sixpence from the lining of one. Murdoch found three shillings. Martha opened her handbag and found five.

'That's not going to keep the baby off the cold floor,' said Bill Bluett. He nodded at the satchel over Martha's shoulder and said: 'Hand over.'

'But that's *The Watchdog* money.'

'We'll have to borrow from it, that's all. We can make it up in collections from the group.' He appropriated the satchel, and counted out two pounds in pennies and three-penny bits, tied the greasy mass of coin in a handkerchief, and said, 'Ta. I'll take this back to the poor bastard and go sick-visiting to please you afterwards. He's four kids and another one coming.'

'Perhaps you should start a birth-control clinic while you're about it,' said Martha, for he had spoken about the four children with dislike, as if they were a form of self-indulgence on the part of the 'poor bastard'.

'Now, now,' said Bill, 'I'm a clean-mouthed working lad, I don't like sex talk like that.'

'Oh go to hell,' said Martha, finally losing her temper, and he laughed, gave her another solemn pantomimic wink and departed along the street.

'You shouldn't get upsides with Bill,' said Murdoch, seriously. 'He only tried to get a rise out of you.'

Martha shrugged irritably; every contact with Bill left her feeling bludgeoned and sore. She capitulated at last by saying: 'Well, I suppose for a worker from Britain we must seem pretty awful.'

Murdoch said: 'Worker, is it? He's no more worker than you. He's proper bourgeois, his father was a painter, a real painter, not what I'd call a painter, mind you.'

'Then I'm getting tired of middle-class wolves in workers' clothing.'

To which Murdoch responded with indignation: 'He's a fine lad.' He added, sentimental again already: 'The lads in the camp think the world of him.'

'Oh let's get back to the exhibition,' she said, too confused and angry to want to think about it. 'Why does he take it out on me if he doesn't like being middle-class?'

'Keep your hair on, Matty,' he said earnestly, following her. 'Keep your hair on.'

They were walking past the Indian store, where the assistant was locking the door for the night. He nodded at them and said shyly: 'How's the Red Army?'

'Fine,' said Martha, her irritation gone because of the reminder of what they all stood for.

'I've collected seventeen shillings for your newspaper.'

'Coming to the exhibition?'

'You let us in?'

'Of course,' said Martha.

'Of course,' he said, ironical but friendly. 'The first time in our fine city Indians can enter an exhibition like that, and you say, "Of course, of course."'

'We don't believe in race prejudice.'

He kept his ironical smile, nodded, and said: 'So the Reds don't believe in race prejudice, and so race prejudice is at an end in our city?' He dropped his irony, and said simply, smiling: 'You are good people, we know who are our friends.' He got on to his bicycle and went off towards the railway lines.

Martha and Murdoch walked along the bicycle-crammed street towards the centre of the town. Murdoch's expression had changed and he was looking steadily sideways at Martha. Martha, responding, thought: If *he* does it too, then . . .

'Let's drop in for a beer at McGrath's,' he said sentimentally.

'But we're half an hour late.'

'Being a Red's as bad as the army,' he said ruefully.

'But we have to have discipline.'

'Not even one wee drappie of beer? Well, you're right. You're right enough.' He sighed. 'It's a fine thing,' he said, 'to see a girl like you giving up everything for the working-class.'

'I don't see that I'm giving up anything.'

'I suppose you can take it that way. I admire you for it, and that's a fact.'

They were pushing their way along crowded pavements, separated at every moment by the press of people. Martha thought: I've delivered *Watchdogs* with him half a dozen times, and sat in the same room with him at meetings. We have nothing in common. Surely it isn't possible . . .

He said: 'What do you say if we get married?'

Martha said: 'But, Murdoch, we hardly know each other.'

'You're a fine comrade,' he said sentimentally. 'And you're an attractive lass too.' As she said nothing, frowning, he added, on his familiar weakly humorous note: 'There's no harm asking, is there?'

'But, Murdoch, how can you go around getting married just like that?'

'There's not much time for courting in the Party.' He said resentfully: 'I can see a working-man's life is not much to tempt you. Specially for you white girls out here – never had to lift a finger for yourselves in your lives. Believe me, you'd make a fine wife for a working-man!'

'Then why ask me?'

'Forget it,' he said, and began to whistle. They walked on, hostile to each other.

'No beer?' he asked, as they passed McGrath's.

'But I would if we weren't so late.'

'Aye, I'll bet you would. Waste five minutes of Party time – not you!' He went off towards the office at Black Ally's, saying: 'I'll change back into my jail-clothes. See you later.'

They had rented a showroom on Main Street for the exhibition which was called: 'Twenty-six years with the Red Army.'

The large room was filled with light movable screens that had posters and photographs pinned all over them. At the table near the door, Jasmine sat with Tommy Brown. He had a book open in front of him, and she was looking over his shoulder.

'Sorry I'm late,' said Martha.

'You *are* late,' said Jasmine, formally, speaking as group secretary. Changing her tone, she said: 'Hey, Matty, what've you done with Murdoch? You haven't let him go, have you – he'll get tight again.'

'I can't help it,' said Martha, furious.

'What's the matter with you?' Jasmine examined Martha calmly, nodded to Tommy to stay where he was, and followed Martha out to the pavement. 'What's eating you?'

Martha said laughing, but in genuine despair: 'Murdoch has just proposed to me.'

'Well, he proposed to me last week. And he proposed to Marjorie the day before yesterday and went and got drunk when she said she was going to marry Colin.'

'They're all mad,' said Martha. 'That means that all the RAF members have proposed to us all in the last month.'

'Oh well,' said Jasmine.

'It obviously doesn't matter to them who they marry.' Martha was laughing but she was filled with dismay and discouragement. She was relieved when Jasmine rolled up her eyes and said sedately, 'It's the spirit of the times.' Jasmine always made such remarks as if they were being made for the first time. Martha felt: Well, it *is* the spirit of the times, and laughed, and Jasmine departed to a hall down-town, where she was helping to organize a public meeting.

Tommy Brown was taking admittance money from a group of girls just out of their offices. They went to examine the posters and photographs of the Civil War that had the look of stills from an old film. Martha recognized the look on their faces, which was an idle, rather startled interest: it represented the feeling she had had herself, a year ago, when the 'Russian Revolution' was offered to her for the first time. She thought: But they'll all be married inside a year, so what's the point?

She sat beside Tommy, who was waiting for her with one finger marking the place in his book. She said: 'It would have been better if this exhibition had been about this war, about the Red Army in this war, instead of the Revolution as well.'

His round eyes searched her face. His face had a look of strain. There was a pause while he thought over what she said. Five minutes with Tommy always made Martha feel frivolous, because of the depths of attention which he offered to all the older members of the group.

'You mean, we shouldn't push communism down their throats?' he asked. He frowned. 'But that's what we are for.'

'Oh I don't know, I don't know, I don't know.'

Outside the door a group of dark-skinned people hesitated, and Martha looked, wondering: Indians? Coloureds? She saw the assistant from the Indian store and smiled. They came in, with nervous glances at the group of white girls who were making their way around the exhibition.

'OK?' said the assistant.

'OK,' said Martha. The group of Indian youths started at the other end of the exhibition from the girls, with an air of wary self-respect, as if to say: We'd prefer not to come here at all if it means trouble.

'Oh hell,' said Martha, suddenly utterly depressed, and instantly felt that to let go into private moods was irresponsible with Tommy.

He said, blushing scarlet: 'I don't think that I can be a communist. I mean to say, I feel bad things all the time. I know it's the way I'm brought up. But when I see Coloured people or Indians in a place like this, then I think of them as different from us, and that's wrong, isn't it?'

'We can't help the way we were brought up.'

'And it's not only that. I mean, sitting here selling tickets, I mean selling tickets to anyone, it makes me feel funny. I feel self-conscious. That's snobbish, isn't it?'

'Well, I felt like that to start with.'

'I mean, ever since I joined the group I feel funny. I don't know what I feel, half the things I feel seem to be wrong but I feel them. I know they are wrong but I can't help it.' He ended, very defiant, his honest urchin's face hot with confusion.

'But, Tommy, it's because we're both brought up in this country. We've got bad attitudes to people with a different colour. We've just got to change our attitudes.'

'But it's so hard to change. Today on the job I did something very bad. I was fitting a pipe with my mate. And one of the Kaffirs brought the wrong pipe and I shouted at him. But if I did different, then the blokes on the job'd think I was mad. I'm just an apprentice, and it's hard to be different from the grown-ups. And there's Piet. I saw him today on the job with some Kaffirs unloading stuff and he was talking to them just the way he always does – and listen to me, I use the word Kaffir and I shouldn't, it just slips out.' He ended in despair, almost in tears.

The group of white girls, having finished their tour, went out. Slowly the group of Indians scattered out of their defensiveness and began wandering around the exhibition at their ease.

'The point is,' said Tommy, 'it's easy for you, because you're better educated.'

She laughed in astonishment. 'I don't think that's true.'

'Well, it is, I'm telling you.'

His finger, insistent on a point in the page, drew Martha's attention. The book was *War and Peace*.

'Did Jasmine tell you to read this?'

'She said it was the greatest novel ever written. Is that right?'

'Yes, I suppose so.'

'But man, it takes such a long time to read. I thought this was the whole book but there are two others when I've finished this.'

On the open page half a dozen phrases had been underlined in pencil, with definitions scribbled opposite.

'*Your eloquence would have taken the king of Prussia's consent by storm*,' she read. And in pencil: 'eloquence: the power of speaking with grace.'

'I don't even understand half the words,' he said.

'But Tommy, you shouldn't read books unless you really want to.'

'I've never read books before, except just adventure stories. Jasmine said this book explained why there was a Russian Revolution; she said if I read this I would understand about Russia before the Revolution. But perhaps there's a shorter book somewhere?'

'Don't you enjoy it?'

His eyes lit into enthusiasm. 'Oh yes, I do. But you don't see what I'm saying, Matty. I watched Jasmine the other day, reading. I thought about the way she reads books. It was just another book to her. Because she's read so many books, don't you see? I asked her about the book she was reading and she said: It's a useful description of reactionary circles in Paris. Then she said: But it's a bad book. Don't you see, I wouldn't know if it was bad or not. It's just a book. When I read this stuff here, I mean about all these generals and maids-in-waiting and the courtiers, it makes me feel . . .' He hesitated, looking angry and stubborn. 'What I mean is, I couldn't say: This is a useful description.' He was suddenly scarlet with anger. 'Don't you see, it's just snobbish when you and Jasmine say things like that. Well, anyway, that's what I think. All the time I'm reading this, I feel – mixed up in it. I mean to say, if I were there, I'd be thinking just what all these generals and old ladies think. I'd be the same as them. And that makes me confused. Because they were all a bunch of reactionaries, weren't they? And this girl, Natasha, I like her.'

'But why shouldn't you like her?'

'She was the daughter of an aristocrat, wasn't she? So why should I like her?'

'But, Tommy, suppose someone wrote a novel about you. The Africans might say: Why should I like that reactionary white man, Tommy Brown? But it would help them to understand the way things are, do you see?'

No, I don't see. That's it,' he said, 'I just don't see. And sometimes when I tell you and Jasmine and Piet what I'm feeling, you have a smile on your faces, and I know you're thinking: Tommy's just a stupid boy.'

'But I haven't got a smile on my face,' said Martha. 'I don't know why you think everything's easy for us either. The thing is, now we're communists we've all got to go on learning for the rest of our lives.'

'I can't say what I mean,' he said. He put up his burned fist and began banging at the top of his head where the tufts of hair stood up. 'You say: "We've got to go on learning," but I don't even know half the words I see.'

'But we'll all help you, we'll all help each other.'

'Do you know what I think, Matty? Well, I know what you are going to say when I tell you. But it's this. I don't think any people brought up here, white people, can ever be good communists. It's different for people like the RAF, because they weren't living here all their lives, and so everything comes easy to them, but I don't think we can change ourselves.'

'But we are changing all the time.'

'Well, all right. I'll try.' He pushed the book towards her. 'If you tell me what the words mean then I won't have to look them up in a dictionary.'

They bent together over the book, but almost at once a large sheet of cardboard slid over the print. It was bordered with black an inch thick, and it was headed 'Homage to Heroes'. Solly Cohen, grinning heavily, stood beyond the piles of pamphlets on the table, hands in his pockets.

A short while before, at a Progressive Club lecture on the necessity for switching support from Michailovitch to Tito, for this was before Michailovitch's collaboration with the Germans had been officially confirmed, Solly had come with a group of local Yugoslavs and stood at the back of the hall chanting steadily, every time Tito was mentioned: 'Communist propaganda, communist propaganda.' At the end of the meeting, when the chairman wound up, Solly had leaped up to shout over and over again: 'Down with Stalin the Assassin.'

In the interval Allied policy had switched: Tito was now officially principal guerrilla leader in Yugoslavia, and Michailovitch a dubious collaborationist. Martha therefore faced Solly triumphantly.

But he seemed unconscious that she had any right to. He indicated the large black-bordered cardboard and said: 'I've brought this for the exhibition.'

Martha examined it. There were on it the names of a couple of hundred Red Army officers, none of which she had heard of. 'What are you up to now?' she asked.

'Short list of Red Army officers murdered by Stalin,' he said. 'Why don't you hang them up too? They died in a good cause.'

She handed him back the cardboard and said: 'You mean you've gone to all the trouble of printing these names just to come here and be irritating?' She was genuinely astounded. Solly continued to grin: he was perfectly satisfied, it seemed, with the reaction he was getting. It was the look of satisfied malice, which he wore now whenever he encountered 'the group' in public, which made it easy for Martha to dismiss him entirely.

'You're so damned childish,' she said.

He said: 'You aren't going to hang that list? You haven't room?' He took a rapid glance around the exhibition and said: 'You could take down one of those six pictures of Father Stalin to make room for it.'

Tommy Brown shouted: 'Capitalist propaganda,' and Solly, delighted, roared with laughter. He sobered to say: 'The truth is what I want. As a Marxist, I want truth.'

'Such as, that Tito was an invention of the communist party?'

He waved this aside, and said: 'This is an exhibition of the Red Army, and I want some of the hundreds of Red

Army officers murdered by Stalin to get some recognition, that's all.'

'You're mad,' said Martha. 'You're corrupted by capitalist propaganda.' And now Solly had got what he had come to get, apparently; for he again burst into peals of laughter and went laughing to the door. There he turned and made a low bow towards the picture of Stalin nearest to him: 'Salaams, Lord, Salaams.' He went out.

Tommy and Martha dismissed the existence of Solly with a contemptuous shrug. Martha tore up the piece of cardboard and, looking for a place to deposit the pieces, found a large packing-case under the table. It was covered in heavy oiled paper, and full of pamphlets called: 'Fascist Vipers Crushed Under Stalin's Heel'. She opened one and read: 'As the Fascist Scum leave their deposits of filth over the sacred soil of our Russian Motherland, our Heroic Russian Soldiers march on, armed with the unerring faith of true patriots and the inspiration of the Glorious Communist Party of the Soviet Union and its leader Comrade Stalin!' She grimaced humorously and looked at Tommy who, however, was not humorous.

'There you are,' he said, again in despair. 'That's what I mean. All that motherland stuff, it simply makes me want to laugh, that's all.'

Some people had come in and were handing their money over. Martha unconsciously slid the pamphlet out of sight. Tommy assisted her in covering the packing-case over, and said: 'Jasmine had them on sale. Everyone who came in saw them and laughed, so she hid them.' He looked guilty. Martha realized she was feeling guilty too. 'After all, it stands to reason the Russians feel more strongly about the war than we do,' she said, weakly.

Tommy said: 'But they say scum. I mean the Germans are human beings. They're soldiers.' He added, hastily: 'Though of course the Russian communist party knows best, doesn't it? Comrade Stalin must know what he's doing.'

'We've got four packing-cases of pamphlets from Russia,' said Martha. 'What are we going to do with them? Well, we'll bring it up at the group meeting and take a formal decision on policy.'

At this point Bill Bluett came in, back in his uniform.

Tommy produced the doubtful pamphlet and showed it to him. He read it, dead-pan, until Martha said: 'What do you think? I think it's silly,' when he reacted instantly with: 'Naughty naughty Russians, so crude, aren't they?'

'It's no use selling pamphlets that make people laugh.'

'They'd laugh out of the other side of their mouths if they had the Germans here.'

'Yes, but we haven't.'

'Well, we'll bring it up at the meeting and Daddy Anton will make a decision for us.'

Martha, confused, for Bill had always seemed to have respect for Anton, said: 'Why, what's wrong with Anton?'

Bill said, grinning: 'But what on earth could be wrong with Daddy Anton?' There was a personal implication in it, and she demanded: 'What's *that* in aid of?' He shrugged and said airily: 'Well, if you'll move, I'll take over now. You should be at the meeting, and you'd better be quick because it's going to rain.'

'You mean, I might get my feet wet?'

'That's right.' But now, as he usually did, he gave in, and his aggression disappeared in a half-cajoling, half-comradely smile. 'Run along, Comrade Matty.'

Tommy took up *War and Peace* and Bill pounced on it. 'Well, well,' he said, 'why not T. S. Eliot?'

'What's the matter with *War and Peace*?'

'You are a bourgeois, aren't you? Why not T. S. Eliot while you're about it.' He began reciting: 'April is the cruellest month, breeding lilacs out of the dead land.'

Martha listened critically: he missed nothing of it. She interrupted to ask: 'If you despise it so much, why do you take the trouble to learn it by heart?'

'That belongs to my decadent period. Thought you'd appreciate it. Ta ta.'

The street was hot and stuffy. The evening sky was loaded with black sulphurous clouds. A few large sparkling drops fell. She ran down the street as the storm broke, feeling the warm sting of the rain on her shoulders with acute pleasure.

By the time she reached the Sympathizers of Russia committee meeting it had already started and she was soaked.

They were discussing how to restore the status of the society, for as Anton had predicted, the episode with Jackie Bolton had caused all the respectable patrons to resign, including the Reverend Mr Gates who had had second thoughts. The policy, exactly the same now as it had been before, was being overseen by Boris Krueger, chairman, Betty Krueger, secretary, and a committee of people co-opted by them. Martha and Marjorie were on it with instructions to keep 'an eye on the Trotskyists'. While the hostility between the Krueger faction and the communist faction was extreme, so that before or after meetings they could scarcely bring themselves to exchange more than the minimum of politeness, their political views, at least so far as this society was concerned, caused the work to go on much faster than it had in the past when the susceptibilities of the respectable had to be pandered to in the wording of every resolution. The Kruegers and Martha and Marjorie were in one way and another raising large sums for Russian Aid, and in addition were selling propaganda leaflets all over town in numbers which took them by surprise. When the meeting was over, Betty Krueger, who had been eyeing Martha with elaborate hostility throughout, suggested she had better go and change her dress before she caught cold. Martha had forgotten she was soaked, and said: 'But I haven't got time.'

'Such busy little bees you Reds are,' said Betty, her fair and delicate face ugly with dislike.

'I thought *you* were a Red,' retorted Martha, and she and Marjorie left.

'Those Trotskyists are really so awfully childish,' said Martha explosively, thinking of Solly that afternoon.

Marjorie said: 'But they are all right for that kind of work.' She was looking embarrassed, and Martha knew why: she liked to slip off for a meal alone with Colin before or between meetings, and always felt as if this submission to 'personal feelings' was disloyal to the group.

'Meeting Colin?' Martha asked; and Marjorie, relieved, said: 'You know we are getting married next week.'

'But that's wonderful.'

Marjorie was hesitating on the edge of the pavement, giving Martha lingering glances of appeal. The wet street swam blue and red and gold as the cars swished by. It was still raining a little, and though it was a warm rain, Martha had started to shiver.

'Do you think I'm doing the right thing?' demanded Marjorie.

'To get married?'

Marjorie's face, usually open with enthusiasm and response, seemed pinched. She was wearing a red shirt, open at the neck, but she was holding it close in front of her throat with her thin brown hand, clenched like a fist.

'What's wrong?' said Martha.

'I don't know; I feel I haven't known Colin very long. He's so nice.' She added humorously – and the moment the humorous note entered the conversation Martha knew that the impulse to confess had passed: 'He's so nice, and he's just what I wanted – a solid man, you know.' She grimaced, staring across the street at the cinema which was showing some war film. Spitfires and Focke-Wulfs dived, spitting fire, across a vast wall-high poster. The reflection from the reddish lights of the cinema shone on her face. 'You know I always said I didn't want that kind of marriage, I mean a dull marriage – I don't mean dull, of course; no, I don't mean that. But I've been playing around quite a bit now and you get fed up . . .'

'You talk as if you were forty,' said Martha, suddenly angry.

'Well, I'm twenty-five, and if you want to have children, though of course if we're in a revolutionary situation we won't be able to have children . . . but I suppose everyone feels like this when they've committed themselves,' she added, smiling, again reaching out firmly for the support of humour. She nodded, and went off, saying hastily: 'I'll see you in half an hour at the meeting.'

So she's not in love, Martha thought, disapproving, feeling that Marjorie had betrayed something. Then she thought: Well, what does it matter, what matters is we should all work hard for the Party. And with this she walked off towards the group office. She had had no lunch and proposed not to have supper. She was still damp and shivering and thought she might warm herself in the office by doing some work, whatever needed to be done.

Anton was first into the office, and at once sat in his chairman's place at the table, looking at his watch. 'We cannot tolerate unpunctuality,' he said. 'The comrades are late.'

Marjorie and Colin came in. She was being gruffly humorous; he was eyeing her uneasily. Martha thought that the supper together must have been an uncomfortable one. They accepted Anton's reproof for being five minutes late with nervous apologies.

Soon Andrew came in with two of the men from the camp: there should have been five more, but he said they had all promised to be here and did not know where they were. They all sat around on the hard benches, waiting, while Anton watched the door.

'Why can't we start?' asked Marjorie.

'This is a full organization meeting; we have one only once a week and everyone should be here.'

'I've a mind that Murdoch will not be with us,' said one of the airforce men.

'And why not?'

'He's had a wee drop too much,' said the lad apologetically.

Anton let his cold eyes settle on him, and Andrew protected him hastily with: 'Murdoch's a good lad. He'll be here if he can.'

Martha remembered the scene of that afternoon, and thought: He couldn't possibly have got drunk just because I said I wouldn't marry him ... Acutely depressed all of a sudden she thought: Are we all going to pair off? But it's like cards being shuffled, something quite arbitrary. It's frightening.

Fifteen minutes passed and Piet and Marie du Preez came in. They were late because they had been at the Hall with Jasmine, who sent a message to say she was not coming.

'And why not?' demanded Anton.

Marjorie said: 'I don't blame her for not wanting to leave, after last time,' but Anton quelled her with his pale glance.

A month before, a representative of the Johannesburg Medical Aid for Russia had paid a visit to this town. He was essentially 'respectable', being a Professor at the Rand University.

On the evening, more than a thousand people, the biggest public meeting the town had seen, were assembled to hear the Professor on the subject of Aid for Russia. The Prime Minister, a Bishop, and half the Cabinet had graced the platform. For an hour and three-quarters the speaker had held forth on the virtues of communism, and the utter decay and corruption of capitalism.

The members of the group had had the time of their lives, while the faces of the Cabinet Ministers had reddened and writhed, and the audience applauded each violently revolutionary sentiment.

But afterwards Anton had broken into the excited chatter of the comrades, when they were discussing the meeting, to say: 'Yes, yes. That was all very amusing, in its way. But it has no political importance at all. The new comrades do not realize that being a communist can be very hard indeed, a matter of life and death. They have joined at a time when any Tom, Dick or Harry calls himself a communist and communism is respectable. If you called a meeting in the middle of the night to discuss social insurance in Siberia they'd turn up and shout slogans. There's no need to lose our heads over it. And there are better ways we can occupy our time than listening to a pack of fools applauding Comrade Rochester from Johannesburg.'

The justice of this had been, with regret, recognized, and as a result, a decision had been taken that this second public meeting should be organized by Jasmine, but that no comrades should waste their time attending it.

'We've taken a decision,' said Anton, 'that this kind of meeting can perfectly well be handled by the Borises and the Bettys. We have better things to do.'

Bill Bluett came in, saying casually: 'Sorry I'm late.'

'Half an hour,' said Anton.

'We are under dscipline but the voluntary helpers are not. The girl who was supposed to take over from me was late.'

'In that case you are excused,' said Anton.

Bill said, 'Thanks' in such a way that Anton raised his head sharply and the two men exchanged a long, thoughtful, challenging look. Bill Bluett, by no means the loser in this contest, waited until Anton had lowered his gaze and added: 'Besides, there was the literature. I had to lug four cases of the stuff over from the exhibition.'

'You, I imagined, were not responsible for the literature. What have you to say, Matty?'

'I didn't have time,' said Martha. 'I was down selling *The Watchdog* in the Coloured Quarter this afternoon. And all the afternoons this week.'

Anton laid down his pen, pushed aside his papers, and sat back, in a way which told them all they could expect the full force of his critical disapproval. But it was deflected by the entrance of Jasmine and Tommy Brown both elated and laughing, because of the mass enthusiasm of the meeting they had come from.

You are both under severe censure,' said Anton to them. Tommy went to sit by big Piet, as if wanting his protection. Jasmine, instantly sobering, took her place beside Anton at the table in the secretary's position.

'We are more or less complete,' said Anton. 'I now declare the meeting open. First item, Party Work. And now I propose to speak unless anybody objects.' He did not pause for objections. 'I propose to talk about discipline. Discipline in a group like this is voluntary. There is no means of enforcing it. But what is the use of making collective agreements if they are not kept. It is an insult to the Party.' He turned to Jasmine. 'Comrade, if you and Comrade Tommy had come away from that meeting in time to be here, would anything have been lost by it – except, of course, your enjoyment at seeing all the bourgeoisie popping up and down in their seats and applauding every time the Soviet Union was mentioned just for the sake of applauding.'

'I can't understand why we bother to organize these meetings if you despise the people who come to them,' said Marie.

'It's not a question of despising, it is a question of assessing a situation rightly. Well, Comrade Jasmine?'

Jasmine said: 'You are quite correct. I apologize to the whole group and promise not to let it happen again.'

'Comrade Tommy?'

Tommy muttered something, banging the top of his head with his fist.

'So that's Comrade Jasmine and Comrade Tommy accounted for. Comrade Murdoch is drunk; there is no excuse for that. Comrades Marie and Piet have apologized. There are five RAF comrades not here. Let us hope they have a good reason.'

'They are down in the Coloured Quarter,' said one of the RAF men. He had just joined the group: a big-boned, hollow-cheeked, passionately serious youth from London, Jimmy Jones, who tended to make violent rhetorical speeches as if at a public meeting. 'They seem to have made valuable contacts in the Quarter.'

'And who took a decision that their contacts are more important than group discipline?'

Jimmy said obstinately: 'They are good contacts. They should be maintained.'

'Is that so?' said Anton. He turned to Martha: 'You have not fulfilled your duties as Literature Secretary because of your work with *The Watchdog*. The correct way to deal with such problems is to come to the group, say you have too much work, and get the work reallocated. Not to leave the work undone.'

At this, Bill Bluett, always derisive about Martha when he met her outside the group meetings, looked sympathetically at her and said: 'Comrade Matty's doing good work in the Coloured Quarter.'

'The Coloured Quarter, yes, yes, yes. But we decided selling *The Watchdog* there would be allocated one afternoon a week. How many afternoons have you all spent running like chickens around the Quarter? And why?'

'There are so many things to do: people in trouble, and the women want advice about their children.'

'You are supposed to be selling *The Watchdog* and not having a social life.'

At this everyone exclaimed, and Bill said: 'Communists should enter into the lives and the problems of the working people. That is what Comrade Matty is doing. And by the way, the group will have to raise two pounds tonight for a bloke with rent trouble – fork out.'

'Comrade Bill,' said Anton.

'Comrade Anton,' said Bill, grinning, and not pleasantly.

'How many Coloured people are there in this Colony? A few thousand. They are unimportant, economically and politically. We can sell *The Watchdog* around the Coloured Quarter from now until doomsday but unless the numbers or the economic position of the Coloured people alter, they will never be a political force.'

Bill nodded, and remained silent.

'Do you agree with my assessment of the Coloured people? I seem to remember it was you who made the analysis for us?'

'Yes,' said Bill reluctantly.

'And may I expect you to draw the correct conclusions from it? We agreed that in principle our work should be done among the Africans who are the proletariat of this country. But that in view of the fact we have no contact at the moment with the Africans, since the political structure is such that no white person can easily make contact, we must work in the progressive white organizations and with the Coloured who are physically accessible. And we decided that one afternoon selling *The Watchdog* would be adequate.'

Here Jimmy burst out: 'I agree we should go among the

Africans, we're wasting our time, my complaint about the work of this group is that we spend all our time with the white people. They're all bourgeois and a waste of time.' At this there was an outburst of agreement from the three RAF men, Bill, Andrew, and Jimmy who reinforced his words with emphatic nods and exclamations.

'Comrades,' said Anton patiently, 'you were all here when we analysed the class situation in this country – well, weren't you?'

Silence.

'And from that analysis we drew certain conclusions and with those conclusions we all agreed, and took a vote on them.'

An uncomfortable and uneasy silence.

'Well, comrades? Is it that you wish us to make a fresh analysis?'

'Jesus, no,' said Jimmy angrily.

'And what does that mean? That such analyses are unnecessary?'

Jimmy said stubbornly: 'All I know is that we have developed good relations with a number of the Coloured people. They are working people, like us – or some of us. We understand each other. And Comrade Matty has been doing good work. Why throw it away? I don't see it.'

'I shall put the question formally,' said Anton. 'Do you wish us to pass a resolution that we should make a fresh analysis of the class forces of this country, and, based on that fresh analysis, review our work?'

'No,' said Jimmy heatedly. 'No, hell, no.'

'In that case, logically, the previous decisions stand. Matty will spend one afternoon in a week selling *The Watchdog* from house to house in the Coloured area. The RAF comrades may help her if necessary. None of you will get involved with rent problems, birth-control problems, or any other such problems. And we shall from now on not only resolve to be punctual, but in fact be punctual. Now, next item on the agenda.'

'Literature,' said Jasmine.

'Just a minute, comrades,' said Marie du Preez. She faced

Anton. Her tone combined anxiety and a sort of easy maternal warmth for him, as if she could only subdue her disapproval of him by a tone of voice she might have used to a child.

'Comrade Marie,' said Piet impatiently.

'I'm not happy about it. But I would find it hard to say why. Logically I agree with you. When you put it logically no one could disagree. But humanly – there is something wrong. Certain comrades here have made real friendly contacts with the Coloured people, and now you say it should all be thrown up and cut short – they are human beings and so are we.'

'Comrade Marie, the work of a communist party in any given country is based on an intellectual analysis of the class structure, the class forces in that country at a given time. It is not based on individual and private feelings. Otherwise it's not a communist party at all.'

Marie frowned, and at last said stubbornly: 'I've told you I can't argue with you intellectually. But I feel you are wrong.'

Her husband, Piet, who had been grinning throughout this exchange, now let out a great laugh, and said: 'Women. She *feels* it is wrong, and so that's enough.'

His wife said: 'That's enough from you.'

'I resent that,' said Marjorie. 'I demand Comrade Piet should withdraw his remark unconditionally.'

'And I too,' said Martha heatedly.

'And I,' said Jasmine.

'I withdraw,' said Piet, still grinning.

'You aren't really withdrawing at all,' said Marjorie. 'You're just humouring us. You're showing a bad attitude towards women.'

Anton said: 'Comrade Marjorie, he has formally withdrawn.'

'Formally,' said Marjorie.

The women looked with resentment at the big, good-natured, laughing trade unionist, who was trying hard to look contrite.

Suddenly Andrew took his pipe out of his mouth and

said, also grinning: 'Comrades, I have to catch the station bus in half an hour and so have the lads.'

'OK,' said Marjorie. 'I see that Comrade Andrew shares Comrade Piet's attitude.'

'As for Comrade Piet,' said Marie, looking at her husband, 'I'll fix him later.'

'Well?' said Anton, 'have we now dealt with this important problem?'

'I hope,' said Marjorie, 'you are not suggesting it is unimportant.'

'As chairman,' said Anton, 'I now propose we take the second item on the agenda. Literature.'

Jasmine said: 'The position is we have four cases of pamphlets from Voks in Moscow. I consider their style is quite unsuited to our present conditions.'

There was another chorus of agreement. It seemed everyone had seen the pamphlets. But on every face was a look of discomfort: they felt disloyal at having to criticize the Soviet Union: more, they felt subtly betrayed, and even threatened.

Anton said calmly: 'I have studied the pamphlets and I agree that the comrades in Moscow are out of touch with our needs and have sent us unsuitable propaganda. I propose we write a serious letter explaining why and suggesting lines on which they might frame more suitable pamphlets.'

'They never answer letters,' said Jasmine, bringing out this fresh criticism of the beloved country with an effort.

'They probably have more important things to do than worry about the problems of Zambesia,' said Anton.

'Then why do they bother to send the pamphlets at all?' said Marjorie.

Anton said coldly: 'I suggest this is not such a very serious problem. Next item on the agenda.'

'I consider you are dealing with this meeting in a very high-handed manner,' said Bill Bluett suddenly.

'So do I,' said Jimmy, who was sitting clenched up, frowning, his big red hands trembling with excitement on his knees.

Anton said: 'There are twenty minutes before the RAF

comrades must leave, and eight items still remaining on the agenda. We will have to cut political instruction because punctuality is not considered important by the comrades.'

'I still think you are high-handed,' said Bill.

'In that case I suggest you elect another chairman?'

Anton sounded huffy and impatient, and Marjorie said: 'I consider your attitude towards Bill's remark incorrect.'

'So do I,' said Jasmine, in her sedate way: 'You should not react like that to criticism.'

Anton lowered his eyes to the table and played with a pencil, jabbing it again and again into some paper. The fine lines were quivering around his mouth.

'Which brings me to something I must say,' said Bill. He got up, fitting his cap over his thick lank hair. 'I propose that this group undertakes to keep its agreement to have criticism and self-criticism.'

'Agreed,' said Jasmine promptly.

'Since it is not a question of taking a vote, but since it is a question of putting into effect a decision already made, there is no need to agree or disagree,' said Anton. To Bill he said politely: 'Thank you for reminding me, comrade. You are quite correct.'

'Oh, don't mention it,' said Bill airily, moving to the door. The other two RAF men followed him.

The remaining people said they would continue the meeting without them, but all at once Anton got up, nodded to them, and said he had to leave. He went, leaving the group headless.

'Surely he's not upset at being criticized?' said Marie.

'Of course not,' said Jasmine. 'He's an old comrade and knows how to take criticism. Let us continue the meeting.' But here Martha, who had been shivering spasmodically throughout the meeting, shivered so deeply that her teeth chattered. They all looked at her, and exclaimed that she was sick. The meeting broke up on this. Marie and Piet du Preez took Martha home and put her into her bed. Martha was thinking feebly that to get sick was an act of irresponsibility and disloyalty to the whole group. She was also thinking that it would be pleasant to be ill for a day or two, to have time to think, and even – this last thought gave her a severe spasm of guilt – to be alone for a little, not always to be surrounded by people.

Part Two

Lenin, as we know, did not spare his opponents.

A. A. ZHDANOV

Chapter One

In the morning Martha woke ill, but above all uneasy because of a weight of guilt: she was ill because she had been careless, and now her work would fall on other people. But the languor of fever was pleasant to her. She had been dreaming and she wished she might return to sleep, for the dreams had had the peculiarly nostalgic quality which she distrusted so much, and yet was so dangerously attractive to her. She had been dreaming of 'that country'; a phrase she used to describe a particular region of sleep which she often visited, or which visited her – and always when she was overtired or sick. 'That country' was pale, misted, flat; gulls cried like children around violet-coloured shores. She stood on coloured chalky rocks with a bitter sea washing around her feet and the smell of salt was strong in her nostrils.

Now she thought: Well, I suppose it's England . . . but how can I be an exile from England when it has nothing to do with me? And do I really have to feel guilty about wanting to sleep when I never sleep enough? She dropped back into a hot sleep, and dreamed she was back in 'the district' standing at the edge of Mr McFarline's great gold-eating pit. But it was abandoned. It had been abandoned centuries before. The enormous gulf in the soil had been worked by a forgotten race which she saw clearly in her dream: a copper-coloured, long-limbed, sharp-featured people, tied together like slaves under the whip of a black overseer. Centuries ago, these people had vanished, and the pit had fallen into disuse, and its sides were covered with a small scrub of bushes and a low rank grass. But near to where she stood was a projection into the pit, a jut of layered rock that spread at its base, like a firmly set animal's foot.

She stood at the extreme edge of the pit, space beneath her, smelling the warm gritty smell of hot African sun on loose dry soil, examining the deep-layered rock. Fold after fold, the growth of the earth showed itself in the side of the pit, a warm red showing the living soil at the top, then the dead layers of rock beneath. She saw that the projection into the pit was not dead, but living. It was not an animal's paw, but the head and the shoulders of an immense lizard, an extinct saurian that had been imprisoned a thousand ages ago, in the rock. It was petrified. The shape of the narrow head, the swell of the shoulders, was visible. A narrow ledge of rock along the grass-grown bottom of the pit was its dead foot. Martha looked again and saw that its eye was steadily regarding her with a sullen and patient query. It was a scaly ancient eye, filmed over with mine-dust, a sorrowful eye. It's alive, she thought. It's alive after so many centuries. And it will take centuries more to die. Perhaps I can dig it out?

But it seemed quite right that the vast half-fossilized extinct creature should be there, alive still in the massive weight of the earth. She looked down at the half-closed patient eye and thought: You must be too old even to see me.

She woke, all her limbs irritated by fever. Now she was awake the dream seemed frightening, but because of its distance from the cold salt-sprayed shores of 'that country'. She thought: Next time I drop off to sleep I might go anywhere, it's like a nightmare, not knowing what's waiting for you ... For the cold salt-sprayed shores and the deep sullen pit seemed to have nothing in common, not to be connected, and their lack of connection was a danger. She realized she was afraid to drop off to sleep again.

It was ten in the morning. Although she was weighted with guilt because of her responsibilities to the group which she would now not fulfil, she had only just remembered her duty to the office where she earned her living. She went to the telephone in the passage and rang Mrs Buss, who was at pains to explain to Martha that she was quite capable of running the office by herself indefinitely. As for herself, she had not had a day's illness during the fifteen years she had been earning her living. Martha found Mrs Carson behind her, listening. 'I'm sick,' she said hastily, to avoid being involved in some new servant crisis. She went back to bed, followed by the white intense face and the dark obsessed eyes of Mrs Carson, who sat on the foot of the bed and told a long story of how once she had been alone on a farm in some remote district, and a whole pack of natives had surrounded the house trying to get in, but – seeing her with her shotgun waiting for them – had contented themselves with peering through the windows and jeering obscenities. Martha lay under piled untidy blankets, shivering, listening to this fantasy, repeating to herself over and over again: I must not lose my temper with her. I must not. She's sick and she can't help it. But finally she said, and was surprised that her voice cracked with tears when she spoke: 'Mrs Carson, I'm ill.'

Mrs Carson, reminded of Martha's existence, slowly stood up, smoothing down her dress with bony hands, looking about the room as if something might be suggested to her. At last she rather helplessly drew the chintz curtains across and returned to stand beside the bed, frowning at Martha.

'Perhaps I should telephone your mother?' she suggested.

Martha sat up in a panic. 'No, no, please don't.'

Mrs Carson, unsurprised, but pleased that nothing was asked of her, said vaguely: 'If you need anything let me know.' She went out remarking: 'It's better with the curtains drawn; *they* can't see in.'

Martha went back to sleep and was woken instantly by bad nightmares which she could not remember but which drove her out of bed. She had undertaken to do certain things and she must do them. She dressed and rode downtown on her bicycle. It was only when she was balancing on waves of sickness on the rocking machine that she understood she was really sick, and had a right to be in bed. But she went to the group office, collected a list of addresses of businessmen who must be approached for donations to Medical Aid for Russia, and spent the day going from office to office. She was surprised to find that habit made it easy for her to switch on her 'money-collecting personality' without effort. She despised this personality: cool, practical, rather flirtatious, humorous to order so as to take the sting out of the business of giving money to Russia. She got the promise of over three hundred pounds. She returned to the group office and left a note to the effect that some other comrade must take over her responsibilities, and climbed back, with difficulty, on to the bicycle. It was in the solemn heavy heat of mid-afternoon. Sun glinted off walls, off the metal of motor cars and bicycles, off the skin of Africans, off the eyes of people passing, off the leaves of trees. Everything hotly glittered. Light struck painfully into her skull through her eyes. She cycled slowly, knowing that cars were hooting at her. She thought: If I'm behaving oddly, then it will be a discredit to the group. I must cycle straight and look normal. If people think I'm drunk, the Party will be blamed for my behaviour.

When she at last got herself into bed in the darkened room, she was thinking miserably: All over the world people are dying, people are being killed, they are suffering indescribably, and I'm being sick. I have no right to be sick.

She slept and dreamed that she was among hordes of war-crushed people for whom she was responsible. She would half-awaken, her eyes closing again at the sight of the strong light on the limp chintz curtains, thinking: That's France, yes – we're holding there (for in her dream she, representing 'the group', had stemmed some flood of violence or act of terror), but there's Germany, the people in the concentration camps in Germany, I'm forgetting them. And when she fell back into sleep, she was in Germany, holding back brutality there, but tormented that she was forgetting France, or Russia, or some other place for which she was responsible. She woke and slept, slept and woke, in a steadily increasing fervour of anxiety, repeatedly visiting in her dreams the chilly shallow shores of nostalgia, where no responsibility existed, or returned for glimpses into the dust-filled half-closed eye of the great petrified saurian.

Once she woke and found a large tray covered by a fly-net by her bed. Mrs Carson, worried that she ought to be doing something for Martha, but unable to come far enough out of her obsession to think what, had arranged a three-course meal: soup, now cold and filmed with grease; roast beef and potatoes congealed in fat; and a slab of wet cold pie. Martha's stomach turned, and she went to the bathroom to be sick. On the way she passed the kitchen where Mrs Carson was sitting in a cretonne wrapper that showed part of her wrinkled bosom, a fly-whisk in her hand, watching her new servant make cakes. She did not notice Martha, who returned to bed, where she dreamed she was responsible for Mrs Carson, and trying to explain to her 'once and for all' that 'she had been on the wrong path' and that 'she should be happy and not waste her life dreaming'. In this dream she saw Mrs Carson as a jolly bouncing card-playing widow with a salacious and friendly wink, who said to Martha: Thank you dear for saving me. You are my true friend.

This dream was so much a nightmare that she struggled out of it, gasping and crying out.

The night passed. In the morning she woke to find Jasmine regarding her from the foot of the bed.

'You OK?' she inquired.

'Of course,' said Martha.

'Want a doctor?'

'Hell, no.'

'Can't stand them either. Well, I'm on my way to work. Give me a ring if you want nursing.' Jasmine, demure and precise as always, her small neat body defined in bright blue flowered linen, frowned at Martha while she adjusted an ear-ring.

'What's going on in the group?' asked Martha, who felt as if she had been exiled from it for several weeks.

'Trouble,' said Jasmine, rolling up her eyes and sighing. 'There was a meeting last night. The RAF are suffering from severe infantile disorders. They want to make a revolution here and now. Jimmy wants us to march into the Location with a red flag, shouting: "Down with the white tyrants."'

'Seriously?'

'Seriously.'

'Perhaps it's not a bad idea at that,' said Martha crossly.

'You'd better stay where you are then,' said Jasmine. 'If you're in a red-flag-waving mood too, then you'll be more of a nuisance than a help.'

'All the same, I've been thinking . . . we talk and talk and analyse and make formulations, but what are we doing? What are we changing?' Her head ached, and she lay still, looking at the cool white ceiling.

'If I were you I'd go to sleep.'

'What else? What else has been happening?'

'Well, the RAF say we are bourgeois.'

'Obviously we are. What then?'

'Because,' said Jasmine composedly, 'we wear lipstick and nail varnish.' She put forward a small foot in a high-heeled blue sandal and examined her scarlet toe-nails with satisfaction. 'They say our origins are betrayed by the way we dress.'

'Who? All women, or just the group women?'

'The women comrades. They say that we are corrupted by the emphasis capitalist society places on sex.' Jasmine offered this last remark to Martha on a serious note of query.

Martha considered it from the depths of her anxiety-ridden dissatisfaction with herself, which made her ready to range herself with anybody who criticized her. But the other side of her perpetual stern rejection of what she was now, was the image of what she wanted to be: to match this image with any of the men in the group was enough to make her reject them entirely. She was thinking: Any *real* man would be able to see what I could be and help me to become it, and all these tom-tiddlers in the group . . . She was dismayed that she was able to think of her male comrades thus, and said angrily: 'Oh, they can talk . . .'

'That's what I said to Jimmy.'

'Of course it was Jimmy, of course.'

'Yes, I said to him, if you disapprove of make-up and high heels and so on, what were you doing in McGrath's with that girl from the reception desk? Because she's got dyed hair to start with. He said he was educating her.'

Martha laughed. Jasmine smiled composedly and said: 'Bloody hypocrites they all are. Every one. Well, so long,

Matty, and look after yourself.' She departed, slinging a satchel bag full of pamphlets over her shoulder.

Next time Martha woke it was night, and Mrs Quest stood where Jasmine had stood earlier, at the foot of the bed.

'I'm glad to see you are getting an early night for once,' she said in a sprightly way.

'Yes.'

'Have you heard from William?'

'Who?'

'That corporal or whoever he was.'

'Yes, I've heard.'

'If you're going to let him down too I shall really wash my hands of you.'

'Mother, I keep telling you, there's no question of my marrying William.'

'You left your husband for him.'

'I did not. I left Douglas for . . .' She stopped, knowing it was useless to explain to her mother why she left Douglas.

Meanwhile, Mrs Quest, cold-eyed and hostile, was examining Martha's naked shoulders. She said: 'That nightgown is indecent. If some of your friends come in . . .'

Martha, who at the first sight of her mother had thought: Thank goodness, she'll look after me, now pulled the blankets up to her face, and said: 'No one's coming in. And I'm sleepy.'

Mrs Quest went to Martha's dressing-table, examined what was on it, and said: 'So you're using rouge now. Well, if you're going to jazz about the way you do, I suppose you'll need rouge at your age. But don't say I didn't warn you.' She returned to the foot of the bed and said: 'Mrs Carson's worried about you.'

'In what way?'

'She says that you don't keep your curtains drawn and the garden boy hangs about to get a sight of you.'

'Oh, do shut up,' said Martha, understanding with dismay that she was able to take this sort of thing from Mrs Carson, but not from her mother, to whom surely she owed much more patience and understanding? Guilt set in about this too, and added to her sick fever.

Mrs Quest had retreated into apologetic embarrassment, and retreated hastily with: 'Well, perhaps she's got it wrong. I won't disturb your beauty sleep any longer.' She went to the door, exaggeratedly quiet. As she went out she said: 'I hear Caroline isn't well, poor little girl.'

The image of Caroline rose to confront Martha, who said to herself tormentedly: I can't think of her now, I really can't. She sternly pushed Caroline into a region of her mind marked No Admittance. Yet as soon as she slept, Caroline emerged from this forbidden place, and confronted Martha: sometimes charming and childish, sometimes sick and plaintive, sometimes hostile to Martha her mother. Martha kept waking, afraid for the first time of the loneliness of this dark shabby hired room, despising herself for being afraid, hating her mother for evoking the image of Caroline.

Another night passed and a slow hot morning. Flies buzzed against the curtains through which the glare beat in threads of yellow. Martha was thinking: If my mother would come in again, and just be kind, instead of hating me so much . . . the weak listlessness of this frightened her again. She thought: Just because I'm sick, I start crying for mother. And I'm probably not sick at all, just trying to get out of something? But what am I trying to get out of? I simply must not give in. And she got limply out of bed, brushed her hair and made up her face. She lay tidily back on her pillows thinking: If I make up my mind to it, I needn't be sick. But almost at once she was back in sleep, and nightmare-ridden delirium.

In the late afternoon she woke to see Anton seated by her bed. The sight of him was an exquisite relief.

'Yes, yes, yes,' he said. 'If people don't look after themselves, they get sick.' He held her wrist tightly: it was partly a brotherly caress and partly because of the necessity for taking her pulse.

'So,' he commented. 'And what does the doctor say?'

'I don't need a doctor.'

'So you don't need a doctor. That may be so, but you must excuse me: I shall telephone your doctor and he will come and visit you.'

He sat smiling at her. Martha could scarcely recognize him. She said to herself: Suddenly he's human. She was also thinking: Suppose he is in love with me? The thought was half-exciting, half pure panic. Oh my God! she thought involuntarily, it's just as bad as the others – just an accident, falling in love, if you can call it that. All the same, a pulse of excitement was beating in her. She looked through her fever at the stiff controlled face, now softened with a small paternal smile, and thought: He may not know it himself, but he's attracted to me.

And now Anton lifted himself up to his height, and stooping, kissed her on the forehead. 'Yes, yes,' he said. 'And now you will lie quite still and the doctor will come.' For a moment they were both embarrassed because of that kiss, and he said quickly: 'I will come in again this evening and see you. It is Dr Stern, isn't it? I will make the arrangements.' And he went out on tiptoe stiffly, like a lean high-stepping bird.

When I'm with him I feel safe? she wondered, remembering how he had said: women's problems are not sufficiently considered, and how she had responded to the promise of understanding. Yes, he's kind, she decided.

Now she was looking forward to the doctor's coming. If Anton took the responsibility for this act of weakness, the act of admitting one was ill, then it was all right, it was off her shoulders.

She lay facing the door, where Dr Stern would come in. When she woke it was to see Jimmy, entering with the same exaggerated caution as Anton had used in leaving, absorbed in his caution. He carried a big bunch of pink zinnias in his large red hand and, thinking Martha was asleep, was looking for some place to put them. He went out again, leaving the door open, and Martha heard him talking to the servant in the kitchen. He was speaking with earnest friendliness, but the man was being nervously evasive: the contrast between Jimmy and Mrs Carson was too much for him. Jimmy returned with the stiff flowers stuck in a big ornamented green vase. Martha could see that he liked the vase, from the proud way he regarded it. She consciously suppressed a wince of disapproval at his bad taste, thinking: That's snobbish, they are right to call us names, middle-class and the rest . . . When he had set the vase down beside her, he found her awake and smiled self-consciously when she thanked him.

Although the sunlight on the curtains was now a pale yellow, and the heat no longer beat into the room, it was stuffy and Jimmy's large bony face was scarlet. He was wearing the thick clumsy uniform issued for winter use.

'Why don't you take off your jacket?' she asked, and all at once was embarrassed. She remembered her mother had said her nightgown was indecent; and she pulled the sheet up high to her chin thinking: I wasn't conscious of it at all when Anton was here, but I am with Jimmy.

It was true that he was frowning with hot disapproval of her. He undid the top button of his jacket, and set himself to improve her situation: having studied her face he said: 'You don't look too good, and that's a fact.'

With which he scientifically studied the arrangement of her bed until he had decided what should be done. 'Now hold it a minute. I'm the boy for this.' He put his hand under her head, lifted it, adjusted her pillows, pulled off a thick wodge of blankets which Martha was not aware were too heavy for her, and said with authority: 'Now lie easy. No good twisting yourself up like that.' Martha obediently unknotted all her limbs.

'That's better. You can take it from me. I've had it myself.'

'Had what?'

'I was in the san for ten months before the war. I know all the gen about being sick.'

'You're cured?' she asked, looking how the red flared on his great bony cheeks.

'I'm in the RAF, so I'm cured.'

She laughed, but he did not. 'That is why I came to see you. You should sweat. You have a temperature.'

He was possessed by his role of nurse. 'You've got a drop of something here? Brandy? Then I'll wrap you up in the blankets and that'll do the trick.'

'But Jimmy, the doctor's coming.'

He said: 'You don't want to trust them. Pack you full of poison and lies when nature can cure.'

'But Dr Stern is coming.'

He said stiffly: 'Oh well, if you feel like that.' He was so offended that he buttoned his jacket again, and made a move towards the door.

'Jimmy, you're surely not going to be cross because I've called the doctor when I'm sick?' Her voice came plaintive, and she frowned, thinking: Well, if I'm going to strike that note, then . . . He had already weakened into a smile and sat down by the bed. 'While I'm here I'll give you the gen about *The Watchdog* round. I've been doing it for you with Murdoch and Bill.' He gave her a report, an almost house-by-house report, and she lay watching the so deeply serious face, silent until he said: 'We've fixed Ronald. He's OK. There's nothing for you to worry about.'

'Ronald? The man dying of . . .' She stopped herself.

'Dying? He's not dying. Let me tell you, comrade, what he needs is some good food and rest. There's no such thing as TB.'

'Well, what have you done?'

'We took a collection among the lads and we've fed him up. We've given him a good feed and paid his rent. These sicknesses are just poverty. That's all, poverty. You wouldn't know, with your class background, but believe you me, when the doctors talk about TB and cancer and all that caper, they're just helping the capitalists. They'd be out of work without poverty.'

Martha's head ached. She said: 'Jimmy, for all that, he's so sick he should be in hospital.'

'Sick? Of course he's sick. He'll be better in a week, with us lads looking after him. And now there's you. How long have you been in bed?'

'I don't know.'

'Why doesn't that old woman look after you?'

'Oh, she's too busy being neurotic about the natives.'

'What do you mean neurotic? What's that kind of talk?'

'If you like it better, she's got the African problem on her mind.'

'You're full of bourgeois talk, comrade, do you know that?'

She said flippantly: 'I'm middle-class to the backbone,' and thought: Now he'll lose his temper, and then laugh.

But his deep-socketed eyes were too indignant for anger.

'If you weren't sick, I'd have it out with you, I would straight. Look at you, comrade, lying here alone in bed with lipstick on. What sort of caper is that?'

'I'm not alone,' she said, 'you're here.' And grinned at him. But he went dark red and said: 'There you are. Listen. Believe you me, there's a lot of rottenness in you you've got to lose before you're a good comrade.'

'Oh God,' said Martha, suddenly angry, 'you're such a bloody prig.'

'And your language. I don't like to hear girls using that kind of language.'

Martha, prickling all over with exasperation, moved angrily about in her bed. Quite unconsciously he reached out his large hand to adjust the covers, as if he were saying: 'Be still.'

'You bourgeois girls, you need a wood working-class husband to teach you a thing or two. When I see you bourgeois girls I think of my mother and what she had to take from her life, and believe you me you could learn a thing or two from her.'

'All of you,' she said, 'all of you working-class men have this damned sentimental thing about your mothers.'

'Sentimental, is it? Let me tell you, it's the working-class woman that takes the rap every time.'

'I imagined that was why we wanted to change things.'

'What do you mean?' he said hotly. He was leaning forward, sweat-covered, scarlet-faced. She was sitting up, clutching the blankets to her, her face running with sweat.

She said, in a change of mood, grimly: 'We'll abolish poverty, and give women freedom and then they'll simmer and boil, sacrificing themselves for everyone – like my mother.' She laughed at the look of bewildered anger on his face. 'There's no good your talking to me about women sacrificing themselves for their families – I've had that one. And I don't want to talk about it either,' she added, as the explosion of his emotion reached his eyes in a hot stare of protest.

'What do you mean, you don't want to talk about it? I'm going to talk you out of this one, believe you me. Women are the salt of the earth. I'm telling you. My mother was the salt of the earth. My dad died when I was ten and she brought up me and my two sisters on what she got by cleaning offices until I went to work and helped her out.'

'Good, then let's arrange things so that women have to work eighteen hours a day and die at fifty, worn out so that you can go on being sentimental about us.'

She collapsed back, shaking with weakness.

He said: 'I don't know what you're saying, comrade, and that's a fact.' He stretched out his hand again to pull the sheet up to her neck. 'And you should be keeping still. I keep telling you, keep still. When my mum was ill once I nursed her three months day and night – you should lie still and let nature take its way. The doctors couldn't do anything for my mum, but I could. They gave her this and they gave her that, but I kept her in bed warm and still for three months. It was the rest she needed and the rest she got, with me helping her. You should let the powers of nature flow through you, comrade. It's a fact.'

'That may be so, but the doctor's coming now – I can hear him.'

She could hear Dr Stern and Anton talking in the passage. Jimmy got up, saying: 'Then I'll make my way outside and wait until he's gone.' He went out through the doors on to the veranda. She could see his big patient shape through the curtains against the red of the setting sun.

Good Lord, she thought, he's taken me over. He's responsible for me. And through the wall on the other side Anton was talking her over with Dr Stern. An old feeling of being hemmed in and disposed of prickled through her. I hate it all, she thought wildly, not knowing what she hated or why she was imprisoned. I wish to God everyone would leave me alone. She had a nightmare feeling of sliding helpless into danger.

When Dr Stern came in, bland and weary as always, she

rememebered she had not seen him since she left her husband, and sat up, thinking: He'll disapprove of me and show it, and I'll pretend not to see it. Besides, there's the bill. I'd forgotten – I simply can't afford to be sick.

But his eyes were professional. 'Well, Mrs Knowell,' he asked, as she heard him so often: 'And what can I do you for?'

She laughed obediently at the joke and lay down as he held her wrist.

'You should have called me in before,' he remarked. 'Who's looking after you?'

'My landlady.'

'I think we'll find a bed for you in hospital.'

'Oh, *no*.' Martha sat up again, in an impulse to escape the whole situation. Dr Stern held her by the shoulder and said: 'If it's a question of paying, then don't worry. There are times when people can pay and times when they can't. You're an old patient of mine, aren't you?'

Martha's eyes filled with tears and she turned away to hide them. But her voice shook as she thanked him.

'Yes, Mrs Knowell, and you've been here all these days with a high temperature letting things ride – and you're a sensible girl, so I've always thought.'

'Perhaps I'm not sensible,' she muttered. 'Dr Stern, I really don't want to go to hospital.'

'And who will nurse you?'

'I have friends.' She thought: If he understands this then he's a real doctor and not just a medicine man. He let his eyes rest on her face for some time: her lips were trembling. At last he nodded and said; 'Mrs Knowell, there are times when we all find life too much for us.'

Oh Lord, she thought, he's trying to make me cry.

'I understand the divorce is going through between yourself and Douglas. Well, that's not my affair. And you must be missing your daughter.'

The reference to Caroline dried Martha's tears at the source. She said: 'Dr Stern, I'll do anything you say, but please make it possible for me to stay here.'

He was annoyed, and – as Martha knew, not because she

wouldn't go to hospital, but because she had closed against him. He said coldly: 'Very well. I can't take the consequences. I'll have the medicines made up. I'll come to see you tomorrow. Does a sensible girl like you have to behave like an uneducated person who is afraid of hospital? You're like my native patients, who think they're going to die in hospital.'

Martha felt as she had with Mr Maynard: Dr Stern, in using such an argument, was so infinitely removed from her that it was as if he had moved back into the past. He stood at the foot of the bed waiting to see if she would react; when she did not he said: 'Very well,' and went out. Again she heard Anton talking to him in the passage. She realized that Anton would be looking after her. When he came in, she had succumbed to being ill; for the first time she was gone under waves of sickness. She was aware that he had again kised her forehead and hot nausea came with the thought: Well, that means now Anton and I will be together. She did not define how they would be together. He sat by her a few minutes, then said he would go to collect the medicines. She did not hear him leave; nor hear Jimmy enter. She opened her eyes to see Jimmy large and looming over her. His attitude expressed something hostile to her.

'Well, comrade, and are you sick?'

'The doctor says so.'

'And he's going to fill you up with medicines?'

'I suppose so.'

'I'll get them for you. I can go on my bycicle.'

'Anton's gone already.'

'I saw him here, I saw him,' he said, accusingly. As she did not reply: 'Tell me, have you and Anton got an agreement?'

'An agreement?' She was angry because he assumed he had the right to ask. It was clear he felt he did have the right. He even looked as if he had been betrayed. 'I mean, are you and Anton getting together?'

'Not as far as I know.' She kept her eyes shut and when she opened them again he had gone.

She was deeply anxious: her stomach was twisting with

anxiety. She thought: I've been irritated because of the way these men just fall for us, from one minute to the next, but what's the difference between that and me and Anton getting involved? Because it seems to me we are involved. If I'd responded to Jimmy or Murdoch over a glass of beer or selling pamphlets, then it would have seemed to me quite right, inevitable, even romantic. Her anxiety rose to a climax, and she felt caged by Anton. But it happens to be Anton . . . why? Is it because he's the leader of the group? But that's despicable. And actually what do we have in common?

These muddled, dismaying thoughts were too much for her, and she went off into a semi-delirium. Her body had taken over from her mind. She lay feeling every pulse of pain, every sensation of heat and cold. Her body, precisely defined in areas of heat and cold, lay stretched out among sheets that felt gritty and sharp, as if she were lying on sand, or on moving ants. But her hands were not hers. They seemed to have swelled. Her hands were enormous, and she could not control their size. At the end of her arms she could feel them, giant's hands, as if she compressed the world inside them. Everything she was had gone into her hands. She moved them, to see if she could shrink them back to size. For a moment they were her own hands again, then out they swelled, and, lying with eyes shut, she felt the tips of her fingers touch the vast balls of her thumbs as if girders had been laid across a ravine. The world lay safe inside her hands. Tenderness filled her. She thought: Because of us, everyone will be saved. She thought: I am holding the world safe, and no one will be hurt and unhappy ever again.

Anton came in later, and lifted her up to take her medicines. She kept her hands away from him: she had to keep them away because of their immense power: he might get hurt if he touched them.

She woke in the dark once to see him sitting by her in the chair, asleep. When she drifted off again, holding humanity safe in her powerful tender hands, she held him too, close and safe: the protector protected; the power-dealer made harmless.

In the morning the fever had gone down because of the drugs and Anton still sat there, smiling at her.

'Aren't you going to work?' He did some kind of clerk's work in an export and import firm. As an enemy alien it was not easy for him to find a job, and she worried that he might lose it because of her. 'Aren't you going?' she insisted.

He shook his head. 'I've telephoned and now you must not worry at all, you must sleep.'

For three days Anton sat by her, scarcely leaving her, taking instructions from the doctor and dealing with Mrs Carson with a gentle ironical patience that she would never have expected from him. Slowly her hands lost size. There was a moment she looked at them, small and thin, and began to cry. Anton took her in his arms and kissed her.

She murmured: 'What about Toni Mandel?' He said: 'Yes, yes, everything has its end. You must not worry about Mrs Mandel.'

Anton was not there when Jimmy came in again, bristling with hostility. He made some remarks about the sale of *The Watchdog*, told her that Ronald was completely cured, and then said: 'I have to tell you, comrade, that I must criticize you for your attitude.'

'What attitude?'

'I don't like lies. I don't mind the truth but I don't like lies.'

'What lies?'

'You and Anton.'

'What the hell's it got to do with you?'

He was again red and angry, very hostile.

She thought: Well, it's true that it might just as well have been Jimmy. Yet the feeling between her and Anton had now grown so that their being together seemed right and inevitable; she could not imagine that any accident (she thought of her sickness and Anton's looking after her as an accident) would bring her and Jimmy together.

'And in any case, comrade, I'd like to tell you straight, I've found a better woman.'

'Well, I'm glad,' she said flatly.

'Yes. I have. A fine working-class woman, like my own kind. You and I wouldn't have done at all.'

'I'm very pleased.' She wondered who he meant. There were no working-class girls in the group. She thought: The receptionist from McGrath's? Then he'll have to stop her using lipstick and dyeing her hair.

He said: 'She's a woman who can take hardship, who knows how to suffer. Yes, those girls down in the Coloured Quarter know how to take life.'

Martha's brain informed her that any reaction she would have to this would be 'white settler' and therefore suspect. All the same, she had to say something. And he was waiting for her to speak, waiting with his whole body expressing challenge and readiness to fight.

'Jimmy, you'll get yourself posted.'

'I'm not taking orders from any bloody colour-minded fascists.'

'You won't be allowed to marry her.'

'The war won't last for ever.'

'And besides, we took a decision that the RAF must not have personal relations with the Coloured women, because it would give the reactionaries a stick to beat us with.'

That was what he had been waiting to hear. He turned the full force of his resentment on her and said: 'Who took decisions? I'm not bound by any colour-minded decisions. If Comrade Anton wants to have colour prejudice, then he should be ashamed, but I'm not bound by it.'

'You know it's not a question of colour prejudice.'

'Is it not then? For me it is. And if you ask me, Comrade Anton should examine his attitudes. I don't like them at all.'

'Then why didn't you say so in the group meeting?'

'There's a lot wrong with the group,' he said.

'Then why don't you say so in the group? It's no use saying so outside.'

'I'll say my mind any place I want to say it. I'm not going to be told what I'm to say or where. I'm telling you, comrade, there's altogether too many middle-class ideas in this group for my taste. And for the taste of the lads from the camp.'

He left the room suddenly, letting the door crash behind him. Martha lay still, arranging in her mind the words she would use to describe the scene to Anton. Instinctively sh

130

softened it. She had an impulse not to say anything: 'Jimmy's personal feelings are his own affair.' But they were not his own affair. It was her duty to tell Anton.

She said to Anton that Jimmy seemed to be in an emotional state, and should be 'handled'. Then she reported what he had said.

At this, Anton's personality changed: the gentleman who had sat by her as a nurse vanished. He became the chairman: stern and cold, with compressed lips and judging eyes.

'There can't be one set of rules for one person and another set for another. A decision was taken, and until the decision is changed by a majority vote of the group, then Comrade Jimmy will have to abide by it.'

'Perhaps I shouldn't have told you,' she asked herself, and Anton. To which he replied: 'It is the duty of a comrade to report infringements of discipline. It is our duty to aid and support each other.'

She felt him to be logically right; she felt him to be inhuman and wrong. There was no way for her to make these two feelings fit together. She was still weak and sick, and she let the problem slide away from her.

Soon she was convalescent; and the members of the group came in to see her, at lunch-hour, or in the intervals of meetings. The RAF, however, did not come: Jasmine reported that they were in a bad mood about something.

It was now accepted that Martha and Anton were a couple.

Chapter Two

Mr Maynard and his wife took breakfast at the opposite ends of the big table which was fully furnished with white damask, silver and cut-glass dishes displaying the yellows, browns, and golds of five different types of marmalade. Mrs Maynard took a cup of coffee and half a piece of toast; Mr Maynard a cup of tea. The problem which occupied the two minds behind the large, dark jowled faces did not reach words: the native servant stood at attention throughout the meal by the sideboard.

Mr Maynard said: 'I have to be at the Magistrates' Court in forty minutes.' Mrs Maynard said: 'I believe the living-room is empty.' Mr Maynard waited by the door of the living-room, watching the morning sun quiver on the glossy leaves of the veranda plants. Mrs Maynard, tucking a white handkerchief into the bosom of her stiff navy-blue dress, where it stood up like a small stiff fan, came to a stop beside him, remarking: 'I think you had better let me see the girl.' She said 'gal'.

He said: 'I saw her last time, and she was quite amenable to persuasion.'

'It's a woman's thing,' she said, but without force.

'How much are we prepared to go to?'

'I shouldn't think we'd get out of it under a hundred.'

'Doesn't do to give that sort of person a handle, I should be careful,' she said. Her eyes were already marshalling her rose bushes, which offered white and pink cups of petal to the wind; they shook gently under a cloud of greenish-white butterflies. She frowned, saying: 'I must get the garden boy to spray those roses this morning.'

He nodded, saying: 'I might not be back for lunch,' and walked off, hands behind his back, towards the gate.

Mrs Maynard, a solid dark blue shape, moved frowning over the crisp lawn, narrowing her eyes at the roses.

Maisie Gale had a room in one of the avenues, and it was not more than five minutes out of Mr Maynard's morning walk to the Magistrates' Court. He was counting on catching her before she left for work. In fact she was just wheeling her bicycle towards the gate when he appeared.

She said amiably: 'Thank you for coming, Mr Maynard,' and leaned the bicycle against the trunk of a jacaranda tree.

Some weeks before, Mr Maynard had visited her, in order to persuade her not to marry his son, or at least to wait until Binkie returned on his next leave. He had expected opposition, but met none. Yesterday she had written him a letter saying she was pregnant. 'I would like to talk this over with you at your convenience, Yours truly, Maisie Gale.'

She seemed to be agreeably surprised that his convenience was so readily at her service.

'I suppose you are quite sure about this?' he inquired.

Maisie leaned against the brown stem of a young jacaranda tree, one bare arm wrapped about it, the other propped on her lazy hip. Her pretty plump face showed blue stains under the eyes. She said: 'Oh, yes, I'm two weeks over.'

'And I suppose you are quite sure Binkie is the father?'

She turned wide blue eyes on him, studying him as dispassionately as he was studying her. 'Oh, yes. You see, we were engaged.' This, offered with the conviction that it must make the ethics of the situation perfectly plain, caused Mr Maynard to frown, and to raise his black brows at her.

'What I thought was this,' she said. 'Binkie told me Mrs Maynard has friends high up in the RAF. I thought Binkie could get compassionate leave. Yes, I know it's a long way off, and they say the lads'll be in Italy by now perhaps, but I thought perhaps it could be worked.'

Mr Maynard's eyes focused on her face with a suddenness he must have felt himself, for he lowered them, allowing himself a small knowing smile.

'I know a girl who had a friend in the office. She got

pregnant, but her boy got compassionate leave and came home to marry her.'

'My dear girl,' he said, his voice weighted with ironical meaning. 'I assure you it is quite out of the question.'

She looked puzzled. She had begun to blush. 'Well, if it is, it is,' she said, and grasped the handlebars of her bicycle.

His face was hard. 'The CO must be pretty well used to the cries of complaint from the girls left behind, you know – whether justified or not.'

She looked even more upset. Her face was a clear scarlet. 'I don't know what you're saying,' she queried.

He did not reply save for the ironical stare. She shrugged and got on to her bicycle.

'Wait,' he said. She waited, moving the bicycle along the earth under her, back and forth, back and forth. He grimaced with irritation. 'There's no need to fly off. What are you going to do?'

Her eyes filled with tears, and she turned her face away.

'The sad thing is this, with my other two husbands I wished I could have a baby, and we didn't do anything but I didn't get pregnant. This time, Binkie and I took precautions because we were only engaged and not married, and I'm pregnant. Well, that's life.' She ended humorously, but the tears were running down her face.

'But my dear girl, you can't have an illegitimate baby,' he said, making his voice scandalized.

She replied coldly, because of the falseness of his tone: 'I never said I should. What I said was, couldn't Binkie come on leave so we could get married and I could have the baby.'

His stare at her was prolonged. She met it with wet eyes. There was a look of distaste on her face.

'You'll need money,' he said on a tentative note.

'I'll go to Joburg,' she said. 'I know a girl who went. It cost her seventy pounds. Fifty for the operation and twenty for the travelling. If you could lend the money, I'm sure Binkie would give it back to you when he comes home.'

'Tell me, what do you get as widow of your two husbands?'

The dislike on her face was now so strong that he began

to feel apologetic and to be angry because he saw no necessity for apology.

'I refused the allowance when my second husband was killed because he had a widow for a mother and she got it. And I didn't get money from my first husband because I didn't like the way his mum and dad behaved after I married him.'

Mr Maynard thought: It's easy to check on the first marriage. I know the parents. This idea expressed itself in a furtive set of his facial muscles, and she saw it, saying hotly: 'There's no need to make inquiries because what I say is true. And it's nothing to do with you either,' she added.

Now they stood opposite each other, antagonists, the bicycle standing between them under the thick green layers of shade.

He said: 'If I make it £150, will that do?'

'But I said an abortion would cost £70.'

'Look here, let's call it £150 and make it quits. But I must have any letters Binkie wrote you, and you must undertake not to make trouble.'

The scarlet flamed up again, over her fair exposed neck, her angry face which was bright against the pale glistening tendrils of hair. Even her arms were red. 'I don't understand you,' she said. 'What's the £150 in aid of? I said £70. That's what it costs. And I don't see why you are making such a thing about it. If I wrote to Binkie he'd send it to me. He's fair. He sees things fair, the way I do. But the posts take so long with the war, and I don't want to wire to get him into trouble.'

His eyes moved fast over her, resting for a full glance on her stomach. Now she smiled sarcastically. 'What are you thinking? You think I'm trying to put something over on you? Well, I'm not. And I'll tell you something else. You needn't think that I don't know why you asked me not to marry Binkie on his leave. You think I'm not good enough. Well, what I think is, if I married Binkie I'd be stuck with you for in-laws, and I wouldn't like it. I don't like the way you think. You've got dirty minds. I like Binkie well enough, he's a fine kid, but you're too much for me. As far as I'm concerned, it's off for always. You can choose him a wife with your ideas, haggling over money when a girl's in trouble. And you can keep your bloody seventy pounds. I'll borrow it somewhere else.' She got on to her bicycle and went off down the avenue, cycling erratically beside a stream of early-morning office-bound cars.

Mr Maynard was left under the jacaranda tree, all his susceptibilities in flux. He thought: Well, she's not much of a hand at blackmail. Then a nerve of justice twitched in him, and he thought: At least the marriage is off, I suppose that's something.

But he was depressed, and frowned and grunted as he walked under the thick trees towards the Courts. All the same, it seems she is pregnant after all. I was wrong. She's got my grandchild inside of her. This hit him hard. He had not put it like that to himself before. Perhaps if I saw her again . . . But he knew it would be useless approaching her again. No good now to offer to bring Binkie down for a wedding, which of course it would be perfectly easy to arrange. No good at all. He'd muffed it. Perhaps his wife would have done better? The conviction that she would not comforted him. Now his mind was filled with the idea that he might have had a grand-daughter and there would be no grand-daughter.

Maisie was several blocks in front of him, knowing that he followed, watching her. She saw trees, buildings, people through blobs of tears. She turned past a statue of Cecil Rhodes side by side with another bicycle. On the bicycle was Martha Knowell, who smiled at her, but in such a way it was easy to do no more than smile back. Maisie suddenly remembered that Martha was a Red, and that the Reds believed in free love.

'Hey, Matty,' she said, 'can you spare a moment?'

Martha came to a stop, resting her foot on the kerb, and Maisie arrived beside her.

'Matty, I hope you don't mind my asking you some advice, but I've got some trouble.' Martha smiled; Maisie, comparing the smile with others in her memory, said: 'What's up with you? You sick?'

'I've been sick. My first day up.'

'Too bad. We all have our troubles.'

'What's yours?'

'Well, Matty, it's like this. I'm preggy.' She anxiously examined Martha's face for signs of disapproval. There were none, so she continued: 'Hell, man, I wish I could die, I do really, because I didn't marry Binkie, his parents asked us not to until the next leave. So now I want to have the kid and I can't, because it would seem Binkie couldn't get compassionate leave.'

Martha frowned and remarked that it was disgraceful that women couldn't have babies if they wanted to, even if they didn't have husbands.

Maisie said reproachfully: 'Hell, man, Matty, but I know a girl who had a baby without a husband and everyone treated her like dirt.'

'I know,' said Martha, 'that's what I mean.' At this point Maisie's distressed face brought her out of the region of principle, and she said: 'Well, you can't have an illegitimate baby in this dump, but don't you go to those wise women, they mess you up.'

'But that means Joburg.'

'Haven't you any money?'

'I can get some from my mum.'

'Will she mind?'

'My mum'll always stand by me,' said Maisie warmly. 'The reason I don't like to tell her is it's because she's not too rich herself. No, I'll get it from somewhere. But the thing is, I've not got the address of that place in Joburg, and my friend that knows, she's away. So do you know?'

'I don't, but surely we can find out?'

'I do so hate this business, Matty. It makes me feel sick. I say to myself: Well, you're a woman and you're going to have a baby, that's all. But already I feel dirty, if you know what I mean. And where's the sense? I mean, there's something funny about it – I have had two husbands, and Binkie, and here I stand, not knowing where to turn.' Tears splashed from Maisie's cheeks into the dust.

Martha said: 'Oh hell, Maisie, don't cry. Why don't you

send a wire to Binkie? He'll fix something. These men always fix things up somehow.'

'But I can't send him a telegram saying what is the truth, because someone might read it and he'd be in trouble. And I asked Mr Maynard but he's very strange, isn't he?'

'He's a damned old reactionary.'

Maisie frowned, waited for Martha to use a word that she could feel with, and when Martha did not, went on: 'I don't understand anything he was getting at except he thought I was trying to put something over on him, and I don't want to have anything to do with people like that. It makes me feel badly about Binkie too. I don't want to marry Binkie if I've got to have types like that in my life. So what shall I do?'

'I'll see if I can get the address of that place in Joburg.'

'I'd like to have the baby, Matty. I've had the three boys – my two husbands, and Binkie, and I wish I could have a baby to myself.'

Martha, seeing that this was a crisis not to be solved by addresses in Johannesburg, said: 'Look, Maisie, you'd better come to see me, and we'll talk it all over.'

'Thanks, Matty, when can I come?'

This was a real problem. Martha, out of bed that morning, had no evenings free as far ahead as she could see. She said: 'Tomorrow evening there's a Progressive Club meeting. I'll meet you and we'll talk. By then I'll have asked my friends about it.'

'But, Matty, I don't want people talking about me.'

'But how can I find out?'

Heavy footsteps sounded beside them. Mr Maynard passed with a stiff nod and a measured smile and a sharp, penetrating prolonged stare at Maisie.

Maisie said, again crying: 'Hell, Matty, these people get me down. My first man's parents were the same, they think in a bad way, they think about life as if it's all money.'

'Come tomorrow and we'll fix something.'

'Well, thanks, Matty, and you're a real pal.'

They cycled off side by side, once again passing Mr Maynard, but without looking at him.

Mr Maynard, now that the image of a grand-daughter possessed him, ached with elderly loss, and he gazed fixedly at the fair plump body moving lazily past on the machine, a body which he saw simply as the casket which housed the heir of his flesh. He thought: She shouldn't be cycling if she's pregnant. He thought: Martha told me she didn't see Maisie these days. Why did she tell me a lie? He was possessed by an irritable anger. I suppose she's behind it . . . this thought switched into: Some communist trick, I suppose. Normally such an idea would not lodge in his critical mind for longer than a second, but now he did not resist it. His mind fumed with all kinds of suspicions: Maisie was one of the Reds, and in some way the appeal for money had a link with communism.

He allowed his mind to play with these ideas of treachery and deception until he reached the Magistrates' Court. He was late, and everyone was waiting for him.

He took his place at the big table, with officials standing on either side. His black interpreter, Elias Phiri, waited beside the small stand where the prisoners would be placed. A black messenger in uniform stood at the door, and, as each offender entered, sent him on his way with an officious push and a word of command.

In the course of thirty minutes Mr Maynard offered twenty-odd African men the choice of a ten-shilling fine or a month in jail for being out in the white part of the town the night before without one or more of the obligatory passes. Most chose prison.

A Coloured man came up on a charge of falling behind on the instalments for his furniture: a stop-order was fixed on his salary.

A white woman stood before the magistrate in order to receive a lecture on improvidence. Having undertaken to pay off five pounds a month on a debt of £130, she had failed to do so. She said she had five children and a drinking husband. Mr Maynard said this was no affair of the Court: she must pay off the arrears of £20 within a week, and keep up the monthly payments in future. She was a middle-aged woman with a thin, lined sunburned face, and a mouth tight with resentment and bitterness.

'And where am I going to get the £20?' she inquired. 'My husband's out of work.'

'Then you should get work.'

'But my baby's six months old.'

'There's a crèche, isn't there? Put the children in a crèche and get a job.'

'But, sir, if I get a job I won't be earning more than fifteen pounds a month and it will cost all of that to keep the children in the crèche.'

'But my dear lady, you should have thought of all that before running yourself into debt.'

'Thank you very much,' she said, 'thank you.' And went out of the Court with fast blind steps, muttering: 'Old owl, bloody old owl,' while Mr Maynard gazed at the space where the next defaulter must stand.

He was a white youth charged with speeding. He earned fifty pounds a month and was fined two pounds.

There followed a black lorry-driver charged with the same offence: he was fined two pounds, but asked for the option of prison, since he earned four pounds a month.

'And what will your family do while you are in prison?'

'I have no family, sir,' said the lorry-driver, smiling broadly.

'Very wise,' said Mr Maynard. 'Right. One month in jail. Next case.'

There were no more cases. The Court rose. That is, all the officials departed save Mr Maynard and the interpreter Elias Phiri.

'Elias, come here.'

'Sir,' Elias stood smiling by the table.

'That lorry-driver, is it true he has no family?'

'I don't know, sir.'

Mr Maynard sharply raised his brows, and Elias said: 'Well, sir, I believe he has a woman.'

'His wife? I suppose not.'

'A spare, sir.'

'And children?'

'Two children.'

'And so why did he want to go to prison?'

'His wife is coming from Nyasaland this week, sir, and he knows there will be trouble between the women. I think he wanted to be out of the way, sir.'

Mr Maynard would normally have laughed at this, but he said sharply: 'Prison is supposed to be a disgrace. What's the use of us sending you people to prison if you don't think of it as a punishment?'

Elias said blandly: 'But, sir, we aren't civilized yet, perhaps that is the reason.'

Mr Maynard did not laugh, as Elias had expected him to do. He said: 'I see absolutely no reason why we should give house-room to your friends to keep them out of domestic trouble.'

'No, sir.'

'Elias.'

'Yes, sir.'

'At these meetings, the communist meetings, is there a young lady, a white missus, who calls herself Maisie?'

'No, sir.'

'Are you sure?'

'Quite sure, sir.'

'And the other meetings, the public meetings, does she go to those?'

'No, sir.'

'Are you still keeping a note of the names?'

'Oh, yes, sir.'

'And so what's going on? Anything new?'

'Oh, a lot of trouble, sir. A lot of quarrelling.'

'Indeed. What about?'

'The men from the camps, the RAF, sir, they want to make a revolution with us natives, but the others, they say no, the time is not yet ripe.'

'Ah? And what are the RAF doing about fomenting a revolution?'

'Nothing, sir. They say it is time to begin, that is all.'

'And what is this I hear about a white man being seen down in the Location last week selling that communist rag?'

141

'I don't know about it, sir.'

'Then you'd better find out, Elias. That's what I'm paying you for.'

Elias, averting his gaze from Mr Maynard's face, said quietly: 'Of course many of the RAF men and some of the baases from the town wait outside the Location gates at night for our girls.'

'Yes,' said Mr Maynard dryly. 'I am aware that they do. But you know that is not what I am talking about.'

'No, sir.'

'I'll expect to talk to you tomorrow, Elias.' He pushed five shillings across the table at Elias, who pocketed it swiftly and as swiftly went out.

Mr Maynard waited a few moments, then shouted: 'Sixpence.'

The Native Court Messenger came in. 'Baas?'

'Have you seen any white men in the Location?'

'No, sir.'

'Have you heard of any white men in the Location?'

Sixpence, otherwise Tabwinga Mleli from the regions north of the Zambesi Valley, stood smiling politely. 'No, sir. Only the superintendents, sir.'

'You idiot, I know about the superintendents. I'm asking you about white men, RAF men, selling newspapers in the Location.'

'No, sir.'

Mr Maynard took a ten-shilling note from his pocket, and rubbed it between his fingers while he gazed at the messenger.

'I know nothing, baas.'

'Very well,' said Mr Maynard, putting back the ten-shilling note, at the sight of which Tabwinga, who earned two pounds a month, let a deep sigh escape him. 'Send in Mathew.'

'Yes, sir.'

A moment later, Mathew, an old man who had been for many years in the service of the Court, came in, with humility.

'Mathew, do you know about white men selling communist newspapers in the Location?'

Mathew's grizzled old face puckered up: the ten-shilling note was again playing bait between Mr Maynard's fingers.

'There are always baases after the girls, sir.'

'Yes, damn it, I know that.'

'I did hear,' said old Mathew, his eyes on the ten-shilling note, 'that there was a white baas last week in Elias's house.'

'Elias? Are you sure?'

'I heard it only. Perhaps I am mistaken.'

Mr Maynard suddenly threw the ten-shilling note on to the floor. Mathew's face, puckered up with distress, turned away, as if he was about to walk off. Then he bent and picked up the money, slowly. He said reproachfully to Mr Maynard: 'I have worked for you for many years, sir.'

'Yes, you old scoundrel, I know you have. Well, get out.'

The old man went to the door like a scuttling old fowl.

Mr Maynard now allowed himself half an hour for serious thought, putting the facts to himself as follows: The girl was not trying blackmail, she is in fact pregnant. The chances are that it is Binkie's child, though of course with these people anything is possible. The girl is a negligible creature, but then, so is any girl Binkie is likely to choose. If I don't do something quickly she will get an abortion and that's the end of Binkie. (Mr Maynard's instinct, not his mind, informed him that this would be the case: he so far discounted Binkie as a person that he had not once considered what Binkie would think of his parents' behaviour.) I must stop her getting an abortion. It is now useless for either myself or my wife to see her. I must approach Martha. Once Martha has made Maisie see reason, I shall explain to Maisie that it would not be in Binkie's interests for her to have anything further to do with the communist element in this town. After all, he is a civil servant.

He telephoned Martha at her office, demanding that she should lunch with him.

That morning Mr Robinson had told Martha that she had altogether too many personal calls in the office. He was at that moment standing impatiently beside her desk with documents to be typed.

'I suppose it's about Maisie,' said Martha.

'It would seem,' said Mr Maynard, his voice heavy with willed urbanity, 'that I've offended that woman without knowing why.'

Martha said nothing. Mr Robinson bent at her elbow. Mrs Buss's fingers were hopping like sparrows over her type-writer at the next table.

'Mr Maynard,' said Martha, noting that Mr Robinson's disapproval vanished at the sound of the magistrate's name, 'I'm not going to do your dirty work for you. I've told you before.'

Mr Robinson let out a gruff: 'I *say*!' and glared at Martha.

'I can't imagine why you should assume it is dirty,' said Mr Maynard.

Martha put down the receiver. Mr Robinson said: 'You take a very cavalier tone with your elders and betters.'

Martha was feeling quite sick with dislike of both him and the magistrate. She was still weak after the illness. Mr Robinson, receiving no answer, examined his typist. Martha knew she must be pale, for she could feel the cold deadness of her cheeks. Mr Robinson escaped from the situation by saying: 'I shouldn't overdo it the first day if I were you, Mrs Knowell. You don't look too good.' Forcing a smile he added: 'And you might bear in mind that as a member of the legal profession, I have a natural desire that my staff should show a modicum of respect to magistrates – at least when they are using my telephone.' He went into the inner office, slamming his door.

Martha would have gone home to bed. But she was thinking of the meeting that night. She had missed three, and longed to be back with the group.

Chapter Three

Seven o'clock in Black Ally's; the smell of hot fat; the spitting and cracking of hot fat from the kitchen; the tables crammed as usual full of the RAF – unbuttoned, at ease, noisy, a thick mass of men under a grey haze of kitchen fumes and cigarette smoke. Anton sat in his usual corner, eating methodically, waiting for Martha. She came in brightly, smiling yet anxious, examining his face so as to match what she had learned of him during the last three weeks with how she had seen him before. He hastened to rise, draw back a chair and settle her; this protective and almost fussy manner belonged to the man who had been a devoted nurse. She was thinking: he wouldn't have done that before. Is he doing it now because I've been sick or because I've become something different for him?

In a corner nearby the RAF group, Andrew, Jimmy, Murdoch and Bill Bluett were steadily taking in eggs, bacon and chips. Jimmy saw Martha, the colour on his big cheekbones deepened, and he gave her a stiff nod. The three others greeted her with the jocular defensiveness they used for any woman, comrade or not, whom they met when they were in a group of the RAF. She saw them give Anton unfriendly looks, and remembered that while she had been away battles of principle had raged. Even Andrew, because he was with the others, allowed himself – while checking disparaging remarks about Anton in a brisk comradely voice – to ally himself with their hostility by smiling connivance. She looked at Anton, to see how he felt, but he seemed unaware. She thought it impossible that he did not know they were hostile to him; therefore he must have decided it was unimportant. This made Martha feel better. Yet she asked: 'Anton, why didn't you sit with them?'

'I was here first.'

'You could have moved and sat with them?'

'I was waiting for you.' There was an awkward gallantry in his manner which struck a note foreign to their relations before her illness, and discordant with the simple kindliness of his manner to her while she was ill.

She thought: I've become something else for him, and it made her uncomfortable and resentful. Again she felt caged and hemmed in: there was a new possessiveness in him, something dogged and cold.

I'm caught for life, she thought: but the words 'for life' released her from anxiety. They all of them saw the future as something short and violent. Somewhere just before them was a dark gulf or chasm, into which they must all disappear. A communist is a dead man on leave, she thought. That's what matters, and not how I feel about Anton. And, anyway, if Anton and I are unhappy it will be easy to separate.

These ideas flashed through her mind all at once, and she smiled at Anton and said: 'Well, of course, I wanted to be with you too.'

They continued their meal. Martha was conscious of the airforce men in the corner, envying them because of the solidarity of their comradeship, even while she told herself it was sentimental to envy them: the comradeship was the uniform, that was all, and had nothing to do with them as individuals. All the same, she was possessed by an old feeling that she was being shut out of some warmth, some beautiful kind of friendship. She watched Anton eat, and told him about Maisie. She was wanting him to say that Maisie should have the baby and defy the world, but he broke a piece of bread carefully between long, thin fingers, and said: 'There's nothing to an abortion if it's properly done.'

At this moment the four airforce men rose from their own table and came to stand by them. There were a few moments of banter, behind which Martha could feel a dislike of Anton which dismayed her. Was it simply because of the RAF solidarity? Because they had seen her choose Anton instead of one of themselves? Her instinct said no.

Andrew said bluntly: 'What are you two love-birds talking about?'

Martha grimaced at the 'love-birds' but, because she trusted Andrew, told him about Maisie: she wanted a more generous reaction than Anton's about the baby.

The three men with Andrew listened seriously, as Andrew did: she was grateful for it – because she was in trouble she became a comrade again, and one of them.

Jimmy said hotly: 'It's a bleeding shame, that's what it is.'

Bill Bluett said: 'Serves her right for not bargaining over the wedding ring, poor bint.'

Andrew said: 'Never mind, we'll put it all right come the Revolution.'

'The Revolution's not going to help her much,' said Martha. 'That is, unless we can make one in the next two or three days.'

Anton said: 'She should have thought of all that before: instead of getting pregnant and then feeling sorry for herself.'

The atmosphere chilled. The four men stiffened inside their thick uniforms, and their eyes exchanged cold messages. Murdoch cried out in derision: 'She should have thought of that before, should she?'

'That's the long and the short of it, mate,' said Jimmy with solemnity – 'look before you leap, a stitch in time saves nine, and if a girl gets caught out, that's her funeral.'

Bill Bluett said to Martha, ignoring Anton: 'See you upstairs.' The other three men followed the jerk of his head towards the door.

Martha got up and said: 'We'll be late.'

Anton said: 'There's five minutes.' He lowered his chin obstinately, and hunched up his shoulders, sitting silent. Then he deliberately reached for the cheese plate and began to eat. Martha, sitting on the edge of her chair, watched him, thinking that the meeting was due to start now, that she had never known him be unpunctual before by so much as half a minute, and he had begun eating again in order to enforce himself against both her and the RAF men.

The fumes of hot wet cabbage and boiling fat filled her throat and she set herself not to feel sick. At the end of five minutes Anton rose and said: 'Now it's time.'

Upstairs there was a full complement of people. Anton went to sit by Jasmine, who was waiting for him with her papers spread ready. Martha sat beside Andrew McGrew, feeling a disloyal pleasure in the way the RAF opened their ranks to her, as if protecting her against Anton. She looked to see how Anton reacted: he had the appearance of someone on trial, and her instinct was confirmed by the expressions of satisfaction on the faces of the RAF men. Jimmy even whispered to her: 'Don't you worry, lass, we'll fix everything.'

At once her emotions swung over: it appeared that there had been some decision among the men to 'fix' Anton? Well, they had no right to it; and no right to take her compliance for granted.

There was a crisis blowing up, and Anton was aware of it, and confident he could handle it.

He said: 'Comrade Jasmine will now read the minutes of the last meeting.'

Jasmine did so in her small voice, effacing herself as a good secretary should with such intensity that there was no need for Anton to sit as he did, gazing severely at the paper from which she read, in order to remind everyone that minutes were no mere formality, but something that needed everyone's attention.

Martha's mind wandered. She blamed herself for not concentrating. She had meant to listen behind the formal words for a sense of what really happened at the last meeting. She thought: Next week, the minutes will read: Minutes of the last meeting, that's all, just a formality, but actually something ugly is happening.

Martha, at the risk of earning Anton's disapproving stare, let her eyes move over the other faces. Elias Phiri, seated at the end of a bench, was staring at the floor. The smooth thick flesh of his forehead was puckering and smoothing and puckering again – like cat's paws of wind on warm smooth water. Martha thought: When illiterate natives – I mean, Africans – listen to something they don't understand, their foreheads pucker and smooth like that – but Elias isn't illiterate. That means he's worried about something. One of his feet shifted. It began to feel and move in rhythm. Listening for the rhythm, Martha heard a pulse of drumming from over the street: they were dancing at McGrath's. Elias swallowed a guilty yawn behind a large hand. Well, *he* wasn't listening either.

Marie and Piet sat side by side. She had her hand on his knee. They both stared before them. Impossible to tell whether they were listening or not.

Carrie Jones, seated beside Tommy, regarded her ten red fingernails which were spread out on her knee. She wore a yellow linen dress as smooth as butter and her face had the smooth prepared surface of a very pretty girl who feels men's eyes play over her like sunlight. Martha thought: She's what I used to be: she looks at herself in the looking-glass, and she sees how her face and body form a sort of painted shell, and she adores herself, but she is waiting for a pair of eyes to melt the paint and shoot through into the dark inside – well, she'll have to wait! . . . Martha examined this idea, in a change of mood, and rejected it. She was again full of violent dissatisfaction. Half the things I think, she thought, are untrue and full of self-pity – I've only got to get tired or be sick, and I'm full of nostalgia again, but the Lord only knows for what! – full of self-pity, and my mind seems to breed dramatic and silly ideas on its own.

She yawned, still watching Carrie. Well, what *is* she doing here? She's such a pretty girl, she doesn't read, she isn't really political at all. There isn't a man in this room she could be interested in. And at this moment she's bored because she's sitting by Tommy – bored and ashamed of being bored.

Carrie, feeling Martha's eyes on her, offered her a companionable but rather tired smile. The tiredness in Carrie's smile restored Martha's mood of five minutes before. She thought: She's fed up with everything. She hates that painted shell of hers and she despises men for the look they get on their faces when they see her. She's become a communist because she wants to be something different. She'll leave us soon – yes, of course. Because there isn't one man here who doesn't think: Carris is such a pretty girl. They all have that defensive and rather shame-faced look, and their voices when they speak of her are different, simply because she's so pretty.

Here Jasmine's voice stopped and Bill Bluett leaned forward to speak. He had obviously been listening to every word of the minutes-reading, for now he challenged three points in their wording. They were unimportant points. Jasmine submitted his order of words to the meeting who accepted them without discussion. The minutes were changed. They all of them knew that Bill had done this, not because he cared about these details, but in order to challenge Anton; Anton knew it too. He initialled the altered minutes and said:

'Anything else of importance, Comrade Bill?'

Bill shook his head, but remained leaning forward, on the alert. Martha looked at his hands, which lay loose on his knees. They were long, fine, white hands, but grimy with oil. He was a fitter. He even smelled of oil. Martha looked at the hands of the other RAF men, and thought: Well, they don't have to have signatures of oil all over them. Bill does because he's middle-class. She had no time to pursue this thought, because Jimmy was speaking.

'Comrade Chairman, I want to put a resolution to this meeting.'

'On what subject?' asked Anton. 'This is item two on the agenda. Political instruction. Comrade Jasmine is to speak.'

'I don't care about item two,' said Jimmy. His face was flaming, his big mouth shovelled out the words. 'I want something done. I want to do something instead of talk, talk, talk.'

'Take it easy, mate,' said Bill, in a low tone aside to Jimmy. Obviously something had been decided between the RAF men, and Jimmy had upset the plan by speaking now.

On the other side of Martha, Andrew shifted his body

uncomfortably. He doesn't like all this, she thought, and looked inquiringly at him. He made a quick wry face, as if to say: I don't understand it either.

'I want to ask the meeting if I can put my resolution,' said Jimmy, glaring around at them all, including his RAF comrades.

'Let's keep to the agenda,' said Marie du Preez good-naturedly. 'Otherwise we'll be yapping all night again.'

Jimmy glowered at her. She smiled at him, maternal and quizzical. He blushed deeper and said, still angry but in a lower voice: 'OK then. Only because the political education is the same thing. Then I demand my right to put a resolution. I demand it, see?'

Anton, ignoring Jimmy, said to Jasmine: 'Comrade, will you now speak.'

Jasmine spoke for fifteen minutes, her wrist-watch propped in front of her, on racial and national hatreds. These, she said, together with any forms of hostility between one group or sub-section of humanity and another, were due to capitalism, and would vanish on the advent of socialism. When she had finished, Anton said: 'We have ten minutes allowed for discussion. Who speaks first?'

'I want to put my resolution,' said Jimmy.

'But this is the time for discussion.'

'You can't just go upsetting the agenda like that,' said Marjorie excitedly.

'I'm not upsetting anything,' said Jimmy. 'I want to put a resolution. It's a resolution about the things Jasmine has just said.'

'I propose we set aside the agenda and let Comrade Jimmy put his resolution,' said Andrew, in the humorous voice he used for difficult moments.

Martha glanced at Bill who was grinning sardonically: apparently he was not unhappy about the way things were going.

'Agreed?' said Anton briefly.

'Agreed, yes, we agree,' said various voices, some resigned, some amused, some impatient.

Jimmy took a piece of paper from his breast pocket,

unfolded it, and held it before him. 'I propose to put the following resolution to the meeting. One: all forms of racial prejudice are artificial, contrary to nature, and created by capitalists in order to divide and rule . . .'

Here Elias Phiri said: 'Wait a minute, I want to ask a question.'

'Comrade Elias,' said Anton, turning to him.

'You are saying,' said the African, looking to Jasmine, 'that racial prejudice is created by capitalism. Is that what you are saying?'

There was a pause. Jasmine said precisely, but rather puzzled: 'Yes, comrade, that was the subject of my talk.'

'I see,' said Elias. 'I see.' He looked back at the floor. His foot still tapped, tapped, stroked the floor, to the time of McGrath's hardly audible drums.

'What is Comrade Elias saying?' asked Marjorie. 'I don't understand.'

'I just wanted to be sure: the communists say racial prejudice is created by capitalism – I wanted to know about that,' Elias explained to Marjorie.

There was an even longer pause. He had said, 'The communists,' as if he wasn't one of them. And it had slipped out, which made it worse. They all felt uncomfortable.

'Can I go on?' asked Jimmy angrily.

'Go on,' said Anton.

'Secondly, that anti-Semitism is just capitalist propaganda.'

'Well, of course,' said Marjorie at once.

'Thirdly, there's no such thing as national difference. It's all nonsense, talking about the British character, the German character, the Japanese character – we're all the same.'

He lowered his paper slightly and gazed about him aggressively: 'We're all the same as each other,' he said.

'Well, go on,' said Anton calmly. Everyone looked puzzled.

'Well,' said Jimmy, frowning at his piece of paper, momentarily at a loss, as if he had expected them to disagree. 'That's not all. That's not all by a long chalk.'

'But I don't see the point,' said Marjorie. 'I mean, we all know that, so what's the point of passing resolutions?'

'I'm just fed up with talking,' said Jimmy. 'I want something settled for once and for all.'

Marjorie shrugged and sat still.

'Fourthly,' said Jimmy, 'that all people are equal, and that everything is a question of education. And that's the most important thing of all – education.'

'I don't understand,' said Marie. 'Of course everyone should have an equal education.'

'It's more than saying of course. It seems that you're just paying lip-service. Lenin said, every cook must govern the State. But when it comes down to it, you don't hold with it at all!'

'But why are you saying all this?' asked Marjorie. She was very excited and angry. Colin, phlegmatic and proprietary beside her, very much the new young husband, laid a large pale hand on her agitated arm. She almost shook it off, then remained still, sitting back, smiling crossly.

'There's no such thing as talent,' said Jimmy. 'It's all just a trick to scare the workers out of trying. Talent is education. Up to now, the educated people have had talent. They write books and that sort of thing. But it's because they have been educated.'

Jasmine was observed to be looking at Anton, as if expecting him to call a halt. But he remained silent, drawing something on his agenda.

Marie said in her direct honest way: 'I don't understand what all this is in aid of, comrade. Are you saying everyone's exactly the same as everyone else?'

Here Piet let out a good-natured guffaw, and said: 'If we are going to pass a resolution abolishing the little difference between men and women, then I'm going back to being a reactionary.'

'*Oh!*' exclaimed his wife, with friendly exasperation. 'Trust *him!*' They exchanged the rapid, understanding, cheerfully antagonistic glances of a well-matched couple. 'Don't you take any notice of my old man. But Jimmy, how can you say that? People are just born different.'

Jimmy sat loosely on the bench inside the thick grey shell of uniform, like a heap of big bones roughly packaged up.

His big face was scarlet, his eyes sombrely unhappy. 'There you are,' he said, 'I knew it would be like that!'

'But Jimmy, you're saying there's no such thing as talent?'

Here Andrew came in again, with his 'humorous' voice saying: 'I think Comrade Jimmy is framing his resolution carelessly. Why don't we put it like this, comrades: Fourthly, that unequal education has so far prevented the workers from making use of their talents.'

'Very well,' said Jimmy aggressively. 'OK. I'll accept that.'

'But I don't see why we have to pass a resolution at all,' said Marjorie. But again she made herself go quiet under the pressure of her husband's hand.

'I want it all clear,' insisted Jimmy. 'I want this meeting to pass this resolution.'

'But we can't pass a resolution about this: it's simply what we all believe anyway,' said Jasmine.

'But I don't believe it,' said Tommy, writhing as usual because of the effort of speaking up in front of everyone. 'I mean, it's not true. Take this book Jasmine made me read, *War and Peace*. Well, I can't see myself writing that in a thousand years, even if I was educated.'

'Yes, you would,' said Jimmy, glaring at him. He raised his voice and shouted: 'There you are! They were all aristocrats! They were bourjoys. So why do you have to sit there and fall for it?'

'Well, I don't see what this is about,' said Marjorie, 'but if Jimmy wants the resolution passed, then I think we should pass it. And then we can get on with the agenda.'

Jimmy said: 'That's just contemptuous. You don't really think so at all, but you are saying, "Let's pass the resolution," just to shut me up.'

'I vote we pass the resolution,' said Bill. As if Anton had been waiting for the sound of Bill's voice, he stopped doodling, and said: 'Any further discussion? Who will second?'

Bill said: 'I will.'

The resolution was put and carried unanimously. They were all smiling awkwardly, feeling foolish.

But Jimmy was clearly almost in tears. He said: 'But it hasn't been done right. I don't feel right about it all.'

'Come off it,' said Piet, brusque and rude. 'Come off it now. You've got your resolution, now shut up and let us get on with the job.'

Jimmy was looking so sad, so puzzled, that they all felt as if they had let him down.

Bill said to him in a low voice, leaning across Martha: 'Come off it now, Jimmy boy. We're not going to end everything that's bad in the world by passing resolutions, are we now?'

Jimmy smiled back at him, but his eyes rejected him and everyone. They were turned inward, on some sore miserable place which – they all felt – had been cruelly touched. They knew he was badly hurt. It was the first time it had occurred to any of them that perhaps he was not in his right mind, or that he was so ill he had become unbalanced.

Now they worked fast through the agenda. Clearly Anton was hurrying everything as much as he could. He was still afraid of some sort of show-down, that was obvious.

At five minutes to ten he said: 'Any other business? We've got five minutes. I propose I formally close the meeting.'

Martha felt Bill straighten and harden. Now, she thought, this is it.

Bill said, almost casually: 'Comrade Chairman, this is the third time that we've scamped an item on the agenda after formally making a decision about it.'

'We have taken a formal decision never to end a meeting later than ten,' said Anton. 'Your proposal, if you remember.'

'We have also taken a formal decision to have self-criticism and criticism.'

'We can't criticize fifteen people in five minutes.'

'The camp bus is not leaving until eleven tonight.'

'It seems on certain occasions not only that the RAF comrades can all come to the meetings, but can also arrange for the bus to leave an hour later,' said Anton.

Bill said unpleasantly: 'Is that a formal criticism of the RAF comrades? If so, will you bring it up in its correct place and in a form in which it can be answered seriously?'

'You are suggesting that we should extend the meeting for an hour for the purpose of criticism? Anyone disagree?'

Marie du Preez grimaced at her husband; Colin attempted to exchange a rueful look with Marjorie; but she said reproachfully: 'Of course we should have criticism. All serious communist groups have criticism.'

'Good,' said Anton. 'I suggest that the order in which the criticism should be conducted be as follows: First, self-criticism. Then, criticism of each other. Then criticism by individual comrades of the group work as a whole. Any objections?'

'Agreed,' said Bill at once.

'I think it would be better to have criticism of each other first, then our self-criticism would be deeper,' said Jasmine seriously.

'Agreed,' said Anton, as impatiently as he ever allowed himself to sound. 'Now, where do we start?'

There were two obvious people, sitting at the extreme ends of a rough semi-circle: one was Jasmine and the other Jimmy. Various people said apprehensively, 'Jasmine. Besides, she is the secretary.'

Jasmine stood up. She was self-possessed, but her hands were trembling. Martha, looking at the small slight girl in her tight flowered dress, her black hair in curls on her head, pale and rather stern in her effort to appear calm, felt protective. She looked around and saw that everyone felt the same. Piet appeared almost comically bewildered. Marie recovered herself first. She hissed at her husband: 'Go on, you old ram, she's a human being as well, isn't she?'

No one said anything for a time.

'Well, comrades?' said Anton. 'Criticism of Comrade Jasmine.' He paused. 'It is a well-known fact that in every person's character is a basic trend or type of weakness which, if he or she is not aware of it, so that it can be corrected, may destroy them as communists and as persons.'

Bill Bluett laughed out aloud. They all laughed.

Andrew said to Anton: 'I wish to pass a belated amendment to the previously passed resolution: namely, that national characteristics are of the utmost importance.' I

156

sounded affectionate. Anton glanced up, studied Andrew's face to see if he were being serious, and said: 'You mean, I am a German? Well, comrades, in reply I would say that if I am pedantic, it is a useful and necessary counter-balance to your British frivolity.'

'Oh, I say,' said Colin, his spectacles flashing.

'Yes, yes, yes,' said Anton. 'If the fundamental fault of the German character is pedantry, then your fault is empiricism and a refusal to base your ideas upon serious analysis.'

'And what happens to Jimmy's resolution?' asked Piet good-humouredly.

'I don't know what empiricism is,' said Jimmy, in such a tone that they all sobered. The thin skin of his cheeks shone scarlet, and his eyes glittered.

Meanwhile, Jasmine stood upright behind the table, waiting. 'It seems no one has any criticism of Comrade Jasmine,' said Anton.

'I have,' said Andrew. Jasmine turned to face him. He said gently: 'Comrade Jasmine, you have a tendency to take on far too much work. I think you take jobs on and do them hurriedly instead of letting other people do them. It is the fault of the very efficient,' he added, smiling at her.

'Yes, I know that is true,' said Jasmine. She looked distressed, and they all felt embarrassed and wished she could sit down.

'Anything else?' said Anton. No one spoke, and he said: 'All right, Comrade Jasmine. Sit down.'

Murdoch said: 'But that's not a fundamental fault, is it? And we've often told Jasmine that before, haven't we?' Jasmine involuntarily stood up again, facing Murdoch who, as she did so, began the familiar half-humorous writhing that he used when he was the focus of attention.

'If there is any criticism of Comrade Jasmine you want to make, then make it,' said Anton.

'But I didn't say there was,' Murdoch cried out, and Jasmine sat down again.

Jimmy said fiercely: 'I want to say something. But it's not just about Jasmine, it's about all the women comrades.' He looked at Martha, then at Carrie Jones. She lifted her indolent dark eyes at him, and he shouted out: 'All of you – lipstick and red nails and fashion magazines. That's not communist. Women should be respected and not behave like . . . well, I can't bring myself to say like what.'

Carrie, who had begun to frown, saw smiles on every face save Jimmy's, and smiled back, rather self-consciously. This self-conscious smile apparently drove Jimmy almost out of his senses, because he stood up and yelled: 'There, you see? You think it's enough just to smile and put lipstick on. Well, I'll tell you something, I've got no time for any girl who messes herself up with paint and plaster.'

'If that's the case,' said Marjorie indignantly, 'why do you take out that girl from McGrath's – she's got dyed hair.'

Bill Bluett snorted with laughter. Now they all laughed, except Jimmy and Anton, who seemed angry.

'I would remind you,' said Anton, 'that this is a communist group. Not a music hall. Comrade Jimmy, you can't bring up a big question like this casually. You are raising the whole question of the position of women. May I suggest that we appoint an evening for the discussion of the position of women?'

Martha watched in herself, and with surprise, because it was contrary to what her instincts told her about Anton, contrary to what she felt when she remembered the Austrian woman, the familiar feeling of trust and relief well up, as if Anton's words built a pillar on which she could support herself. *Draping myself like a silly clinging vine on anything that sounds strong*, she told herself disgustedly.

Andrew said: 'Comrade Anton, you're behaving like a capitalist government asked an awkward question – they always appoint a select committee and hope everything will blow over before the report is published.'

'But it is a question of the position of women,' said Martha.

'*You* say that,' said Jimmy, furious, direct to her, and it was at once obvious to everyone that his attack had from the first been directed at her. 'You say that. You're worse than anyone.' Jasmine said: 'I think Comrade Jimmy's attitude is very sectarian. I see no reason at all why women comrades should look ugly.'

'I didn't say ugly,' said Jimmy.

Jasmine said, with defiance, blushing: 'If a majority vote decides that we should give up cosmetics, then I shall regard it as masculine domination – it's nine to five. I personally consider that all men, whether communists or not, have remnants in them of middle-class ideas about women. Even Lenin. Even Lenin talked about greasy glasses.'

'Hear, hear,' said Marjorie. 'Men make me sick.'

Martha said: 'I quite agree.' She laughed, however, and Jimmy turned on her and said: 'And I want to criticize you, Comrade Matty. You're flippant. You aren't serious. Middle-class comrades are all the same.'

'But Matty isn't being criticized,' said Bill Bluett.

'Well, I'm criticizing her.'

'I agree with Jimmy,' said Tommy. He was perspiring, and his eyes begged apology from Martha, even while his whole body insisted on his right to say what was very important to him. 'I've been thinking about it. Comrade Matty isn't serious. I mean, she acts seriously, but she doesn't talk seriously. Well, I've been reading this book – I've said about it before, this Count Tolstoy. Well, and I've discovered from that book that her manner is a middle-class manner. The middle-class say things that are serious in an unserious way. Jasmine and Matty and Marjorie all do it, but Matty worse than anyone. It's contemptuous. They say something and you have to think, do they mean it or don't they?'

'I protest,' said Andrew. 'I protest against two things: first, the working people are not grim as Tommy seems to think, he seems to suggest the middle-class have a monopoly of humour – '

'Not being funny,' said Tommy earnestly. 'Not that. But saying things as if you're poking fun at yourself for saying them. It's snobbish.'

' – and secondly,' continued Andrew, 'Matty isn't under discussion at all at the moment. The next comrade on the list for criticism is Anton.'

'That's right,' said Bill. 'And I'm surprised at our chairman

159

for not stopping the discussion before. So irregular too, and not a word out of Comrade Anton.' To Martha he said, mock-serious, 'We'll deal with your flippant manner later.'

'Comrade Anton,' said Andrew. 'Comrade Anton, kindly stand up for criticism.'

Martha understood that both Bill and Andrew were protecting her. Also, that Andrew was about to protect Anton from Bill.

Anton slowly stood up. His hands, hanging down by his sides, were quite steady.

'And now I'm going to let you have it,' said Andrew to Anton, in a gruff humorous voice. 'You're an arrogant, stiff-necked, domineering bastard. You're a pedant and a hair-splitter . . .'

Anton was smiling slightly. He knew Andrew was protecting him from Bill, and resented it. The lines around his mouth quivered into life, giving his face a crumpled look, like a used table napkin.

'You're a bureaucrat, Comrade Anton. You're the image of a bureaucrat. I'd like to take you to a low pub every night for a week and see you drunk and making a fool of yourself. Then you might begin to be a good comrade. At the moment you're a pain in the neck.'

Everyone was laughing. Elias Phiri was rolling on his bench with laughter. Anton, still smiling very slightly, nodded at Andrew.

'Anyone disagree with this criticism?' he inquired.

'No, we all agree,' said Marie pleasantly. 'You're just too good to be true, comrade. I wish you'd let up a little.'

Elias Phiri, spluttering out laughter, said: 'Ho, ho, ho,' and tossed his feet up. Then, seeing that everyone was watching him, smiling, he stopped himself laughing and sat shaking his head, internal amusement shaking his whole frame, while his face remained grave.

'The point is,' said Bill to Anton, 'do *you* agree with these criticisms?'

Anton said stiffly: 'Yes, comrade, I am well aware that I tend to be a bureaucrat . . .' It seemed he had been going to say something more, but he stopped.

'Right,' said Andrew. 'You may sit down, Comrade Anton. And mend your ways or we'll get another chairman.'

Anton sat down. He glanced at Bill as he did so; Andrew also looked, with some apprehension, towards Bill. Bill was lolling back, arms folded. He said: 'Comrade Andrew has taken the words out of my mouth. I'll bring up certain other criticisms later.'

There was a pause, then Carrie Jones stood up for criticism. But a note of frivolity had crept into the thing. She listened good-humouredly to criticisms of her 'excessive attention to her personal appearance', and sat down, nodding. Before Tommy stood up, Anton warned them that this was a serious matter. But the rest of the criticism went fast, with plenty of laughter. Again, when they reached Martha, Anton insisted that they were being 'fundamentally irresponsible', but it did no good: Martha, Andrew, Jimmy and Murdoch were criticized fast, in a rapid crossfire of good-humoured phrases from all over the room. Anton then said: 'That's it, comrades. It's half-past ten, and I suggest we leave the group criticism and self-criticism until next week.'

Bill Bluett uncoiled his long thin body in one fast movement, sat forward and said: 'Oh, no, oh, no, you don't. Now we're going to be serious.'

Anton laid down his pencil, and sat up, on the defensive. 'I was under the impression we were being serious.'

'You know perfectly well that this has been a farce. This is not how criticism is conducted in a serious communist group.'

'You're suggesting we should begin again?'

'No, since it is apparently impossible to conduct criticism properly in this group – at least, as presently constituted, then I propose we have general criticism.'

Andrew said, slowly packing tobacco into his pipe: 'Comrade Bill, haven't our criticisms been covered by the criticisms made of Comrade Anton?'

'Your criticisms,' said Anton promptly, on the alert: he had been waiting for this, as they could all see: 'Do I understand you to say that the RAF comrades are making a criticism, as a group, of the group as a whole?'

161

'Yes,' said Andrew, 'you're of course right if you are suggesting that is factionalism, but there are special circumstances here. Of course it is factionalism. And I would like to say in advance that I do not go all the way with the RAF comrades.' He turned to Bill and urged: 'Comrade, wouldn't you agree that what we intended to say has already been covered?'

'No, I would not.'

'I'm not accepting the criticism of an inner group,' said Anton. 'That is contrary to every party principle.'

'If it makes you easy,' said Bill, 'I'll say I'm making criticisms for myself.'

'I agree with Comrade Bill, though,' said Murdoch excitedly.

'And so do I,' said Jimmy.

'I will not, as chairman, accept factionalism,' insisted Anton.

'Oh let up, Anton,' said Marie, as she might have spoken to one of her children. 'Let up, do.'

Bill said: 'I insist on saying this: the work of the whole group is a complete waste of time.'

'Indeed?' said Anton. 'You are proposing, I gather, that we need a fresh analysis of our work? In that case I shall put it on the agenda for next week. Make a note of it, Jasmine.'

Bill said: 'Oh, no, you don't. Next week it would seem that we are discussing the position of women in capitalist society, in order that our lady comrades will know whether to use lipstick or not. Jesus!'

Anton said: 'If you will kindly make detailed criticisms instead of broad generalizations, we can proceed to discuss what you have to say.'

But before Bill could say anything, Murdoch shrilled out on the humorous defensive note he had been criticized for five minutes before: 'Och, but it's a fact. And to my mind it's your doing, Comrade Anton. It's your attitude that does it.'

'Comrade Anton has already been criticized and has accepted the criticism,' said Andrew.

'Will you please be specific,' said Anton. Now he was furious: his face quivered with anger.

'Hell, man — anyone can see it. OK then — take your attitude to Matty's friend who got herself in the family way. You're not human.' He mimicked Anton's voice: '"She should have thought of that before." Hell, what sort of attitude is that for a communist?'

Marie said: 'What's all this, Matty? What's it about?'

Martha said: 'A girl I know got herself pregnant. We were discussing it. That's all.'

Anton said: 'Am I to take it, comrades, that this group, a communist group, now proposed to discuss seriously what to do about a girl who needs an abortion?'

'But she doesn't want to have an abortion,' said Martha.

'This group is now going to accept the responsibility of finding abortionists or husbands for all the girls in the Colony who've got themselves pregnant?'

'There you are,' cried Jimmy. 'That's what I mean. That's how you talk.'

'You are criticizing me for a tone of voice?' inquired Anton.

Andrew said: 'I agree with Anton that all this is quite irregular, but there's nothing wrong with us trying to help someone who's in trouble. I remember one of our lassies back home got herself in trouble and we fixed her up with a husband.'

Anton said: 'In that case, Comrade Andrew, since it seems that you are familiar with this type of important party work, may we leave it that you will be responsible, with Comrade Matty, for the problems of this girl? And now, since that is dealt with, may we continue?'

Andrew said to Martha: 'I'll be in town tomorrow for lunch. I'll have it with you and we'll talk it over.'

'Thanks,' said Martha gratefully, moving closer to him. He put his arm around her, and said: 'Comrade Matty and I constitute ourselves a sub-committee for the solving of personal problems.'

Anton had been watching them, in cold patience.

Bill said: 'All of our energies go into the white minority in this country.'

Anton allowed himself to appear ironically surprised.

'Again?' he said. 'This has come up at every meeting we've

had for the last six weeks. Every time it is the same thing. Do we really have to go through it again?'

Bill said: 'Yes, we do.'

Anton and Bill faced each other for the fight that both had been manoeuvring for all evening, but Jimmy interposed. He said: 'You say, we can't make contact with the Africans. But I have. While you town types sit on your arses and talk red revolution, and tell these white settlers about the glorious Red Army, I've been selling *The Watchdog* in the Location. Ask Elias if I haven't.'

Elias moved unhappily on his bench. Again the soft brown skin above his brows was puckering. He said, sighing: 'Yes, comrades, but it is not easy.'

'It was a group decision that the RAF lads should not go into the Location,' said Anton sharply. 'And now I have come to my criticism of you – you have no discipline, you come to the meetings or not, as you feel inclined, you do party work or not as the mood takes you, you are all absolutely unreliable.'

'That's right,' said Jimmy roughly. 'And we break the sacred rules of the Colony by having Coloured girls as friends.'

Marie said impatiently: 'We discussed all that last week. You know why we took the decision we did.'

Here Tommy began to shift on his bench, grinning unhappily, in the way they all recognized and respected because of his desperate sincerity.

'I want to say something,' he said. 'It's this. There's something wrong. We say, we don't believe in inequality, we don't believe in the colour bar and that. But when it gets down to it, we take a decision to behave like everyone else. We say, Don't let's upset people.' He said apologetically to Elias: 'I must say straight, comrade, that I don't think it's right for black and white to marry, but I know it's because I've been brought up here – I'm just trying to say what I think . . .'

Elias nodded, his eyes lowered.

'But that's what we say we believe. Yet when Comrade Jimmy there falls in love . . .' he hesitated and changed it

164

'. . . likes a girl from the Coloured Quarter, then we say no. Because it would make people say bad things about communists. But it seems to me there is something wrong with it all.'

'You're telling me,' said Jimmy, direct to him.

'Comrades,' said Anton, weary with exasperation. 'If we all of us, at this moment, made ourselves red flags and walked out of this room and down into the Location, shouting: Arise, ye starvelings from your slumbers – then what would happen? I would be put into the internment camp. Every RAF member would be posted. The two government servants, Marjorie and Colin, would get the sack. Piet would be asked to resign from his job in the trade union. And anyone else would be deported. Is that what you want? Well, is it? Because that's the logical conclusion of what you're saying. And if you want this group to shout out about sexual equality, then it's the one way to get ourselves in trouble with everyone. Would it help matters if every single man here married an African or a Coloured girl tomorrow – not that it would be possible. Or if we all took Coloured mistresses? There's nothing new about white men sleeping with Coloured and African girls. Is there? The basic problem is economic and not social. Use your heads, comrades.'

'Why do you have to make every simple human problem into a big question of principle?' said Bill suddenly.

'Are we communists or aren't we?'

Jasmine said earnestly to Jimmy: 'Your attitude is very bad, comrade. We explained everything last week and took decisions. But it makes no difference to you what decisions we take – you just go straight on doing what you like in any case. I don't see why you bother to come here at all – if you're a group member you have to accept discipline.'

Jimmy stood up, straightening his tunic, tucking his cap over his heavy hair. 'That's right,' he said, 'I don't know why I bother to come here either.' Murdoch stood up beside him grinning weakly, adjusting his cap. Bill Bluett rose and joined them.

Jimmy looked slowly around at them all, his fevered face

165

and eyes burning. 'You can count me out.' He remarked to the wall above Martha's head: 'I've got myself a real working-girl, a girl like myself, and I've got myself comrades in the Coloured Quarter and in the Location I can talk to as man to man. But I can't be a member any more of this talking shop.'

He crashed out of the room; Murdoch went after him saying, 'So long' in a hasty friendly way. Bill, nodding at them all around in an impartial manner, followed them.

Andrew stuffed his pipe away quickly, and said: 'Well, comrades, I'm sorry about that, but I'll see what I can do about it.' He, too, hurried out.

Elias, who had been looking under his eyebrows at them all, frowning, said: 'And I must go too. I haven't got a pass to be out.' He departed, while they said good night, good night, good night, after him.

'I suggest, ' said Anton, as if nothing in particular had happened, 'that we now end this meeting.'

'But aren't we going to do something?' asked Marjorie.

'Comrade Andrew will do what he can. If he can't, then we shall work without the RAF comrades. Anything else? Then I declare the meeting closed.' He slid his books and papers together, and went with the same abruptness as the others.

Jasmine was almost in tears. Marjorie seemed stunned. 'But what's happened?' she said, appealing to everyone, 'what's happened, I don't understand.'

Colin patted her shoulder, and she irritably shrugged him away.

Carrie shrugged, slinging a soft white wool coat over her shoulders, as she went to the door. 'Perhaps communism isn't suited to this country?' she remarked. 'Well, good night, I must get some beauty sleep.' And she, too, departed.

The du Preez, standing side by side, gazed unhappily at the place where Anton had sat, as if he might rematerialize and solve all these problems. At last Marie sighed and said: 'That boy, Jimmy, what he needs is a good doctor, if you ask me. He's dying on his feet of TB – anyone can see it by looking.'

Piet said, grinning: 'Women! We'd better make a rule that

no one can come to group meetings unless their temperature is normal.'

Tommy said: 'But it wasn't Jimmy, it was Bill, wasn't it? I mean, Jimmy did the talking, but you could see it was Bill all the time.'

Piet affectionately thumped the side of his fist against the boy's head and told him: 'Now you shut up for tonight, and we'll give you a lift home. Who's for a lift?'

Down in the street the 'town types' saw Jimmy under a lamp at a corner, surrounded by the three other RAF men. He was shouting and gesticulating; they were, apparently, trying to stop him from doing something.

Then they saw Andrew, obviously in a bad temper, going off by himself away from the others. The three: Bill, Murdoch and Jimmy, linked arms and strolled down the pavement, three abreast, so that the groups of townspeople coming the other way, out of the pictures, had to move off the pavement to make room for them.

'Bloody Raff,' said Piet, angrily, 'time they all went home to where they belonged.'

Chapter Four

Murdoch said, after Andrew's square back: 'Bloody arse-licker.'

Bill said: 'That's right. All things to all men, that's Andrew.'

The men had come out of the group office united in hostility towards 'the people from the town'. Andrew had joined the others in making disparaging jokes all the way down the stairs. Already he had left them: he had said to Jimmy, 'You made a proper balls-up of that, mate.' Bill had responded instantly with a jeering: 'Stoo-pid, ain't we?' Andrew maintained a gruff mateyness while he said: 'We didn't want to smash everything up, but just to change the policy.'

At which Jimmy had exclaimed: 'I'd like to smash it up – smash this whole bleeding town and everything in it.' He let out a short quivering shout of rage, his fists clenched: the others laid calming hands on him, but he shook them off, scowling at them and at the people passing. Then, when he was quiet, Andrew said: 'Well, I'm going to catch that bus if you aren't,' and left them.

When Bill said: 'That's right, all things to all men . . .' the other two nodded fierce agreement. Yet almost instantly they felt hostility for Bill too: his tone was too jaunty. Jimmy and Murdoch were tense, angry and miserable because of what had happened. Bill was not: they saw that his alert grey eyes held nothing but interested speculation. He was not with them. He said: 'Are we going to take the bus? Because I haven't got an all-night pass.'

'To hell with the bus,' said Murdoch, but in such a way that the others knew he would catch it at the last moment.

They linked arms and swung down the street. Main Street at eleven o'clock; the cinemas emptying, the hotels filling. The three young men, their uniforms slack and untidy, charged along the pavement, watching out of the corners of their eyes how the groups of townspeople moved aside to let them pass. Had any man shouldered them, or said anything challenging, their fists were tightened for the fight. But the men, most of whom were accompanied by women, gave them acute thoughtful glances, and saw to it that the pavement was clear half a dozen paces before contact became likely. After the three airmen had gone past, some of the townsmen muttered: 'One of these days I'm going to beat up those . . .'

Half-way down, Carrie Jones, accompanied by a girl-friend, came into view walking towards the airmen. As the two girls saw the three airforce men, their bodies tightened defensively, and they moved out to the edge of the pavement. Half an hour earlier Carrie had sat in the same room with them, but now they had become 'the RAF' and she was careful not to look at them. Murdoch let out a wolf-whistle when he was four yards off. The colour deepened in the girls' cheeks and they looked distressed. Bill said, with authority: 'Here, let up, man!' Murdoch, his face and hair glowing in one wild red flame of aggression, whistled again. As they swung past the two girls, Bill said, grinning: 'Comrade Carrie.' She turned fast, saw who it was, and nodded, while her whole body expressed hurt and resentment.

'What are you treating our girls like that for?' said Bill. Again he spoke jauntily: it was the form of reproach. Murdoch stopped dead, Jimmy with him. 'What's that for?' Murdoch demanded. 'Who're you getting at? She didn't even look at us. *Comrades.*'

Bill said, in the same tentative way, as if he might be testing, or finding out something: 'You frightened her. That's a stoopid way to go on.'

'Och, hell,' said Murdoch. His heated, wild, unhappy face seemed to be flying apart, and his light wild Scots blue eyes were furious.

Jimmy said, with his usual desperate earnestness: 'Whose

side are you on? I don't hold with whistling at our girls, but she just treated us like dirt.'

Bill fell back from the other two; he had, it seemed, lost interest in them. 'We're going to miss the bus,' he said, already moving off. Jimmy and Murdoch linked arms, and said with hostility: 'Go to bed then,' and 'Tuck yourself up warm.'

Bill walked back the way they had come towards the bus, his back, like Andrew's earlier, set self-consciously against their critical stares.

Jimmy and Murdoch, deflated, all the aggression gone out of them, leaned against a pillar outside a shop. Murdoch lit a cigarette, hunching one shoulder out against the wind, cupping the flame close inside his hands – it was a cool, absolutely still night, the stars blazing high above the low coloured glare that spread above the small town.

Murdoch said: 'Och, well – let's get ourselves back to camp.'

Jimmy said nothing. He was breathing deep and hoarsely, and his eyes were fixed. He had an all-night pass, but for some reason had lost interest in what he had been going to do. Murdoch nudged him, and he automatically followed Murdoch along the pavement without speaking. The street was now almost empty of townspeople, but odd groups of them still made their way along the pavement, and now the two airmen gave way to them, not looking at them. When they reached the bus-stop, the bus was just reversing towards them. They jumped on as it went forward. Andrew was seated well up towards the front, reading. Bill was sprawled out, apparently asleep. Jimmy and Murdoch settled at the back, close together.

'Back to the concentration camp,' said Murdoch.

'That's right,' said Jimmy gloomily. But there was pleasure in these remarks, a masochistic pride in their fate.

'There's that match against Guineafowl tomorrow,' said Murdoch. Now he was smiling and relaxed again. 'We'll win it,' he added. 'We've not lost a match yet.'

Jimmy did not answer. The half-jocular 'concentration camp' made him think of the great barred gates of the camp, the high wire fence. He shifted his shoulders inside the thick confining uniform. He had an all-night pass. Why was he here then? If he got off outside the gates and made his way back to the main road, he could thumb a lift back to town – if one of those bastards could bring himself to stop for an airman! It was a permanent source of bitterness in the camp that many of the townspeople refused lifts to airmen. But he remained with the others. The men descended together from the bus, and, feeling the constriction of the high wire barricade all around them, like a pressure on their minds, moved forward in a body for a dozen steps, before drifting off in ones and twos towards their huts. Bill and Andrew went off in different directions by themselves; Jimmy and Murdoch did not see them: they were locked together in a warm sentimental mood that excluded everyone else. Walking very close they ambled towards the crude shed which had been home to them and to eighteen other men for two years. It had a flattened, crouching look under the big sky; dozens of exactly similar huts surrounded them. Murdoch said in his real voice – seldom heard and, surprisingly even to himself, a voice neither rueful, nor humorously pained; but quiet, earnest: the voice of a boy confronting wonder: 'Do you know what this mucking place reminds me of, Jimmy boy, do you know?' The movement of his progress, which was loose and wild, like that of a tenderly-gawky stick-insect, stopped in a defensive pose. Jimmy came to a standstill beside him. They were so close they could feel the heat of each other's sides.

'What?' said Jimmy, as Murdoch's breathing continued to frost the moonlit air.

'Think of the maintenance bench. Do you see what I mean?'

Both men, fitters, worked from a long, grimed and shiny table littered, though methodically littered, with dozens of small, hard and angular bits of metal.

Jimmy staring, his mouth half-open, saw the sheds and huts of the camp diminished to the scale of their workbench, an arrangement of precisely-made machine parts. He felt, as Murdoch did, imprisoned, but the warm substance of his body insisted against the vision. There was a moment of painful striving between the two: the ugly mechanical regularity of the camp, that had the obstinate look of metal parts and tools, and the full hot insistence of his breathing body.

He said slowly: 'That's it. You're right. Everything's just machines these days.' But even as he said it, and saw Murdoch's face ease away from the painful knowledge of failed communication, into a smile of grateful comradeship, he felt, in the flesh of his finger-tips, the engine parts he handled all day. His big bony fingers moved unconsciously, in mastery of metal. In the tips of his fingers he felt inert, lazy steel, uncommunicative until he touched it and it took on life. Now his ears, that had been sealed from habit, against noise, opened to a roar of aircraft: several hundreds of yards away on the runway, an aeroplane stood roaring and quivering under a beam of arc-lights, and the sound made Jimmy see the plane he had worked on that morning. He had slid into its proper place a tiny smooth glob of metal, and the dead part of the machine sang into life.

Murdoch insisted again, clutching his arm. 'See what I mean?'

'I think I'll stick to aircraft when the war's over,' said Jimmy.

Murdoch let his hand fall: he felt as if Jimmy had turned and walked away from him. He dreamed of something different when the war was finished. He did not know what, but his uncle had a small fish and chips bar in Edinburgh, and recently he had been thinking of writing to him. He thought: Jimmy'll be in a san by the time the war's over, the way he's going on, silly bugger, and no one can tell him he's sick, no one can tell him anything.

He said: 'I'm hungry.' He was thinking of the warm smell of food that pervaded his uncle's fish shop.

Jimmy said: 'I've got some chocolate in my locker.'

The door of their hut was open, half a dozen paces ahead, an oblong warm light. Their beds were at opposite ends of the hut. In fact these two men had not felt close before; both had other mates, beside whom they worked and with whom they went out into the town, when the group gave them time.

Jimmy remembered that as well as the chocolate there were several dozen *Watchdogs*, still unsold from last week. He said fiercely: 'I'd like to see one of those comrades, they call themselves, taking on a working-woman's job – it'd kill them in a day.'

'That's right,' said Murdoch. 'They don't know what hard work is, and that's a fact.'

They drew together again, thinking with bitterness of the girls in the group, who had rejected them, treated them with contempt – so they felt.

They went forward into the hut. The men were lying or sitting on their beds. The radio was on. Nostalgia filled the hut. Vera Lynn was singing: *When You Come Home Again.*

Jimmy's bed was nearest the door. Murdoch, not wanting to separate from his friend, sat on the foot of it. A youth sprawling on the next bed looked up and said with an automatic friendliness: 'Joe for King.'

These two, Jimmy and Murdoch, were the Reds of the hut. It was known they were members of a secret group in the town. They sold several dozen *Watchdogs* each week. The airmen bought willingly, but seldom read the newspaper. They were buying a share in the current mood of optimism, which they felt but could not define. Russia was doing well; they felt goodwill towards the Red Army because they felt that in some complicated ways its successes showed their own government as incompetent. Each one of these men thought of every man above him, from corporal up, as incompetent, slovenly, and out for himself. They hated the whole officer hierarchy with a cheerful impersonal bitterness.

They also felt that after the war things could not possibly go on as they had before. They had jeered at the Atlantic Charter, and greeted the patriot speeches of the high-ups about better times coming after the war with a steady contempt as bait for suckers, the suckers being themselves. But all the same . . . things could not go on as they had; and the victories of the Red Army in some way proved this.

Yet they protected themselves against disappointment by

disbelief. All round the camp men greeted each other with 'Joe for King,' but it was jaunty, and the clenched fist of the greeting quivered in a parody of fervour. They bought the *Watchdog*, gave three times the proper price for it, but did not bother to read it. They would leave copies lying about the canteens, the reading-rooms, or sticking out of their pockets to annoy officers. There were several home-made red flags in the camp, and they would be brought out sometimes and flaunted about to the accompaniment of wild, insurrectionary but always self-parodying speeches.

Over the beds of the men in this hut were pictures of girls, family photographs, and several had pictures of Stalin, captioned: Joe for King, or Uncle Joe.

Both Jimmy and Murdoch had large pictures of Stalin torn out of newspapers, but theirs were inscribed: Comrade Stalin.

Jimmy returned the greeting to the next bed, sat himself down beside Murdoch, and became angry with himself for being here at all. He said: 'I'm thinking of getting back into town.'

Murdoch said: 'Take it easy, Jimmy boy.'

'I mean it.'

'But you won't get out again now.'

'I know how. You can come too.'

'I haven't got a pass.'

'You can get back the same way.'

Murdoch was uneasy. He recognized the set and inflamed stare of Jimmy's eyes. Privately he thought of Jimmy as not only sick, but crazy. And in spite of his own reputation as a firebrand, which he was proud of, he was a young man who liked order, and was uncomfortable breaking rules.

Jimmy said: 'You coming or not?'

Murdoch had not expected the challenge so quickly. Jimmy was standing up, tightening his belt.

'Och, man,' he said, laughing weakly, 'I need my kip.' He got off the bed.

Vera Lynn's voice was so loud and strong and sweet that the bright thick air in the hut throbbed. The men were singing with her in a group around the radio, and Murdoch wanted to join them.

Jimmy shouted: 'You're scared, that's it!' Now his whole being was concentrated behind the desire that Murdoch should come with him. He glared at his friend, hating him.

'Scared, is it?' said Murdoch, affronted. Then, seeing where this would get him, he slid off into his familiar humorous plaint: 'I'm dead with sleep, and that's the truth.' He did not allow himself to meet Jimmy's set and aggressive jaw; but said: 'I'm for bed,' and moved off fast.

Jimmy felt himself betrayed. Murdoch had left him. One by one, all evening, his friends had left him. Earlier he had been one of fifteen people in a room of comrades – for the purpose of this dream he forgot the tensions and the animosities and remembered only the warmth. Then there had been the group of four RAF – one by one, all gone, now even Murdoch. He thought: There's only one man in the whole town I like and that's Elias. I'll go and see Elias.

Now it was quite easy to decide what to do. He fitted his cap on to his head automatically, and left the hut, feeling that Murdoch was staring after him. He hardened his shoulders against the stare.

There were few people about now; the airmen were in their huts. It was brightly lit, in the centre of the camp. Briefly, Jimmy thought of going to the gate, and trying to slip past the sentries when a group of people from the officers' mess went out. He had done it before, but it would mean hanging about. Perhaps he could get into a car? He went cautiously to the officers' mess, and poked about a bit among the cars. Most of them had necking couples inside. Quite likely they'd take him in, since they had been drinking, but again, it would mean hanging about, taking his time and, above all, talking. He did not want to talk.

He went fast through the camp to where some trees had been left standing against the wire, and stood under a tree, the moonlight sifting over him, listening to the dance music from the officers' mess. A hundred yards off, the great wire fence stood glinting. Some days before he had noticed there was a small depression in the earth at one place, under the wire. One of the African camp guards came strolling down beside the wire. Jimmy stepped out of the shadow towards him. The man recognized him, and said: 'Comrade Baas?' Jimmy had fed this man with copies of *The Watchdog* and pamphlets from the South about racial equality. But still he called Jimmy and the other airmen, who, taking their cue from 'the Reds', were friendly to him, 'Comrade Baas'.

Jimmy said fiercely: 'Hold that wire for me while I get under.'

The man looked frightened. 'But Comrade Baas, you'll get into trouble.' He meant – get me into trouble.

Jimmy said angrily: 'Go and f — yourself if you're scared to.' Then, seeing the alert frightened look on the man's face, he felt warmth for him, and pity. He said, in the same sentimental tone he had using with Murdoch earlier: 'Come on, mate, give us a hand, no one'll see.' He went straight on beside the fence. The African hesitated, then followed. The lowest strand of wire was six inches from the earth, and Jimmy was a thick man. The guard gave a last despairing look around, saw no one, caught the insistent gleam of Jimmy's eyes, bent down and heaved at the taut slippery wire with all his strength. 'No, not there,' said Jimmy crouching a few yards further down, where the hollow was.

Again the African looked around, very frightened. They were in full view. The moonlight poured down, and between them and the first huts were only a few stunted trees. At this moment a group of officers came out of the mess with some girls, and could have seen them by turning their heads.

'Come on,' said Jimmy again. He was lying on the earth beside the fence. The African bent himself and heaved. Jimmy rolled over, under the tight strand. His shoulders stuck. 'More,' he said. The man put all his strength into it; the wire quivered and twanged with the quivering of his straining body. Jimmy got his shoulders through, then his body. He lay on the earth on the other side of the fence, then rolled over and over like a bottle into the dark shade under some tall grass.

'Thanks, mate,' the African heard.

He said: 'Good night, Comrade Baas,' and walked off

himself, very fast, shooting frightened glances in every direction. But it seemed no one had noticed.

Jimmy wriggled to a thicker clump of grass and got his back to it and to the camp. He lay on his elbow resting. Save for the thin pulse of music coming from the officers' mess, he might be miles away from people. The camp held the lives of several thousand men within its tall taut encircling wires; held them close and tidy and confined. Jimmy thought that for all those months he had lived in a simple repetitive cycle of movement: sleep in the hut; work by the air-strip; jaunts into town in the camp bus from the gaunt gates on the main road. Yet here, ten yards from the camp, the trees stood dark and whole under the moon, the grass was tall and unflattened. The wish to move on had ebbed out of him. It was the wire fence he had wished to escape, the eternal pressure of the wire fence, as if steel cobwebs confined him, pressing on his flesh every time he moved out of line. He thought: I'll stay here until morning, and then walk around the wire through the trees to the main road, and present myself at the gate with my pass. No one'll know. There's no harm sleeping out. He settled himself, head back, motionless, moving his eyes only to take in the moon, the trees, the grass, the soft gleaming trash that littered the soil. City boy from blackened, cold streets, he breathed the fresh tart air of the high-veld in and out of tainted lungs, fingered grains of heavy soil that clung to his fingers, frowned at the moonlight about him and thought: This is something like it. Never see a sky like this at home. The grass behind him was a solid wall, grown to its July strength, the sap no longer running, each stem taut and slippery as fine steel, massed together in a resilient antagonist to his back. He swung himself slightly, away from it and back again, and found himself laughing out loud out of a deep startled pleasure because of the toughness of the resisting grass. But the laugh frightened him. He heard it raucous and sudden, not his. Now his ears were opened to sound, and above the whine and distant roaring of engines on the strip in the camp, he heard the soft noises of the night all around him. Grasses, leaves, earth kept up a perpetual soft movement of sound. There was a steady clicking and singing from the grasses. Birds? he wondered, frowning again. Frogs? He listened carefully, and became conscious that the grass smelled sweet. Over his head bent tall soft fronds, feathered like oats. He looked up, seeing the strands clear and individual and black against the silvery star-swarming sky, and thought: Behind my back as tough as – metal. Over my head they bend, separate. Soft. Moving because of the wind. And again his nostrils filled with a sweet sharp breath of scent. His mouth fell open, his eyes stared and glazed a little, his body was tense, trying to absorb noises, scents. He was thinking, I'll get my fill of this and then I'll sleep. The sun'll wake me. The sun comes up hot and sudden and it'll wake me ... His eyes, wide on the black-defined fronds above him, blinked, then again – there was something in his eye. No, he had stared too long at the fine black outline, because it had clotted, on the delicate feather was a black knot. He blinked, hard and sharp, hearing, just above him, a sudden outburst of noise, as loud as machine-gun fire. And from behind his back, in the grass-stems, another. He shifted uneasily, his blood pounding, his nerves tight. He looked and waited. All of a sudden he realized that the black knot was an insect, it was making that noise. And behind him too. He rolled sharply away from the grass-clump and examined it. All over the thick gleaming grass, dark knots. Some moved as he watched. They were silent again, the small machine-gun fire had ceased. My God, he thought, they were making that noise, the insects. His flesh crawled with fear. Looking down at himself, as he crouched in the grass, he saw his legs and body splotched with dark objects. My God, they were all over him, large, horny beetle-insects, clumsily waving their feelers and moving up over him. He let out a yell of fear, and brushed them off with frantic hands. The insects clung, and when they fell off, fell heavily into the grass and lay waving their legs – like some kind of monster, he thought wildly, every particle of his flesh crawling with loathing. Five, six, ten – while he lay there, on the soil, they had been crawling on to him, and had even started to make their noise, as if he had not been there at all.

178

Now as he stood, half-crouched, his eyes moving warily about him, he saw them everywhere in the grass, and half a dozen paces away they were still clicking and singing as if he didn't exist. But they were everywhere! He let out another yell of pure terror and ran off fast away from the camp into the trees, beating at his legs and body with his hands as if he were on fire and he were beating out the flames.

He ran clumsily, sobbing out his breath and muttering: Filthy, dirty, disgusting ... and he glanced continually down at himself, as if he had been soiled and contaminated. He came into a clearing free of grass between trees that made deep dark patterns of shadow. There he stopped. Where was he running to? The veld sloped gently down in front of him. Three miles away the night sky flared up pinky-mauve, the lights of the city. He was running towards the lights. But he wanted to see Elias; and where he lived the sparse light made no glow in the sky. If he headed towards the sky-glow, he would arrive in the white town. He turned himself to the left, thinking: But shall I cross the river?

The river was a dirty little stream, and a dozen medical officers had lectured the men on not letting one drop of that water, or any other wild water touch their flesh. Disease lived in the water, which might keep them under treatment for months.

Jimmy came sharp down into a gully, saw a gleam of wet, and thought: I'll jump it. The sides of the gully were steep. He jumped and crouched down to the water-level and made a wild leap, landing knee-deep in water, clutching at slippery stiff grasses for support. Here the vegetation was silent, but his flesh was crawling again: Those little buggers are waiting for me in the grass, he thought. I've stopped their filthy row, but they are there all right. Still in the water, feeling the sluggish flow of it tug at his legs inside his wet and heavy trousers, he looked up at the steep grass side of the gully, hesitating, not wanting to leave the water because of the insects. At last he pulled himself up and out, and crawled through the grass, crouched double, his arms folded around himself in protection. He came out in low ankle-length grass the other side. The moon was lower now, throwing long shadows. Half a mile away were the flanks of the white town, the walls of villas glaring sharp in the moonlight. A few hundreds of yards away on the left, a shamble of tall dark huts or sheds, like sentry-boxes or outdoor lavatories each with its long jagged shadow. He inspected himself loathingly for insects, found one, threw it off, cursing, and moved off towards the dark huts. He was moving through a foul smell; and he turned his head from side to side trying to evade it. He realized the smell came from the grass he was moving through, not from the huts, and moved on tiptoe, clenched in horror. Around the brick huts was a flat ungrassed space. There was a smell of grain, a soft sweet smell. Threads of light around the doors of the huts. A banjo was playing inside one. Jimmy knocked on its door, the banjo at once stopped. He knocked again. The door slightly opened, a dark face looked out, the jaw dropping fast at the sight of a white face.

Jimmy said: 'Here, mate, let me in.' He stopped, because the dark face stared and was frightened. The white eyeballs glistened in the moonlight.

Jimmy said: 'Listen, mate, I just want to ask you something, that's all.'

The door shut. The light vanished. In the other dozen or so huts that stood up tall under the moon the lights went out. They might all have been deserted.

Jimmy thought wildly, incredulous: He was scared of me! Of *me*. Then – poor buggers! Then, muck them, muck the lot of them, muck all these white bastards.

Jimmy the social being had been revived. He stood humped up, frowning, thinking, outside the door that had been closed in his face: I must be off my chump, knocking at doors like that in this bloody fascist dump – could get them into trouble – if I go and see Elias like this, he might get properly into trouble too.

He stripped off his jacket. But even so, with his shirt and trousers he was, at one glance, from the camp. He was shivering. It was cold now. The cold lay heavily around him all over the grass, a thin moving mist. He put on his jacket again, and moved forward towards the Location thinking: I'll be careful, and it'll be all right.

Again he moved through foul-smelling grass, found a hard-beaten path and followed it. Meandering, it led towards the Location. A mile further on and he was on the outskirts of the place. There was a wire fence confining the Location, but these thousands of people, too swarming for the amount of earth allotted to them, overflowed out over the fence into hundreds of ugly little shacks and boxes. They were all dark and silent. He walked through them, Gulliver in Lilliput, for he was taller than some of these houses. Inside each, he knew, a dozen people might be sleeping: this was one of the shanty-towns, he had heard about them from Elias. He came up against the fence. It was low and rusted. He thought ironically: We airforce types rate a ten-foot fence. Comrade Baas, that's us, with a fine fence. He saluted himself, the comrade baas. Fences, fences, everywhere you look, concentration camps everywhere and fences. He thought of the concentration camps in Europe and without any feeling of being alien. He felt identified with them, and with the people sleeping all around him in their little boxes and shacks. If we got to the moon, he thought, we'd put up fences and keep people inside them. He was looking up at the moon, now at eye-level, a small silver-bright disc. Standing just inside the fence he saluted the moon, derisively, thinking: Well, mate? We'll have you nice and tidy before you know it.

Inside the fence there was order, of a kind. Streets there were none: they were tracks of dust between lines of houses, unsurfaced and badly potholed. Dozens of minute houses, dolls' houses, stretched around him. He moved through them, unconsciously trying to make himself smaller, for he felt enormous in this clear shallow night. Now he knew where he was going. Last time he entered the Location, selling *Watchdogs*, he had found a warm and accepting comradeship in a certain building that could not be far from here. City boy with tidy numbered streets, he moved his big face this way and that like a dog sniffing, and moved off, certain of his direction, into a part of the Location that consisted of parallel brick lines, rooms built side by side under a long single tin roof. He moved, crouched low, breathing hard. There was not a light anywhere. On his own flesh he felt the pressure of the people sleeping massed along the brick lines. The memories of his own flesh shared their experience. Now he came to a building that was like the smaller courts of the Coloured Quarter, built in a square, with a gap in front like a missing tooth. Each side consisted of a dozen rooms. He moved into the court which smelled thick of vegetables and grains, for in the day it was a market. The room he was looking for showed a thin light below the door. He heard, very soft, the beat of drums. He knocked. The drum-beat stopped. The door opened and a face he knew appeared and instantly showed fear. 'Let me in, mate,' said Jimmy urgently, and the door opened and he was inside. The room was about twelve feet square. It was low, and its ceiling and walls were white-washed but stained. The floor was of rough red brick. Half a dozen young men sat on the floor, leaning their backs against the walls. They had mouth organs, a banjo, a guitar, a native-style tom-tom. One young man sat on the only chair. He had a set of drums, old and battered, but real drums and he was playing them softly, watching Jimmy; another had a trumpet, but he was fingering and loving it with his hands, silently playing it. Sometimes he lifted it to make a long soft note under cover of the music, but it was too loud to play safely. Jimmy stood there smiling, feeling warmed because this door had opened to admit him; and looked on while the young men smiled white teeth at him out of dark shining faces, and continued to play, soft, softly, a breath of music, because this was long after hours, long after the time when regulations said lights out, no more music, sleep now so that you will be fresh for the white man's work in the morning.

Jimmy let his back slide down the rough wall, and he sat as the Africans did, on his haunches, his arms resting loose on his knees, listening. He did not know music and he did not know what they were playing.

The white dance bands in the city played many kinds of jazz, but when they played wild it was fast, Chicago-style, white man's jazz – there were no Africans in the white town's bands. Here they played wild too, what these boys had heard from listening outside walls, outside windows while white people danced inside to the jazz born in the head of Chicago, the city on the river up from New Orleans. Sometimes, when the trumpet had time and space to sing, it sang slowly, more sorrowful; and sometimes the drums beat, not from the memory of what the white man's drums did at the dances in the town, but because drums had beaten through the childhood of all these dark boys, city boys now, but bred in the villages of a country where drums were seldom silent. In this small damp room now, and it was one of a couple of dozen similar rooms in this location, stood the hide-covered wooden drum from the villages, and it stood beside the metal-shining drums bought second-hand from a white man's band, and often, late at night, the two kinds of drum spoke together against each other, as if talking each other out in argument.

Sometimes, late at night, because it was long past the time for music, it was time for sleep, the sleep that feeds conscientious and reliable work – sometimes, because of the necessity for caution and secrecy, a soft music came into life that sang and questioned and hesitated, music born out of secrecy, double-talk and the brotherhood of oppression.

Jimmy sat loose, humped against the wall, breathing easy, listening like the others for the sounds of official steps outside, listening to the soft beat of the music, and thought: I feel at home here. This is the only place in this bloody country I've felt at home.

The mouth organs and the guitar fell silent. The drums competed for a moment. The trumpeter lifted his trumpet and let out one dark defiant note, and then clapped his hand over its mouth as if to shut it up, shutting himself up. Now there was silence and the young man who had let Jimmy in sang out, as if continuing the music: 'Comrade Jimmy, Jimmy man, and what you doing here, so late, Jimmy man, but you'll get us all into fine trouble, man.'

Jimmy blurted, breaking the rhythm, 'I got fed up with that camp.'

'It's the high jump for you, man, if they catch you,' said the trumpeter.

Jimmy saw it was not enough to say, simply, that he wanted to be here, he saw, now that the music was finished, their eyes held a look which said he must prove himself.

He said nervously: 'I wanted to talk to Elias.' He added quickly, seeing that eyes met each other and quickly withdrew: 'I need to ask him something.'

'Elias Phiri?' said the drummer, and beat out a dozen thudding notes on the tom-tom, ending with a double thud on the cymbals, silencing the cymbals with a snatch of his hand.

'The government interpreter?' said the trumpeter.

'He's all right,' said Jimmy.

'Ya, man, government officials are all right,' said a youth with a mouth organ. He blew a discordant noise, and let it groan out, in derision.

'What's the matter?' said Jimmy, looking hotly from one to another. 'Isn't he OK then?'

'OK, he's OK,' said the youth who had let him in. He wore a bright yellow shirt and a purple flowing tie, and he now stood up, hunching on a sharp-shouldered jacket. The trumpeter stood up, hiding the trumpet under a jacket folded over his arm. The man with the tom-tom wrapped it in brown paper like a store parcel.

Jimmy rose, repeating: 'What's wrong? What's the matter?'

The man who sat behind the set of drums was lifting it into a large packing-case and fitting down the lid. The packing-case had stencilled on it in black paint: Heinz Baked Beans and Tomato Sauce. He sang out, softly, with a rolling-eyed smile at the others: 'We Kaffirs are an unreliable lot, an unreliable lot, we Kaffirs yes, man.' Two of the young men sharply opened the door, stood listening, listening, glancing fast around the empty moon-shadowed space in the court of the building, then ran out on silent feet towards the opening in front. They vanished. The trumpeter and the tom-tom player stood like divers on the edge of a pool, and dived out into the moonlight and disappeared. Jimmy said to the remaining young men: 'What've I done wrong, I don't get it.'

'Nothing, boy, nothing,' said the young man who had admitted him. He was grinning. He laid his hand on Jimmy's shoulder, and rocked him back and forth a moment. 'Nothing, boy,' he repeated. Then he looked at the door. Jimmy went out. The three young men worked on locking and fixing the door. Then, without another look at Jimmy they ran hard through the court and swung out of sight into the road.

Jimmy went after them, stumbling over cabbage stalks and maize cobs. By the time he reached the opening, there was not a soul in sight. He stood in the shadow of a wall, a shadow six inches deep, and waited. At the end of the road, two native policemen came into sight, swinging their clubs. They strolled down the moon-filled space between the brick-rows, not seeing him. Whey they had gone Jimmy went up towards Elias's house, his heart swollen into a hot and angry and pounding fist that seemed to fill all his chest. He was thinking, poisoned by a sense of injustice: They were scared of me. They don't trust me. They were frightened.

It hurt him so much he wanted to cry out, explain himself to them. But it hurt too much to sustain, and a hot pity took the place of the hot anger, and he felt protectiveness, a need to shelter them. He thought: I'll get to Elias, we'll work out something. He wanted to destroy and to punish; to protect and to save.

Elias's house was one of the best houses, since Elias was a government employee. It stood in a short road of such houses. They all had two small rooms and a sentry-box-like lavatory standing at the back. They were all quite dark. It was about three in the morning.

Jimmy found the house, and stood for a while under a mango tree that grew close against the wooden steps. He was getting back his breath. He then climbed noiselessly on to the veranda and knocked on a dark window-pane.

After some time, Elias's face appeared, dark against darkness, frightened, ready to duck.

Jimmy said: 'Elias, it's me.'

Elias said: 'But baas, but baas . . .'

'It's me,' said Jimmy, in appeal against the 'baas'.

'Wait,' said Elias, after a moment's silence.

He disappeared from the window and the door opened. Elias was wearing his shirt and his legs were long and bare. He stood just inside the door dragging on his trousers.

'I want to talk to you,' said Jimmy.

Elias said: 'Baas, you shouldn't be here. I told you, you should not come here.' A strong smell filled the tiny stuffy room. A light went on in the next room. The sound of a woman's voice and then a child crying. Of course he has kids, Jimmy remembered, remembering how last time he had been here, early one evening, the place had been full of small children.

He said: 'Elias, I must talk to you.' He smelled the sharp smell again. He understood it was Elias, sweating. He thought, understanding slowly, Elias is so frightened that he's sweating.

The idea that Elias was frightened because of him, Jimmy, made him angry, though not with Elias.

'Listen, mate,' he said, in soft and urgent appeal, 'I'm not doing any harm. I must talk. I've come to talk.' Elias, now fully dressed, stood close by the door, waiting, his hand on the knob.

'What is it?' said Elias resentfully, his eyes continually returning to the square of the window.

'I want to discuss plans.'

'Plans?'

'We're socialists, Elias. We're comrades. I want to talk to you about the future. I've got an all-night pass. I thought we'd spend the night talking.'

At the word comrades, Elias's body gave a sharp tug of fear. 'You should not be here,' he said, now sharp and angry.

The next room was dark again, and silent, but there was a soft movement beyond the door. Jimmy thought: His wife is listening on the other side of the door. For the first time it struck him that he should not have come: After all, he thought, it's common enough for a wife not to agree with a man's politics. Perhaps she doesn't know.

186

'But, Comrade Elias, I want to discuss with you how we can work to deliver your people from their bondage.'

Elias was silent. Jimmy realized he had used the words: deliver from bondage. They struck him as inaccurate – unpolitical. But they filled him again with a warm and protective emotion, and he laid his hand on Elias's shoulder and said: 'We must help each other, comrade.'

Elias's voice rose in a wail of angry fear: 'You must go now, baas, you must not be here. Go now.' He shifted his shoulder away from under Jimmy's hand, and opened the door, pushing Jimmy out. 'Go now, baas. Please go now.' His voice was high on the *please*. Jimmy said: 'I've got free time tomorrow afternoon. Can I come and talk then?'

'No,' said Elias. 'No. Go away now, please, baas.' He shut the door. Jimmy stood, feeling the blood pour up over his face. He was shaking with the heat of his body, a dry pounding heat which shook him like hands. Then he, too, was in a drench of sweat and felt cold. He turned slowly from the house and walked past the mango tree, whose leaves shone hard, almost green, the size of moons, all over the branches. Careless of police, he stumbled off across sharp dusty ruts. He was careless from tiredness and from sorrow. The sharp reflecting moonlight on leaves, stone, windows was like eyes mocking him. He found himself on a lot of empty rutted earth where the food-stalls were. A dozen little vans with shutters that could be let down to make selling counters stood untidily in the lot. He leaned against one of them. It had painted roughly on its side: MRS SMART'S HOT DOG STORE. BEST HOT DOGS. BEST FANCY CAKES. BEST TEA IN TOWN. WE HAVE THE BEST IN THE WORLD! COCA-COLA. FRIED FISH. BOILED MEALIES.

Jimmy thought: If I go back to camp across country I'll have to go through all that dirty grass, and then those beetles or whatever they are. The river too – his trousers still flapped heavy and wet around his ankles. A mile up town was the Coloured Quarter. He would go and sleep on the floor in Ron's room.

He turned out of the Location gates into the main road which ran south, here a narrow hump of tarmac that gave off a grey glitter of cold light. Soon he passed the white cemetery, its trees and monuments all a pale gleam of light above black jagged shadows. Then came the railway lines, a double line of whitely-glittering steel. He stopped. The power station beyond raised cooling towers against the shoulder of a steep hill. The white towers curved finely inwards under clouds of dark smoke that were solidified by the surrounding clarity of chill white light. Across the lines, arising out of a mess of soiled grass, railway sleepers, old tin cans, was a small tree, white-stemmed, a cloud of fine leaves rising into the moonlight like the spray of a fountain. The swollen sore place inside Jimmy slowly cooled and soothed. He was conscious of a feeling of emptiness. He stared at the proud young tree, the squat shapes of the cooling towers, the great masses of dark smoke carved like thunder clouds by star-light and moonlight, and understood that ever since that afternoon he had been driven from action to crazy action, not knowing what he was doing, not responsible for himself.

I'm a silly sod, he said aloud to himself, standing alone on the Location side of the railway lines, shivering with cold. Yet it was not quite enough to say it: it still hurt, what had happened between him and the jazz-players, between himself and Elias.

He'll see things different in the morning, he decided, refusing to believe that Elias did not trust him, and that he was really rejected by the jazz-players. He set himself to walk on, down into the Coloured Quarter. When he came to the court where Ronald lived, it was silent and dark. He moved quietly along the veranda and knocked. He had to knock several times. He expected Ronald to come to the door – recently he had been better, apparently over his fever, and able to walk and talk to his RAF visitors. Now he remembered Ronald's mother. It was odd he had forgotten her, for when he had told Martha that he had 'found a better woman, a fine working-class lass like his own kind,' he had meant Mrs Spikes, Ronald's mother. Yet he had done no more than talk to her in Ronald's presence and dreamed wildy of inviting her to England when the war was over.

After a long wait, and repeated soft knocking, the door opened to show Mrs Spikes. She had flung an old coat over the petticoat she had been sleeping in. She blinked at him, sleepily – too sleepy to be frightened.

'Mrs Spikes,' said Jimmy in a low confidential tone, 'I came to ask Ron if I could sleep on the floor until morning.'

Mrs Spikes clung to the door-frame for steadiness, because she was so weary, and said: 'Ron went to the hospital this afternoon in the ambulance. He's bad, and they came in the ambulance. He will die, the doctor says.'

A child started to cry in the room behind. He had forgotten the little girl, Ronald's sister.

Mrs Spikes said into the dark room: 'Hush there. Hush and be quiet.' She shut the door and leaned against it, yawning. It was quite bright on the veranda, because of the moonlight in the court. Jimmy gazed at the half-clad woman and thought she looked young and pitiful. A thin coil of dark hair had come undone and lay on her thin neck. Jimmy looked at the shadow under the hair, and wanted to dive into it and be forgotten. She was still vague from tiredness. Her eyes were not on Jimmy, but on the doors ranged along the wall opposite. She returned her eyes to him, from politeness, and said: 'In this place everybody knows everyone's business.'

He saw he was embarrassing her. He could not sleep here with Ronald gone. He thought bitterly that even while he was consumed by a passion to protect her, even while he yearned to sink into the comfort of the shadow which was her hair and her arms, he was embarrassing her and making things hard for her. This thought came out of the sober self that had been revived in the cool mood that had come on him while he stood by the railway lines.

He said in a different, responsible voice: 'Sorry, Mrs Spikes. I'll go. And don't worry about Ron. Those doctors don't know nothing.'

'He'll die,' she said, her voice hard and angry. 'You got somewhere to sleep? There's the hostel in town.'

'Yes. I'll go to the hostel.' He hesitated. He was on the point of saying: 'Mrs Spikes, I like you. Please marry me.'

Realizing this, he told himself: You silly sod, you're crackers.

'I'll be seeing you soon,' he said. At the tone of his voice, she put up a thin hand and began twisting at her loosened coil of hair, regarding him with thoughtful troubled eyes. It struck him that the first thought she had, in a moment when she knew a man liked her was *trouble*. This made him angry: only then did it strike him that the *trouble* she expected was more simple; he had again forgotten he was a white man in forbidden territory. Meanwhile the whole set of her body had changed; she looked wary and stubborn. She was waiting for him to go.

'Good night,' he said.

'Good night,' she said, with a quick smile. Because she was now free to go inside, away from the neighbours' eyes, away from him, her smile showed a touch of consciousness, acknowledged him as a man. As the door closed softly in his face, he hated her for the smile, and remembered that across the yard, men from the camps came to lie with the women of the court. She's probably had offers enough, he thought bitterly, offers enough and to spare. it was only with a great effort that he conquered this bitterness, thinking: She's a decent woman, she's not that sort . . .

He stood silent on the veranda, wondering where to go. As he did so, a door opposite opened and he saw a man's shape emerge. It was one of the men from the camp. Jimmy thought: I'll stop him and ask him where he puts up at this time of night – too late to get to the hostel now, it's nearly morning. He changed his mind, remembering the girl from the room, whom he had seen often enough when visiting Ronald. She was pretty, sinuous and male-antagonistic.

He waited until his fellow from the camp disappeared. The he crossed the court and knocked on the door. He was thinking: I'll explain to her, I'll tell her . . . for he was again filled with a passionate pity for women, and loathing for the man who had left. Phrases passed through his mind: this life you are leading; victims of economic system; men, women . . .

He knocked again and the door opened an inch. 'What do you want?'

Before he could answer, the door opened fully. The girl stood there half-naked, her arms thrust roughly into a wrapper. A rich full smell of sex and sweat came from her and made his head turn.

'How much?' she said, standing in front of him, twisting up the long masses of her black hair.

'I don't want it,' he said. Then, as she laughed, he said, 'Don't you remember me? You've seen me.'

'Yes, I remember,' she said. She looked him up and down and said something in Afrikaans over her shoulder. An old woman came out, ducking under her daughter's naked arm where it was propped against the door-frame. She held in her hand a candlebox and was jamming an old hat on her head, skewering it into place with broken knitting needles. She passed, muttering obscenities at him, but impersonally, for her bright old eyes searched his face curiously, until she had set the candlebox down full in the moonlight by the veranda, and had sat herself on it, swaying to and fro, while the knitting needles in her squashed hat flashed out light.

'Come in,' said the girl.

Jimmy, his throat thick, half with lust and half with a longing to cry, said: 'But listen, I just want to . . .'

'You coming in or not?'

Behind her a candle-flame appeared in the dark, floating at first on deeper dark, like a flame on dark water. Then the shape of a bottle appeared beneath the flame and the candle, and then a naked arm. Jimmy saw the inside of the room dimly lit. A bed, already slept in, from which the girl and the man who had left the court had emerged. A rough mess of blankets on the floor, where the old woman had been settling herself down before being disturbed by this new customer. And another narrow bed by the wall, where another girl lay, her sharp chin dug into a cushion, watching him with interest. Behind her a man lay sleeping.

Jimmy said: 'Sorry, mistake.' He turned and fled out of the court. He heard sharp angry voices and a door slammed.

He stood quiet in the street, waiting for his blood to run more tranquilly. The sky was greying, the stars going out.

In the few minutes he had been in the court, the night had ended. There were sounds of movement in the street. A couple of bicycles went past, men bent over the handlebars. A group of men came, sleep-wearily, carrying hoes, then a couple of young women, pedalling slowly, not noticing anything, the machines swaying clumsily because of the sleepiness of the riders. Then all at once the street was crowded with people, on their way to work on foot or on bicycles.

Jimmy loitered along the pavements, watching them, and thinking: At home I'd join in, I'd be one of them, but just because I've got a white skin . . . He remembered his uniform – he was doubly separated from them.

He would have to lie low for a couple of hours. It was only just after four now. Or perhaps he could walk slowly back to camp and present himself at the gates in plenty of time for breakfast. Jimmy set himself to walk the five miles back, thinking: I'll get hold of that silly clot Elias this afternoon and talk some sense into him.

Meanwhile, Elias was on his way to Mr Maynard, after an agitated frightened quarrel with his wife. About the time that Jimmy reached the centre of the town, which lay silent in the grey dawn, Elias was banging on Mr Maynard's front door.

Mr Maynard had gone to bed very late the night before, and heard the banging with annoyance. Swearing steadily under his breath, while looking over his shoulder at his wife's shut bedroom door, he went to the veranda in his pyjamas. Elias stood there, grey with fright.

He babbled about insurrection, about communism, about RAF inciting the Africans to an uprising.

Mr Maynard told him to stay where he was, and went back into the house to find himself a dressing-gown and a finger of whisky. Then, standing like a magistrate in front of Elias, he cross-examined him until he got the story.

He perceived that what troubled Elias was that he was afraid that other people, most probably old Mathew, the other Court Messenger, who lived in the house opposite to his in the Location, would come with tales about him, say that white men had been visiting his house at night. Were it not for this fear, Elias would not be standing here.

Mr Maynard continued to cross-examine Elias until he was convinced that his lies and stumbling were from fear and not from policy, and out of contempt for the man and for his whole race, began to laugh at Elias, making jokes.

'So the RAF men are making a revolution, is that it?'

'But sir, he was in my house this morning at three and a half minutes past three o'clock. You can ask my wife, she wrote down the time.'

'And we can expect the Red Flag to fly over the Location any day now, is that it?'

'But sir, it is the truth. I swear it is the truth.'

'Oh, go back home,' said Mr Maynard, and went indoors with a slam of the door. Elias walked down to the Magistrates' Court, where he laid himself down on a bench and slept.

Mr Maynard also slept. At the breakfast-table he told his wife that it would be advisable if she communicated certain names to her cousin in the Administration of the Airforce, in order that they should be posted at once. The names were Aircraftsmen James Jones, William Bolton, and Murdoch Mathews. Andrew McGrew was not mentioned, because in his fright, Elias had forgotten him.

Mr Maynard made his way to the Court, regretting that he had been so sharp with Elias. After all, he did not want this source to dry up. He would tip him well – ten shillings, or something like that.

Part Three

My friendship for him began by my being struck by the stand he took on certain political questions.

OLIVE SCHREINER'S LETTERS

Chapter One

For several weeks of group meetings the little office above Black Ally's was filled with civilians; the grey-blue uniforms had withdrawn themselves. Then, unheralded, Bill Bluett walked into a meeting and, begging their permission to insert his item thus arbitrarily on to the agenda, stood in the middle of the room and read them a resolution on behalf of the communists in the camp. This was a document of two foolscap pages, beginning: Comrades!

It stated that the group in town were petty-bourgeois social democrats infected with Trotskyism, right-wing deviationism and white-settler ideology and that because of these facts the RAF members intended to sever all connection with them.

Having finished reading this statement, Bill crumpled it up into his pocket, and stood waiting for their comments. As there were none, he began again, in a different tone: 'Comrades, it's really much simpler this way. We'll run our group in the camp and maintain a liaison with yours.' Wry smiles appeared on various faces, but it seemed Bill could see no reason for them. 'We'll need you, anyway, to get supplies of pamphlets and *The Watchdog*. I'll drop in one of these days and make arrangements with Matty – that is, if she's still Lit Sec and not too absorbed in welfare work.' Here he offered Martha a lopsided grin that said he approved of the welfare work, looked at his watch, nodded with perfect friendliness all around and left them. They saw him no more: he, Jimmy and Murdoch were posted from the Colony that same week.

Andrew returned to his place on the bench beside the literature cupboard as if nothing had happened. This man, whose respect for discipline was as great as Anton's, seemed unaware that his behaviour had been at all incorrect. And Anton said nothing. More: from that time on, men from the camp announcing themselves as communists from this part of the world or that, would drop in to group meetings, coming in late, leaving early, as if the group were no more than a club. And still Anton said nothing. It seemed that for them, for these individuals from the armed camp, discipline need not exist. Meanwhile, for the people in the town, discipline had reached a point where, if someone arrived two minutes late, the group felt a collective grief on his or her behalf, coupled with a collective determination to assist and support this comrade to better self-organization.

This two-way process, a simultaneous loosening and tightening, was showing itself in other ways.

For instance, there was the question of criticism. Every week these people stood up before their comrades and criticized themselves: with sincerity, and after considerable heart-searching. Yet they did not again launch criticisms at each other, nor was it even suggested. Mutual criticism was dropped from their programme, without any formal decision being taken: at the most they nodded, as it were impartially, when one of them made a point against himself.

Again, there was the question of allies: even more time than before was spent on analysing the exact degree of apostasy on the part of people like the Kruegers, yet Jasmine for one, had revived her friendship with them. As for the du Preez couple, all their social life was devoted to people whom they agreed, at least on one night of the week, were in one way or the other enemies of socialism.

And finally, whereas once all the multifarious responsibilities of the group were organized from the dusty little room over the restaurant, now the headquarters seemed to have become the du Preez' house. For one thing, it was central – not practically, for it was on the outskirts of the town, but spiritually, situated in a suburb whose fringes spread on the verges of a vlei whose grass flanks would soon vanish under new houses, but which now stood a mile from the Location and was not far from the Coloured Quarter. It was felt that when the group spread links among the African proletariat, it would be easier from a house within walking distance of the African ghetto. For these people continued to feel, deeper than anything else, a continual hurt and embarrassment on behalf of the Africans.

This hurt had been crystallized by the defection of Elias Phiri who vanished from group life after the meeting which was also the last for the RAF group. Jasmine had gone down to the Magistrates' Court to inquire from him, urging his attendance on behalf of his nation. When he arrived at the next meeting he was drunk, sat through two items of the agenda with a look of sullen withdrawal, and then interrupted with a long speech, delivered on his feet as if he were at a public meeting, against his people who, he said, were all backward savages and fit for nothing but servitude. He left them at the conclusion of his speech, which was: 'I tell you, they're all pigs and Kaffir-dogs!'

Jasmine had gone down to the Court again, and had explained to him, with many historical illustrations, the incorrectness of his attitude. She had made little impression, however.

Soon they were saying that his character was unstable. In short, Elias, like the Kruegers and the RAF group, was spoken of thus: 'He was never a communist at all. If he had been he couldn't have left.'

Meanwhile, the remaining members of the group worked together in a honey of amity, but perhaps with less efficiency, because of the way minutes, papers and pamphlets were distributed between the du Preez' house and the group office.

Various changes had occurred in the personal lives of the members.

Marjorie was pregnant after four months of marriage. Martha noted the girl's efficiency, recognized a certain emotional competency; noted, too, a characteristic set to Colin's fat shoulders, something both complacent and wary, and thought: Well? It's no good expecting me to believe in it . . .

One afternoon the two young women were addressing

envelopes for the Progressive Club on the du Preez' veranda, and talking about Europe after the war. Italy was certain to be communist, and so was France. In five years there would be a communist Europe. They imagined it as a release into freedom, a sudden flowering into goodness and justice. They already felt themselves to be part of it.

'I'd prefer Italy, I think,' Marjorie said. 'Yes, I was there on a holiday once. I like the Italians because their temperament is so different from mine – I have such a tendency to worry and fuss. When the war is over I'll go to Italy and the comrades there will give me a job for a year or so.'

She had forgotten about Colin and about the baby. Almost at once her expression changed into the dry humour that had already absorbed the eager earnest charm that had been hers a few weeks before, and she said: 'It's hard to remember one isn't free. It's funny, isn't it, Matty? Just because of . . . the baby, I'll never be free again.' She had been going to say: Because of Colin. 'But I won't stay in this country, I won't!' she concluded fiercely, looking with hate at the rows of identical little gardened villas of which the du Preez' house was one. 'You're free, though,' she added, smiling encouragingly at Martha.

'Having a baby ought to make everything fuller, not narrow everything,' said Martha. And by a natural transition which Marjorie easily followed, she went on to: 'In the Soviet Union, with the crèches and nursery schools, everything must be different, relations between men and women must be quite different, there must be real equality.' For some time, they spoke of the lives of the women in the Soviet Union. They lapsed into silence, smiling, pursuing the same fantasy: They were in the Soviet Union. They walked into some factory or industry, which was run by a woman, who was their age, or perhaps a little older, someone competent, matter-of-fact, sympathetic. There would be little need for talk even; a smile and a squeeze of the hand would be enough, for this woman would understand at once why they needed to be given work which would absorb the best of themselves, why they needed time for study. 'Under capitalism,' she might have said, though it was hardly necessary to do so, 'women have to diminish themselves. Women like you, already part of the future, because you can imagine how diferent human beings will be, are entitled to spend a year or so in the socialist world, so as to strengthen your vision and carry it back home with you, and hand it on to others.'

From this fantasy, Martha fell to thinking about Marjorie's words: You're free, though . . .

For something had occurred which had left her feeling less than free.

For some weeks Anton and she, although regarded by themselves and by the others as a couple, had not made love. Martha had decided that some delicacy was causing him to wait until their relationship had reached a natural moment of fruition. She rested in this belief of his fine feeling with something not far off love.

A week ago he had suggested they go to the pictures together. They had never done anything together that was not associated with the group activities. He had said: 'Even the best comrades need relaxation sometimes.' There had been a consciousness in his smile that had made Martha think: Surely he can't be doing anything so vulgar as to take me to the pictures in order to set the mood for going to bed?

After the film she went back with him to his hotel room. She had not been there before. She was thinking of the Austrian woman who still lived in the hotel, when Anton got determinedly off the bed where he had been sitting, took her by the hand and raised her from her chair and towards the bed in one movement that had in it a mixture of gallantry, which she was able to tolerate, although it was hard to associate with him ordinarily, an uncertain appeal, which warmed her to him, and a complacency which she hated.

The act of sex was short and violent, so short she was uninvolved. She thought that perhaps he might have been nervous. He did not, however, seem nervous. She gave no hint of her feelings, and listened to him talk of his experiences in the revolutionary movement in Germany.

She worried over this for some days and came to some

201

contradictory conclusions. There was something essentially contradictory between the image of the revolutionary, essentially masculine, powerful and brave, and how Anton had behaved with her in bed. Yet the need in her to admire and be instructed was so great that she was on the point of telling herself: It must be my fault and not his. And yet no sooner had she reached this point of self-abnegation than her experience told her there was something wrong with Anton. And yet – here was another indisputable fact: with each man she had been with, she had been something different. Although various totally despicable because dishonest psychological pressures made her wish to say she had never enjoyed Douglas, never had pleasure with William – for both these men, from the moment she became Anton's, seemed faintly distasteful and very distant – yet she knew this to be untrue. What it amounted to, then, was that she must wait for Anton to create her into something new? But after half a dozen times the honest voice of her femininity remarked that 'Anton was hopeless'. Or, to salvage her image of the man: 'We are sexually incompatible.'

At the time of her conversation with Marjorie on the du Preez' veranda, she had decided to tell Anton that she was not for him: more diplomatically, so as to save his pride, that he was not for her. She played with fantasies of how the Austrian woman would burst into the room, making scenes, claiming him back. She, Martha, would say: But Anton, it's only fair, she's known you so much longer than I have.

But the Austrian woman was nowhere to be seen. When Martha asked about her, Anton said: 'But my little one, she's a sensible girl, believe me.' This with a fond and protective smile.

My little one moved Martha, filled her with repose, even though she despised the emotion. *She's a sensible girl* repelled her because of its complacency. Anton had chosen to be sensible and left Toni Mandel no alternative but to choose sense? Presumably. After all, she was a middle-aged woman and a very tired one. But would *he* be sensible if she, Martha, decided to be? Her instinct said not. She imagined herself saying: Anton, I'm sorry, we've made a mistake. How, then, would he react? The man who made a special journey at lunch-hour to buy cinema tickets and order a table for two in a mood of dogged determination to do what he thought was the right thing, who fetched her gallantly from her room, and settled her into the front seat of the car he had borrowed for the occasion, and all this with the creaking kindliness he never used towards her when they were both being, simply, members of the group – that man she imagined as capable of ugly vanity. She was afraid.

But not as afraid as of the man she imagined stiffening into hurt, saying in the cold voice he used when preserving a shell of pride: 'Well, of course, if you feel like that . . .'

Yet all this was unimportant; after the war they would be scattered into the revolutionary battle-fronts of Europe. Personal unhappiness was irrelevant. All the same, she would speak to Anton about their unsuitedness to each other not later than tonight . . . well, if not tonight, then at some suitable moment when neither was tired, and both could be reasonable.

In the meantime there were a hundred things to be seen to. She saw to them: the organizing of meetings, the study groups, the addressing of envelopes. There was also the question of Maisie.

She did not speak to Anton of Maisie because he continued to refer, with disapproval, to 'charitable activities'.

Martha had been present at the first interview between Andrew and Maisie. It had been brief. Andrew, brisk and kindly, had said he was prepared to marry Maisie, and would allow her to divorce him when the child was born. He thought he could get permission from the CO to marry. If it came to the worst he would say he had got a girl into trouble. He said this with a smile, his eyes warm on Maisie's calm but unhappy face. She asked for time to think it over. He insisted that he would do whatever she wanted, and that she should send a message to him through Martha. Then he left the two girls together. They were sitting in Black Ally's on either side of a tomato-sauce-stained tablecloth. Maisie drank strong tea in silence, thinking, until she asked at last:

'But, Matty, I don't get it. Why should he? I mean, he doesn't get anything out of it but the bother of a divorce. Is it because he's a communist?'

'We don't think babies should be killed simply because of nonsense about illegitimacy,' said Martha. She added, feeling she had been partly dishonest: 'I don't know why it should be Andrew – but he's a kind man.'

'Yes, he is,' Maisie agreed at once.

Martha heard nothing of her for a week. Then she came into the office and invited Martha for lunch.

Her mood had manifestly changed. For the first time since she had known her, Martha saw Maisie anxious.

'It's like this,' she said. 'I'm worried. Suppose I get fond of Andrew and I don't want him to divorce me, then he won't like it and I'll be unhappy. Well, I don't want to be unhappy. I've got enough troubles.'

This statement caused Martha to feel a pang which she recognized with disapproval as jealousy. For the kindliness of Andrew over Maisie's baby had caused her to feel warm towards him, and she had even been thinking: I was a fool to let myself get involved with Anton instead of Andrew. She saw that Maisie had already become fond of Andrew.

Martha said: 'He'll be going back to England after the war.'

'I know. And I'm sure I'd hate England. But don't you see, Matty, there's something not right about this, it's too cold-hearted.'

Martha sent a message to Andrew. He came into town that afternoon, and she set herself to convey to him, without actually saying so, that Maisie's objection to this practical arrangement was the fact that it was practical. She watched Andrew's face change from complacency into gratitude. He said: 'Well, I'm quite partial to the lass myself. Where does she live?'

The group maintained a discreet silence about Maisie and Andrew for several days. This was hard to do, the signs of joy were so strong on Andrew's face that it seemed positively dishonest not to notice them. Then he announced that he was marrying Maisie, and with the pride of a man in love. He was looking for a flat for Maisie. He even said he did not approve of women working while they were pregnant, adding with a calm nod towards Anton that he didn't give a damn what they thought in the Soviet Union on this subject – he was old-fashioned. No one said a word of criticism.

They were delighted. The group was filled with a spirit of warm, though wry pleasure; as if something wilfully beautiful had been offered to them. That is, they were all delighted save Anton, who invited them to consider the consequences.

Marjorie remarked, smiling dryly: 'The group is going to have a baby – but it's not my baby!'

Meanwhile, new decisions had been taken about the work of the group. A 'fundamentally new policy' had come into being, and, oddly enough, not as a result of the fundamental analysis demanded by Anton, but because of a remark of Jasmine's.

They were all assembled in the du Preez' living-room, engaged in the routine management of the half-dozen societies they were now responsible for, when Jasmine said: 'I met Mrs Van der Bylt in the street today, and she wanted to know why I had dropped my work in the Labour Party. Well, of course I couldn't say I couldn't stand that bunch of social democrats any longer.'

'But Jasmine,' said Marie du Preez, 'I'm still a member. Surely you're wrong? I didn't know we were expected to stop being members. Why should we?'

The questions of principle raised here were immense, but not gone into: Anton said calmly that of course Jasmine had been wrong.

Jasmine went to a Labour Party Committee meeting, to which she was invited to go as an observer, and returned saying that it would be quite easy to co-opt four or five of the group members on to the committee. Mrs Van, who was a really progressive person, not at all like the others on the committee, had said she would be pleased to have them there. She proposed to co-opt them.

Martha, Marjorie, Colin, Marie and Piet were instructed to attend the next committee meeting. Carrie Jones, invited to do so, refused. She took this opportunity of saying that she wished them luck, but she felt she would never make a communist. Next day it was announced in the *News* that she was engaged to the manager of the firm to which she was secretary.

The group, feeling that this had been inevitable, congratulated her and afterwards did no more than describe her as fundamentally petty bourgeois. In fact, Carrie Jones, who had always been less of a communist than any of them, incurred less censure from them than any of the other renegades. They continued to greet her when they saw her, and spoke of her with amiable contempt.

Within a month, the balance of the group activities had entirely changed. The societies such as the Progressive Club and Sympathizers of Russia ran almost by themselves. The committees of these organizations were practically interchangeable, with one or two outside people on each for respectability's sake. *The Watchdog*, farmed out to dozens of sub-agents, sold phenomenally, and with so little trouble that Martha could never rid herself of a feeling that there must be something wrong with a political activity that needed so little effort.

After the five had been co-opted on to the Labour Party Committee, there was a meeting at the du Preez' house at which Anton, after lengthy analysis, decided that it was their task to influence the Labour Party.

It was a meeting at which there were two new faces.

Maisie was present, listening lazily, watching Andrew, who was now her husband, with affection.

Also there was a new man from the camp, a Greek fresh from fighting in the mountains with the communist forces. He was now training to be a pilot. He was a small, dark, lean man, with burning serious eyes and an impressive gift of silence.

He said nothing about the political decisions taken that evening, on the grounds that he did not understand the conditions in the Colony.

Andrew and Maisie left early. Anton remarked that he did not think Andrew should have brought Maisie without asking them first. The Greek asked who she was, and they told him the history of the couple.

He listened gravely. At last he nodded, saying: 'That is good. That I like to hear very much.' He leaned forward, his thin brown hands pressed between his two knees, looking into their faces. 'Comrades, we live in a terrible and ugly time, we live when capitalism is a beast who murders us, starves us, keeps from us the joy of life. As communists we must try to live a life as if the ugliness was already dead. We must try and live like socialists who care for each other and for people, even while we are hurt all the time by capitalism which is cruel. And so I am happy to hear about these two comrades. That shows we in this room are real communists. I am proud and happy to be with you in this room.' With which he rose, nodding at them all gravely, in turn, saying he would attend the group meetings when he could.

Anton said nothing. Athen, newly arrived guerrilla fighter from the mountains of Greece, had more right than he to make judgments. So they all felt, and he knew it.

Chapter Two

The six, Jasmine, Martha, Marjorie, Colin and the du Preez entered their first executive meeting together, and five minutes late. The room was familiar to them, because they had rented it for various meetings of their own. It was a large brown dusty room, of the kind in which it seemed they spent most of their lives now, but distinguished from their own office by two large pictures, one of Ramsay Macdonald and one of Keir Hardie. With themselves, there were twenty people present. At the table of office sat Mrs Van, and beside her an elderly clergyman, a tall greyhound of a man with a thin pleasant face, who surveyed them all, impartially, with determined goodwill. Mrs Van was a large woman, Dutch by origin, calm, matter-of-fact, controlled. Short grey hair lay flat beside serene cheeks. Her eyes were small, blue, direct. She wore a dress that looked like an overall.

A big untidy Scotsman was speaking as they settled themselves. Martha recognized him. He was Mr McFarline, whose existence she had forgotten, since it belonged to three incarnations ago, her girlhood on the farm. His fist rhythmically jabbed into the air beside him, and he was chanting the classic phrases of the socialist credo with every appearance of passionate belief. Martha was stunned, in spite of expecting to find such evidences of hypocrisy in the Labour Party. Mr McFarline was the richest man in 'the district'. One of the richest men, they said, in the Colony, especially since he had bought up a lot of city property which was in the path of new development. He was famous for the ill-treatment of his African workers, and was probably not able to number the half-caste children who shared his features in the compounds of the mines he owned, but did not run.

This man orated about the brotherhood of humanity while the six listened, careful to keep from their faces any look of irony. They were determined to make a good impression. It was obvious to these connoisseurs of political meetings that a good deal was going on under the orderly surface that Mrs Van was so ably preserving.

There was something else: a sense, in the way people spoke, of weight and consequence. They were all being reminded that in the group meetings they might represent world communism, but that what decisions they took affected little but themselves. This was the executive of the Social Democratic Party which had seven members of Parliament and was the official opposition to the Government. What was decided in this room presumably had some effect on the course events took in the Colony. If the atmosphere of self-dedication which was the natural air they breathed was absent here, they were being introduced unexpectedly to a feeling of power. Why had they been invited here at all?

The item on the agenda which made it clear was soon reached. Mrs Van remarked that six newly formed branches of the Party had asked the Executive Committee to appoint delegates to attend meetings on their behalf: the branches were remote, three of them several hundred miles away, and they could not afford to send delegates. Mrs Van reminded the meeting that she had put forward the six names of the new delegates to the last meeting, and they had been approved. She then paused and waited for comment.

Mr McFarline was whispering to the man beside him who was nodding vehemently. The words 'barely a quorum last time', were audible. It seemed, then, that Mrs Van had put forward the names at a time to suit herself, and that the faction who would have opposed them was represented by the Parliamentary members, who made their feelings quite plain by directing long hard stares towards the six communists.

Mrs Van had, in short, put a fast one over on her opponents, and they were taking their defeat badly. And yet these men were expressing admiration as well as resentment in their scarcely-concealed grimacing grins towards the table where the chairman and the secretary sat. And Mrs Van, although she was placidly in command of herself, could not refrain from directing at them a single steady beam of quiet triumph. It was as if she had laughed out loud.

And so, the six were thinking, they were here as pawns in some internal battle they did not yet understand. Mrs Van, who was notoriously unsympathetic to communism, a lady of the utmost respectability (she had been a town councillor for many years now) felt so passionately about something, some issue, that she was prepared to saddle her own side with the weight of six communists? The meeting wore on. It was conducted with such devotion to the rules that they could only admire Mrs Van, for it was clearly she who had brought this job lot of people to such a pitch of discipline. The chairman, a delightfully sympathetic man, was obviously chairman by virtue of his personality, and not because of his efficiency. He lost his way in the agenda, slipped up continually over resolutions and amendments, and corrected himself with self-deprecating charm when Mrs Van put him right, which she instantly, firmly, and maternally did.

Meanwhile, the seven members of Parliament continued to lounge and smoke, arms crossed, legs outstretched, in the poses of men who have sat too long on hard benches.,

It was not until the end of the agenda that the six understood why they were here. It was an item called African Membership, and now the members of Parliament showed by their sudden attention that this was why they were here too.

Mr McFarline rose to his feet and said that while there was no one in the Colony more passionately devoted to the welfare of the blacks than himself, he thought the establishment of African membership was inopportune because . . . But he was ruled out of order, Mrs Van pointing out that the decision to have African members had been taken at the last meeting, and the question now was: What form was this to take? She added that if the Parliamentary members attended executive meetings more often, or read the minutes with

210

attention, they would not be quite so out of touch with the affairs of the Party.

At this, Mr McFarline's neighbour, a dark and lean man with the rancorous speech and eye of the self-hater, delivered himself of half a dozen brief remarks about Kaffir-lovers and do-gooders.

He was ruled out of order with the same maternal severity.

Mrs Van said with the utmost amiability that in view of the lateness of the hour and the heatedness of people's feelings, the whole subject had better be left to the next meeting.

'But it's been put off twice already,' said Mr Playfair.

'It has been put off,' said Mrs Van, 'because of the inability of certain Parliamentary members to attend, but I am quite prepared to put it off again if everyone agrees?'

Anger broke out from the opposing faction, and during the noise Mr McFarline was heard ejaculating to his dark lieutenant: 'That lot will have the vote next time; they haven't got it this meeting.' And he nodded with dislike towards the six communists.

'We can discuss it now or at the next meeting, as you prefer,' remarked Mr Playfair, after Mrs Van had whispered to him.

The dark man put his lips to Mr McFarline's ear. Mr McFarline, grinning, said: 'I'm in agreement with a postponement.' He added: 'There are a lot of branches that have lapsed and need whipping up.' In short, he intended to strengthen his own side as Mrs Van had strengthened hers. His look at her was triumphant. But she nodded, a small smile at the corners of her mouth: she could not have said more clearly: You think you've done me but you haven't.

Mr McFarline hesitated, apparently wondering who would have the advantage from a postponement devoted to the 'whipping-up' of the constituencies.

He was seen to cast a practised eye over the people present now, counting up his supporters. Mrs Van did the same.

He said: 'I think it would save time if we took a vote now.'

Mrs Van agreed. They all agreed. Whereupon Mrs Van blandly pointed out that the six newly co-opted members were entitled to vote on this issue according to ... here she produced the constitution and read the relevant clause.

Mr McFarline frowned, but had to agree she was in the right.

The vote was then put, the six communists voting with Mrs Van's faction: African membership of the Party was confirmed; and their votes were to count the same in the affairs of the Party as the white members. The question as to whether they should form themselves into special branches or not was to be discussed in a fortnight's time.

The meeting broke up. The six communists remained where they were, watching how people would disperse for clues as to how they were aligned. They were waiting, too, for some kind of explanation from Mrs Van.

Martha was watching Mr McFarline. She half-wanted him to remember her. Throughout the meeting his eyes had been on her, sometimes with the hard glance which she earned as a member of the communist faction, sometimes with the frankly assessing stockman's look of a woman-lover, and this she resented now for the same reason she had years before – he was an elderly man and had no right to look at her like that!

Now he came over to her, a big smiling man, easy with the good-nature of power, and said: 'Lassie, don't I know you?'

She was confused when she did not want to be; Mr McFarline, lover of women, was shedding on her an impersonal kindly warmth, his brown eyes were extraordinarily shrewd and even gentle. She felt herself instinctively raising her hand to her hair in a coquettish gesture. She let it drop, and said: 'I was Martha Quest.' Mr McFarline nodded, fitting his memories together. He said, tentative and inviting: 'So now we're going to be comrades in arms?'

Martha said: 'Hardly comrades, Mr McFarline!'

He nodded, laughed out, switched off the warmth of his attention, and turned away. His bilious lieutenant who had been watching him during his passage with the communist faction now went after him with a taut cold face. Three other members of Parliament went with them.

Piet du Preez said to Martha: 'You'd better watch it. That's an old swine if there ever was one. He boasts that if all the women he's had were laid end to end they would cover the railway lines between the Zambesi and the Limpopo – only he doesn't express himself quite so nicely!' His eyes were enjoying Martha's confusion. It was one of the moments she was made to learn something about herself: the men of the group were all watching her and she felt exposed.

Marie came to her rescue by shaking her husband's arm and saying: 'That's enough from you – if I didn't keep you in order you'd be as bad.'

Colin and Marjorie stood to one side, listening. He had his hand on her elbow; her forearm dangled loose below it, and her hand was a fist. Marjorie said: 'What's the joke?' moving a step nearer, stopped by Colin's grasp. Martha, still irritable because she had responded to Mr McFarline, noted the proprietary hand, the stiff resenting forearm, and thought, disliking Marjorie: Why did she marry him? What for? She doesn't love him ... I'll tell Anton today it's no good us going on.

At this point Mrs Van came towards them. Mr Playfair had remained, and one of the members of Parliament, a small battling Scotsman, Jack Dobie; also a tall thin freckled man, grey-haired and eager-faced – this was Johnny Lindsay, an old miner from the Rand.

Mrs Van said smiling: 'I am very pleased to see you all here.'

Jasmine and Piet, both old friends of hers, stood forward, like official representatives of the group.

Mrs Van laughed, a warm girlish laugh, and said: 'Well, we've won that round – and it serves those old so-and-sos right for not attending meetings.'

The group laughed in response, but not as frankly: being allies of Mrs Van had its difficulties, since, by their definition, she and her friends were all reactionaries.

Johnny Lindsay said cheerfully: 'That's one thing we can count on you communists for – you're fine on racial questions.'

Here Mrs Van, Jack Dobie, Mr Playfair and Johnny Lindsay all nodded and smiled together, and the group finally understood exactly why they had been co-opted on to the executive.

'That lot can't stand you,' said Jack. His small fighting face was lifted by the chin, aggresively thrust out in a character- istic gesture, as if presenting itself to enemies with every belief in the power of that sharp point to repel no matter how strong a fist. 'They hate your guts,' he added, but with a mock-threat in it now, like a growl. 'And, comrades, let me tell you – I'm from the Clyde, I've worked with the Reds all my days, and so you'd better not get up to any of your tricks. I'm warning you, you won't get away with it.'

And now they all laughed together in a relief of tension, liking each other.

Jasmine said in her demure way: 'But, Jack, communists are always prepared to work with the labourites on certain issues.'

He growled out: 'So you're prepared to work with us, is that it? Well, I was a member of the CP myself once, so I know it all – and watch your step.'

Mrs Van said, stern and formidable: 'You can be commu- nists outside this room, but in here you're members of our Party and please remember that.' She gave them an emphatic nod. 'We're in the habit of taking our rules and regulations as seriously as you take yours!'

At which Johnny said: 'And our Mrs Van is a mistress of rules and regulations – and aren't that bunch sorry for it now!'

The general laugh was led by Mrs Van's full-throated ringing peal, the laugh of a girl who was still buried somewhere in that large, placid matron's body. 'Come and have a cup of tea in my office,' she said. 'We need to do a little plotting.'

Mrs Van's personal office was in the same building, across the court – the usual dingy square of soil surrounded by a veranda off which rooms opened.

The six group members, with Mr Playfair, Johnny Lindsay and Jack Dobie, sat themselves around Mrs Van's tidy paper- filed, filing-cabineted office, noting that above Mrs Van's head hung two portraits: Nehru and Gandhi. They drank tea and did not plot; there was no need to, for they were all in harmony. The issue was clear. These were all people who felt deeply about the situation of the Africans of the Colony; they did not need to support each other in their belief that Africans, though deprived of a vote, should somehow be introduced, even if in small ways, to political responsibility, and if being members of this particular political party was a small way, it was better than nothing. Mrs Van's faction wanted the African members to form a branch because it would educate them in democratic procedure. The reactionaries, led by the members of Parliament, did not want black men in the Party at all. Jack Dobie, member of Parliament and therefore a traitor to *his* group, since he did not stand with them on this issue, spoke of them as career men and white trade unionists.

And yet he was himself a white trade unionist, elected by white railway workers.

Piet, white trade unionist, challenged him, saying that they weren't all anti-African.

'Is that so?' demanded Jack. 'You say that to me?'

'You're sitting here, aren't you?' said Jasmine.

'Not because of my views on the Native Question.'

It was clear to them all that his particular quality, the one which got him elected, no matter how much his views contradicted those of the men who elected him, was one that the other members of the Parliamentary group did not have. Jack had the quality of honesty; a simple, unself-regarding honesty. The others were politicians. One could not sit in the same room with him for five minutes and not feel the difference between him and them.

They played the white trade unionist line. He would stand on a platform before a couple of hundred railway workers, all of them Kaffir-hating, wage-jealous white men, telling them they should be ashamed not to consider the Africans as brothers and fellow-workers!

'They elect you,' said Mrs Van, 'because they have consciences after all.'

'Is that it? I'd like to think so.' He added, grimly: 'They elect me because they have it both ways: they have the

215

satisfaction of knowing they're electing someone with the principles they ought to have – and they know that since there's only one of me it won't make any difference to the policy of the Parliamentary group – and that's why *you* aren't out on your ear, Brother Piet, don't you make any mistake about it!' With which he gave them all an efficient nod, thumped Piet on the shoulder, and left them for his duties in the House.

Mr Playfair departed also: he had a church service to manage. Mrs Van and Johnny Lindsay sat together, talking.

The six communists watched them a while and then exchanged smiles. Mrs Van and Johnny were discussing how to use the rules of procedure in order to get their way over the African Branch. They were talking like old friends, which they were, but it was more than that: the white-haired man with his sunburned boyish face and startlingly young blue eyes, and the fat matronly woman, calm with self-command, their heads bent together over four sheets of printed Rules and Constitution, gave such an impression of warmth and of trust that more than one member of the group involuntarily sighed and envied them.

Martha was again feeling her old pain, that she was excluded from some good, some warmth, that she had never known. She thought: They are like lovers – though of course they aren't.

Mrs Van, a fat forefinger half-way down a page, raised her grey head, looked triumphant and said: 'There, see that? That'll cook their goose for them.' And Johnny, alive with the delights of intrigue, nodded vigorously, with 'That's the stuff. That'll dish them!' They were like a pair of conspiring children, and the group, seeing they were no longer wanted, said good-bye and left. The du Preez went home saying they must put the children to bed, but later, it went without saying, their house was available for group activity.

Marjorie and Colin walked away together. Martha saw that Marjorie now had her hand inside Colin's broad elbow. It was a contrite and affectionate hand, and Martha thought: She's feeling guilty, because she resents him so much . . . I really must talk to Anton tonight.

Jasmine and Martha lingered on the pavement. Both of them had watched Colin and Marjorie go off, and their smile at each other afterwards was accompanied by a dry lift of the brows.

'I'm not going to get married,' said Jasmine suddenly, startling Martha, for this self-contained girl never spoke about 'personal matters'.

It was dusk: cars were streaking past in showers of light; the stars were coming out.

Jasmine said: 'There was that business with Jackie – I must have been mad. I mean, not to have an affair, but thinking of marrying.' She spoke without heat, good-natured and rueful. 'I loved that other man – you never knew him, he was killed in the Spanish Civil War.' She paused, frowning, and sighed. 'There's something about marriage, whenever I see it, I feel ... but of course you've been married and I haven't.' In the dusk she was a small figure: always Jasmine gave this impression, against all the facts of what she was and the life she led, of smallness, forlornness, and isolated courage. 'I'm not going to get married,' she announced. She shyly squeezed Martha's arm and said: 'And don't you go and get married either, Matty. There's no sense in your breaking up one marriage and then getting married again, is there?' She nodded, and trotted off to where her car was parked, leaving Martha thinking: She knows I'm in a dilemma about Anton, and she's warning me. Yet she admires Anton.

It's like someone outside a danger-zone warning someone in it. And if the position were reversed, I'd certainly warn her – if she gave me the chance, which she wouldn't, because she's far too reserved – not to get married to anyone yet.

Martha was meeting Anton in an hour for supper. She knew she ought to use that hour for thinking, but she walked off up the street towards Maisie's flat, which was five minutes away. All the members of the group had assured themselves and each other that it was only right to leave Maisie and Andrew alone together as much as possible because of the delicate situation they were in.

Martha excused herself by thinking: Well, it's only for an hour. The door was opened, however, by Tommy, and behind him she could see Athen from Greece, sitting at his ease and smiling with pleasure at, presumably, Maisie. Martha went in. It was a two-roomed flat, furnished hastily and cheaply. This front room had a couple of chairs bought at a sale, and a divan in one corner covered with an army blanket. Maisie sat upright on one of the hard chairs, her hands folded loose in her plump lap. She wore a blue maternity smock and the mound of her pregnancy showed firm and placid behind the folds of blue. Her fair glistening hair had evidently just been brushed, for it was not untidy, as it ordinarily was, but she was not made up. She looked young and appealing, and she was smiling with calm attention at Athen. Tommy, his urchin hair standing up all over his head, was pouring out tea which he had just made for them. He was handing Maisie a cup of tea as if it were a present. Altogether, the pretty, lazy girl had the look of someone worshipped and adored.

She greeted Martha with a Hi there!, smiled, but did not move. Martha felt at peace. She sat on the divan beside Athen the Greek, and thought: There's Maisie, in such a complicated mess, and she's quite calm and happy – I never was. I never do anything right. I should have been happy when I was pregnant, but I was fighting everything.

Athen was talking to Maisie about the guerrillas in the mountains. The thin dark keen face was frowning with attention for the words he was using, because his English was uncertain, but his eyes smiled gently and steadily at Maisie. And she, Martha knew, was not listening: the words, guerrilla, war, fighting, communist, fascist, went by her, she was forming no picture at all of what they meant. She merely liked Athen and his feeling for her.

Athen, realizing this, stopped talking and said: 'But you must ask your husband to explain all this to you.'

She said: 'Andrew tells me all this stuff.' She shrugged. Martha noted how her shoulders moved in a tranquil acceptance of the shrug while the heavy hips remained planted on the chair; the lower part of her body was absorbed in a life of its own.

Envy shook Martha. She thought, Lord help me, I'm going to start wanting another baby just because Maisie's having one. Stop it, stop it at once – in less than an hour I'll be meeting Anton.

Andrew came in, unbuttoning his jacket and flinging off his cap. Maisie turned her head towards him, the blue of her eyes deepening in a smile.

The group of course wondered secretly about the relations of these two. While they wondered, they felt ashamed – or rather, felt they should be ashamed.

Andrew said: 'How's it, Maisie?' and poured himself tea while Maisie watched him. She had the appearance of a very young girl who has just been introduced to a man her parents think will make a suitable husband and to whom, half against her will, she is attracted.

The outward form of their life was that of two people on trial with each other.

The two rooms were arranged as separate rooms. The inner room, where Maisie slept, was a girl's room. It had a single bed covered with a fat shining blue eiderdown, and all kinds of trinkets and bits of nonsense stood on her dressing-table – small dolls, china ladies and so on. There were two photographs on a shelf of her two dead husbands, but none of Binkie, her baby's father.

As for Andrew, it was understood that the bed covered with an army blanket was his: he camped in this front room when he had a pass for the night or for the week-end.

He turned with a cup of tea in his hand, and examined Maisie frankly: he had not seen her for three days. Since his marriage he had changed a good deal. Before, gruffly good-humoured, practical, responsible, he was a man with whom one associated no sentiment. A little sentimentality perhaps: the conventional sentimental jokes and tributes to emotion of a man who has no time for it. But now the broad face had softened and his eyes had acquired a new expression, as if they were saying: 'Hullo! I didn't expect *this* . . .'

It became clear to the three visitors at the same moment

that Andrew wanted them to go. He had taken two steps towards Maisie, but propriety stopped him, and he remained standing by Athen. He even exchanged half a dozen camp jokes with the Greek, but it was pure form, for his eyes kept returning to Maisie.

Tommy jumped up, in confusion, exclaiming that he had to go off and get some supper.

Athen, who had been watching the couple with grave approval, rose also, saying: 'I'll come with you, Tommy.' Martha followed them to the door.

Maisie and Andrew nodded a good-bye to their visitors, and their eyes instantly returned to each other, in the prolonged, serious, respectful gaze that the group knew so well, and which always made them envious.

As they left the room they heard Andrew's voice: 'Well, lass? And how's that little bastard been since I left you?'

Maisie's voice, queenly, and kind: 'You shouldn't use that word bastard, Andrew, because it's not right, don't you see?'

Then their laughter, warmed by the wonder of joy.

Tommy said in a shocked whisper: 'That's a funny joke, I *don't* think.'

Athen laid a hand on the boy's shoulder and said: 'No, it's good – all of it is very good, comrade.'

On the pavement they stood, the three of them, looking up at the uncurtained windows a few feet above them, whose light seemed shed from the happiness of Maisie and Andrew. Athen's and Martha's eyes meeting, they unconsciously exchanged a regretful smile. Tommy, still crimson, fierce with incomprehension, said angrily: 'Well, I don't get it. That's not even his kid. It's someone else's kid.' He stubbed his foot again and again against the pavement edge, glaring away from the lighted windows to a group of scrubby gum-trees that stood in a waste lot a few yards off.

Athen said gently: 'But, Comrade Tommy, don't you see what selfishness it all is – *my* child, *my* son, *my* daughter – don't you see, that's all finished now? Well, it will soon be finished in the world. What it is is just: a baby is being born. A new human being. That's all, comrade.'

Tommy's face twisted into an unwilling grin.

Athen smiled: his smile on the lean stern Southern face was extraordinarily tender. He said: 'When a baby is born it is born to everyone – don't you see that? It is my child and your child and Martha's child.'

Tommy said: 'I don't think that's why Andrew is so pleased with himself. I mean, he's pleased because he likes Maisie. I don't think the baby's got anything to do with it.'

Athen said: 'He likes Maisie and so he likes the baby too. But it is because Maisie is a good girl. She is a good good girl.'

Martha sighed, and Athen heard it. She saw the stern little man look at her in comprehension. She imagined it was disapproval. He said: 'Maisie is a lucky one, she has a gift.'

'What gift, why lucky?' insisted Tommy, almost in despair, still angrily banging his toe at the pavement.

Athen said, not looking at Martha: 'It has seemed to me like this for a long time – that this is a time which is difficult for women. Some women know it and fight. Some women, like Maisie, they don't know it.'

'All the same,' said Tommy. 'All the same – it's not Andrew's kid at all.'

'Andrew is a good man,' Athen pronounced. 'He is a good comrade. Yes, there are very good people in the world in spite of everything.'

And you are a good man too, Martha thought, adding involuntarily: I would be perfectly safe with this man. Instantly the word safe confused her. What do I want with safety? What do I mean, safe? Well, then, is Anton a good man? But now she felt even more confused.

Athen said to Tommy: 'And now we will go and eat before the meeting, comrade.' He gave the obstinately unhappy boy his stern, gentle smile, and said: 'And you are a good boy too, Tommy. You should not make things so hard for yourself. Life is simple, comrade. All the real things are very simple. Why do you make it so difficult? What is this now? A baby is being born and a woman needs a man to look after her. That's all, that's all, Comrade Tommy. It is a good man and a good woman and they help each other. That's all, and nothing else.'

Martha said: 'I'll see you both at the meeting,' and walked off. She wanted to cry, and was frightened because of the tears threatening her. At the corner, under the bunch of dusty gum-trees, she turned to watch the two men out of sight: the small fine-made Greek, who had his hand on the shoulder of the big clumsy youth, his face leaned towards him in persuasion. She thought: I wish I had had somebody like Athen to explain things to me when I was eighteen. She thought: Here it is again, this feeling that I am being shut out of something beautiful and simple. Well, it's nothing but sentimentality.

Yet she did not really believe it was sentimental: there was something very good about Athen being with Tommy, and in the relation between Mrs Van and Johnny Lindsay, the old miner.

The smell of dry dust filled her nostrils; an odour of dry sun-harshened leaves descended from the darkening gum-trees above. She thought: and it was a moment of illumination, a flash of light: I don't know anything about anything yet. I must try and keep myself free and open, and try to think more, try not to drift into things.

The heavy bells from the Catholic Church down the road tumbled out a warning of the time: it was seven, and she began walking very fast towards Black Ally's. Already the old feeling of impatience was snapping at her heels and the moment of knowledge had gone.

Why should I be so afraid to face Anton now? It's absurd to feel caged. It might have been any one of these men, any one, it was simply luck, or some kind of choice I don't understand. But not *my* choice. If Jasmine had been sick, Anton would have – kissed her on the forehead, and I would be thinking of Jasmine now as she is thinking of me – *Don't be a fool.*

She was in a fever of irritable bewilderment. At the door of Black Ally's she remembered she had not agreed to meet Anton here but at the Grill down the street.

She liked the atmosphere of Black Ally's although the food was so bad. The Grill was expensive and was used for special occasions. She thought that ever since Anton had 'kissed her on the forehead' he had been taking her formally to the Grill once or twice a week. On these occasions his manner towards her was different.

Why does he do it? I don't like it, she thought, feeling she was unjust, but too full of irritation to care. It's the way he does it – everything so careful and so planned, as if he were saying: Tonight I shall sleep with you and this is a preparation for it. Most of the week I'm a comrade, a friend, and then he turns me into something else. I simply don't like any of it.

She reached the Grill, which was a small room, flashing with white linen and well-polished cutlery and highly uniformed waiters. Anton waited in a corner. He rose at the sight of her and stood, slightly bowed, until she sat down, reaffirming her decision to end the thing: this tall stiff pale man, watching me from his pale eyes – good Lord, he's got nothing to do with me, and never could have. Well, I'll say something when we reach the end of the meal.

Meanwhile, Anton was ordering. It pleased him to treat her as if she were still convalescent, and he said with a heavy, fatherly playfulness: 'You must have a good underdone steak – yes.' And he smiled at her as if he were surprised it could be so easy and so pleasant to smile.

She put her elbows on the table and chattered to him about the meeting that afternoon in a way she knew irritated him. She was giving him all the essential information, but making fun of it, including the six communists. 'We imagined we went there to influence them, but it turns out we're part of some plot of Mrs Van's . . .' She saw his forehead set into patience against her irresponsibility which he had no intention of condoning but which, since this was a special occasion, he would make allowances for.

Lately, with her, the set of his shoulders and the careful bend of his head had become more easy, more relaxed. Tonight he had regained his self-contained watchfulness – something that caught at her heart because it was a protection against possible pain and she knew it.

'What's the matter?' she inquired, seeing that there was

something very much the matter and she ought to have noticed it before.

He said: 'There is something, yes, but let us finish our food first.'

Now they ate in silence.

Martha was thinking: Perhaps he wants to break it off? Perversely, a feeling of loss and panic swept over her. She noted this with dismay: I'd be capable of talking him into going on simply because it was he who wanted to break it off! Well, if that's what it is, I'll resist a little, so as not to hurt his feelings, and then agree.

Having reached this decision she talked of Maisie and Andrew, although she knew he disapproved of the couple. She was even making some kind of a test of it: if he said something warm and generous about them, it would mean they could be happy together.

She saw he was not listening. He said: 'Matty, something has happened and we must make a decision.'

He talked slowly, every word weighed. It appeared that his employer had taken him aside that morning and told him the CID had paid an informal visit to say that Anton Hesse, an enemy alien, was known to be having an affair with a British woman. Such relationships were frowned upon. It had been pointed out, but in such a way that it need not be taken as an actual threat, that in the past enemy aliens misconducting themselves had been returned to the internment camp. The employer had been 'very upset'. He had not said in so many words that he insisted on Mr Hesse breaking off this affair, but – flurried, bad-tempered from guilt, apologetic for his bad temper, and very verbose – had talked for two hours, finally divesting himself of any responsibility, leaving it on the shoulders of the CID whose very existence he of course totally deplored. The matter had in fact been conducted in the great British tradition: no one had actually threatened anyone, or brought any direct pressure to bear; not only the employer but the CID man had been extremely uncomfortable; it was nobody's fault; nevertheless, the effect was that Anton must toe the line or lose his job and possibly return to the internment camp.

Martha noted that the stiff resentment in Anton's voice was due to only one thing, as usual: that he was anti-fascist and anti-Hitler and yet treated like an enemy.

He was not even trying to influence her. He was stating the position as simply as he could.

When she tried to interrupt he said: 'Wait, Matty, wait. You must let me say everything first.'

He finished with: 'And so if we analyse the position it is this: we must break this off, or we must get married and become respectable. And that is not the lightest decision to make.'

And so he ended, leaving it to her.

Martha was silent. She saw how he had, as she put it, gone into his shell. She noted how his mouth had set in patient resignation. He has taken it for granted, she thought, that she would decide to break it off.

'You must think it over,' he said. 'You must say nothing now, but you think it over when you're alone.'

He really cares for me, she thought; it was interesting that this was the first time she had told herself he cared for her.

'Supposing we break off,' she asked, 'is it still a bad mark against you, having an affair with a British girl?

He said reluctantly: 'Yes, yes, yes.' He added: 'And of course it is not sensible, taking part in all these communist activities – it is more than possible that this is these gentlemen's way of warning me against all this running around at meetings.'

It was this remark that made up Martha's mind for her. She thought: Andrew could marry Maisie to help her out – that was a good thing to do, everyone feels it. (She did not remind herself now that everyone felt it except Anton.) And if I marry Anton, and it's nothing but a formality after all, it will make things easy for him.

She obeyed his insistence that she should not make up her mind now, but later, when that evening's meeting was over, she took his hand hurriedly on the pavement as he was turning away from her with a quiet, patient: 'Good night, Matty,' and said: 'Don't worry about anything, Anton. We'll get married.'

His face lit into gratitude and relief, and with a suddenness that took away her speech. She thought again: So he does really care for me.

They kissed hurriedly, separating for the night out of an instinct that not to separate would be dangerous. Martha, walking home by herself, examined the look that appeared on Anton's face at the moment she had said she would marry him, and saw something else: dependence, something almost childlike. This filled her with unease.

But already she was feeling, under the pressure of the snapping jaws of impatience, the need to move forwards, as if the marriage with Anton and what she might become as a result of it were already done and accomplished. It was as if her whole being had concentrated itself into a movement of taking in and absorbing, as if she were swallowing something whole and hurrying on.

As she went to sleep that night she was thinking: Perhaps Andrew felt like this when he said he would marry Maisie: and only afterwards he discovered he was happy and was surprised he was happy. She went to sleep depressed, and dreamed she was with Maisie, who was due to have her baby, and they were hurrying from door to door trying to find a house which would take her in. But the doors remained closed against them both.

Chapter Three

On the Saturday morning Martha was due to be married for the second time she woke late; she had half an hour to dress and reach the Magistrates' Court. None of them had got to bed the night before until nearly three. Andrew and Anton, appointed Policy Sub-Committee for the Communist Party of Zambesia, had finally produced a 150-page document setting out how the territory would be run if the communists were to take power. This admirable document began with a page-long clause on how racial prejudice was to be made illegal, laying down the penalties for any expression of it whatsoever, direct or indirect, continued through detailed analyses of the industrial, economic and cultural position of the Colony, made provisions for dealing with any sort of contingency, ranging from war launched by other white-settled parts of Africa and backed by British and American capital to economic boycotts, and ended (the style of this part of the document was different from the rest, which was sober and precise) in an impassioned appeal to the masses to support the people's government.

They had all undertaken to study this document in detail, but had been too busy to do more than read it through. It was voted on clause by clause, and accepted. All this took place in the du Preez' living-room, a large and comfortable place whose sideboard was stacked with bottles of beer. Piet said he couldn't face a whole evening's argy-bargy without beer – he wouldn't do it for his union and he was damned if he would do it for the Party. Anton disapproved, but nevertheless these days they sat around on the floor drinking beer in an atmosphere of friendly ease quite different from the early meetings in the office over Black Ally's.

Towards the end, contented with themselves and with the document, they were preparing to leave for bed when Maisie, who had joined the group in order, as she explained, 'to save argument with Andrew', spoke for the first time. She said: 'What I want to know is this. I mean to say, what's the point? You – I mean, we, aren't even standing for elections, so there's no chance of putting any of it into practice. And Andrew explained to me yesterday about there's no revolutionary situation now, so you aren't thinking of being in power at all. So why go to all this trouble?'

Anton said: 'But Comrade Maisie, it is our responsibility to put forward a policy so that the people will know where we stand.'

'But you're a secret group, so they can't know, can they?'

Here Athen intervened, speaking direct to Maisie, as was his way – he never made general speeches to the group: 'Maisie, you must try to understand it. We may be only a few here. But we are more than just a few people. We are the communist ideal. The leadership of ELAS in the mountains spoke like the government, with the authority of a government, to give self-respect to the people. And if two communists find themselves somewhere – let us say suddenly in a strange town, they know they are not just two people, but that they are communism. And they must behave with self-respect because they represent the idea. And if there is even one communist – suppose any one of us finds himself alone somewhere, or perhaps in prison or sentenced to death, then he must never feel himself alone – except as a man, because as a man he is alone and that is good. But he is a communist and therefore not alone.' He smiled at Maisie, and she, after a thoughtful silence, smiled back, afterwards letting her eyes return, with a serious query in them, to her husband, who took his pipe out of his mouth and nodded at her, as if to say: Yes, that's true.

Piet said jocularly: 'Well, we can take over the Government any day now. All we need is to explain to our white fellow-citizens that we're the men for the job. After all, we don't seem to have any Africans with us, do we?' Anton frowned, but said nothing. For some time Piet had been making remarks of this nature: he had become the privileged clown of the group, who could say things no one else could.

They went home feeling – in spite of the fact that Maisie's as it were lay objections had struck home uncomfortably into each of them – cheered and supported by the existence of the long and workmanlike Policy which, could they put it into practice, could have the whole territory well on the way to socialism in five years.

Martha woke thinking of the document – thinking confusedly, something like this: Anton and Andrew drew up the programme, yet they are such different men, and they don't like each other. (She wondered if they knew they disliked each other.) They had no difficulty in agreeing on it; in fact they drew up the first draft in two evenings. Anton once said: Two communists on either side of the world, ought, if presented with the same set of facts, to come to exactly the same conclusions – that is the strength of Marxism. She remembered the stern proud look on his face as he said it. Yet, if someone in the same intransigent mood as Bill Bluett or Jackie Bolton had been in the room last night, then they would have fought every clause, and the rest of the group would not have known what to think. (Now she felt uneasy because the group had agreed so readily, almost gaily to the programme.) What does that mean, then? That a group runs harmoniously when there are a couple of leaders agreed on something, putting it forward for 'the rabbits'. Yes, that must be it. If there was only one leader, we'd be uneasy about it. But two strong personalities supporting each other, and everyone feels confident. Yet it is not as if they didn't invite us to criticize and discuss: both of them keep saying, every time we quote Stalin: Kindly do Comrade Stalin the favour of thinking for yourselves instead of quoting him. All the same, we passed that programme clause after clause as if it were simply a formality to vote at all. There's something wrong somewhere, something I ought to be understanding: the group can only work if the two strongest people in it are in agreement? I must think about it. But how can I? I don't know enough, I simply don't know anything about anything. Yet I'm quite ready to vote on a programme that might affect a whole country . . .

She told herself, dryly, in a change of mood: Luckily there's no danger of any such responsibility. She examined the word *luckily*, told herself that the other comrades were quite correct to criticize her for flippancy, discovered she was acutely depressed, and examined herself for the reason: of course, she was going to get married that morning.

She hurried out of bed, taking dresses down from the cupboard, and discarded them. She should have ironed one last night, they were all crumpled and in fact there were only two fit to wear at all. Why should I bother, she thought: it's nothing but a formality for both of us. Yet, having put on one dress, she removed it and tried the other, and looked at herself in the glass with the old feeling of cautious expectation. It seemed that she had not had time for months to examine her image – and her nail varnish was chipped too, and her hair needed attention. Her face, rather pale, with heavily shadowed dark eyes gazed back at her. She was in a fever of anxiety, the familiar strained irritation, as if she were juggling half a dozen objects in the air at the same time, and knowing she was bound to drop one of them. She examined the severe young face and thought: If I didn't know myself, what would I think? Well, I certainly wouldn't guess all the things that have happened to *her* in the last year, getting divorced, being a communist, getting married again, all the complications and never sleeping enough. No, it's all nonsense, people talking about faces. Faces don't give things away at all – that face says nothing.

Martha, even more discouraged, swung the mirror back, and passed her hand downwards over her body. I'm in one of my thin phases, she thought. Well, I suppose that's something. But I really can't go and get married without stockings – well, why not? No one would even notice. She hastily turned out her drawers, looking for stockings, but they all had ladders in them.

At this point Jasmine came in, and Martha said in despair: 'All my stockings have ladders.'

'Well, don't panic,' said Jasmine composedly, already

sitting down on the bed to strip off her own. As her sunburned legs came into view she glanced at them with approval, and tossed the stockings over to Martha, who put them on. 'You'd better have a cigarette,' she said, lighting one and coming over to put it between Martha's lips. At the same time she gave Martha a cool, diagnostic look and smiled faintly. Martha understood Jasmine's ironic, compassionate expression very well. She even smiled back, with the same irony, but almost immediately she sighed and said: 'We'd better go and get it over with.'

'Take it easy,' said Jasmine, nodding at a chair, and Martha sat in it obediently. 'I saw Mrs Van in the street and she says we should both drop into her office before lunch. So as soon as you've signed on the dotted line, we'll go across.' She said this as if offering a prophylactic against despair, and Martha laughed. Jasmine came clumsily across, put her arms around Martha in a timid squeeze, and said hurriedly: 'It's all right, don't worry.' She nodded, with a shy smile, instantly became serious, and said: 'Then let's go.'

They drove in silence down to the Magistrates' Court. Anton was waiting on the pavement outside it. He was wearing a flower in his jacket, and Martha was upset when she saw it, because if she were wearing a flower it would be dishonest.

But she greeted him with a bright smile, noting that he was smiling with tenderness. But I didn't bargain for it, I didn't bargain for it at all, she thought: she was in danger of bursting into tears. The three of them went into the Court. Mr Maynard was waiting for them. Martha had not remembered that he had married her last time; she was worried that he might mention the coincidence, in case Anton might resent it. But how could he resent it – it would be so inconsistent! But she was relieved that Mr Maynard did not attempt to catch her eye, and was purely the magistrate as he asked the necessary questions. It was all over in two minutes, and Martha saw Mr Maynard turn away with a fourth person, a young man called in from the passage to act as witness, saying: 'Any more for the high jump this morning?' From the unpleasantness of the smile on the young official's face Martha saw that this marriage had been the subject of malicious gossip that morning. Well, of course, she thought, swallowing the idea whole as it were – they are bound to talk, I suppose. They can't approve of me marrying Anton: no money, and an enemy alien at that. Well, let them . . . this defiance made her feel better, although she knew it was childish that she should. Anton had his hand under her elbow. He said in the manner which had been born in the moment Martha had said she would marry him – half fatherly, yet subtly deferential: 'We must go and have a drink to celebrate.'

Martha said quickly: 'But we must go to Mrs Van's office, she wants to see us.' Jasmine, with a demure look, said: 'That's right, Matty's back on duty, wedding or no wedding.' Martha felt there was something possessive in Jasmine when she said this. She took Anton's arm between her hands, and said: 'We'll meet you in the Grill as soon as we've finished,' asserting her identity with him and not with Jasmine.

Relieved, Anton said: 'Of course you must go to Mrs Van. I'll be waiting.' He gave Martha his unused grateful smile and went off by himself, while the two young women directed themselves towards Mrs Van, whose office when they reached it seemed so full of people there was scarcely room for them to squeeze in. The Parliamentary members were all there, together, with Mr Playfair, Johnny Lindsay, Jack Dobie, Marie and Piet du Preez and the African Mr Matushi.

It seemed there was a crisis, which had come about in the following way:

The office of Mrs Van – many years a town councillor, and chairman of half a dozen welfare organizations, was always full of people asking for advice and help. Recently there had been far more Africans and Coloured people than usual. Several African organizations had sprung up, in form and spirit similar to the mutual aid associations characteristic of early British trade unionism but with a flavour peculiar to African development of this period: something sorrowful, bewildered and tentative. The leaders of these new societies found themselves very often in Mrs Van's office. Very often indeed this leader was Mr Matushi, who shared with Mrs Van, and indeed with Jasmine and the group members, the quality of being able to speak at any given moment in half a dozen different capacities. That week, Mr Matushi, asking for Mrs Van's guidance in his capacity as Chairman of the African Advancement League, had slipped into his role as leader of the African Branch of the Labour, or Social Democratic Party – if this Branch were to be allowed to come into being. Mrs Van exclaimed that it would be useful to have a member of Parliament or two to go down to the Township to explain to the Africans certain points of law. Mr Matushi had enthusiastically agreed. Mrs Van had asked the Location Superintendent – a gentleman deferential to her in her role as Town Councillor, to let her have the Location Hall for that Saturday afternoon. Mr Matushi, confirming this, had done so in the name of the African members of the Social Democratic Party.

When Jasmine and Martha had understood how this very delicate situation had arisen, they could not help exchanging glances of amused comprehension – and at once Mrs Van gave them a stern look, as if to say that this was no occasion for private jokes. Perfectly obvious now why Mr McFarline, the green-visaged Mr Thompson and even Mr Playfair were looking so agitated, and why Jack Dobie, Johnny Lindsay and the du Preez were ironically appreciative. In short, the reactionaries believed that Mrs Van had again presented them with a *fait accompli*, while the truth was that the hunger of the Africans for advice and support was so strong it had forced its way through this crack in the white crust – the crack being Mrs Van's maternally concerned heart, and had created a situation before even Mrs Van wanted it.

Mr McFarline, having heard Mrs Van out, said firmly that no African Branch existed, since the Party had not yet taken a vote on whether there should be one. Therefore this meeting could not be described as a meeting of the African Branch. Therefore, since it seemed the meeting could not now be stopped, he suggested it be described as an informal gathering of Africans addressed by a few Europeans.

Mr Thompson said: 'I'm responsible to the people who elected me, and I know that not one of them would agree to white people agitating in the Locations.'

Mrs Van said smoothly that obviously it would be better to have very responsible people addressing this meeting, and she urged Mr McFarline to be one of them.

Mr McFarline said hastily that there was a Select Committee that afternoon. Mr Thompson was booked for the same committee. Five other Parliamentary members were returning to their constituencies that afternoon. There would therefore be only one member of Parliament at the meeting, Jack Dobie. Who, with a small smile, inquired of his fellows whether they would be happy to have their views represented to the Africans by himself.

Mr McFarline said grimly that if Jack Dobie committed the Party to anything at all, he'd be in trouble with his colleagues.

To which Jack retorted that he would speak in his personal capacity with pleasure, because he had no intention of putting forward his dear colleagues' views on the Native Question – they would stick in his throat.

At which Mr Thompson said that obviously the important thing was to make sure the press did not hear a word about what was going forward, because if it got into the newspapers they would all lose their seats.

Mrs Van agreeing to this, the Parliamentary members left in a body, leaving Jack, Johnny, Jasmine, Martha and the du Preez.

Mrs Van then instructed these people as to how they were to conduct themselves that afternoon. Mr Playfair and Jack should be on the platform with herself and Mr Matushi – Mr Matushi had been sitting quietly all this time, watching Mr McFarline and his group with a suspicious and watchful smile – while Marie and Piet and Martha and Jasmine should be responsible for a table for the sale of literature.

The literature was stacked ready. Mrs Van, welfare worker for so many years, had had printed at her own expense several useful pamphlets: How to Keep Your Baby Clean. How to Feed Your Family. Kill those Flies! Three others expressed Mrs Van's other and perhaps deeper self: African Woman, you are not a Slave! How to Conduct a Meeting Properly. The Principles of Trade Unionism.

Mrs Van, still seated behind her table, offered the four communists a smile which was both sprightly and firm, and said: 'Yes, I know you'd rather be selling something about the Red Army, but please restrain yourselves for just one afternoon.'

Jasmine and Martha returned towards the Grill, talking about the meeting. For one thing, neither of them had been inside the Location before; for another, they were confused about whether they ought, as revolutionaries, to be selling pamphlets of such a domestic character. But Jasmine settled this problem by saying: 'In the early days of the Russian Revolution the comrades were out in the backward areas liquidating illiteracy and teaching hygiene, so it must be all right, mustn't it?'

Anton was waiting for them. Maisie and Andrew were there too. The three had been drinking wine and were already festive, and Martha and Jasmine had to remind themselves that this was after all a wedding lunch. A big meal had been ordered. Martha ate loyally, watching herself become gay in proportion as her sense of unease deepened. She made jokes and chattered, carrying on a dialogue with herself at the same time. But if Anton had not arranged something special, wouldn't I have been hurt? I would have thought him unimaginative? So why do I hate this so much? Yesterday he said, and I liked the way he said it, But, Matty, you must not think I would ever be unreasonable. This is not a marriage that would have taken place had it not been for the special circumstances, so we will both be reasonable . . . but I wish we could have done like Marjorie and Colin, and Andrew and Maisie – they got married and told us about it afterwards. But I simply can't stand Anton when he's trying to be gay, and doing the right thing . . .

This miserable inner current took its own way throughout the long meal in the small hot overladen dining-room which was full of businessmen concluding deals over lunch.

Towards its end Maisie asked Martha if she were sure she

had to be at the meeting – 'surely they could do without you for once?' And Martha, while she knew quite well it would make no difference at all whether she were there or not, insisted that she was expected and must go. Again she felt Jasmine's comprehending inspection of her.

They separated on the pavement, Anton kissing Martha before them all, with an awkward jocularity quite foreign to him.

Again Martha and Jasmine hurried away together, this time towards Jasmine's car, in which the pamphlets had been stacked by Mrs Van's office boy. Martha felt guilty: she should have gone with Anton. Jasmine was saying nothing. Martha, as she got into the car, burst out in the falsely jocular voice that reminded her of Anton's a few moments ago: 'I think the whole institution of marriage should be abolished.' Jasmine, determined to protect Martha against herself, said quickly: 'Anton certainly did us all well.' She examined Martha's set face, and said apologetically: 'You know, Matty, I read something just lately: when the middle-class rebel, they become bohemians. When the working-class first break out, it's important they do everything just right.'

Martha understood that Jasmine was referring to them both, and she wanted to laugh at the idea of this demure and sensible girl thinking of herself as bohemian. So the root of Anton's dogged determination to be correct in his behaviour was his working-class origin? In that case, she was being a snob. But she did not believe it, and said so to Jasmine, who insisted that 'it was a well-known fact', and continued to speak of the dangers of bohemianism lying in wait for them both all the way to the Location. The entrance to the place was marked by the fact that the good road gave way to rutted areas of red dust. The car bumped and hooted its way through masses of shouting, laughing, gesticulating Africans with their bicycles.

The hall, a dusty little barn, with a clump of dust-filled trees beside it, was marked out for the afternoon's event by five sleek cars that stood beside it. Jasmine's made the sixth.

The benches of the hall were crammed with men in the threadbare patched clothes of decent poverty, and they sat in silence, watching the platform, where Mrs Van presided. A woman who did not care about clothes, she was wearing a formal afternoon dress which normally she would have lifted down from her wardrobe for a garden party or to open a bazaar with a feeling of irritation that such conventions had to be heeded, but which she had chosen today to show she intended to do honour to an occasion. Beside her sat Johnny Lindsay in shirt-sleeves, his fine craggy face alternately giving encouragement to the Africans and tender approval to Mrs Van. Jack Dobie, representing Parliament, sat on her other side, his small and vigorous body held in readiness, his head cocked sideways, as if he were listening to something off-stage which heralded a humorous disaster.

The literature table was by the door. None of the Africans came to buy. There were no women in the audience at all, so the sellers stacked the welfare pamphlets, How to Keep Your Baby Clean, etc., to one side.

When Mrs Van stood up to speak the men in the hall rose in one movement and began a rhythmic clapping, and would not stop until she pressed them back on to their benches with a Canute-like gesture. She then proceeded to make some sensible and cautionary remarks in the spirit of the informal meeting which had taken place in her office that morning. This was not a meeting of the Social Democratic Party, commonly referred to as the Labour Party, the platform was in no sense to be considered representative of the Party, they were all individuals and speaking as such. The listening men leaned forward, frowning, their brows puckering. And before Mrs Van had come to the end of her speech, Mr Matushi was on his feet, saying passionately that every man present was a signed and paid-up member of the Labour Party – he corrected himself to say: Social Democratic Party, and the white people present were all members of the Executive, and he was speaking for every man present in welcoming the Social Democratic Party to the first political meeting ever to be held in the Location. It was at this point that the Location Superintendent, who had been standing like a sentinel at the door, his face grim with disapproval, left the Hall, obviously on his way to telephone to someone in authority.

Now Johnny Lindsay stood up, and in the face of storms of applause which drowned every word he said, tried to insist that they were all individuals.

The audience were on their feet again, a dozen men trying to out-shout each other. Mrs Van nodded at one of them, who cried out, his face working: 'Now at last we know that there are some Europeans whose hearts are turned in kindness towards us, now we know that we have friends among the Europeans.' There was a roar of grateful approval, and the three people on the platform nodded at each other, wryly, but delighted, relinquishing from that moment on all attempts to stem the flood.

Now a man who had been sitting by himself at the end of a row stood up. It was Elias Phiri, who demanded to know, and with great command of bland language, if this was or was not officially a Social Democratic Party meeting, and if the audience was or was not to take what the platform said as official policy. He noted that Mr Dobie was present, and he, as everyone knew, was a member of Parliament: he was looking forward very much to hearing Mr Dobie speak. He sat down in silence; all the Africans in the Hall were looking at this, their apparent spokesman, with something like apprehension. There was a noise in the Hall like a hiss – the sharp involuntary intake of breath. Slowly the eyes turned to Jack Dobie who was on his feet.

Jack began by saying that he was a supporter of African advancement . . . but a man leaped up to shout: 'Advancement, Mr Dobie? You mean equality – we have for many years read your brave speeches, Mr Dobie. You have spoken for us, you have spoken for our equality.'

Jack Dobie, head cocked on one side, smiling dryly, hesitated very slightly, and then remarked into the still attentiveness of the waiting audience that he was an old socialist, he came from a place in Scotland famed for its militancy and its socialist traditions, he came from the Clyde, and as a socialist he stood for the brotherhood of man . . . it was at this point that the audience finally swept up like a flame into passionate unity with the platform, who abandoned any attempt to keep the words and sentences measured by any thought of electors, white citizens or newspapers.

One after another men rose from the body of the Hall, keen, fervent, desperately earnest men, holding small pieces of paper in their hands which they never looked at, since the flood of their anger or their hope fed words into their mouths which kept the audience laughing, clapping, groaning approval. One after another they demanded justice, freedom, brotherhood, kindness, understanding; they aired all the injustices that hurt them – phrased formally in the words of blue-books or white papers – the question of education for their children, the Pass laws, the fact that they had no vote, that their cattle were being killed in the Reserves – but every one of these bricks in the building of their servitude served as a stepping-stone to impassioned oratory. The platform answered questions, made small corrections of fact, sat smiling, and the four communists sat by the literature table, watching and listening, caught up in the hunger, the unity and the brotherhood that beat through the Hall like drums, and feeling that at last they were coming somewhere near the source of their need for service.

And it was not long before the division between the platform and the literature sellers broke: one of the men in the Hall demanded why it was that the white workers – 'for they work with their hands, they are workers, they call themselves workers' – did not support the Africans, their fellow-workers, in their fight for their right to skilled work. Mrs Van nodded at Piet, Executive Committee member for the building trades, who leaped up on his great clumsy legs on to the platform and spoke for half an hour on the principles of trade unionism. There was a point, too, when Mrs Van interrupted a lean, bent, spectacled teacher who was demanding education – 'for if we are children, as the Europeans say we are, then as children we demand education as a right so that we may grow to men' – to say: 'Men *and* women, sir, may I point out that there is not a woman here this afternoon? And why not? Are your wives fit for

239

cooking and bearing your children but not to stand side by side with you in your struggle?'

The audience seemed abashed, but rather in deference to Mrs Van's qualities than to the force of her arguments. Whereupon Mrs Van invited Marie du Preez, in her capacity as secretary for a women's organization, and therefore an expert on the subject, to address the audience on women's advancement. Marie met a sideways grin from her husband with a dignified lift of her head, and went soberly to the platform. She, like Mrs Van, had put on an afternoon dress to do honour to the Africans, and, as she stood facing the audience, broad-faced, rather flushed, her capable body draped in flowered silk, her feet restless in high shoes which were hurting her (she had kicked them off under the literature sales table), she looked the image of a white 'missus' long used to handling servants. 'This question of women's rights,' she began, in a reasonable voice, 'is a complicated one . . .' At which Piet, sitting between Martha and Jasmine, both of whom told him he should be ashamed, said loudly, while maintaining a husbandly grin: 'You're telling me.' Marie stopped in the middle of a sentence, glaring at him. She put her hands on her hips, her body took on an Amazon's pose, she allowed her eyes to return, slowly, to the audience, after a slow, diminishing inspection of her husband, and began: 'The whole lot of you ought to be damned well ashamed of yourselves. Men! If there's one thing that teaches me there's no such thing as colour it is that men are men, black and white. You can't tell me! There you sit, sixty of you, every man jack of you with a little woman at home running after you like great boobies with your food and your comforts, and out *you* come, lords and masters, to sit talking, making decisions, and when you get back home you'll say: Is the supper ready!'

The men listening, not sure how to take her, saw her husband lolling back in his chair and watching her with appreciative derision, and slowly they began to smile, and then to laugh, but with her, not against her. Marie, standing on two firmly planted legs, one hand on her hip, admonished them collectively with a dignified forefinger, and

launched into an abridged account of the suffragette movement, the history of which she told them they would do
well to study because if they, the so-called intelligentsia of
the Africans, continued to treat their women as they were
doing now she, Marie du Preez, would personally make it
her business to see that the African women of the town
started a suffragette movement of their own.

At this point the Superintendent came back, scowling as
bad-temperedly as when he had left. He stood, rather puzzled, at the door for a moment: Marie was declaiming at the
top of her voice, calling the men in front of her a lot of
conscienceless exploiters of human labour, arrogant slave-
drivers, petty domestic dictators. Then, giving it up, he went
to the platform and informed Mrs Van that the meeting had
overrun its alloted span by half an hour and must close at
once.

The lecture on women's rights thus abruptly being brought
to an end, Marie returned to her husband's side, remarking:
'There, you old ram, that's a piece of my mind for you and
for all of you – a communist you call yourself.' To which he
replied, pretending to cringe and writhe: 'What've you got
for my supper?' And she, with great dignity: 'Wait and see.'
But she was unable to maintain it. She suddenly flushed
and smiled at him in reply to his broad smile, and said in a
normal voice: 'All the same, you're a pain in the neck and
that's a fact.'

People were already rising to their feet, and as the three
descended from the platform, groups of Africans surged
around them in anxious insistence, as if this personal
contact might bring their collective hunger nearer to
appeasement. Some of them crowded around the literature
table. In a few moments all the copies of Principles of Trade
Unionism and How to Conduct a Meeting had gone, while
the welfare pamphlets remained untouched. The Superintendent stood by the table watching, and making notes of
the titles of the pamphlets.

As the white people left the Hall, a group of women who
had been standing under the bunch of trees came forward,
pushing in front of them some small children holding

bouquets. After urging, the children presented a bouquet to each of the white people. There was a great deal of nodding, smiling, shy curtsies.

Martha and Jasmine sat in their car, the bouquets on their knees, both profoundly depressed. Jasmine was nearly in tears.

'It doesn't matter what one does in this bloody place,' she burst out, 'all we are is a bunch of do-gooders uplifting the poor. And do you know, Matty, what I was feeling all the time, I was hating those men for being so damned grateful, and I could feel myself becoming more and more condescending and pleased with myself inside . . .' Here she burst into tears, and Martha put her arm around her. She had been feeling the same, and disliked herself for it.

Almost at once Jasmine stopped herself crying and said: 'Sorry, Matty, I'd forgotten this was a special day for you. Well, I won't offer to help move your things – I expect you'd rather be alone. And I'll spend the evening with my parents for a change.'

'Are they speaking to you yet?'

'They're trying to marry me off to a business friend of Dad's.'

She tried to laugh, but failed. 'You know, Matty, I've been thinking . . . I don't know how to say it – but I go home, and there's the house, nothing ever changes, Mum and Dad always the same, and when I'm in it it is hard to believe how the world is changing, and what it's like in the group. And I think, suppose I married this man, well, he's quite nice, in a couple of years I'd be just like them, and I'd be thinking like them . . . don't you see, Matty – well, there are times when everything scares me.'

Here she hurriedly squeezed Martha's shoulders with a convulsive pressure of her arm, and said with forlorn cheerfulness: 'Well, never mind, we'll all be dead in a hundred years!'

Martha found Anton, surrounded by packed suitcases and piles of books, seated on his bed in his hotel, waiting for her. It seemed that the lease for the new flat had not been signed and that he wanted her to go down to the lawyer's office to sign it. She had expected him to have dealt with it, for she had searched for the flat, interviewed lawyers and landlord and made terms.

'But I was at the meeting,' she said, 'I thought you'd fix it.' She sounded peevish, and she hastened to alter the tone of her voice to a plaintive humour. 'But, Anton, all you had to do was to sign the thing.'

He said quickly, with a note in his voice she had not heard before, something grumpy and accusing: 'But, Matty, you're good at these things and I'm not.'

Martha was silent from surprise. She had never considered herself good at practical things; while Anton was surely a practical man above anything else?

But she said she would rush down to the office before it closed, sign the lease, get the keys and meet Anton at the flat.

'But Matty, all this luggage here, how can I move it?' He gazed at her patiently, waiting for her to solve this problem.

'Anton, for God's sake! Call a taxi, or ring up Jasmine and borrow her car.'

There was a gleam of dislike in his eyes. She was amazed and frightened. Then she turned this corner of crisis by using the tone she despised, becoming gay and coaxing: 'But, Anton darling, how can you be so *silly*?'

She kissed him, he brightened, and said grumpily: 'Well, Matty, of course you're right.'

She left him, running, for it was late, and almost collided with a young man on the pavement, who said: 'Mrs Knowell, just a moment.' She stopped. 'Were you at that meeting in the Location this afternoon? Would you care to make a statement about it?'

'What for?'

'I'm from the *News*.'

Martha instantly sobered, and said: 'You must see Mrs Van der Bylt.'

'But she's not in her office and I can't get her at her house.'

'Well, I'm sorry – and I'm very late for something.' Martha ran off, thinking: Trouble, trouble, trouble! But she forgot about it, because there was the signing of the lease, and then getting the flat into some sort of shape so they could sleep in it, and she hadn't bought any food yet. She had understood that from now on all the practical details of life would have to be dealt with by herself. This was such a reversal of her idea of Anton that she needed time to think about it.

Chapter Four

When Mrs Van returned to her home from 'the meeting in the Location' (the reporters used this phrase first; and it stuck: thereafter, when anybody said, 'the meeting in the Location', it was in the way one might say: the year war broke out) she found herself faced with immediate demands on her temper and time of the kind she was very familiar with. As she entered the house her husband put his head around the door of his study and demanded to know where the servant had put his spectacles. Simultaneously, the house-boy – the servant in question – appeared to say that a missus was waiting in the living-room to see her.

'Missus wants to see you very bad, missus,' said this young man, in the intimate easy way of a contented servant in a good feudal household.

'Who is it, Mutisi?'

'Mrs Maynard, missus.'

'Please tell her that I shall come as soon as I can, but that might be kept a few minutes.'

Mrs Van entered her husband's study after knocking and receiving permission to enter.

Mr Van der Bylt was one of the town's half-dozen barristers. A lean, grey-haired, dryly humorous gentleman of precise vocabulary, he was as well known in his way as his wife was in hers. He was associated with the type of case which in a small town is followed by the more humble citizens like a protracted sports contest, but with a delighted, tongue-in-cheek malice. He was expert in company law, mining law, land rights: expert, that is, in everything to do with the conflicts of property, but on the highest possible level. He had never, except very early in his career, taken on cases which concerned murder, robbery, violence, or debt. The conflicts of human passion bored him; the expression on his face when as a young lawyer he had unwillingly become involved in them suggested a faintly tolerant distaste. But when a couple of large mining companies disputed, or one newspaper group grappled with another, or a chain store competed for the soul of a town with its rival, then he was at his ease. On such occasions he would shut himself in his study for weeks at a time, studying the refinements of the law like a chess-player. The busy lawyers who briefed him for such cases did so with relief, for it was not necessary to do the usual spadework of preparation when he was Counsel for defence or prosecution. Nobody understood why a man who was by temperament a lawyer took silk except his wife, who knew it was because as a lawyer he would not have been able to avoid involving himself in those other, lower, sordid cases of emotion and crime. When Mrs Van had first understood this, very early in their marriage, her eyes had been used to rest on him – not in irony, for this she would never have allowed herself, but with a certain quality of calm quizzical appraisal.

Yet interestingly enough, for the white citizenry of the town Mr Van played the same role in his field as she did in hers. This nation of petty bourgeoisie were all able to defend and explain in its manifold branches and guises the theory which is expressed in popular language by the phrases: 'If a man has anything in him he can make good,' 'A man must rely on himself,' 'A man must have initiative.' They hated 'big business' more than the devil or even the blacks of the Colony. They hated cartels, trusts, combines, and syndicates, hated above all 'the company' which had once governed this territory, been officially dispossessed by the Legislative Assemblies, but which had, so to speak, gone underground, transmogrifying itself in a hundred different names and shapes. Therefore, when Mr Van's name appeared in the pages of the *News* day after day for weeks during the course of some battle between giants, those independence-loving citizens felt that his dry cold phrase in some way expressed their hatred of finance capital, their delight when 'the dirty work at the top' was exposed to them. Nothing would have surprised Mr Van more than this view of himself, for he would have scorned to take his stand on anything more than a point of the law.

Recently, however, he had accepted a case quite out of his usual run. Two small Afrikaans farmers from E— had been feuding for years over some boundary fence. A hundred yards of ground was in question. Their hatred for each other had reached a pitch which one had started a veld fire inside the other's fence (he claimed it was his land and he had a right to burn it) and destroyed not only his rival's but his own grazing for the season. Mr Van had plunged into this case with a salty relish quite foreign to him. He was a member of a younger branch of an old and respected Cape family, a family which drew its strength from the soil even now. During these weeks Mrs Van had been tending her husband with a new and even gay appreciation. Mr Van did not understand the reason for it; it disquieted him.

He was a man who needed a great deal of attention from his wife. In his home he remained in his study, wearing an old dressing-gown and slippers, and continually summoned his wife to play cards with him, to read to him, or arrange his cushions and find his books. He was, it was understood, an invalid.

On this evening the telephone had been ringing for over an hour from the *News*. He had repeated a dozen times that his wife's business was not his, and he knew nothing that could be of any interest to the newspapers. Now, when Mrs Van had found his spectacles, he said to her: 'Well, my dear, have you had a satisfactory afternoon?' and the dry and courteous voice familiar to the city's courts sounded like the creak of a closing door.

She said: 'I think quite satisfactory on the whole.' She sat in a stiff chair, holding her back rigid. For some months she had been suffering from a pain in her back. She was overworking, she thought. Later 'when things were not so busy' she would rest. By this she meant, when the political crisis was over: in her own way, Mrs Van suffered from the prevalent mood of apocalyptism. Things were so bad, she

247

thought, 'the native problem' so acute, there were so many unhappy people, that the situation could not possibly continue. Common sense must prevail, and then she could rest. Meanwhile she waited opposite her husband, conscious that Mrs Maynard, two rooms away, was fretting for her arrival. But it had been understood from the beginning of this marriage that Mrs Van's duties were first to her children, then to her husband, and finally to her work. Mrs Maynard must wait.

Mr Van der Bylt was this evening preparing a complicated transfer of shares from a gold mine to a copper mine. The controlling interest in both mines was owned by the same company which under another name was part of the complex of capital in a major group on the Rand. The transfer was being disputed, but almost humorously (or at least, that is how Mr Van saw it), for the party who objected to the transfer was, in another guise, the party who wanted it. In short, this was one of the shadowy and ambiguous negotiations in which Mr Van took so much pleasure, and he was looking forward to an evening of law-chopping. But the telephone had been ringing for an hour; he knew that there was going to be yet another newspaper fuss in which his name would be prominent. His wife sat before him talking about some meeting or other, her eyes resting on him indeed, but warm with remembered political passion.

The relations between this couple were, as the phrase goes, very well adjusted, and though Mr Van was in the habit of remarking: 'Marriage is a question of compromise,' while Mrs Van marked her agreement with him by a calm but emphatic nod, this state of affairs was due to decisions taken by her, and a very long time ago.

There had been two great illuminations in this woman's life. The first, when she was a girl of eighteen, already engaged to the promising young solicitor who was the son of a friend of her father's, she had been taken to England and to Switzerland by her aunt in order to broaden her mind. Like her future husband she was a member of an old Cape family, solid comfort behind and around her, brought up in a small sleepy South African village which was the centre of a fruit-farming district. Her aunt was a decent capable woman who was fond of saying to her niece: 'You must remember, my dear, that over in Europe they have no idea at all about our problems with the Kaffirs, so it is much better not to discuss that sort of thing.' During the voyage over, the girl had read *The Story of a South African Farm* and this had begun an intellectual revolution in her. But not a sign of this appeared in her face or in her behaviour, for she allowed herself to be taken to dances, introduced to distant relatives and walked around the London parks, the very model of a well-chaperoned young girl. The year was 1913. At night she read behind locked doors, got hold of suffragist and socialist newspapers and by the time the year was over had come to a conclusion. It was that she had been brought up in a backward part of a country whose ideas were decades behind the times, and that although several hundred pounds had been spent on her education she knew nothing about the world. The second conclusion was that while she was in sympathy with the ideas of the suffragettes and that section of the socialist movement with ideas which she characterized as 'pacifist', she could never hope to participate emotionally in all these exciting European currents. More, to allow herself to be stirred by them before she even understood them would be foolish. She formulated this quite clearly, and on a certain occasion. It was after having told her aunt she was going to church, she had slipped out for a couple of hours to attend an international socialist congress in Berne. She listened to the speakers without opening her mouth once or talking to any of the other people there, and returned to her hotel, where she sat in her room for several hours with her hands folded, her calm blue eyes fixed on the wall. She told herself, while she remembered the fervour of the socialist speakers: 'In South Africa we haven't reached that stage yet. And besides, I shall be marrying Jan quite soon. When I'm married and independent I shall educate myself and find out what I ought to do.' She imagined herself discussing her new ideas with her husband. She imagined how they would act together.

When she returned home, she considered her Jan seriously

in the light of what she had learned in Europe and decided that her parents had chosen well for her. Her fiancé's dryly humorous and judicious manner seemed to her a proof that she could count on him to share her ideas. She married him and a month later had understood she had been mistaken: she was superior to her husband. But she did not do what nearly all women do when they understand they have made a bad bargain – create an image and fight a losing battle sometimes for years, in the no-man's-land between image and the truth. She told herself that her development must depend on her own efforts and that they must be secret efforts.

This had become plain to her one night when her husband had come to bed after sitting up late to prepare a case and had found her reading Ingersoll. He had already taken her into his arms when he saw the title of the book lying beside her pillow. At this he had withdrawn his arms and turned away, remarking in his humorously dry voice: 'I see you have better company than me, my dear. Sleep well.' That night she had lain awake, and again it was emotion that she decided she must ban from her life. Emotion was dangerous. It could destroy her.

She was already pregnant, but her first child was her husband, and she thereby put herself beyond being hurt by him.

She had seven children during the next fifteen years, and was a devoted mother and a good housewife. At night she read and studied; books and newspapers came from Britain and from America. In complete isolation, for there was no one in that small village with whom she could share her ideas, she became an atheist, a socialist, and a believer in racial equality – this last was the hardest, because of the way she had been brought up.

When her husband moved the family northwards she had welcomed the change: she was going to a capital, though it was the capital of a country even more backward than her own. She settled the family in and then looked about her. She began by working for the women's and welfare organizations, became a town councillor and a member of the embryo Social Democratic Party, at that stage consisting of a few white trade unionists who used the slogans of socialism in defence of their own position, which was to protect their living standards against the black workers. Soon she was secretary. It had taken her seven years of patient work to get this socialist party to accept the principle that when it got into power it would nationalize the means of production, distribution and exchange. On the day this was accepted by Congress, Mrs Van had celebrated her victory – not by herself, as for years she had celebrated her private achievements, with a present to herself of a new book or a library subscription, but with two dear friends, Jack Dobie and Johnny Lindsay. They opened a bottle of wine in Johnny's tiny house which was on the edge of the Coloured Quarter, and drank to the victory of world socialism and to the brotherhood of mankind.

Since then the Social Democratic Party had become official opposition to the Government. Her children were grown-up. She had nine grandchildren. She was a happy woman, at the height of her powers, looking forward to a seat in Parliament and (she hoped secretly) in the Cabinet, for she knew herself to be more capable than all but one of the present Cabinet, the Prime Minister himself, and more efficient than any of the possible Government save for Mr McFarline, whose knowledge of finance she respected although she despised his principles.

Mr Van had watched his wife's determined advance towards her own goal, made his small dry comments, flicked little whips of sarcasm at her, supported her publicly, and privately thought her a cold and unpassionate woman. Even more privately he was relieved. And perhaps he was even relieved that she was immune from being hurt by him. Yet in his own way he redressed the balances. Throughout their early married life Mrs Van had been used to being woken, after a hard day with her young children, and after her session of study with her books (for never once had he broken into her hours of reading; it was as if they had come to an agreement that he should not) with a demand for attention of some kind. And never once had she failed him.

251

With indomitable cheerfulness, even if she had perhaps slept an hour or a couple of hours a night for weeks, she would arouse herself, rub his back, make him tea, play chess with him, and discuss interminably whether his symptoms might be those of sciatica or lumbago. It was as if he were saying: If I'm one of your children then I demand the same attention.

Now she sat, hands folded, in front of him, telling him about the meeting in which he was quite uninterested, listened to his variations on the theme that he might be losing the sight of one eye, agreed with him that the dust this year was particularly bad and the grandchildren might expect to suffer from stomach complaints because of it, and did not move until he said: 'Well, my dear, I expect you have more interesting things than me to attend to.' At which she rose, carefully, for her back hurt her, kissed his cheek, said that they would meet for dinner in half an hour, and went to her living-room. In the few seconds it took her to reach it she had considered all the reasons that might have brought Mrs Maynard to her, and decided it must be something to do about rehousing the Coloured community, a question they agreed on. They hardly ever agreed about anything.

But as soon as she saw Mrs Maynard, who rose quickly at her entrance, a long rope of pearls sliding over her black lace-shrouded bosom, her face flushed, her dark eyes sombre and agitated, she knew there was something else, something she had not made allowances for. She offered Mrs Maynard a drink, and Mrs Maynard said violently: 'Yes, a stiff one please.' Mrs Van rang for the servant, ordered the drinks to be brought in, and the two women sat facing each other inquiring about each other's husbands until the servant made himself scarce so they could get down to business.

These two women had been working together on the city's committees for many years, respected each other's capacities, and disapproved of each other utterly.

But there was something more. During interminable committee meetings, at which they nearly always took opposite viewpoints, they would sometimes watch each other with a private and rather uneasy speculation.

For here was Mrs Van, radical by conviction, known to everyone as 'a Kaffir-lover', a socialist and a libertarian. And yet surely she was deeply conservative by nature and by temperament? The pattern of her life showed it, with its ranks of solid, unradical children, its complement of well-brought-up grandchildren, its comfort and its order.

And here was Mrs Maynard, conservative by conviction, unegalitarian, aristocratic. Yet surely there was something romantically anarchistic in her that was shown by her cabinet of wire-pulling ladies, and her passion for intrigue and even her handsome husband with his discreet but of course gossiped-about liaisons – particularly his long-standing affair with Mrs Talbot, who had been hovering in the wings of Mrs Maynard's life for so long, beautiful, outrageous and victorious. Then there was the one son in contrast to Mrs Van's well-founded family, the unsatisfactory Binkie. And no grandchildren at all. When Mrs Maynard came to the Van der Bylt house, there were grandchildren playing on the veranda or in the garden, but in her own home, only the bridge-playing women, the committees of self-appointed vigilantes of public order. No grandchildren, and no sign of any grandchildren.

Mrs Maynard had made a hundred attempts to win Mrs Van over to become a member of her 'cabinet', partly because of her rival's ability, partly out of her curiosity about the hidden anomaly which both matched and contradicted her own.

But Mrs Van, the radical, would have nothing to do with the secret processes of private government. She rested herself on the processes of democratic government: committee work, agenda-balancing and election. She preferred to do solid boring detailed work in an organization for seven years in order to prove that she was worthy of election at the end of them. Mrs Van, the socialist, did everything by the book, according to the rules, and in the open.

This then was the contradiction which made them watch

each other and reflect about themselves. It was this contradiction which was going to show itself now. Both knew it and showed that they knew it by the way they waited for the servant to leave the room and close the door behind him.

'Well, Mrs Maynard?' said Mrs Van, nodding as if she were a chairman giving a signal to speak.

'Look here, my dear,' said Mrs Maynard, brusquely. 'I've got to ask you something. And it's something pretty tricky.'

Mrs Van merely nodded.

'You know that gal Maisie Gale? She's one of the communists. At least, they've got hold of her. Something like that.'

Mrs Van reviewed a dozen faces in her memory, and shook her head.

'But you must know. She runs around with them. At any rate, this is the thing. She was engaged to my son Binkie. She got herself in the family way. Instead of coming to us about it like a sensible gal, the next thing we heard was she married one of the airmen, a sergeant I believe, or something like that.'

Mrs Van noted that Mrs Maynard was almost incoherent with spite.

'This girl Maisie, didn't she tell your son she was pregnant?'

'Not a word,' said Mrs Maynard dramatically. 'And when my husband went to see her she was abominably rude.'

'How did you get to know she was pregnant?'

Mrs Maynard said quickly: 'We heard it. But the point is Binkie is heart-broken. He's got compassionate leave. He will be here in a month. And of course it's impossible to get the gal to see reason.'

'You say she has married someone else?'

'Oh some ridiculous person, a man from the camp.'

Mrs Van said nothing. She filled Mrs Maynard's empty glass and sat waiting.

'You have influence,' said Mrs Maynard. 'You know them. And there's that Quest girl. She's a friend of Maisie's.'

'I know Mrs Knowell of course.'

'Mrs Hesse now. She married that German.'

Mrs Van said, surprised: 'Really, when?'

'My husband married them this morning – absurd. But that's not the point. It's Binkie's child. And that gal Maisie will not answer my letters or even see my husband.'

Mrs Van thought: She got married this morning and was at the meeting this afternoon. She was touched for a thousand private reasons. Yet she disapproved of Martha. To leave a husband was pardonable although – as she had herself proved, hardly necessary. To leave a child was unforgivable. Yet she was moved, deeply, and where she did not want to be touched at all.

She came out of private reflections to hear Mrs Maynard say: 'And so I would be very grateful if you'd undertake to talk to that Maisie creature, or get the Quest gal to talk to her.'

Mrs Van said: 'But, Mrs Maynard, I really don't understand you. The girl's presumably of age. She married this man of her own free will. It's her affair.' She added, since Mrs Maynard showed complete incredulity: 'It's not my affair. And it's not yours either. If she's married she's married. Are you suggesting she should divorce this man again to marry your son?'

'But it's all a mistake. It's all a terrible terrible mistake,' Mrs Maynard cried out, and her eyes were full of tears. She directed them hopefully at her antagonist, realized that completely divergent principles were in conflict and stood up saying: 'These RAF – they should never have been allowed into the country.'

'But my dear, they are here after all because of the war.'

Mrs Maynard, with a wistful glance at a small table on which stood framed photographs of half a dozen small children, said: 'I'm sorry to have taken up your time,' and departed in an energetic wave of black lace.

Mrs Van had not yet had a chance to ring for dinner when the servant announced yet another 'missus' and a woman she did not know came hurriedly into the room saying: 'I'm sorry to disturb you but I simply must ask you . . .' Mrs Van urged her to sit down – but she would not; offered her a drink, but she refused it. She was Mrs Quest, she said, and she simply had to know . . .

Mrs Quest, in a severe tailored dress and a severe dark hat, was almost as girlishly agitated as Mrs Maynard had been. Mrs Van, whose thoughts had already returned to housing estates and public meetings, again recognized personal crises, and again in a matron as old as herself – at an age, that is, to be past them.

Mrs Quest cried out that her daughter had married a German, had not even told her parents, and perhaps Mrs Van could . . . she burst into tears, dried them with a look of annoyance, and said briskly: 'Perhaps if you could talk to her she would see reason.'

For the second time that evening Mrs Van said: 'But she's married, isn't she?' as if saying all there could possibly be said.

Mrs Van felt herself divided. One half she was a mother disapproving of a daughter who had behaved badly. But the other was occupied with brooding, almost wistful thoughts which hovered on the border of a region of her mind marked *Danger*. Mrs Van's common-sensical self soothed Mrs Quest, made her take a drink, murmured that young people these days had no standards, but it was due to the war and the unsettled times we lived in. At the same time she was thinking: She got married this morning, but she came to the meeting this afternoon, she cares so much about that she put it before getting married . . . but there's something wrong somewhere.

Mrs Quest left at last, as flurried as when she had come, saying that she had no intention of going anywhere near Martha until the girl had come to her parents and apologized for her behaviour. Mrs Van gave her husband his dinner, ate sensibly herself, although she was not hungry, talked about the prices of copper and the rise in copper shares, and saw to it that Mr Van was settled comfortably for the evening.

Afterwards she stood on her dark veranda, observing the moonlight that flooded her garden. The garden boy had left the sprinkler on. Fine gleams of light played over a sparkling dark lawn. The dark trees that edged the road stood massively still. An earthy, cold and secret perfume came again and again to her face: she turned herself towards it. It was from her rose garden which, catching a wide-flung spray of water from the sprinkler, glistened distantly under the trees. Mrs Van took a pair of secateurs from a shelf on the veranda, went swiftly into her garden and cut a great bunch of roses that, as she gathered them together, flung drops of water off into the grass where they lay glinting like small hard jewels. She carried the prickling bunch of roses in her arms to the car, laid them carefully on the seat, and drove herself off down-town towards the flat where Mrs Quest had said Martha had moved that day. She drove fast and even recklessly through the stream of cars that were pouring towards the cinemas. She was full of an uneasy emotion which she did not recognize, for she felt it so seldom – guilt. She was guilty because of what she felt about that girl, Mrs Quest's daughter; and now the full soft perfume of the roses, loosening and warming in the car, irritated her so that she rolled down a window to let the cool air in.

When she knocked on the door of that flat there was a noise of laughter and voices and she thought: I'm glad there's a wedding party, I'll stay five minutes and leave the roses.

The room was full of faces she knew, but little furniture. There were two narrow beds, not yet made up, both loaded with people. On one perched her old friends Johnny Lindsay and Jack Dobie, as well as Jasmine, and Marie and Piet du Preez. On the floor sat a large pretty fair girl who held the hand of a man in uniform. Mrs Van gave this couple a swift second glance and as it were inwardly nodded: Yes, that'll do, they respect each other. She did not say of young couples: They're in love. When her daughters had brought their young men to the house she had diagnosed: She respects him. Or: She does not respect him, and took up an attitude accordingly. Now she saw the warm trustful look on the pregnant girl's face, liked Andrew, and thought: I hope that Maynard woman'll leave them alone. I'd like him for a son-in-law.

Beside Maisie sat Tommy. Mrs Van greeted this youth with an especial smile: he had come, inarticulate with emotion, into her office the day before to demand advice as to whether he should 'throw everything up' and 'make his way somehow, I'll find a way, you'll see' – to China, where he proposed to fight with the Chinese Red Army. Mrs Van had advised him against this, had suggested various books to read, notably a history of the British Labour Movement. He returned her smile with the abashed and earnest blush of a boy.

On the other bed were Anton Hesse and Martha and several men in uniform. On an up-ended suitcase on the floor was a young South African journalist from the *News*. Mrs Van allowed him to rise and offer her the suitcase on which she sat, spreading full skirts. He stood against the empty wall and said: 'Mrs Van, we've been trying to reach you all evening. Your husband said you were out.'

'I was out. And then I was busy,' she returned, her hands still full of the roses, which no one had remarked on. She felt put out because she was back in her usual role: she noted that even her dear friends and allies Jack and Johnny were sitting back and ready to let her do battle for them. 'And now,' she said, smiling towards the Hesse couple, 'I'm here for a wedding celebration. I'm off duty.'

'But I say!' said the journalist, 'that's not good enough, you know. And you'll blame us if we get our facts wrong tomorrow.'

At this everyone burst into a loud and spontaneous laughter, while the journalist frowned, and remained frowning.

But the atmosphere was friendly enough. They all knew him. He was fresh on the job of attending their meetings. He took them aside afterwards to say that he sympathized with their ideas and they were not to blame him if the editor ordered him sometimes to alter the wording of his reports.

Mrs Van said smiling: 'But Mr Roberts, I sent in a report of the meeting to the editor this afternoon. Didn't he get it?'

'He sent me out to see you,' said Mr Roberts, who was both embarrassed and aggressive. 'Mr Dankwertz' – this was the Location Superintendent – 'rang us up to say that it was a very important occasion.'

'In that case Mr Dankwertz needs to be spoken to,' said

the Town Councillor. 'It is not his job to give reports to the press.'

'Come on, man, have a drink,' said Jack Dobie, his small face crinkled up with a mixture of disgust and amusement: his expression whenever faced with any representative of what he always referred to as the capitalist press.

Two bottles of Cape wine stood on the bare boards of the floor. Anton Hesse unfolded himself from his place in the corner, poured red wine into a cheap tumbler, and handed it to the journalist. Mrs Van thought: He looks pleased with himself. She looked at Martha and thought: No, she does not respect him.

The door opened again with violence. Another young man came in, who nodded professionally at Mr Roberts and at once took out a notebook. People exchanged glances and put themselves on the alert. This was a senior sub-editor, a tough and ambitious young man, quite a different proposition from the still unhardened Roberts. Mrs Van said to him: 'Mr du Plessis, if you're looking for me I'm here on personal business, and I'm not ready to be interviewed.'

Mr du Plessis stiffened. He was thin and wiry, with a hard and pushing face and his eyes had the combative stare of an enemy never off guard.

'Mrs Van der Bylt, I'd like to interview you about your Party's activities in the Location this afternoon. I have half an hour before it must go to the printers.'

'I sent the editor a report.'

'I'd like to ask you some questions. I've been chasing you since five o'clock this afternoon,' he added with open hostility.

'These people are having a party,' she said. 'I really do think you might have asked before coming in.'

'Were all the people in this room in the Location this afternoon?'

'A full list of the names of the people present has been given to the editor.'

Mr du Plessis examined, one after another, the faces of the people around him, lingering on Piet du Preez.

'I understand you were making speeches about trade

unionism,' he remarked. 'Trade unionism and political organization.'

'And women's rights,' remarked Martha, suddenly laughing. At the sound of the laugh Mrs Van turned her attention to her, noting that the laugh seemed to break the young woman's face up: the lower half seemed to grimace while the dark eyes remained serious and watchful. Mrs Van involuntarily looked down at the still water-fresh roses. But scarlet petals had already scattered on to the bare boards beside her sturdy brown shoes.

Mr du Plessis, bursting into open combat before he had intended to, because of the general laugh which had followed Martha's, said: 'Mrs Van, if you will not answer any questions you can take the consequences.'

'If there are any inaccuracies in the paper tomorrow the Party's lawyers will see to it,' she replied emphatically, and turned her back on him.

Mr du Plessis shut his notebook and nodded peremptorily at Roberts, who was embarrassed because of his colleague's behaviour: he had been standing silent against the wall, with an ashamed smile, glancing in appeal at the young people sitting on the beds, as if to say: 'Don't blame me for it!' Now he gave another appealing glance around, said: 'So long!' and followed du Plessis out.

Mrs Van said: 'Poor boy,' sounding maternally contemptuous.

Instantly Jack said: 'Poor boy my foot. He's half an inch from being as bad as du Plessis. Don't you start wasting your sympathy on that bunch of vultures.'

Again everyone laughed; and Mrs Van smiled patiently until she was able to remark: 'All the same, he's not a bad boy. He's ignorant, but he's learning.'

'Learning what?' said Jack. 'He doesn't resign when the editor re-writes his pieces for him and that's enough for me.'

At this Mrs Van and Johnny exchanged the loving glances of tolerant people for a hot-headed intransigent, although both of them in the past had played the role of intolerant while the others smiled.

Mrs Van's eyes again came to rest on the roses while she

wondered how best to present them. She observed that Martha was pale and withdrawn, sitting against the wall with her arms locked around her knees. Anton was watching her with a look of fond pride. Mrs Van saw how Martha, in response to a whisper from Anton, first tightened herself in an involuntary movement towards isolation, and then turned to him, smiling. She took Anton's hand and held it.

All the same, thought Mrs Van, it's not right at all. Suddenly very tired, and unaccountably sorrowful, she thought: I'll take Johnny and Jack with me, we can have a drink somewhere.

Johnny said: 'What do you think of these two? They got married this morning and told no one. Jack and I heard it by accident and dropped over to congratulate them.'

This was a signal for laughter and joking all around, and Mrs Van, nodding and agreeing that these young people took life altogether too seriously, saw that Martha flashed up into vivacity in response to the teasing, joked with old Johnny, told Jack (but with a certain dry self-punishing irony) that 'we communists haven't got time for all this middle-class self-indulgence,' while the others of the group cried out that she should speak for herself; laughed, flirted and played the part of a spoiled bride for just so long as she was the centre of attention, after which she lapsed back into listless withdrawal. Meanwhile, as the older woman noted with a lightening of her heart, she clung to Anton's hand as if it were a lifebuoy.

She tried to catch Johnny's and Jack's attention: she had understood that these two men, dropping in on an impulse as she had done, had interrupted a communist meeting and now these young people wanted them to leave. Jack and Johnny both met her glances with a slight dryness which said simultaneously that while they disliked communism utterly, they liked these communists personally, agreed that they had the right to hold meetings if they wished, but that they disagreed totally with an ethic which allowed a young woman to spend her wedding night at a political meeting.

The two men got up as Mrs Van rose from her suitcase, making jokes because of the stiffness of her back.

'We'll leave you to your deliberations and have some of our own,' said Mrs Van, with a calculated stiffness in her manner which was designed to let the group know she was aware they were having a meeting. She was still holding the roses.

She said to Martha: 'Is there a kitchen? Have you something I can put these in?' Martha noticed the flowers – until that moment it had not occurred to her they were for her, and now she felt inadequate because she had not – scrambled down off the bed, and accompanied Mrs Van next door, where there was a small stove in a tiny room.

Mrs Van said: 'Well, my dear, it's not much of a wedding present, but it was the best I could do at a moment's notice.'

Martha went pink, her eyes filled with tears and she frowned.

Mrs Van, seeing the tears, nodded, as if to say, Yes, that's right, and at the sight of it Martha's eyes widened in incredulity, as if at a cruelty.

Mrs Van thought hurriedly: She ought to cry, it's right she should. She's too – hard, almost. But at the same time she knew she was feeling something she ought not.

Martha stood grasping the prickly bunch of roses whose red petals fell slowly on to the pale wood of the table, and thought: She's given me flowers, it was kind of her, so why am I disliking her so much? And why should she, when I scarcely know her? And Jack and old Johnny drop in to congratulate me, why? Just because it's a marriage, I suppose. But what has it got to do with me?

It seemed to her that the smile on Mrs Van's face was complacent, and she thought confusedly: There she is, with that dry old husband of hers, and all those children, every one of them a pillar of society, and grandchildren by the half-dozen, and everything tidy and safe and nothing painful anywhere. So then, why the roses? The pain of the thorny stems in Martha's hands seemed like a warning. She concluded: But her life can't have anything to do with mine, she could never understand all this in a million years. (By *all this* Martha meant something dark and unhappy and essentially driven, something essentially foreign to everything Mrs Van was and ever could be.) She can't understand me, so she is not giving the roses to me, she's giving them to somebody else.

Mrs Van said gently: 'My dear, I was so touched when I heard you'd come to our meeting after you got married this morning.' She stopped. Martha had turned pale. Mrs Van searched Martha's face with a severe but tranquil gaze. She had understood that she wanted Martha to break down and cry; she was telling herself that if Martha wept, flinging herself on to her for comfort and support, then it would be good for her, good for the marriage.

At that moment there flashed into her mind a memory of the occasion which she always referred to as 'that night'. She did not remember any of the emotions of that night, she saw it at a long distance, like a shot from a film: a young girl lying awake in a small dark bedroom beside her husband. This girl was crying, but without a sound; the cold tears had run down over her cheeks all night. Her cold bare arm lay at a skin's distance from her husband's muscular arm. But she did not move her arm; it lay still and trembled with the effort not to move it, while she thought: He wants me to let my arm touch his, but if I do, he will see it as a kind of an apology, a promise. He will forgive me.

Now, after all those years, Mrs Van remembered the image that had filled the girl's mind through those long hours while she lay awake by a man who also lay awake, waiting for her to turn to him. The image was of something deep, soft, dark and vulnerable, and of a very sharp sword stabbing into it, again and again. She had not moved, and not let her arm relax into contact with her husband's, and so the sword had not stabbed into her, never again, the soft dark painful place which she felt to be somewhere under her heart had remained untouched. She had remained herself.

For the flash of an instant Mrs Van felt the pain of that night, so that the small bright harmless picture was radiant with a real feeling. Mrs Van abruptly turned away from Martha. She said gruffly: 'My dear, I know all these things are very difficult, they are all very difficult . . .' Her voice shook, and she said hastily: 'My dear, I hope you will be very happy.' This conventional remark released Martha, who turned to her and thanked her, smiling, laying the roses down on the table.

Mrs Van said suddenly: 'Your mother came to see me tonight.'

'I didn't know you knew her.'

'I think you should have told her you were getting married.'

Martha's eyebrows went up, as if to say: And what's it got to do with you?

Mrs Van, regretting she had mentioned Mrs Quest, said with severity: 'All the same, you should have told her.'

Martha exclaimed: 'Do you imagine I wanted to make all this bloody farce even worse?'

Mrs Van positively started. Then she walked out of the kitchen with a gesture that repudiated Martha completely.

The main room was silent and held a new element. This was Mrs Quest, who had just entered, and had stopped inside the door, whatever she had been going to say swallowed by the surprise of seeing so many people. She could not see Martha, and as her daughter came into view behind Mrs Van, she said in a friendly and even sprightly voice: 'Oh, so there you are.'

Mrs Quest, who had vowed never to speak to her daughter again, had in the interval since she had seen Mrs Van whipped herself up into a mood of violent anger. All kinds of scenes of reproach, recrimination and reconciliation had been passing through her mind. In the midst of her anger, Mr Roberts, in pursuit of Mrs Van, had approached her to find out where Martha could be found, and dropped the information that Martha had that afternoon been 'inciting the blacks to revolution'. Martha said helplessly: 'Well, mother?' – and began the business of introduction. But she gave it up.

Mrs Quest demanded: 'Where's my son-in-law?' Five minutes before she had been pursuing a fantasy where she announced to him that with the co-operation of the authorities she would have him deported from the Colony, but now she sounded no more than humorously grieved.

Anton extricated himself from the mess of people on the bed, held out his hand, and found that he was being kissed by an elderly British matron on whom he had never set eyes before, gave her a stiff and awkward nod, said he was very pleased to make her acquaintance, and then, feeling that more was being asked of him, bent to give her a courtly kiss on the hand. 'Gnädige Frau!' he murmured.

Mrs Quest blushed and cried out to Martha that if she were having a party to celebrate the wedding the least she could do was to invite her father, who would be very hurt indeed when he heard.

Martha was still helpless in the middle of the room. She was looking with apprehension at a wad of paper in Mrs Quest's hand. Everyone was watching the scene, most with half-suppressed grins on their faces. Mrs Van was stern with disapproval.

'But it isn't a party, it's a meeting,' Martha said, her voice harsh with humour. She was feeling as if farce, the spirit of total incongruity that seemed to lie in wait for her behind everything she did, had finally overwhelmed her.

'A meeting,' cried Mrs Quest. This revived her anger. Looking around for means to express it, her eyes discovered the papers in her hands. These she thrust energetically into the hands of the people closest to her. In a moment, the heads of everyone in the room were bent over cuttings from the *Zambesia News*.

Mrs Quest was in the habit of cutting from the *News* all the letters signed White Settler, Old Hand, or Fair Play, most of which began: 'After forty years of handling the native, etc.'

Jack Dobie read out aloud, very seriously, his face expressing the queerest mixture of amusement and anger: 'It is my opinion that the cheek and the insolence of the Kaffirs is largely due to the propaganda of certain liberals in this town, and Britain's greatest mistake is her belief in equality: let charity begin at home, and let her take her hands off our natives.'

He handed the cutting back to Mrs Quest, with a polite: 'Thanks.'

Mrs Quest now handed the cutting to Martha: 'You see,' she said, 'the Kaffirs are getting out of hand.' But she was smiling. Her anger, contained in the bits of newspaper, was now distributed around the room, and she wanted to be invited to join the party. She was looking at the bottles of wine on the floor. Martha took the cutting, and poured her mother out a glass of wine. But there was nowhere for her to sit down.

Besides, the meeting, which had been due to start at eight, was now two hours delayed. 'The group' were handing bits of paper from hand to hand with delighted and satirical smiles.

Mrs Van, whose instinct for saving a situation was always stronger than any other, said: 'Those cuttings will be very useful for my collection.' She had a file headed: 'White settler imbecilities', filled with articles and letters of a similar tone, which she sent to newspapers and magazines overseas as evidence of the deplorable state of affairs in Zambesia.

Mrs Quest, delighted to find an ally in a woman she had heard of as Kaffir-lover, delighted that this Town Councillor, by repute so dangerous, was in fact sound, now grasped Mrs Van by the hand and said: 'My dear, I'm so pleased you agree with me. It is really awful, isn't it, these agitators should all be shot.' She kept her hand on Mrs Van's arm while she remarked generally around the room: 'You see, it is really very dangerous what you are doing. I've always said so.'

Mrs Van said: 'I'm going back home now. Perhaps you'd like a lift?'

Mrs Quest, uncertain what to do with her glass of wine, looked about for a place to set it down, saw nothing but bare boards, hastily drank it, said: 'Thank you, my dear! And I would like to discuss this native problem with you – I think responsible people like ourselves ought to get together and form some vigilantes committees, because the Government doesn't do anything, and we must protect ourselves.'

'That would be a very good idea,' said Mrs Van. She turned and said in a low voice to Martha, with an emphatic and rather angry nod: 'If things are done in a regular manner, these situations need not arise!'

Martha said: 'Regular? What's regular about anything that happens? Don't you see that it's all a farce, everything . . .' She turned away from Mrs Van and returned to her place on the bed.

Mrs Van, shrugging crossly, signalled to her allies Jack and Johnny, who followed her to the door, grinning with delight at the situation. There Mrs Quest remembered Martha, and said: 'Go to bed early, you naughty girl, and get some sleep.' She remembered her daughter had just got married, frowned, said hastily that she would see her in a few days, smiled at the company and went out.

People showed signs of dissolving into laughter, but Martha looked gloomy and strained, and nothing happened, until Athen inquired seriously: 'I did not understand that woman, Comrade Matty. Is she your mother?'

Martha shrugged.

'And what did she want you to do with these reactionary letters in the newspapers?'

'We should read them and acquire a correct outlook on life.'

'I do not understand you, Comrade Matty.' Martha again shrugged. The Greek examined her for a moment, in silent severity, and then, speaking to her direct, as if they were alone, said: 'I feel I should say something. There is a kind of laughter that is very bad. It is a mocking at the truth.'

'Well, yes, I dare say.'

At this Maisie said: 'I think Matty is upset, and I don't blame her. I don't think we ought to have a meeting when Matty and Anton haven't even arranged their room yet.'

But Tommy, who had been waiting impatiently for some time, unable to understand the undercurrents, unhappy and disapproving of this marriage which he found even more irregular than Maisie's and Andrew's, burst out: 'No, comrades, we must discuss something, I have to get my mind clear about something.'

So the meeting started, on the burst of Tommy's furious

demand for clarity, and for the first time without chairman, secretary, or any sort of formality.

'The point is this. As I see it there is a fight blowing up in the Labour Party – I mean the Social Democratic Party – and I want to say something else too, all these names, all these names all the time, meaning different things all the time, Social Democratic used to mean revolutionary as far as I can see, and now they use it to be respectable . . .' He banged his fists on the top of his head. 'But that isn't the point. It's the African Branch that bothers me. As I see it, an African Branch is reactionary. It's democratic to have natives, I mean Africans, as members of the Labour Party just like everyone else, going to meetings as individuals. An African Branch is segregation. Well, isn't it? But Mrs Van and Johnny and Jack are good types, not colour-minded at all, and they support an African Branch and all the reactionaries support what is democratic. Well, I don't get it. I simply don't get any of it.'

Athen the Greek directed his firm, unsmiling sympathetic face towards Tommy and said: 'That's a good boy, comrade, you must always speak up for what you feel.'

Piet du Preez said with comic and clowning despair: 'We should of course get our line straight about this little point. We should always have our line straight.'

Anton recovered himself from his lapse into irresponsibility and personal feelings, and sat up, swung his legs down to the floor, and said: 'Comrades, it seems clear that we must analyse the situation.'

The meeting broke up at four next morning, and everyone went to sleep where they were, on the floor, or in loose bundles of tired flesh on the two beds. They were woken at six again by Maisie's house-boy, who regarded his employers as friends and allies. He had brought them that day's copy of the *News*, which had big black headlines: Agitators Inciting Africans to Revolt.

'Baas, bass,' he called out through the half-open door to Andrew, nervously averting his eyes from the dishevelled bodies all over the room. 'Baas, baas! It's the newspaper. It is saying bad things about you, baas. Oh it is wicked. It is saying wicked things.'

Part Four

The origin of states gets lost in a myth in which one may believe but one may not discuss.

KARL MARX

Chapter One

The walls and pillars of the du Preez' veranda, which had been absorbing the sun all day, still quivered off heat at eight in the evening. The members of the group, who had thought it might be cooler out in the quiet heavy-lying hot night air, changed their minds and returned to the big heat-sodden living-room. It was only half the group. Last night Anton had said: 'Group meeting tomorrow, eight o'clock.'

There were present Anton, Marjorie, Andrew and Marie.

'Where's Piet?' Anton demanded before he had so much as sat down. He was angry, but with a new kind of stiff anger, as if with each new infringement of discipline he were inwardly nodding and saying: Yes, it was only to be expected.

Marie said: 'He's at the union meeting. And Tommy's with him.' It was now assumed that trade union and labour meetings came before group meetings; or rather, it was not so much an assumption, which would have needed decisions on a fundamental policy, as a fact. Ever since 'the meeting in the Location' the group had been shaken, pressured, squeezed this way and that because of the repercussions from that great event. In Piet's trade union a battle raged. Piet had given a lecture on trade unionism to the Kaffirs, and this raised principles whose discussion brought men to the union meetings who normally never went near them.

In the living-room easy chairs were set in a circle. Stacks of literature on Russia stood everywhere among the children's toys. The room had a look of easy family good-humour. Marie said: 'We'll have a spot of the drop that cheers – we might as well while we're waiting.'

Anton said: 'This is a communist group meeting.'

Andrew said: 'I'll have a beer.' Marjorie said: 'Me too.' Children defying teacher. Anton said nothing. He held his notes on his knees ready for his lecture, which was to be on the course of the war on the Eastern Front.

Marie brought in beer bottles, frosted with cold. The heat sagged through the room and the thunder rolled slowly overhead.

'I've a notion we'll have to wait some time,' said Andrew. 'Matty and Colin have gone to Jack Dobie's lecture on India.'

'They had no right to.'

'Jack came to our place and asked Colin to come – Colin's been studying up on India. And Matty was there and she said she would go with Colin.'

At the sound of his wife's name Anton settled back into pale stoicism.

'Oh, go on, have a beer, man,' said Marie, and thrust a glass into Anton's hand. He set the glass down without looking at it and asked: 'And is Athen on duty? If not, why is he not here?'

'Don't ask me,' said Andrew. 'And Maisie's not here because she's not feeling so good.' Anton never inquired after Maisie. It was his way of saying that he did not count her as a group member. Andrew always insisted on accounting for her. The tension between the two men had become acute.

Marie said: 'For crying out aloud we'll start slitting each other's throats because it's hot in a minute.'

She sat down yawning and spreading her legs.

'Perhaps we should take a decision to have cocktails with our group meetings,' said Anton with bitterness. It was true that the scene might have been set for a sundowner party.

'Oh come off it,' said Andrew. 'Come off it. If things have gone wrong tonight, we can put them right next time.'

'Yes, yes,' said Anton, 'here we sit, drinking beer, and meanwhile our comrades are dying for us.'

He picked up a newspaper which had been lying on the floor. Its headlines were: German Front Cracking. General

Frost Beats German High Command. German Armies Perishing of Cold.

All that winter the Russian armies, the German armies had been struggling together, millions of men struggling and dying, locked in cold and snow, locked together over hundreds of miles of front that stretched over wind-swept, blizzard-torn, frost-bitten plains, Northern plains tilted away from the sun into darkness and ice. Headlines, reports from the fronts, newsreels, gave messages of heroism and misery, but the voices came out of a terrible cold, like distant shouts from people struggling through a snowstorm.

Marjorie looked down at the big black print on the newspaper, saying Cold, Snow, Blizzard, Death and remarked: 'We could do with a bit of that cold here.' Her face was beaded with sweat, and she moved her big body continually into easier positions. She was trying to sound humorous.

Anton said: 'Comrade Marjorie, is that your idea of a joke?' Ever since her marriage, he had spoken to her as if he disliked her, and she met it with her own brand of dry tolerance. Now she frankly and loudly sighed, and Marie ostentatiously sighed with her.

Andrew said quickly: 'Why don't you give your lecture to us, Comrade Anton. After all, it's better than wasting it.'

Anton raised his cold eyes towards him, lowered them to examine his watch, gathered his notes and began his lecture. It was analysis of this particular stage of the war, with emphasis on the reasons why there was no second front. Normally he spoke for half an hour. Tonight he finished it in ten minutes.

Marjorie said: 'All the same, it's like Napoleon, all those masses of men dying in the cold.'

Anton said: 'Comrade Marjorie, historical parallels are sometimes useful, but don't you feel this one is rather far-fetched?'

Marjorie said tiredly: 'No, why? Of course, this is socialism fighting for its life. But men are still dying of cold.'

'Poor buggers,' said Marie, splashing beer into her glass and spreading her legs out wider in front of her. 'Poor bloody bastards. I wish the spring would come for their sake.'

'You are, I presume, referring to the Red Army?' asked Anton.

'I was referring to the Germans as well.'

'Comrade Ehrenburg has I think made the line quite clear. The Germans have proved themselves barbarians and fascists and must be considered as such. Put yourself into the place of the Russians.'

Marie said: 'If the Russians hate the guts of all the Germans, then it's natural. But speaking for myself, there are times when Comrade Ehrenburg makes me sick. I don't see what all that nationalist drum-beating has got to do with socialism, and that's a fact.' She said this with a deliberate challenge, as if she had planned to say it for some time. She added, 'And I keep thinking of those German boys, poor sods, fascists or no fascists, they're human beings.'

Anton got to his feet. Marie stayed where she was, frankly played out, frankly indifferent. Her face was scarlet with the heat, and her arms and legs were slowly mottling with some kind of heat rash. The thunder was rolling overhead.

'Wish to God it'd rain,' said Andrew, in the bluff, let's-have-no-trouble voice which meant he was back in command of himself. He gave Anton a clout across the shoulders and said: 'Do let up, there's a good chap. We can all get our political lines straight when it starts to rain.'

Anton said: 'Since there is no group meeting, I consider it's our duty to go and support Matty and Colin at the meeting on India.'

'Duty or no duty,' said Marie, fanning herself, eyes closed, 'I've had it until it rains.'

Marjorie, Andrew and Anton left her, and stood together on the veranda. Beyond the pillars the sky massed itself, darkly thunderous, lightning spurted and ran from one cloud mountain to another. The air was dry. For a week the clouds had been packing along the horizons, piling up, and thickening, but the rain held off. Tonight the air quivered and sang with the dry heat, and the dust shifted along dry earth under a small feverish wind.

'Coming to the meeting?' Anton said to Andrew.

Andrew said, after hesitation, 'I suppose so.' But he was ashamed, for he added heartily: 'Jack Dobie knows his stuff and we should support him.'

When the car passed the flats where Marjorie lived she said apologetically: 'I'm not feeling too good. This baby's beginning to make itself felt.'

They dropped her, and drove to the hall where the meeting was. It was full. Andrew said: 'Not bad, three hundred people for a meeting on India in this weather. And for God's sake,' he added, 'don't say anything about the heroism of the Russians or I'll leave you and go to the pictures.'

Anton permitted himself to smile. They settled themselves, standing, against a wall, while Jack Dobie, an energetic little figure alone on the platform, worked himself up to his peroration: 'Having bled India dry for hundreds of years it is our moral duty, etc.' Meanwhile a short, gingery, Cape-brandy-complexioned man jumped up and down and shouted: 'Go back to the Clydeside. We don't want you here.' A group of local Indians, shopkeepers and teachers from the segregated Indian school, stood by themselves in a corner, kept their eyes fixed on the speaker, and from time to time muttered, 'Shame, shame!', shaking their heads sorrowfully. The body of the citizens listened in silence to the subversive views being put to them with the look of those prepared to keep an open mind about everything. The meeting, in short, was like all the meetings of that short epoch 1942 to 1945. The walls of the hall were still covered with posters from last night's meeting, the Sympathizers of Russia's Brains Trust on 'Soviet Man – a New Species?' Lenin, Stalin, and an assortment of Soviet generals gazed at each other over the heads of the crowd. Words like liberty, freedom, democracy, revolution drove one brave sentence into the next. If Lenin himself had appeared before these white-skinned petty-bourgeois, consigning them and their kind to the dust-heaps of history, invoking over their heads the masses of Africans (none were present that night, they were all safely asleep in the Location), he would have been immune from them, protected by the spirit of the time, and the image of a red-starred, hammered-and-sickled, frost-bitten, weary, blood-stained peasant. Along hundreds of miles of battle-front that stretched across dark and winter-bitten plains, the Red Army fought in choking snow and cold, and a breath of this cold air came into the hot and sultry little hall where men sweated in shirt-sleeves and the women fanned themselves with programmes emblazoned: 'Let India Go Free!' Jack Dobie marched from one end of the platform to the other, his Scots eyes blazing, shaking his fist at them and telling them they were blood-sucking imperialists and that freedom was indivisible.

Anton looked along the upturned faces for Martha. She was not there and must have gone home. Andrew was thinking of Maisie: he had reasons to be with her tonight. But both men knew that because of their rivalry they would stay out the meeting to its end, and afterwards take Jack Dobie off for coffee. He had been officially pigeon-holed by the group as 'sincere, but too much of an individualist, and needed guidance by Marxists'. Unless it rained and although the thunder rolled above the tin roof, often drumming out the sound of Jack's voice, there was no sign of rain, there would be no excuse to go home.

Five hundred yards away in a small bright hot room, Maisie Gale, briefly Maisie York, briefly Maisie Denham, now Maisie McGrew, a girl of twenty-four in the full of her pregnancy, sat with her belly resting on her sweaty thighs on the bed which was in the dayime a divan, and hollowed her hands around a small highly-coloured globe, her eyes fixed on the sandy-coloured area which represented the Sudan. Opposite her on a stiff chair sat Athen the Greek, his small brown muscular hands resting on his khaki knees, watching her with a brotherly and patient concern. At eight o'clock, under the impression the group meeting was at the Hesses' flat above this one, he had knocked and found it empty, descended to this room to make inquiries about where the group was meeting, and found Maisie moving fast and clumsy about the small room, holding her stomach away from the sharp corners of chairs and tables, her fair baby-hair glued to her head with sweat so that her face lengthened beneath it into a heavy, yellowish, stiff-staring mass of unhappiness. She had offered him tea, coffee, beer, told him to cook himself supper if he were hungry, sat down, got up, sighed, stood staring out of the window into the electric-crackling darkness, and finally informed him in a voice full of resentment that Andrew had gone to a meeting, but she hoped he would be back soon.

That morning Mrs Maynard had opened the door without knocking and informed the girl in a curt but at the same time obsequious way that Binkie had been given compassionate leave and would be in the town tomorrow. Since Maisie had said nothing at all, Mrs Maynard had left again, with a dignity that suggested a patient readiness to suffer injustice.

Then Maisie collapsed. She had ignored letters, telephone calls and even telegrams from the Maynards, but the actual presence of the black-browed and peremptory matron who was Binkie's mother, whom Binkie so much resembled, had forced her to think: Binkie is coming. And then: The father of my child is coming. He will be here tomorrow.

Now she sat with one white, pudgy, rather grubby forefinger on the pink splodge that was Italy, and the other on the tiny black dot which was the city she lived in. She let her gaze move down across the blue of the Mediterranean where at that moment a naval battle was in progress, across the yellow of Egypt and the sands of the Sudan, down over Abyssinia, down across the great crack in the earth which was the Rift Valley, across the lakes and forests of Nyasaland and the empty dryness of Northern Rhodesia which produced copper, wasted in war, south to where she sat now in the small, shallow, heat-filled room. Then back her frowning puzzled eyes moved to Italy. Perhaps Binkie had not yet left? Perhaps he had been held up and she could have a few days' grace? But most likely he was now somewhere in the air above Egypt, the Sudan, Abyssinia, travelling down over the curve of the earth, south and away from the cold of the war in Italy which was tilted darkwards away from the sun, south over the belly of Africa thrust forward into the sun, thrust into summer, where she sat and sweated and waited. She saw a tiny fly-like aeroplane move down over the earth's curve, the sunlight deepening on its wings, and she lifted her eyes to Athen and said miserably: 'I don't know what to do. I don't know what's right and what's wrong.' Athen said for the tenth time that evening: 'But Maisie, you knew he would come some time. You knew that.'

'I didn't know I would feel so bad when I saw him.'

'You haven't seen him yet,' he said, smiling gently.

'And when I told Andrew that Binkie was coming, all he said was: Well, see him, tell him where he stands and get it over.'

'That was very sensible,' said Athen, noting the look of hostility on her face as she mentioned her husband. Every time his name had occurred that evening her face had put on that same look of hurt, angry resentment.

'You love Andrew,' he said, grave and reproachful.

'I was married twice before.'

'But now you are married to Andrew.'

'They were both killed.'

Athen leaned forward, his two burned muscular thin hands gripping his knees. Maisie watched his hands with the same puzzled frown. 'Maisie, you loved them, and they were killed, but it is not your fault.'

'Love,' she said sullenly. 'Sometimes I wonder what it means.'

'Do you think of them?'

She made an impatient movement with her shoulders.

'But it is no disloyalty to Andrew to think of them. It is bad not to think of people who are dead when you have loved them.'

'But why are you talking about them? I don't see why?'

'I had good comrades killed,' he said, still leaning forward, still searching her face. 'I think of them often. Don't you see, Maisie, if someone loves you he loves you for everything you have been. Therefore it is right to think of those two men, if you loved them, and they were good honest men.'

Her whole body stiffened. 'Why do you keep on about them? It's Binkie I'm thinking about. I wish this baby was Andrew's baby. And do you know what I was thinking this afternoon? I was thinking if Binkie was killed it would make everything easier.' She looked at him defiantly.

'That is very bad,' he pronounced gravely, and, as if she had been waiting for this, she let her body slump and sighed.

'I know it is bad. And after that I thought: Well, if Andrew got killed I'd be a widow for the third time.'

'Maisie, why do you have to kill these men? You have to decide which you want, that is all.'

'I've been thinking. When Andrew talks about how he lives in England, then I can't see myself.'

'He expects you to go with him to England after the war?'

'After the war! It might be years and years. Sometimes I think there'll be a hundred years' war like there was once before. Sometimes we say things like: When we are in London, but it's not serious.'

'It's serious for him, Maisie.'

'No,' she said with unexpected firmness. 'I don't think he's ever really thought. It all just happened. He was kind and he'd marry me to give the baby a name, and then – we grew fond of each other.' She said this last with a touch of the sullenness he had come to expect.

'Maisie, you aren't deciding between the two men, you are deciding between two different ways of living. If you go back to your child's father, you will be the wife of a rich man . . .'

'*Rich?*'

'For me such a life would be rich,' he said with a small smile. 'Maisie, the white people of this country live like only a few of the people in the world live. Don't you know that? You take it for granted. You will be a comfortable wife with servants. But if you go with Andrew you will be the wife of a communist and you will have a hard life and a good one.'

'Communism,' she said. 'You know, there's something silly about it. Oh I know it's all right for you. You are a poor man, you said you sold newspapers on the streets in Athens.

So there's some sense in you being a communist. But sometimes I want to laugh, seeing Matty and Marjorie and the rest of them – and besides, communism would be bad for the blacks, say what you like.'

He smiled again, gravely, at this phrase resurrected from her life before she joined the group.

Her answering smile was sour but determined. 'Oh I know you are thinking that I should know better now than to say things like that. But that isn't the point, don't you see? What I keep thinking about is this: If I stayed married to Andrew, then I'll be a communist. But if I take Binkie, then I'd never think about it again. Well, and so it makes me feel as if I'm nothing in myself.'

'But, Maisie, how nothing? You are you. You aren't just the wife of a man.'

She said resentfully: 'Andrew talks, you know how he talks, I might be a child.'

'That isn't true, Maisie.'

'Yes, and he's always right, always, no one can ever be right but him.'

Athen said with authority: 'Maisie, do you know what you are doing? You want an excuse to blame him for something, you want to dislike him, and so you are making up reasons for it.'

She resumed her restless progress about the room. She looked clumsy and distressed. From shoulders to thighs her big body was the anonymous body of a pregnant woman. But her young arms and brown legs were a girl's; and her steady puzzled blue eyes were maidenly and severe; as severe as his dark, stern, judging eyes. She drifted to the divan, sat on it, laid her arms over the globe and her head down on her arms and began to cry.

Now Athen gently pushed her back on the bed so that she lay stretched on Andrew's army blankets, lifted a pillow, made her raise her knees, put the pillow under her knees and sat beside her. 'That is how I did my sister when she was sick and having a baby. Is it comfortable?'

'Yes.'

He laid his thin brown hand on the mound of her stomach. She tensed up and then lay still.

'There now,' he said. 'That is good. I can feel your child. I like it.'

She lay still, looking up at the ceiling, frowning, feeling the little man's hand lying on her stomach. Her face began to ease out of its yellow tension.

'You are perhaps a woman for whom the man is not so important. That is not a bad thing. So what you must think of, it is what is good for the child. You must bring him up to be a good man, with knowledge of the world, a man who will fight for justice and for peace.'

'He!'

'Is this child a girl then?'

'Who'd be a woman?'

'So you insist on a girl, because you need a companion in all your suffering?'

She laughed out, and as if ashamed of it, thrust the side of her hand into her mouth and bit it.

'You are not yourself tonight, Maisie.' He began gently to stroke the mound of her stomach. His own face was extraordinarily gentle, and his eyes were full of a fierce joy. 'So now ask yourself: Which of these two men will bring up your son or your daughter to be a good person, understanding the world and living to make it better? That is all you must ask yourself.'

'Go on doing that,' said Maisie. 'It makes me feel good.' After a pause she said: 'If it had been you – you might have married me to do me a good turn, and then we should have loved – we should have had a good time for a while.'

'Loved,' said Athen. 'You should not now say to yourself you have not loved Andrew. If you have loved someone even for a short time, then it is a good thing, and you should know it and say it and not pretend to yourself it wasn't so.'

'Love,' said Maisie lazily, in her normal easy voice. 'Love. Sometimes I think it doesn't exist.' She lifted her plump and childish hand from the pillow beside her and yawned against it. Athen turned off the big light; the room was now dimly lit. 'You must try now to be still, and perhaps to sleep, and remember you are a person, you must find out what you want for yourself and not blame other people for your weaknesses.' She yawned again, let her hand fall back beside her face, smiled at him and let her eyes close. Athen continued to sit by her, stroking the big swollen lumpy mound of her stomach until her breathing changed. Then he quietly went out, switching off the lights.

Half an hour later Andrew came in, switched on the ceiling light, saw Maisie lying asleep, switched it off, tiptoed clumsily to the bed, and turned on the small lamp. He sat where Athen had sat, beside the sleeping girl. He was full of apprehension. That morning Maisie had told him Mrs Maynard had been and that Binkie was coming. All afternoon, which he had arranged with considerable difficulty to have free from the camp, she had been evasive, nervous, guilty and silent. All evening, at the meeting, and afterwards drinking coffee with Anton and Jack Dobie, he had been half-dreading, half-longing for this moment when he might, as he put it to himself, 'be with' Maisie again. It seemed to him that all that afternoon she had been a stranger. Now she opened her eyes and smiled at him, and his heart eased into a comfortable warm beat – he realized it had been pounding with anxiety. Then her face changed, she gave a hasty yawn, and turned over on her side.

'And how's the little bugger tonight?' he said in the gruff and humorous voice he always used for this routine query.

'OK,' she said, not responding, and added politely: 'How was the meeting?'

'Not bad.'

She was staring into the room over the curve of the pillow. He examined her and found with surprise that her swollen body was repulsive to him. He remembered that earlier that day, when she said Binkie was coming, he had had the same feeling: he looked across at her, finding her hideous.

He had lived with the growth and the change of her body, hardly noticing it, burying his face at night thankfully in her warm full shoulders, greeting the child under her flesh with his hands, never thinking that it was not his own. Now, because Binkie was coming, he kept thinking: This is not my child, and her pregnancy was strange and distasteful. Maisie reached out her hand for his wrist, and laid his hand on her stomach. There was the stiffness of reluctance in his arm, he let his hand lie a moment, and it fell away. Maisie gave him a deep, blue, reproachful look.

His anxiety exploded against his will into the question: 'Still worrying about Binkie?'

'Well, it's natural I should, isn't it?' She was looking through her lashes at his big clumsy hand resting beside her body on the blanket. He said with a clumsy attack: 'Look, Maisie, I've got to get this straight, I want to know where I stand with you, it seems to me you turned against me from the moment you knew Binkie was coming.'

She did not move, lying big and clumsy and swollen, and he felt physical distaste like a sickness. She said breathlessly: 'So I changed did I? I changed? I said he was coming and you looked at me and I felt like dirt.'

He was silent, thinking: She surely couldn't have noticed how I felt then? He said aggressively: 'The moment you knew he was coming, it started.'

She said: 'He is the father of the baby.'

'So much so that I had to marry you to give the little bugger a name.'

She sat up and stared at him. She was thinking: It would have been fair to say that if he had just married me and said good-bye afterwards. But not after we'd loved each other. (She had been going to say, had a good time together, but because of Athen, used the word love.) So now he has no right to say that, she concluded, lying down again, this time turned away from him. 'No one made you marry me. You offered.'

'I'm sorry. I shouldn't have said it.'

'No, you shouldn't.'

The silence after this became unbearable. He said stiffly: 'Do you want me to sleep in your room? You needn't move from here if you'd rather not.'

'If you like,' she said indifferently. He was about to go next door without another word when he saw her eyes were wet. He gave a contrite exclamation, tugged off his uniform, and got on to the rough hot blanket beside her. 'You should get into your nighty,' he said. 'It's too hot to be dressed.'

Now she hastily flung off her clothes, noticing as she did so that he was careful not to look at her. A look of hurt came on to her face, and she slipped quickly under the sheet and lay with her back to him. He lay close behind her, as he had done recently at night, so that her head lay on his shoulder, and his arm, resting on the high curve of her stomach, supported her big loosened breasts. Suddenly he felt at ease.

'Hullo, Maisie,' he said thickly into her damp hair, and she snuggled back against him. He understood that the soft searching pressure of her buttocks meant she was trying to discover if he was big for her. They had made love easily since the beginning, adjusting themselves without thinking to her altering shape. Tonight he understood that his new physical distaste for her made it impossible for him to make love. He held the upper part of her body close to him, and kissed the side of her throat and said: 'Maisie, we mustn't quarrel.'

She had gone tense. She said: 'Quarrel? This isn't a quarrel. You don't love me any more.'

'But I do, Maisie, I do.'

She took his hand and directed it in a gentle stroking movement over her belly. He let her direct the massage for a moment, then her hand fell away from his, and he held it: her hand was friendly to him, but her body alien.

They lay still, filled with dismay. Then she said: 'I think I'd better sleep by myself tonight, I don't feel comfortable.'

This was the first time they had not lain together at night. He got quickly out of the bed without a word, and went into her bedroom next door. The photographs of her husbands were still on the walls. He gave them both an ironical nod of greeting, and thought: I suppose when Binkie comes back she'll put my photograph up beside theirs. He forced himself to sleep, unwilling to face a night of wakeful misery, but even more afraid that Maisie might come in, for reassurance, lie beside him, and he should again betray his new, instinctive repulsion.

Immediately above Andrew, through the thin ceiling, in a

284

room identical in shape, lay Martha in a damp petticoat, watching the dry and rainless lightning flash among unbroken masses of cloud. She was smoking heavily, and was so tense with heat, irritation and exhaustion that she could not lie still. She felt guilty because she had so easily found a reason not to go to the group meeting. She felt worse because, having reached the meeting on India with Colin, she almost at once crept out again. She knew everything Jack Dobie was going to say, agreed with it, in fact might have made the same speech herself. And Colin irritated her. Having decided that he needed to 'specialize' in something, and chosen India, he had in his conscientious way immersed himself in the subject. He sat in the meeting beside her nodding or shaking his head with phlegmatic attention to Jack, and whispering asides to her if there was a small fact or a detail wrong. She soon apologized and went home, in search of solitude. She was in a fever to be alone. In the flat she found two RAF men from the Progressive Club. Ever since she and Anton had married, the focus of the group had shifted from the du Preez' house to this flat. She had understood this when people had begun to drop in, and the pamphlets, books and files had begun to accumulate in the living-room. Naturally, since this was central, and the du Preez' house was not; and since the du Preez were a family with children, and this had the flexibility of the young married couple's flat. Once Martha had understood that she could always expect to find people asleep on the living-room floor, or even in the bath when she woke in the morning, and that people would drop in for meals, she accepted the fact and liked it. She knew she was pleased not to be alone too much with Anton.

But she was surprised to find Anton resented it. It seemed a new personality had been born in Anton with the marriage. To begin with he had doggedly, almost furtively, with a look of secret satisfaction, bought furniture for the two rooms which seemed to her ugly and conventional. She would have preferred rooms like Maisie's bare living-room, a place to camp in, furnished with the help of friends and ingenuity. But Anton, when she had said so, told her in a new voice, also acquired since marriage, that she had bohemian tastes. The two rooms could now have gone on exhibition as a cosy suburban home and Martha hated them. Also, Anton had spent all his small savings on the furniture, and had several times reminded her of it. Martha said nothing, but had made a note that their ideas on money did not coincide. Further, Anton showed he had a talent for domesticity and expected it. She understood that he wanted his life divided carefully into three areas: the time he spent working as a clerk, working conscientiously and without interruption from his other lives; the time he spent at meetings or talking to people in the interests of communism; and the time he spent at home, into which politics or irregularity should not intrude.

But it appeared that he was himself ashamed of this last trait, for although he would watch Martha talking, cooking, welcoming the people who dropped in, watch her closely and critically, he did no more than grumble that they were turning into an hotel. 'I should have thought,' Martha remarked, 'that if we believe in comradeship and sharing things then we shouldn't think of feeding people or giving them a place to sleep as being an hotel?' This query was half genuinely indignant, and half uneasy, because she knew her motives were partly dishonest.

'Yes, yes, but we can't afford it.'

At this Martha took a decision. Mr Robinson had been suggesting for some time that she might learn to do the firm's books. She had refused, because she preferred to devote the time to her other interests. She now told Anton that her salary would be going up by ten pounds a month and that should cover the entertaining they did.

On that evening she asked the two RAF men to go away, because she had to do some work. They said cheerfully that there was no need for her to worry, they would entertain themselves. She sat on her bed, listening to their loud voices through the thin wall and wishing she might have just this one evening to herself. Yet if she had done her duty she would be at one or other of two meetings, and here she sat, idle. There was plenty of work for her to do here. For instance, there was the work in connection with the campaign against Mrs Van. Ever since 'the meeting in the Location' the *News* had been printing several letters a day which described how tools of Moscow were fermenting revolution among the blacks. Mrs Van's name was always used in such a way that she must be regarded as a leader of these activities. Further, there had been a spate of anonymous leaflets and pamphlets. There were two in particular, one describing 'certain communist agitators among the Kaffirs', a pamphlet full of personal innuendo; the other a factual account of Mrs Van's work from a certain angle which, since she had been campaigning for many years for better conditions for the Africans, and had made several dozen speeches on the subject, could be made to sound as if she had never done anything else in her life. 'We want public men and women who work for the benefit of all races,' this pamphlet said, 'not people who are interested only in the blacks.' There was nothing offensive in this pamphlet from the point of view of libel: but since it had been delivered at the same time as the other on all the doorsteps of the town, they had been read together, and Mrs Van's name must therefore be associated with the venom of the first.

Martha had been given the task by Mrs Van of going through all her speeches, seeing if she had been correctly quoted, and making sure there was nothing libellous. She had finished checking the speeches. That afternoon she had finished the work in connection with the letters. This had involved an interview with the editor of the *News*. In all the weeks since the meeting in the Location, there had been precisely one letter supporting it, or rather inviting the citizens to keep their heads and a sense of proportion. But other letters had been written, as Martha knew, since she had been given the job of seeing that they should be written. Some time before, a sub-committee of the group had been set up to see that all reactionary letters in the *News* should be instantly replied to. This had needed so much time that the sub-committee (Martha and Marjorie) had been, so to speak, standing at ease. With the new crisis it hastily sprang to attention and some thirty people who regarded themselves as liberal agreed to write letters to the editor pointing out that the meeting in the Location had other aspects besides the subversive. But not one had been printed. Martha had therefore demanded an interview with Mr Haggerty which had taken place that afternoon.

Mr Haggerty was a South African born and bred, and met Martha in the first few sentences with the information that he had no time for Kaffir-lovers. Almost at once it became an argument on principles.

In the first place, Martha demanded, was it democratic that there should be only one newspaper in the Colony, and that an offshoot of a chain of newspapers operating in the Union and connected with the Chamber of Mines? No, said Mr Haggerty, it was not, but there was nothing to stop another newspaper being started.

Nothing but a lack of capital, said Martha.

That was not his fault, said Mr Haggarty.

Was it democratic, inquired Martha, that since there was only one newspaper, which should therefore be more than usually aware of its responsibilities, it should print only one letter supporting the meeting in the Location to several dozen against?

Perfectly, said Mr Haggerty. According to his reckoning there might perhaps be fifty people in the Colony who might agree with such goings-on, and that fifty were more than represented by the single letter.

Fifty white people, said Martha.

That's right, Mr Haggerty said, and then, seeing his impasse, explained that he regarded the *News* as a mouthpiece of black opinion as well as of white, but that he was convinced that the 'mass of the blacks' only wanted to be left alone. At this Martha laughed, and Mr Haggerty tapped his desk in irritation.

She asked to be told how he, as an editor, would define the basic policy of his newspaper.

He replied that it was the policy of the paper to support the existing government.

And, inquired Martha, was that democratic?

Of course, said Mr Haggerty: the Government was elected by the people and therefore it was democratic to support it.

By the white people, said Martha, and proceeded to recite paragraphs from the American Declaration of Independence, quotations from Tom Paine, Milton, Jefferson, Shelley and Byron. To which Mr Haggerty, listening with suspicion, replied that he was not interested in communist propaganda. To which Martha, delighted, made suitable reply.

To which Mr Haggerty said that if Jefferson, Paine or Milton had lived in a colony like this, they would have had more sense than to talk about liberty.

To which Martha said he had no historical feeling at all.

Liberty, said Mr Haggerty, having the last word, should be the property of the washed and the educated, and what the Kaffirs needed was discipline and hygiene.

The interview then ended, with ill-feeling on both sides.

Martha had tried to see Mrs Van that afternoon, but she was not in her office.

Now she thought: I could go and see her at home. But to visit Mrs Van in her office was one thing, to visit her at home another. For ever since that day she got married there had been hostility between herself and Mrs Van. She did not understand why, since she knew she admired and liked the older woman.

The roses had stood in the bedroom long after they should have been thrown away. Martha had watched the petals soften, crumple and fade, thinking: If I don't want to throw them away, then I must have been touched that night. Yet she gave the roses to someone else, not to me, and so therefore it is all dishonest.

Yet the roses remained, and Martha watched in herself the growth of an extraordinarily unpleasant and upsetting emotion, a self-mockery, a self-parody, as if she both allowed herself an emotion she did not approve of, allowed it and enjoyed it, but at the same time cancelled it out by the mockery. 'How do I know what I feel and what I don't? I've only to hear a boy scouts' brass band on Sunday afternoon and tears come into my eyes. Anton has only to call me "little one" and a lump comes into my throat. Mrs Van gives me roses and I want to cry. It's all dishonest. It's as if somewhere inside me there was a big sack of greasy tears and if a pin were stuck into me they'd spill out . . .'

Martha, having decided she would not go and see Mrs Van, lay down on her bed, tossed there for half an hour, and then found herself up and collecting the files and papers to take to Mrs Van.

She went quietly through the front room. Now there were five people in it. A young pilot who had just finished his course was getting himself drunk in a corner on Cape brandy. The two original RAF men had been joined by their girls, and they were all lying around on the floor, discussing what they would do after the war. They were agreeing in the half-wistful, half-jocular tone which was the note of the period (the jocularity Martha recognized as a cousin to her self-parody) that they would go to the Soviet Union, present themselves to Stalin, and demand some difficult and danger-ous work. 'After all,' one of the girls was saying as Martha went past, 'they can't have achieved a perfect socialism yet. I'd like to help develop Siberia, something like that.'

They greeted Martha as if she were a fellow-guest, and continued with their day-dreaming while Martha took her bicycle and went up to Mrs Van's house in the avenues.

When Mrs Van seated herself opposite Martha, composed and straight-backed as always, she said she was pleased to see her and in a way which suggested she should have seen her before. Martha felt hurt, and gave an account of her stewardship – the interview with the editor, details of the interview with a lawyer about possible libel, the extracts from the speeches. Mrs Van listened, extracting the core of the situation at once, which was that she had no legal redress, and that her political reputation was probably permanently damaged. She dismissed this with a tranquil nod, and went on to say: 'And now I have to discuss the question of Saturday's committee. I'm not at all satisfied with the attitude of you people. There's this major crisis developing, and I wonder if you realize it.'

'But Mrs Van, we spend hours of our time discussing what is the right thing to do.'

Mrs Van said coldly: 'I dare say you do, but I do not recognize the rights of the communists to decide policy separately.'

Martha instinctively got up, as if to leave. She was now angry as well as hurt. Why then, she wanted to ask, did you arrange things so that we should be on the committee? You made use of us, and now you say 'the communists' in that tone of voice. She noted that Mrs Van's large working hands were engaged in a movement she knew: agitatedly smoothing down the stuff of her dress over her thighs. She knew, from her mother, that this meant distress. Mrs Van had not meant to say that; she was expressing some sort of private irritation. So she sat down again and waited.

Mrs Van, controlling herself, said in a different voice, which was genial and quizzical: 'I should be glad to know what *line* you've agreed on?'

'Yours,' said Martha. 'But the fact is, we're bothered by a question of principle. There's something fundamentally undemocratic about an African Branch and . . .'

But she could not finish. Again Mrs Van exploded out of her private irritation: 'It really is extraordinary how you communists always tend to side with the right wing . . .' But she again stopped herself, sighed and said patiently: 'I'm sorry, but I'm worried about a number of things. Of course it's undemocratic. I'm always surprised how often in this country progressives have to fight on bad moral grounds. You might remember', she added smiling, 'that white trade unionism has kept the Africans of South Africa and this country out of skilled work for generations on the sound moral argument that it is unfair for black workers to be paid less than white workers . . . well?'

'Well, we've decided to support you, but all the same, there's something wrong about the whole thing.'

'I'm glad to hear that *we* are being so sensible,' said Mrs Van, returning without apology to an extreme, irritated dryness.

Martha again got up. This time she sat down because of Mrs Van's peremptory nod towards a chair. Martha sat and listened for some minutes while Mrs Van gave her views on the 'line' she expected the communist faction to adopt. Martha found it humorous that she was expected to be a messenger from Mrs Van to the group, but she knew that Mrs Van did not find it so. She listened, assured Mrs Van they would all be there on Saturday, assured her of their support, rose to go, and saw that Mrs Van was disappointed.

There was a moment of hesitation. Mrs Van offered her a drink. Martha drank and listened while Mrs Van talked about marriage, trying to discover what lesson was being offered to her. At last she saw that Mrs Van was talking to herself. It upset her, that the composure of this woman could be destroyed. It had been. Her voice was harsh and it trembled. Marriage, she kept repeating, was a question of compromise. Marriage was a matter of tolerance. Yet there were times when one wondered if one should compromise on a principle . . . She went on to talk of the law, of court cases, of her husband's attitude towards the law.

She was disturbed by something her husband had done? But why now? And why was she talking of it to Martha?

Martha only knew that the solidity of this older woman was necessary to her and that to see her as she was now was deeply painful. And surely it would be painful to her, afterwards, remembering the scene? Mrs Van did not look at Martha at all. She talked on in a harsh wondering voice. Her small blue eyes moved from one article of furniture to another and her hands plucked at her dress until at last the servant came in with the announcement that Baas wanted to see the Missus at once, at which Mrs Van sighed, sat still a moment, then rose and thanked Martha for coming in her usual kindly and formal way.

Back in the flat Martha found only the drunken pilot. He was a fair, slight, childish young man, his face flushed up with drink and sleep. He was lying on his side on the floor, a brandy bottle rolling empty beside him. Martha knelt by him to put a cushion under his head. She thought he must be hot in the thick jacket, tried to remove it, found the heavy limbs impossible to move, and left him, consciously suppressing a maternal love for him. So many of the pilots who had been near the group had been killed. This one too, most likely, she thought; in a few months' time I'll hear he's dead. I can't stand any more of these deaths and being unhappy afterwards. She shut out the thought of the pilot, and decided that since it was now ten o'clock, Anton would soon be home, and if she were to think about her position she had a very short time to do it in. The beginning of her thinking was to take from Anton's handkerchief drawer the photograph of a young woman, which she studied carefully. This was Anton's dead wife. He had never mentioned her until after his marriage to Martha. Since then he had talked of her constantly, until Martha had come to feel the dead woman was haunting her. She looked at this photograph often, with respect, with resentment, and with – oddly enough, envy. It was a lean, sad, dark-eyed face, full-lipped but severe. The dark hair was cut like a man's, but she was not masculine, not at all. Martha felt drawn to this woman, but she could not imagine how she had married Anton. For the life of her she could not connect the two. It appeared that she had been among the first communists to be arrested by the Nazis and had died in the concentration camp. Anton and she had been married for three years, but had spent very little time together because of the demands of the Party. As Anton said: 'She was a woman who had given herself to the Revolution. She did not care about herself at all.'

And was this a criticism of Martha? She did not think so. When Anton talked of his dead wife it was with a look of stoically regretful and at the same time puzzled pride. Grete had been a fine public speaker. She had great physical bravery. She had 'a mind like a man's' – Martha made a note of this with a feeling that it said a good deal about Anton. Also, 'the workers loved her.' And why should the workers not love her? It seemed she was the daughter of a rich family and had left it for the cause. (That Anton, so bitterly proletarian, should have married a middle-class woman was another fact that Martha stored up for examination, feeling that it said something of importance about him.)

Evening after evening Anton talked of Grete, and Martha listened. The moment they were left alone it was the signal for the entry of Grete. Once Martha said impatiently: 'But,

Anton, why do you talk so much of Grete?' and he replied, 'But she was a fine comrade, Matty, a fine woman.'

At which Martha shrugged. The shrug said everything about the marriage. 'Why should I bother when it's not a marriage at all?' (Yet outwardly she was affectionate and compliant with her husband.) The truth is, she concluded, he's probably still married to Grete. She returned the photograph to its drawer, took off her dress, and lay on the bed, feeling the sweat crawl and prickle over her flesh. The bed was under the window. She looked straight up into a black, dry sky, clashing with barren thunder, split with dry lightning. Storms excited her sexually, and she was on the point of indulging in fantasies of the faceless man who waited in the wings of the future, waiting to free the Martha who was in cold storage – but she suppressed them. Anton would be coming soon. She had learned to protect herself against him sexually. She had consulted a book on sex which belonged to Marjorie and discovered that Anton was suffering from something called premature ejaculation. But she rejected the phrase. Anton's combination of complacent pride with, as far as she was concerned, a total incapacity, expressed something in his personality and had nothing to do with Latin text-book phrases. The deepest of instincts taught her that it was wrong ever to let him suspect the depth of her disappointment with him, and she was becoming the most accomplished of sexual liars. But this was only possible if she were not moved by him. Martha was not a woman who could ever use such phrases as 'the sexual side of marriage'. From the moment when she understood that 'going to bed' with Anton was something she regarded as apart from and subversive of what she felt for him, which was a dry and increasingly critical affection, she restored her own wholeness by resting in imagination on the man who would enter her life and make her be what she knew she could be. She felt this man, rather than saw him, a person perhaps rather in the line of a masculine counterpart to Grete. From the safety this man's image gave her, she was kind to Anton. But there was always a bad moment or two before they went to bed. Luckily it was always very late, they were seldom alone

294

together for longer than a few minutes, and in the mornings there were usually people in the flat who needed to be given breakfast. When the war is over, thought Martha, we will go our own ways. This was beginning to have desperation in it, because it occurred to her that Anton did not take it for granted, as she did, that they must separate.

There was, in short, a well of desperation slowly filling below the attitude represented by a shrug of the shoulders. Anton was coming to depend on her, and in a way she did not like. He saw something in her that she did not recognize as being any part of herself. It had entered her mind more than once, listening to him talk of Grete, that if she died, Anton would talk to his next wife or woman of her, Martha, and in the same way: Martha and Grete would be not so much offered to this new woman as past experience, but stated, laid down, propositions, bits of property from Anton's past. (The last phrase was definitely satirical – for Anton had a sense of property which Martha had not, yet he never ceased to condemn her middle-class attitudes.)

It followed then that she must wonder: Since I could not conceivably be presented to this future woman like Grete, who was a heroine, what qualities do I possess? He must have some idea of her to give him the complacent and uxorious look she hated. So what was it? At this point Martha would sometimes examine herself in the mirror. (On this evening of heat and thunder she examined herself, found herself ugly, and returned to her bed unable to care that she was ugly.) She was attractive, but not particularly so. She had not changed much. When she saw herself from outside there she was as she had always been, rather tense, over-critical, awkward and abrupt. Nothing to give Anton cause for pride. Yet he felt pride and showed it. In which case there was something she did not understand; she was being stupid, and probably, as usual, egotistical, and it was her duty . . .

When Anton came in rather late Martha was asleep. He switched the centre light on and began to undress. Martha woke and said Hullo. He did not respond. She realized he was angry and roused herself to listen to the lecture she felt she deserved for not going to the meetings. But he still did not speak, although she swung her legs over the side of the bed and sat waiting. After two or three questions from her which he answered abruptly, he began an attack on Jack Dobie which she had heard before: Jack was an old-fashioned socialist freebooter without discipline or any real understanding of politics. Martha was more bad-tempered than she knew, for she found herself, when she had decided to say nothing, remarking that he might be a weak-minded social democrat but that it was something of an achievement to get himself elected for one term after another by a collection of white trade unionists who disliked everything Jack stood for, but who respected his character so much they would vote for no one else.

Anton, as if he had been waiting for her to say this, turned a cold gaze on her and said: 'Yes, yes, but it's not our function to run around like a lot of schoolgirls admiring popular politicians.'

He was now moving around the bedroom in his pyjamas putting his things away. She had been interested to find that he bought expensive pyjamas and wore them carefully. He was very tidy. When he was ready for bed, the room once again looked as if it were on display in a shop: two neat little beds, two chests of drawers, a wardrobe, everything correct. Everything except me, Martha thought, knowing that Anton found it irritating that she should lie sprawling in her petticoat under the open window.

'We've got to reorganize the group,' Anton remarked. 'We've got to take ourselves in hand. We arrange meetings and half the members don't turn up. It's got to stop.'

'But, Anton, everyone was doing something important.'

'The Party comes first,' he said with finality. 'The Party is always first.' He sat on his bed and wound up his watch carefully. When he had finished he asked: 'Aren't you going to get undressed?'

'But it's so hot.' However, she sprang up, hastily put on a nightdress, and laid herself down again.

For God's sake, she thought, he's not going to talk about

Grete now? For that particular self-absorbed inward-looking frown meant he was back in the past.

'Yes, Matty,' he said at last, amicable but severe: 'The Party is first, always. That is the first principle.'

She noted that his eyes had returned to the present and to her. Then I must be looking attractive tonight after all, she thought. But I hate the whole attitude: I'm attractive to him tonight, or I'm not attractive tonight. Yet he's an attractive man, I suppose, tall, broad-shouldered and fair wavy hair – it sounds like a description in a women's magazine. But there's something cynical about it all, and I don't like it and it's got nothing to do with me. At which point he arrived at her side and looked down at her with the small complacent smile she was used to seeing at such moments.

'It's terribly hot, Anton,' she said, and took his hand quickly to soften the refusal. His face changed, he nodded at her stiffly and went back to his bed, which he got into without speaking.

Just as if the episode had not occurred he began again, but in a lecturing tone: 'It is the correct organization and the discipline of the Party that matters above all. We must call the comrades at the earliest opportunity and completely reorganize ourselves.'

Martha remarked, with the intention of making a joke: 'Well, discipline may be the highest goal of us all, but I gather Uncle Joe has his moments when he dispenses with it.'

He jerked up on his elbow and stared at her. 'You are referring, I gather, to Comrade Stalin?'

'Anton, don't be so solemn!'

'There are some subjects which I consider sacred and on which I do not permit jokes.' With which he lay flat again, reaching up his hand to switch off the light. They lay side by side, separated by the width of a room, which was now continuously and irregularly illuminated by lightning. It's like the light from gunfire, Martha thought, her imagination returning to the Eastern Front.

As soon as it did, she felt not so much guilty as dismayed: squabbling and pettiness, and men being killed – she lay in an ugly little room, thousands of miles away from where the future of the world was decided, full of anger about nothing.

She said: 'Anton, we aren't seriously going to quarrel becuase I called Stalin Uncle Joe – which everyone does?'

He said: 'Your way of speaking betrays an attitude of mind. It betrays a dangerous way of looking at things. You should be careful, Matty.'

You should be careful was like a threat. Martha considered it for a while, then said: 'Oh, good night, I'm not going to quarrel about it even if you are.'

But in the morning Anton would not speak to her. Before going to work he said that he expected her to see that all the group members should be present that night at seven o'clock sharp for a group meeting. Then he left, stepping past the still sleeping pilot, who lay sprawled under the window in the full hot morning sunlight, with a look of sharp impatient distaste.

Chapter Two

It was not until lunch-hour that Martha was free to round up the group members. Jasmine was not in her own office. Martha ran across the street to the group office and found her there with Mr Matushi. For some days they had been meeting at lunch-time, at his request, so she might give him lectures in political organization, but these had turned into lessons in English. Mr Matushi, who spoke four African dialects, and spoke and read English passably well, considered himself illiterate. When Martha entered, Jasmine was correcting the grammar of a letter he had written to the editor of the *News* about the meeting in the Location. It had not been published, and Mr Matushi was under the impression it was due to his incorrect use of the language.

Jasmine was secured, and Marjorie came next. Martha found her in bed sick, but she said she would tell Colin the group meeting that night had 'first priority'. Maisie was sitting by the window fanning herself. She listened to Martha indifferently, said she had troubles just now and could not come. Would she tell Andrew? 'But, Matty, I told you I've got troubles. Binkie's coming today, and Andrew and I are having trouble.'

'Well, you get rid of Binkie,' said Martha. 'He's no right to bother you now anyway.'

'That's right,' said Maisie.

'What's the matter?'

'They all make me sick.'

Martha laughed, and left, but as she ran fast down the street she felt insecurity grip her stomach. She thought: If Andrew and Maisie are going to allow themselves to be messed about by that idiot Binkie ... She was extraordinarily dismayed, and protected herself by allowing herself to feel a small contempt for Maisie, an onset of distaste. To the extent to which the happiness between a man and a woman has been a symbol for others, they can expect a corresponding disapproval when that happiness collapses. Martha was thinking: There was Mrs Van last night, and now Maisie and Andrew ... she did not conclude her thought, which was: Then there's no hope for me. She was almost in tears.

Martha tried to telephone Athen at the camp, failed to reach him. She tried the du Preez house. Marie was not home. It was half-past one. She cycled to the outskirts of the town where Piet was at work on a building site. Midday, and the sky was loaded from horizon to horizon with the massive, solemn, rolling cloud mountains that still had no promise of rain. The sun broke through the cloud-masses here and there over the plain in indirect spasmodic shafts of light. It was a heavy, orange, ominous sunlight, and the air was pricklingly dry. On the top of a half-finished wall Piet sat straddled, setting bricks into place which were handed up to him by a black man. The rule was that Africans might mix mortar, collect bricks, hand mortar and bricks to the white men, but they might not set the bricks into place, which was skilled work reserved for the white men. Piet saw Martha and, annoyed, gave her a hasty nod.

'I'm sorry, Piet,' she said, standing ten feet below him, looking up into the great sweat-running red face of the white man, and into the lively sweat-dewed black face beside it, 'but Anton says there must be a group meeting tonight.'

'Oh he does, does he?' Piet slapped bricks down, one after another, while the African leaned over with the trowel to smooth off the rough edges of the mortar. He continued this work without looking down until Martha said: 'Piet, look, he insists we've all got to be there.'

'I've got a trade union meeting.'

'Anton says it's important.'

Piet wiped his forehead with the flapping sleeve of his khaki shirt, and said: 'Matty, I'm on the mat again with my mates. I'm in trouble. At five o'clock. You tell our old man that all this is getting a bit much. And besides, how am I to get from the Trades Hall to the flat? If you think I'm going to go running around in all this heat, you can think again.'

'I'll get Jasmine's car and pick you up.'

'If I'm through. Which I doubt.' He fitted another brick into place, nodded at the black man and said: 'Hey, you, hurry up.' Martha thought: Six months ago I would have considered it my duty to criticize Piet for the way he speaks to Africans!

'You'd better tell Marie,' she said. 'I can't find her.'

'One of the kids is sick and she's taken him to hospital.'

'And where's Tommy, can you tell him?'

'He's over there.' Piet inclined his head sideways towards another part of the building site, and then forwards to the African, who handed him another brick.

Martha walked over the rough, hot, brick-littered earth past another white man with his attendant African, to where apprentice Tommy stood by a tangle of piping with a spanner in his hand, being instructed by an older white man. Both were attended by a group of six Africans who were supposed to fetch and carry for them.

Tommy was embarrassed to see Martha. He came across to her, wiping the flat of his hands against his thighs. He said shyly: 'Hey, Matty, what're you doing here?' with an uneasy glance back at the watching men.

Martha gave her message. Tommy said he had plans for that evening.

'Well, we all had plans, didn't we?' Martha heard her voice becoming peremptory, disliked herself, and said: 'Please, Tommy, come if you can, and I've got to get back to my office.'

She was late back at the office, and Mrs Buss said tartly: 'Mr Robinson says he wants that Memorandum typed out even if you have to stay late.'

The Memorandum was not finished until six. Martha, irritable with hunger, a condition she had become so used to she was beginning to wonder secretly if she had some illness, met Jasmine at Black Ally's where the smell of food informed her she had not eaten that day. She bought a bag of sausage rolls, which she ate hastily, sitting beside Jasmine who was driving. Jasmine was talking about Mr Matushi who, she said, needed a lot of working on. Perhaps Martha would take over Mr Matushi since she was going away. Martha did not take this in until she realized that Jasmine had announced she was going to Johannesburg where 'her political development would be advanced by wider experience'.

Martha snapped: 'You can't leave a town without permission from the group,' heard for the second time that day the hectoring note in her voice, and was depressed into silence by the suspicion that she was becoming a shrew.

Jasmine said: 'I feel the group would not be within its rights to refuse permission.' She added that she had bought the train ticket.

Martha, feeling good temper return as the chemical results of the sausage rolls reached her bloodstream, said with a sigh that she envied Jasmine, but there wasn't going to be much left of the group if this went on.

At the Trades Hall Jasmine announced she would fetch Piet from his meeting. Martha said it would embarrass him. Jasmine said that this was too bad, and departed inside the hall. Martha reflected that a week ago Jasmine would not have said it: like everyone else, as soon as she was due to leave the Colony she betrayed her real opinion of its importance. Jasmine emerged a moment later saying: 'Piet's getting it hot.' She added: 'Bloody silly little country, every little incident gets blown up into a major drama.'

They waited for nearly an hour. Then Piet came out saying: 'Well, comrades, that's a bright bit of behaviour – you two are known all over the dorp as a pair of flaming Reds, and Jasmine comes right into the room ordering me to come out, and you sit here in the car in full view, and I'm falling over backwards trying to be respectable.'

'Keep your hair on,' said Jasmine, but Piet went on: 'I've got the whole pack at my throat for subverting the blacks, I've tried to keep them sweet and easy about me being a Red, and you have to push it down their bloody throats.' He was too angry to allow himself to say more. They drove in silence back to the flat.

Anton, Marjorie and Marie were waiting in the Hesse living-room.

Marie was looking wearily humorous. Marjorie was wrapped in a blanket in spite of the heat, for she was shivering and sick. Anton was grimly silent.

'Well?' said Piet. 'Let's get a move on.'

'There are other comrades to come,' said Anton. 'And it's nearly eight. The meeting was convened for seven.'

Marjorie said: 'Anton, I told you Colin can't come.'

'Colin must come.'

Marjorie appealed to the others past Anton: 'There's trouble over Jack Dobie's meeting last night. One of the men from the printers' union went to Jack and told him that there are a lot more anonymous pamphlets being printed – Jack is spreading seditious propaganda about the British Empire. And Colin is with Jack, working out what to do. What's the use,' she demanded plaintively, 'of Colin's making himself an expert on India if he can't use it in a crisis?'

'There's no excuse,' said Anton. To Martha, whom he had not seen since that morning, he said: 'And where are Andrew and Athen?'

'You know they can't be reached easily at the camp.'

'They should be here.'

'Perhaps you should have given people longer notice?'

Marie backed Martha up with: 'Yes, comrade, it's not reasonable to expect full attendance with such short notice.'

Piet said impatiently: 'For God's sake, let's get cracking.'

Ignoring him, Anton said to Martha: 'And where's Tommy?'

Piet said: 'I told Tommy he needn't come. There's a bright lad on the building site, a black from Nyasaland, and Tommy's made a friend of him . . .' Anton began to speak, but Piet steadily spoke him down: 'Yes, it's not easy for a boy like Tommy, a fine member of the herrenvolk, to become friends with a black, and it's more important he should keep his date with this lad than come to this meeting.'

Anton said: 'Who made this decision?'

Piet said: 'Who made the decision to have this meeting? You did. It was not a group decision.'

Anton said: 'I'm chairman, and have a right to convene emergency meetings. And now since this is all we can expect tonight, we can begin.'

'It's not all,' said Marjorie. 'There's Maisie.'

'I do not think we will suffer from the absence of *Comrade* Maisie,' said Anton, with such naked contempt that they all glanced at each other, taking sides against him. There was a mutter of critical exclamations. He sat stubbornly silent, waiting. Then, seeing how the others were looking at him, said impatiently to Martha: 'Then run along downstairs and see what Maisie is doing.'

Martha was angry at his tone, but she nevertheless went downstairs. Maisie's door was shut. She knocked on it, knocked again. At last it opened. Maisie was there, and beyond her stood a tall broad-shouldered young man – Binkie. The war had thinned him, apparently made him taller, straightened him, given him a look of responsibility. Martha would not have recognized him. 'I'm sorry,' said Martha, and retreated. It seemed she had interrupted some speech or declaration by Maisie, for before the door shut again Maisie, having nodded an impatient greeting at Martha, went on: 'And so you see, Binkie, that's how things are, and you've got to face up to it.'

Martha ran back upstairs, thinking delightedly: 'So Andrew and Maisie are all right after all.' She burst into the living-room with the exclamation: 'It's all right – Maisie's standing up to Binkie.'

'I'm glad to hear about Maisie's matrimonial problems,' said Anton, 'but I suggest we now start work.'

'First,' said Piet. 'I told the lads I'd be back by nine. They're dealing with other business in the meantime. I've got twenty minutes.'

Anton said: 'This is a communist party meeting and you'll stay until it's finished.'

Marie gave her husband a startled glance, and clicked her tongue: Tch, tch, tch. She laughed, saying to Anton: 'Oh come off it. And I've got to go too. My kid's sick and the cook's looking after him. Tell us what's important and then we'll push off.'

Anton now began his planned speech: 'Comrades, it is urgently necessary that we should recover our sense of discipline. We are communists. Last night and tonight have shown us to what a distance we have moved from communist behaviour . . .'

Piet broke in with: 'Cut the cackle. What have you brought us here for?'

Anton said: 'My concrete proposal is that we have a series of lectures on the history of the communist party.'

Marie again glanced with humorous concern towards her husband, whose mouth had literally fallen open. After a moment he said blankly: 'Do you mean to say you've got us all together to say that?'

'Yes, yes, yes,' said Anton.

Piet got up, Marie rose and stood beside him.

Piet said: 'Comrade Anton, if you want us to agree formally to a series of lectures on party history, I'm in favour. But I want to say this: You're just out of touch with reality. Or you've got a touch of the sun. What is the position? We're all neck-deep in trouble. My trade union, unless things are handled carefully, is in danger of passing a racist resolution that might stand for years – and I'm fighting to stop it. I'm in danger of losing my position on the Trades Council. The Social Democratic Party is facing a crisis – it might split if things aren't handled properly. We've all of us worked so hard that we've got positions of responsibility in the town and we have influence out of all proportion to our numbers. Yet we're expected to drop everything and run along here to . . .' He was so angry he could not finish.

Marie said in a conciliatory voice: 'Have a heart, Comrade Anton. Sometimes I think you're just a little nuts, if you want to know.'

Anton said steadily: 'I'm not interested in your personal opinions as to my character. I now formally propose that we start our series of lectures tomorrow, or the day after tomorrow if you're all so busy you can't find time for the Party.'

'The day after tomorrow is the Social Democratic Executive.'

'It ends at six,' said Anton.

'But you know quite well that the most important part of these meetings is the discussion that goes on afterwards in the pubs.'

'I'm sorry to hear you say so, Comrade Piet. Sorry, but I must say, not surprised,' said Anton.

Piet said: 'Oh muck it.' And went out. Marie with a final humorously appealing glance at Anton followed him.

Marjorie got up and said: 'I'm really sick, Anton. I must go. The doctor said I shouldn't be out of bed at all.'

'If the doctor said so, Comrade, then obviously you shouldn't have come.'

Marjorie let out a small gasp of anger and hurt, and went out after the du Preez.

Jasmine, who had not opened her mouth, remarked: 'I'll take it upon myself to convene a meeting at a suitable time for everyone. And I hereby give notice that I intend to leave the Colony in ten days' time. And now good night all.' She departed, with a placid smile.

Martha, left alone with Anton, waited for him to say something. But he carefully collected his papers and without a glance at her went next door where he laid himself down on his bed and proceeded to read Lenin.

Martha understood she was sent to Coventry. She went next door and said: 'Anton, you're being absolutely child-ish.' He did not reply. She waited a while, and then walked down the stairs to Maisie's flat. She had heard the noise of a car moving off, and hoped it might be Binkie's. Maisie was alone, and greeted Martha with: 'Matty, I'm sorry I was rude just now, but I was so upset, but he's gone and do have some tea or something.'

'Is everything all right?'

'He cried,' said Maisie, her eyes full of wonder and distaste. 'He cried, Matty. It made me feel so bad. But I don't like it, a man crying. I mean, of course men cry, but he cried as if to influence me, and I didn't like that at all. And it seems to me, it was rather late in the day – of course it's not his fault his parents are such dirty old people, thinking of nothing but money, but . . .' She burst into tears, crying as openly as a child, making no attempt to wipe away her tears, but sitting and swaying slightly from side to side while the water ran fast from her open eyes down her face.

Martha spent the evening with her. Maisie was now hard set against both men, Binkie and Andrew. She spoke of them with a shuddering dismay and dislike. 'They all make me tired, Matty,' she said again and again. 'Sometimes I wonder why we bother with any of them.'

Martha told her she was in a bad mood and would feel better in the morning. She was unable to face the thought that Maisie's and Andrew's love was at an end.

When she went up to her own flat, Anton was asleep, or pretending to be asleep.

Chapter Three

The Executive Committee meeting had been scheduled to start at two. At one the rain came roaring across the veld from the north and enclosed the town in a hot downpour. At two o'clock only half the delegates had arrived; others came in hastily, exclaiming and shaking the wet from their clothes. It was a room whose only illumination was the door, the light had to be switched on because of the teeming dark-grey gloom outside. It was intolerably hot; the noise of the storm made it impossible to hear a word, and soon the delegates left the room to stand around the walls of the courtyard, waiting for the rain to stop. It was even noisier here under the low tin roof of the veranda. As other delegates came in from the street they moved towards their natural allegiances like two armies forming, surveying each other through the driving mists of rain that filled the courtyard between them with a skilled distrust which changed, as they turned to greet the members of their own side, into the hard gay excitement that precedes the decisive battles of the committee rooms. It was a sporting excitement which at moments drew even the opponents together. For instance, when Mr McFarline entered with his sour-faced second, his shrewd brown campaigning eyes summed up the forces on both sides in a single glance, and then greeted Mrs Van, his chief enemy, with a quick and almost amused nod. She nodded briskly and gaily back. Mr McFarline took up his position among the new recruits, the delegates from hastily-formed branches all over the country, and he as much as the 'Red' faction regarded them with interest since, although they were trade unionists and therefore by presumption against the African Branch, no one really knew where they stood.

On the 'Red' side of the courtyard, the ranks were thinner. Colin Black and Jack Dobie stood side by side, united by their common passion for the continent of India. Mrs Van had Johnny Lindsay beside her. His blue eyes were crackling, every line of his tall body expressing the enjoyments of pugnacity in a good cause. On her other side the Reverend Mr Playfair, melancholy with the nobilities of enforced impartiality, studied the agenda with attention. It was an extremely long agenda, the rain showed no sign of weakening, and the meeting was scheduled to end at six. All the delegates were attentive over the agenda, studying the battle-ground, looking for ambushes concealed in sub-clauses, the surprise attack lurking in an order of words. It was clear to everyone that again the conflict would be focused in two items: The African Branch and Any Other Business. Jasmine, who was as at home among agendas as Mrs Van, that other natural committee woman, was leaning over Mr Playfair's arm pointing out how various dreary stretches of unimportant ground could be outflanked by a judicious manipulation of words. Martha and Marjorie were with the du Preez, supporting them in their efforts to explain the agenda to Tommy, who was positively anguished with incomprehension. He kept doggedly repeating: 'Everybody here knows we are going to have a fight about the African Branch, so I don't see why Mr Playfair shouldn't say: "Let's vote and be done with it." I don't see why we should have to mess about when it's all so simple.'

'Democracy, Tommy lad, democracy – that's the point,' Piet kept saying, jocularly aggressive. He was continuously laughing and making jokes, and all the efforts of Jasmine and Martha, who were consciously engaged in making a recalcitrant comrade see reason, were met by the same jocular hostility. They had discussed Piet, decided he was in a mood when he might very well leave the group, and he needed 'working on'.

In a self-contained group further down the veranda Mr

Matushi and two other Africans from the Location waited patiently.

They all had to wait until past three, when the courtyard, until then a square of dark-grey wet, lightened into a drizzle already weakly radiant from an emerging sun.

The office filled. There were thirty people in a room used to accommodate a dozen. Antagonists and friends were crammed together on hard chairs in a press of hot, damp flesh.

Mr Playfair's opening speech was weighted with sincere feeling. The whole Colony watched their deliberations here today; the issues at stake were universal ones – and so on. Mrs Van was observed, after about fifteen minutes, to give him a stern glance. At which he pulled himself up, his good-humour concealing a deep hurt because no one shared his belief that a sufficient number of nobly worded phrases should be enough to enforce noble behaviour on them all.

The work began, and went on fast; it was the clearing away of superfluous scrub from the battleground, both sides having assured themselves that no traps were hidden in items to do with subscription rates and similar matters.

Meanwhile, the new faces were being carefully studied. The 'Red' faction had believed that their perfectly open position was a disadvantage. Now they saw they might have been wrong. It was for the other side to manoeuvre: they were in the position of a small outnumbered army entrenched on high ground. For the half-dozen new men represented more than themselves. Mr McFarline and his aides had travelled through the outlying districts reviving dormant branches and creating new ones, but the branches after all consisted of people with, presumably, ideas of their own. There were two possibilities: that these ideas might turn out, by some fluke of public opinion, to support the African Branch or – more probably – that these men, used to the rough-and-ready methods of conducting meetings possible in small groups far from the embattled centres of opinion, might not understand the formalities of serious agenda-manipulation and therefore vote against their own intentions.

But it was not until five o'clock that the item 'African Branch' was reached. Piet opened for the 'Red' side with a brief and formal statement: The African Branch was an earnest of the good intentions of organized white labour towards the African worker; if the white man was to be taken seriously in his claim to be a tutor to the backward and uncivilized he must be prepared to accept an at least token advance towards democracy; and if the African members were to be disbarred because of the pressure of ignorant and backward opinion, the Social Democratic Party (otherwise, he reminded them, the Labour Party, the party of Labour) could never claim to be anything more than the party of white labour.

After which McFarline counter-attacked with: The African members naturally inspired the citizens of the Colony with distrust, since they, the white citizens, did not understand (here he gave a suave nod towards Mr Matushi and his two friends) the fundamentally reasonable character of the signed-up Africans, but suspected them of conspiring together behind the backs of the white members for reasons of their own. Here he laughed, and there was a good deal of embarrassed laughter, and the three Africans continued politely to say nothing. And in any case the whole idea of an African Branch was undemocratic. He formally proposed that there should be no African Branch, but that African members should, if they wished, attend ordinary branch meetings as ordinary members.

The two trumpets had been blown for either side, and now battle could be joined. Both sides turned their eyes towards the new members who sat by themselves along a bench. The natural leader of this group was already obvious. He was an Afrikaner, Danie du Toit, a railway worker from G—, a squat strong man with a powerfully shaped head, a broad tough face, calm hard eyes. He now remarked that as a newcomer he would like to have some points made clear. Speaking as a labour man who never believed a word he read in the capitalist press, he discounted everything he had read about the meeting in the Location; the capitalists were out to discredit the Labour Party and that was all there was to it. So unless people present could give him any relevant information about that meeting he proposed to skip it and get down to the business in hand. 'It's this question of the proposed African Branch. We all have a great respect for Mr McFarline and what he has done for the workers, but I don't agree with him. If you're going to have African members – and to be honest I must say I disagree with it, it seems to me they are not ripe for politics – present company excepted,' he added quickly, 'but it's nothing but hypocrisy to say they should be ordinary members with the white members. I don't know what's accepted in the towns . . .' He said this in the voice of one who knows perfectly well what's accepted in the towns – 'but in my district the meetings are held in my house, and I know I'd never recruit another member if they knew they had to sit down man to man with Kaffirs. No offence meant,' he added with another glance at Mr Matushi, who was preserving his appearance of sorrowful and patient dignity. 'So it's as good as saying we'll keep the blacks out of meetings. My wife wouldn't have a Kaffir in her house and that's that. I'm for the African Branch. It's not democratic but it's practical.'

Mr Matushi and his friends nodded. Mr McFarline's battalions seemed unhappy. The 'Red' faction could scarcely preserve their impartial expressions.

Mrs Van whispered to Mr Playfair who asked if she should put the vote. Mr McFarline instantly rose to say that he refused to be steam-rollered. His faction nodded impressively. Mr McFarline made a speech direct to his supposed supporters, Danie du Toit and his group, delegates of branches that he, Mr McFarline, had caused to come into existence. He repeated his warnings that the members of the Party, let alone the Colony's citizens, would never stand for the African Branch. To which Danie du Toit replied that the situation should never have been allowed to arise, African members were asking for trouble, but since it had arisen, they had to find a compromise, and the African Branch seemed to him such a compromise.

The argument then broke out all over the room. For an hour the two sides hammered home their points, repeating themselves and shouting at each other. At six o'clock the meeting was extended. The principles of trade unionism and the history of the British Labour Party were explained and offered by both sides as support for their attitudes. The equality of man and brotherhood of races were pressed into service. A debate raged about whether or not races were fundamentally different: scientific evidence for one point of view was offered by the 'Red' faction, much passionate emotion by the other. (The Africans did not contribute at all to this part of the debate.) At seven o'clock they were no nearer agreement; the four men with Danie du Toit had not opened their mouths; and it was impossible to tell how they would vote.

Finally it was agreed that the vote should be put.

The voting was even, sixteen to sixteen, two of the du Toit contingent voting with the 'Red' faction, and two with Mr McFarline. It fell to Mr Playfair to settle the thing with his casting vote. But he rose and said that while everyone knew his sympathies lay with the African Branch, in issues like this he was not prepared to accept such a responsibility. At which Mr McFarline demanded a Congress to settle the matter.

Everyone suddenly collapsed into renewed frustration and irritability. Nothing was settled, everything would have to be fought out again. The Congress was fixed for a month ahead.

The meeting then gave an impressive demonstration of how fast an agenda can be worked through if everyone wishes it. They were all yawning and impatient, voting with scarcely any discussion. Mr Playfair finally announced the item Any Other Business, and was already saying: 'And so I conclude the meeting . . .' when Danie du Toit rose to say he had points to make, his branch had insisted on his making them. They all settled down again.

He demanded to know three things. First, Jack Dobie. They had been informed that Brother Dobie, who was of course respected by every worker in the Colony, had been addressing meetings of the Progressive Club, a communist-organized club, on India. As a result of this, the town had been flooded with anonymous pamphlets against Brother Dobie. Secondly, Mrs Van der Bylt: she had been similarly attacked by anonymous pamphleteers for inciting the Africans. Thirdly, Piet du Preez, who had, they heard, been giving lectures to the Africans on trade unionism. These people were all members of the Party and had no right to compromise it in this way. He demanded an explanation.

At this point it became clear to everyone that far from being over, the meeting was just beginning.

Mr Playfair demanded to know if the meeting should be adjourned for half an hour so that the delegates could get something to eat. The 'Red' faction instantly opposed this: they did not want Mr McFarline to take Danie du Toit aside and explain how he was not fulfilling his, Mr McFarline's, hopes of him. For the same reason, Mr McFarline's faction wanted an adjournment. A vote was taken, it went on the side of everyone's 'staying here till morning if necessary' to get the matter thrashed out.

And now Mrs Van, Piet, Jack and Johnny all made speeches in defence of their right to say anything they wished, in their private capacity, to any sort of organization they wished.

To which the entire McFarline faction openly and violently hostile at last said they had no right. Four of their potential candidates, Mrs Van, Piet, Jack and Johnny, had now been branded as communists and Kaffir-lovers – no offence meant, of course, to Mr Matushi and his friends – and would be lucky not to lose their deposits. An election was likely at any moment. The Party could not afford to throw away four good candidates. It was urgently essential that these four people should publicly disown, in the form of letters to the *News*, any association with communism or any ideas of jumping up the blacks to equality with the whites.

Mrs Van, in a dignified speech, refused.

Piet and Johnny followed suit.

Jack Dobie said that far from apologizing he intended to sue the authors of the anonymous pamphlets for libel.

And how could he sue anonymous people at all?

He couldn't, said Jack, sticking out his sharp and pugnacious chin. But he could and would sue the printer. In fact legal proceedings had already been put in train.

Had Brother Jack in fact said the things he was supposed to have said?

Every word, said Jack. In his view the British were rapacious imperialist exploiters of India and he insisted on his right to say so any time or any place he wanted.

Then the pamphlets were not libellous but accurate?

'It is a question of principle,' said Jack. 'Besides, a court case will give publicity to the socialist view on India.' He emphasized the word socialist, looking around at these executive committee members of a socialist party.

Danie du Toit wished to know what Brother Jack's constituents thought of his attitude. He had never in his life met a railway worker with Brother Jack's ideas, and he did not believe the railway workers in Brother Jack's constituency were different from those in his own.

Jack retorted that he had paid a visit to his constituency the night before, and seen as many of the railway workers as was possible in the time, and found them 'once the principles were explained' in agreement that he had the right to express any views he held.

And had Brother Jack called a public meeting?

No, said Jack, he had not, for the good reason that it was not possible to convene a meeting at a day's notice.

Danie du Toit repeated his disapproval of Brother Jack's action. Jack repeated his defiance. Johnny Lindsay and Piet reaffirmed their principles, and once again the meeting became a free-for-all on brotherhood, freedom and racial equality. In the midst of this Mr Matushi and his two friends left, for the reason they always had to leave meetings early: it was after curfew time and they had no passes to be out late.

When they had gone the argument became suddenly very free, Mr McFarline's side expressing with vigour their conviction that the Kaffirs, the blacks, the natives were savage and childish, and quite unready for political organization; while the 'Red' faction argued against them.

At twelve o'clock the meeting ended from sheer exhaustion. Nothing had been settled save that a Congress would endeavour to reconcile obviously irreconcilable opponents.

New currents of ill-feeling had been sprung. For instance, Mr McFarline, all suavity gone, had been heard to remark to his faction that if Mrs Van were the last woman alive in the world he couldn't bring himself to f—her. Mrs Van had heard this, as she had been meant to, and had given Mr McFarline a look of such contempt that he had raised his voice as he departed along the rain-wet verandas to insist: 'As far as I am concerned there's not a woman in the world who's not a woman for me, old or young, black or white, but Mrs Van's without c— or t— for me and that's the truth.'

Mrs Van, attempting to smile at this, had burst into tears with annoyance. Jack and Johnny had gone to her, cosseting her, helping her with her papers and the business of putting things away.

Further, Danie du Toit on leaving the office had said to Jack: 'You've stabbed us in the back, brother, you've done us a bad turn with all this loving-our-heathen-brethren stuff. If the Party fails at the next election it's your doing and remember that.'

To which Jack had retorted that if the Party had no principles it did not deserve to get in, but Danie du Toit had already left.

Finally, one of Mr McFarline's block of members of Parliament who had been watching Marjorie's persistent shiftings and changings of position (she was nearing the end of her pregnancy) had said to her: 'Well, if it's communism to expect a woman who should be in bed to sit up at meetings till all hours in all this smoke and bad air, then communism is not for me.'

To which Marjorie had replied with a statement of the rights of women, but he interrupted with: 'Well, I wouldn't have my wife behaving so,' and moved off fast, so he did not hear her irritated: 'I'd be surprised if you ever let your wife open her mouth in public – petty dictator, that's what you are!'

Marjorie dropped Martha off at the flat, saying with the

grim humour that had completely swallowed all the impulsive charm they had once known her for: 'As far as I can see when we get socialism we'll have to fight another revolution against men – lot of hidebound reactionaries, that's what they are! Colin told me today he didn't believe in women working after marriage – lucky for him he never mentioned it before!'

As for Martha she was too tired to answer. She was thinking that Anton had still to be faced before she could sleep. He had not spoken a single word to her since their quarrel.

Chapter Four

The case of Dobie versus Johnson was set down in the High Court for eleven that Saturday morning. The famous Congress was due to start at three, 150 miles away, in G—. This meant that Jack and his supporters must drive like maniacs to be at the Congress in time.

At eleven the case of Van Rensburg versus Welty was still in progress; and the token representatives of the 'Reds' – Martha, Jack and Mrs Van, could scarcely find room on benches packed with Afrikaans farmers and their wives who had come to see the final round in the long battle over the boundary fence. Mr Robinson was lawyer for the Van Rensbergs and Martha knew there would be no glorious climax of finality that day; Mr Van, briefed by Mr Robinson as Counsel, had found some obscure law which would keep the pot boiling for possibly several months. These comfortable, solid country people, their faces sharpened and shrewd with the enjoyment of the law, were looking puzzled. And with good reason: Martha knew that Mr Robinson was puzzled himself: he had exclaimed the day before that he hoped Mr Van knew what he was doing, but for his part he was fed up with the whole business – meanwhile the fees were filling page after page of the ledgers. Half a dozen cases, offshoots of the great central case, were in progress. A Welty had assaulted a Van Rensberg in a bar; a Van Rensberg wife had insulted a Welty aunt. A Van Rensberg girl had fallen in love with a Welty boy, and they had run away together. They had been brought back, and since the girl was a minor, the Van Rensberg parents were suing the Weltys for abduction. The young couple were both present that morning, eyeing each other from where they sat well guarded by relatives: the two factions, despite the press on the benches, kept twelve inches of distance from each other, into which frosty no-man's-land Martha, Jack and Mr Van were able to fit themselves.

Meanwhile, the lawyers and the counsels were swapping clauses and sub-clauses and the English judge, his wig rather crooked over his pale, handsome humorous face, occasionally allowed himself an impartial and appreciative nod, as if saying: 'Well played, sir.'

Mr Van's clever handling of the obscure sub-clause won him a postponement of the case until next week, by which time he expected to have proof that the Weltys, on the moral ground that the Van Rensbergs had burned out their grazing, had been running their cattle on the Van Rensberg land. Martha noted that Mr Van, usually so legal and lean, was animated by enjoyment; the Afrikaans lilt was strong in his voice, and the almost English dryness of his personality had vanished because of his absorption in the case. He kept allowing his eyes to meet those of his audience, as if expecting them to share his relish. They did share it; or would have done if they could have understood the complications of the battle. Van Rensberg versus Welty came to an end, or rather a suspension, and as the two factions jostled out of the Court, individual members on opposing sides could be seen commiserating with each other because they had lost a morning's work on their respective farms and would have to come up to town again next week.

For five minutes the courtroom was empty. It was a high room, on whose glossy, dark-wood-panelled sides moved gleams of light, the reflections of people moving to their places. It was a silent room in the heart of the building, and not even the drone and the roar of the aeroplanes from the camp could be heard.

Mr Van moved from one side of the Court to the other, thus marking the fact that he was now Counsel for the Defence. Martha and Jack refrained from looking at Mrs Van whle he did so. They knew she felt it keenly that he had undertaken to defend her dearest friend's opponent. Yet she had never, out of loyalty to her husband, made any criticism of him. She had merely remarked, in a voice stiff with the effort of restraint, her eyes averted, that 'Mr Van has never agreed with me that there are cases he should not accept.'

For a month now, anonymous letters, letters to the newspaper, editorials, anonymous leaflets, had been describing Jack Dobie as a traitor to the British and even as 'A gift to the Nazis'. Through all this he had kept his stubborn sharp little chin high, had refused to answer his critics, and had spent his time preparing statistics and facts about British rule in India. He had called three meetings in his constituency to explain his position to the railway workers. That they were not satisfied was proved by the fact that when the Court refilled after the Afrikaner farmers had filed out, there was a bloc of eight railway workers who had made the journey from U—to see how their Parliamentary representative would comport himself. There were also three men from the Trades Council, of whom Piet was one, elected for the sake of fair play, since he was known to support Jack, to balance the other two, who did not. The right wing of the Social Democratic Party had sent half a dozen observers. All thse people were impatient to leave for the Congress.

Jack had insisted on conducting his own case, on the grounds that he wasn't going to have those damned lawyers wriggling out of the political facts into a mesh of red tape.

He left Martha and Mrs Van with a cocky, grim little grimace, and stood across the Court opposite to Mr Van who was formal in his wig and his black forked robes.

He took up the stance of a man about to address a public meeting. While he waited for the preliminary formalities to be done with, he reassured himself that he remembered the main facts of his argument by consulting his notes. They were the notes he had used for his address to the Progressive Club and for the meetings with his constituents, and as soon as the Judge nodded at him he proceeded to make the same speech, with, however, rather more statistics than usual. The Judge rested his cheek on his hand and gazed down the Court. The lawyers for the opposing sides exchanged glances of professional disapproval at this amateurishness which was disgracing their smooth machinery. Mr Van confidently made notes and bided his time. He interrupted Jack ten minutes after he had begun his speech with: 'Am I to take it that you are resting your case on the poverty of the Indian people after three hundred years of British rule?' To which Jack replied energetically that he was; whereupon Mr Van sat down again and continued to make notes. He had supplied himself with three witnesses: a Major, retired from the British Indian Army; a businessman who had operated from Calcutta for several years; and the widow of an Indian Civil Service District Officer, now living on her pension in a large house in the suburbs which she had named Simla Nights. This lady, in appearance like a newly washed Sealyham, with fluffy white hair under which fierce but faded eyes peeped out; and the Major, who was red-faced and puffy, were exactly what one expected them to be, and made extremely angry by every word that Jack Dobie said, exchanging energetic nods of disapproval and mutters of Shame! Disgrace! and so on. The businessman, however, was a mild, bowed, grey person, known to be an authority on the Upanishads. He had offered to address the Progressive Club on the subject. He showed no signs of wishing to be associated with his fellow-witnesses, moved as far as he could away from their duet of puffs and grunts, and visibly approved when the Judge silenced them with a benevolent but urgent stare. Mr Van, thus prompted, whispered to his two witnesses who fell indignantly silent.

Meanwhile, Jack continued his oration. The listening trade unionists, obviously stretched by a dozen conflicting loyalties, were shifting about and frowning and whispering. The Defence lawyer and Counsel waited and fingered their documents. The printer, who was being sued, a choleric little tradesman furious at having to waste his time thus, kept glancing about him suspiciously at the panoply and fancy-dress of the High Court and openly marvelled that all this could have anything to do with his newly established modest printing firm which aimed at nothing more ambitious than to make enough to send his two children to University at the Cape.

Suddenly the Judge raised his voice to inquire how long

Mr Dobie intended to speak. 'Until I've made my case,' said Jack.

'Ah,' said the Judge and allowed his cheek to return to rest against his palm.

A moment later Jack brought in the abolishment of illiteracy in the Soviet Union; whereupon the Judge raised himself to remark in an absent, almost dreamy tone, that he did not see what the Soviet Union had to do with India.

Jack, ready for this, raised his voice to claim that in his view it was perfectly relevant to compare the thirty years of Soviet rule over backward peoples with the British rule in India.

'I'm afraid,' drawled the Judge, 'that I cannot agree.'

At this the whole tone of the case changed. The Left, delighted, sat up and took notice. The Defence, lawyers and laymen, nodded vigorous agreement with the Judge.

'I must insist,' said Jack. 'I want to make the point that it is possible for backwardness to be abolished in a country if there is a will to abolish it.'

The Judge, without removing his interested gaze from the far end of the room, interrupted with: 'My dear sir, I must absolutely forbid you to make Soviet propaganda in this Court.' He added: 'Or for that matter any sort of propaganda.'

'Are you suggesting that I have been making propaganda?' demanded Jack. His eyes encountered Mrs Van's. They exchanged what might have been described as suppressed winks. Jack took it for granted he would lose the case, and regarded this as an opportunity to make propaganda for the cause. He therefore simultaneously felt indignation because he was stopped from making propaganda, amusement that he was able to make it here, and contempt for the arguments of the Defence – a sort of complicated relish, delight, and loathing of the whole proceeding, all of which was expressed, against his will, in his face and which of course annoyed his trade union critics as much as it was annoying the Defence. An irritable and gloomy impatience was being infused into the atmosphere: it was after twelve, Jack had been speaking for half an hour; at least half of the spectators wanted to leave for the Congress.

'In that case,' said Jack, 'I shall rest my case.' He did so, crossing one leg over the other, and pointing his sharp chin Judgewards. He had in any case finished his speech, but it was generally appreciated that he had chosen a good moment to sit down, giving an impression of being suppressed and silenced.

Now Mr Van began cross-examining the widow of the District Officer. Mottled with anger and with heat, she said that she had lived for forty years in India and that the relations between Indians and British were perfect, and that speaking for herself she had always kept her servants for years. 'My Ayah was my closest friend,' she exclaimed belligerently, 'and my husband always used to say . . .' The Judge gave something like a yawn and Mr Van hastened to interrupt. Martha imagined for a moment that perhaps Mr Van had undertaken to defend this case only to use his skill to make the Defence seem ridiculous, but she saw from Mrs Van's face, which was severe and sorrowful, that she was wrong.

The good widow answered half a dozen questions from Mr Van from which it emerged that she always wrote to her Ayah at Christmas, that she had paid her cook 'very fair wages for those days' and that she had paid to send his eldest son to school 'because they are quite improvident, and if we hadn't educated them they would all be completely illiterate'. Also, in her opinion the climate of India was responsible for its poverty, because its inhabitants lacked energy, and the heat during the monsoon was impossible to imagine 'and the poor things couldn't get to the hills the way we did'.

She was thanked courteously by Mr Van who, it seemed, was pleased with her. He then called the businessman, who offered smiles of fellow-feeling across the Court to Jack, as if to say: Let the best man win.

In his opinion the conditions of poverty in India 'which no one in their senses would deny' were irrelevant, because true culture did not depend upon money, and as an authority upon the Upanishads – 'purely on an amateur level of course' he could say that India was probably the most cultured and spiritual nation in the world. (At this point the widow and the Major nearly died with indignation.) As a lover of India for nearly fifty years – he was happy to say he had been born in it, he could only say in reply to Counsel that while he had every sympathy with Mr Dobie's point of view, it took no account of the most important question of all: Was it or was it not harder for a rich man to get to heaven than for a camel to get through the eye of a needle? (Here he again smiled tolerantly at Jack as if to say: I have no real desire to make you appear like a gross materialist, but I am afraid Truth leaves me no alternative.)

Mr Van dismissed his second witness with the same politeness and called his third, the Major, on whom he obviously set great store.

The Major exploded into the witness-box like a bursting shell, and had to be called to order by the Judge at the end of the first sentence.

'I must remind the witness that this is a court of law,' he remarked, without taking his gaze off the far wall, or removing his tired cheek from his hand.

'Well, that damned fellow has been making speeches for an hour,' said the Major.

'I dare say,' said the Judge. 'I dare say. But I do so hope that you aren't going to.'

Mr Van leaned over to whisper to his witness, who said loudly: 'Oh very well, damn it, but I'm going to have my say.'

He said that as everyone knew who 'understood anything whatsoever about India' the cause of poverty in that continent 'was obvious to the meanest intelligence'. It was that the women spent all their money on jewellery. If they had the sense to invest it, instead of hanging it in their noses or wrapping it around their arms or their necks, they could accumulate capital and . . .

Here Jack remarked, grinning, that the annual average income was a few shillings a year.

The trade unionists had started to smile. A friendly current of feeling had set in between Jack and them, on account of this natural enemy of them both: the fat, red-faced, vowel-twisting damn-you-all major.

Martha and Mrs Van were both shaking with laughter.

The Judge smiled, very gravely, at the wall.

Mr Van, as correct as a Court Order, continued to cross-examine the Major: 'You would say that the causes of poverty in India are . . .'

At this interesting point, Martha noticed the agitated face of her servant in a side door left open to get a draught through the hot and stuffy Court. She left Mrs Van with an apology saying she would be back at once. The servant had a message from Anton saying she must come home.

'But I told the Baas I was going down to the Congress.'

'But the Baas said, you must come now.'

'Very well, then, I'll come.'

She lingered a moment at the door, listening. The Major was making a speech across the Court to Jack, about some occasion when his life had been saved by a Sikh, which proved that the Indians, far from hating the British, loved them. 'Greater love has no man!' he exclaimed angrily, 'than to lay down his life for his friend.'

It seemed as if the case was drawing to an end. Groups of trade unionists were leaving. A couple went past Martha and she heard one of them say: 'Well, I had a Zulu woman as a nurse when I was a kid and . . .' They went off down the panelled corridors. It had not occurred to Martha that anyone could find the arguments of Mr Van's defence anything but absurd, but it seemed he had known what he was doing.

She ran down the street towards the flat, her eyes on an aircraft that roared straight down over Main Street. She was imagining herself to be in a city in Europe, the plane an enemy plane, machine-gunning the street. This was because one of the pilots who came to the meetings – the boy who had got drunk that night a month before, had said that he hated this little town and the country so much that every time he flew over it he imagined he was 'shooting the bloody place and the bloody white herrenvolk up'. Her ears, after the silence of the Court, which had held only the sound of arguing voices, were irritably resisting the roar of the aeroplane. She reached her flat almost in tears because of the noise, found it empty, and banged shut the windows of the small bedroom which was stuffy enough with them open. But two more planes turning in to land overhead made the air tremble, and she sat on the edge of her bed with her hands clenched across her ears. She longed to sleep. For the month before the Congress she had been woken every morning by the roar and grind of the aircraft overhead. Normally a person who slept like the dead, it occurred to her that for her sleep to be so light she must be very tired. She was being carried on the wave of a powerful driving exhaustion, which had reached a pitch where, before going to sleep, she was always filled with a terror that if she allowed herself to sleep too deeply she might not wake up for days; as if a deep sleep were an abyss into which she might fall and vanish. All that month she woke continually at night to see the winking landing lights, red and green, of the aircraft, like silver moths in the moonlight, and she felt the drum of the engines through her entire body in a pulse of irritation or of anger.

All that month Anton had not spoken a single word to her. For the first week she had appealed to him. 'We can't conceivably be quarrelling because I made a bad joke about Stalin!' But he moved about the flat, ate, slept, as if she did not exist.

After that she also became silent, not from policy but from bewilderment, and flung herself into even more concentrated activity. But soon she saw that something very frightening was happening. The cold set distance of his body changed; she saw there was a dogged appeal in a glance or a movement of his shoulders. She understood that what she had to do was to put her arms around him and apologize. But she was fighting against the final collapse of her conception of him. She knew that the moment she put her arms about him, to coax him out of his silence, that creature in herself she despised would be born again: she would be capricious, charming, filial: to this compliant little girl Anton would be kind – and patronizing, as she repeated to herself over and over again, in a fierce resentment. But this would be a mask for his being dependent on her; she would not be his child, but he hers. She found herself saying: Why, he's not a man at all – in anything!

Meanwhile she was dreaming persistently of that man who must surely be somewhere close and who would allow her to be herself.

It was Maisie who used the phrase which broke Martha's determination.

Martha was spending all the free time she had with Maisie, who was alone. Maisie had refused to see Binkie again: at the end of two days' fruitless efforts to see her he had cut short his leave and gone back to Italy. Andrew had been posted a week later, because of the intervention of Mrs Maynard who had told Mrs Van she had considered it her duty to 'protect that stupid gal from herself'. During that week Maisie and Andrew had been together, trying to reach each other in a way which Martha found painful. They were trying to regain the simple and tender gaiety of the time before Binkie came on leave. They made the same jokes and said the same things but across barriers of hurt and pride. The night before Andrew left they quarrelled. Martha heard the quarrel through the thin floor, and, locked in the frozen silence with Anton, envied them for the ability to quarrel. But next day Andrew was gone; and they had agreed to start divorce proceedings.

Maisie was bitter, puzzled, hurt. She said: 'They neither of them cared about me, not really. They talked about each other more than me.' She was standing in the middle of her small room, a body of massive swollen flesh, from which her two mild and maidenly eyes looked forth, untouched. She passed her hands over her great body again and again, and said: 'What I can't understand, Matty, is this – suddenly it wasn't me any more that either of them was fond of. But *I* feel just the same.' This was the nearest Martha was ever to get to what had so hurt Maisie: 'Do you know, Matty, I suddenly felt that Andrew hated me?'

'But, Maisie, how could he hate you? It made us all happy to see you two together. He loved you.'

Maisie repeated obstinately, her eyes clouding with remembered pain: 'No, suddenly he didn't like me. You can always tell, Matty, even if they pretend. I can't stand pretence. I felt insulted. *I* was just the same all the time, but suddenly he wasn't.'

She was in the last month of her pregnancy, suffering with the heat and with the pride of her loneliness. She saw no one but Martha. Athen, of whom she spoke often, had been sent to another camp three hundred miles away for some part of his training. The other members of the group were hostile to her; Martha defended her, even more heatedly because she felt the same hostility. But she knew why: she was mourning as if a happiness of her own had collapsed.

When Maisie's had her baby, and she's in two parts, she'll need a man again – then she'll be different. But who? I believe she loves Athen, but that's no good . . .

For some reason Martha preferred to think of Maisie as she was now, fiercely self-sufficient, and self-absorbed. But not as self-absorbed as Martha thought, for one day she remarked, as if this were part of something they had discussed, as if they were continuing a thought they shared: 'And it must be hard for Anton, all this. I always thought that if he cracked up, he'd take it badly.'

Offered the information that Anton was cracking up, Martha at first rejected it. She examined the pale closed face of this man she had inexplicably married, and thought him as self-sufficient as a fortress: 'a petty-bourgeois interested only in his furniture'. But her heart had begun to ache for him. The night before the Saturday of the Congress she had slipped into bed beside him, and he murmured: 'My little one, so you're sorry for being so silly?'

It was going to be a marriage after all. She accepted the fact with a mixture of dismay and of protective tenderness. It could not last longer than the war – on that point she was determined, but while it lasted she would be open to feeling.

Above all it was going to be a fight because she had understood it would please him if she became less of a communist. That morning he had said reproachfully: 'So you're going to the Congress and leaving me behind?' She had not expected it; had never imagined it possible that this formidable revolutionary from Europe possessed by memories of a wife who had above all been a political being, could wish her to fold her hands and become passive. She understood that he did not know this himself, for when she remonstrated that she had been elected a delegate and must go, he had agreed that of course she must, but in a tone which said clearly that he would have agreed as easily if she had said she would allow her alternate delegate to go instead.

Now the message from Anton had made her fearful that he was going to prevent her from leaving with the others for the Congress.

He was not in the flat. The servant had gone for his midday meal. Soon it would be one o'clock and she ought to be at the High Court. She continued to sit on the edge of the bed, waiting for him, fighting against the need to sleep. At last she caught sight of a piece of paper pinned to the pillow: My little one, Maisie is not well. I thought she would like to see you before you left.

At first Martha felt gratitude that Anton had at last come to like Maisie; then she saw that this was a means to stop her going. This second fact she repressed – it made her too angry.

She ran downstairs to Maisie's flat, and saw a group of three people in the entrance, black against the glare of the street. They were Mrs Van, Piet and Jack. Martha ran down to where she could see their faces. They were angry but they had been laughing together on the pavement.

'You've lost the case,' Martha exclaimed.

'£150 costs. The law's an expensive ass,' Jack commented. In spite of his annoyance he could not prevent his eyes lighting up at the memory of the droning farcical scene in the Court.

Mrs Van said: 'It seems that the judge found the Major's argument about the Indian women wasting the national income on jewellery unanswerable.' She choked with laughter, leaning against the wall of the entrance. Her fat body shook all over, and Piet and Jack, on either side of her, took her by the arms, smiling at each other and at her, with the delicate amused respect that her friends always gave Mrs Van at these moments when the girl imprisoned in the great body laughed out in irrepressible enjoyment.

'It's all very well,' said Mrs Van reprovingly to herself. 'But it's a serious matter.' Being serious she said to Martha: 'Are you ready? We must hurry.'

The door of Maisie's flat opened and Maisie came out, her face glistening with sweat. 'Oh, Matty,' she said, clasping Martha's arm, 'I'm so glad you've come. Anton said you would.'

'Your baby's started?' said Martha.

She knew she was going to miss the Congress. She looked towards Mrs Van as if she could find a way out of this conflict of loyalties. But Mrs Van was a mother and a grandmother first.

'Of course Matty's staying with you. We'll take her alternate.'

'I've sent for the nurse,' said Maisie, and burst into tears.

Big Piet instinctively took command, helping Maisie back into her flat, saying: 'Now take it easy, settle yourself down, crying's not going to get the little brat into the light of day.' He held Maisie around her shoulders, receiving floods of tears on his arm; he was showing an awkward, warm, tender gallantry that made them all like him.

Also, Martha was feeling that for the first time since her marriage Mrs Van was liking her. Why? She thought: She's been feeling hostile to me; it's the same sort of hostility I've been feeling for Maisie – well, then, does that mean I let her down in some way: she wanted my getting married to mean something, and it didn't. Martha put this thought away for later examination: it meant there was something in Mrs Van's life she did not understand.

For a few minutes the four of them stood about, fussing over Maisie until she wiped her eyes and said: 'I'm sorry to be such a fool, I was alone and I got scared.'

Mrs Van said to Martha: 'Your alternate's Marjorie, isn't it? Well, she's due to have her baby too. This is all nonsense: I'll appoint an alternate myself, it's quite regular!'

Jack and Piet laughed at her; Martha was too disappointed to laugh. Seeing how she felt, Mrs Van turned at the door and said they would ring her that night from G—to tell her how the voting went.

'I expect Anton'd be interested to hear too,' added Mrs Van with a detachment that told Martha how much Mrs Van disapproved of Anton.

The sound of Anton's name made Piet's face change. He said abruptly to Martha: 'I'd like a word with you.' Martha followed him into the hallway. Mrs Van and Jack went ahead with a tact which showed they knew what Piet had planned to say.

Piet said: 'Look here, Matty, I meant to do this formally, but there's no time like the present, and I've got to the point where the less I see of your old man the better.'

'Oh, Piet, why don't you think it over?' She had been expecting for some days that Piet and Marie would leave the group.

'I've had enough,' said Piet. His face was flaming with anger and with embarrassment. 'It's a bloody farce. Communists we call ourselves. The truth is, ordinary people wouldn't even understand the language we speak. I'm telling you, when I go to one of the union meetings from one of our meetings, I'm scared stiff I might use some of the bloody jargon by accident – they'd think I'd gone off my rocker. There's half a dozen of us, slaving ourselves to death, we could do exactly the same things if we weren't group members at all.'

'If you disapprove of party policy, the correct way is to stay inside and change it,' said Martha, with earnestness.

'Oh to hell,' said Piet. 'We've got to the point where we spend more time calling each other names than we do on real work. I've had it. Anyway, that's all. And that goes for Marie too.' A car hooted outside. 'No hard feelings,' he said, going out. 'You're going to take a formal decision I'm a fascist traitor, but no hard feelings as far as I'm concerned.'

Martha went back to Maisie, who was now walking up and down the room, frowning with concentration.

Maisie had lapsed from the group without any formal

announcement. Marie and Piet had left, which meant that Tommy would too. Of the RAF men there was only Athen, and he would be leaving the Colony soon. Jasmine had gone to Johannesburg. The Communist Party of Southern Zambesia now consisted of Anton, Marjorie, herself and Colin. Colin had been warned by the head of his Department that he would not hold his job if he did not break his connection with the communists. He had said he could continue to consider himself a communist but he would no longer attend meetings.

In short, the group was at an end. At this, Martha felt herself cut off from everything that had fed her imagination: until this moment she had been part of the grandeur of the struggle in Europe, part of the Red Army, the guerrillas in China, the French underground, and the partisans in Italy, Yugoslavia and Greece.

She was recalled from her sense of futility by the sound of Maisie's heavy breathing: the girl was marching up and down the room with her heavy rolling gait, the sweat pouring off her face.

'Maisie, it's no use getting yourself all tensed up so soon,' Martha said, but helplessly, remembering how she herself had tensed up and been unable to prevent it. 'What exactly did the nurse say?'

'She said there was no hurry,' Maisie said sullenly. 'The pains started, or I thought they did . . .' Maisie lowered herself on to the edge of the bed, and sat limp, her slender arms dangling. In other words it was probably a false alarm.

'You'd better sleep,' said Martha, trying not to resent Maisie for keeping her from the Congress. Maisie obediently laid herself on her side and shut her eyes. Martha drew the curtains. A thin threaded glare of white light lay across the bed, across the heavy body. An aeroplane roared overhead, making the hot air throb.

'Sleep,' said Martha again. The childish lashes lying on Maisie's fat cheeks were trembling with the effort to sleep.

Martha went upstairs to her flat. Anton was there. As she entered he said: 'Well, my little one, I'm so happy you're still here.'

She said dryly: 'I should have thought you would have wanted me to be at the Congress.'

He said in the same fond voice: 'Poor Maisie was so uncomfortable. I thought she would be happy to have you. And how is your patient?' he added.

'It seems it was a false alarm.' She thought that very likely Anton had put it into Maisie's head that her labour was starting. If so . . . She was acutely depressed. We're all mad, she thought, trying to make it humorous. She recognized Marjorie's dry and humorous tone, and thought: Why is it I listen for the echoes of other people in my voice and what I do all the time? The fact is, I'm not a person at all, I'm nothing yet – perhaps I never will be.

She sat on her bed under the window and looked up into the full, hot blue sky where, very high up, a couple of tiny silver insects glittered. Anton was watching her over the top of his book.

'Piet's just told me he and Marie are leaving the Party,' she remarked.

He said: 'So? It does not surprise me. I heard he's becoming a builder on his own account – he's going to be a boss now.' He sounded full of contempt.

'All the same,' Martha said, in the same dry humorous tone: 'there are three of us left now. It seems we ought to discuss whether or not we've been wrong.'

'Yes, yes, as communists we ought always to admit our faults and correct them.' There was a very long silence. Martha was thinking: That's another two years of my life gone. The phrase two years seemed meaningless: they had been years of such hard work, excitement, happiness and learning that they seemed more important than all the time she had lived before. She thought: Well, that's over. She wanted desperately to sleep, but she was following in her mind the car in which Piet, Mrs Van, Jack, and whoever Mrs Van had found to replace herself, were speeding towards the Congress.

She remarked: 'I wonder which side is going to win?'

'Yes, yes, thse social democrats always take themselves so seriously.'

After a pause he added: 'I remember that joke Grete used to make – I remember she used to say . . .'

Martha found herself saying: 'For God's sake, will you shut up about Grete!'

He said with cold reproof: 'She was a very good comrade.'

'I dare say she was,' said Martha.

He waited for her to apologize, but since she did not, lifted his book and shut her out with it.

Martha went downstairs to Maisie, who was asleep.

She came upstairs again, and waited out the long afternoon until the telephone rang. The Congress had come to a sudden end. The 'Red' faction having won on a vote, that the African Branch should remain, the losing side had there and then split off and formed a new party. In other words the 'Left', such as it was, was fragmented: there were two parties, the Social Democratic Party, representing, or at least giving tokens of goodwill towards, the Africans; and the newborn Labour Party, representing white Labour. Any chance of either defeating the Government at the next election was over.

Anton, hearing the news, remarked: 'Yes, the development in this country accurately reflects the same development in the Union of South Africa, and it is proof of the necessity for a communist party.'

'But Anton, there are only three of us left.' Martha was examining two very clear convictions that existed simultaneously in her mind. One, it was inevitable that everything should have happened in exactly the way it had happened: no one could have behaved differently. Two, that everything which had happened was unreal, grotesque, and irrelevant.

'Yes, yes, but that is because of the objective political situation. We must make a fresh analysis of the position and begin again.'

But it's not possible that both can be true, Martha thought. She was overwhelmed with futility. She lay down on the bed, her back to Anton, who was already freshly analysing the situation, and allowed herself to slide into sleep like a diver weighted with lead.